01.

THE BLACK ROOD

By Stephen Lawhead

Dream Thief
Empyrion
The Search for Fierra
The Siege of Dome

In the Hall of the Dragon King
Warlords of Nin
The Sword and the Flame

THE PENDRAGON CYCLE
Book 1: *Taliesin*
Book 2: *Merlin*
Book 3: *Arthur*
Book 4: *Pendragon*
Book 5: *Grail*

THE SONG OF ALBION SERIES
The Paradise War
The Silver Hand
The Endless Knot

Byzantium

THE CELTIC CRUSADES
Book 1: *The Iron Lance*
Book 2: *The Black Rood*

Avalon

Voyager

THE BLACK ROOD

THE CELTIC CRUSADES: BOOK II

STEPHEN LAWHEAD

HarperCollins*Publishers*

0002 246 66X 3102

Voyager
An Imprint of HarperCollins*Publishers*
77–85 Fulham Palace Road,
Hammersmith, London W6 8JB

www.voyager-books.com

Published by *Voyager* 2000
1 3 5 7 9 8 6 4 2

ISBN 0 00 224666 X

Typeset in Postscript Linotype Minion and Galliard
by Palimpsest Book Production Limited,
Polmont, Stirlingshire
Printed and bound in Great Britain by
Caledonian International Book Manufacturing Ltd, Glasgow

For
Fred and Catherine

THE BLACK ROOD

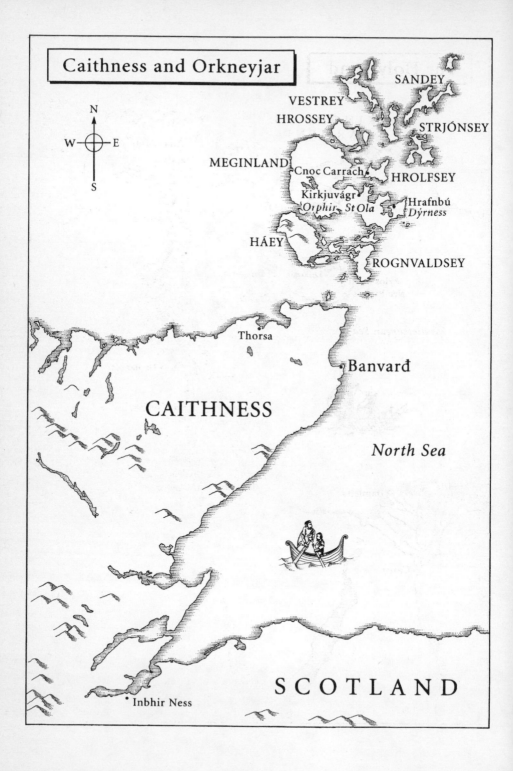

Caithness and Orkneyjar

N
W—E
S

SANDEY

VESTREY
HROSSEY
STRJÓNSEY

MEGINLAND
Cnoc Carrach
HROLFSEY

Kirkjuvágr
Orphir St Ola
Hrafnbú
Dýrness

HÁEY

ROGNVALDSEY

Thorsa

Banvarð

CAITHNESS

North Sea

SCOTLAND

Inbhir Ness

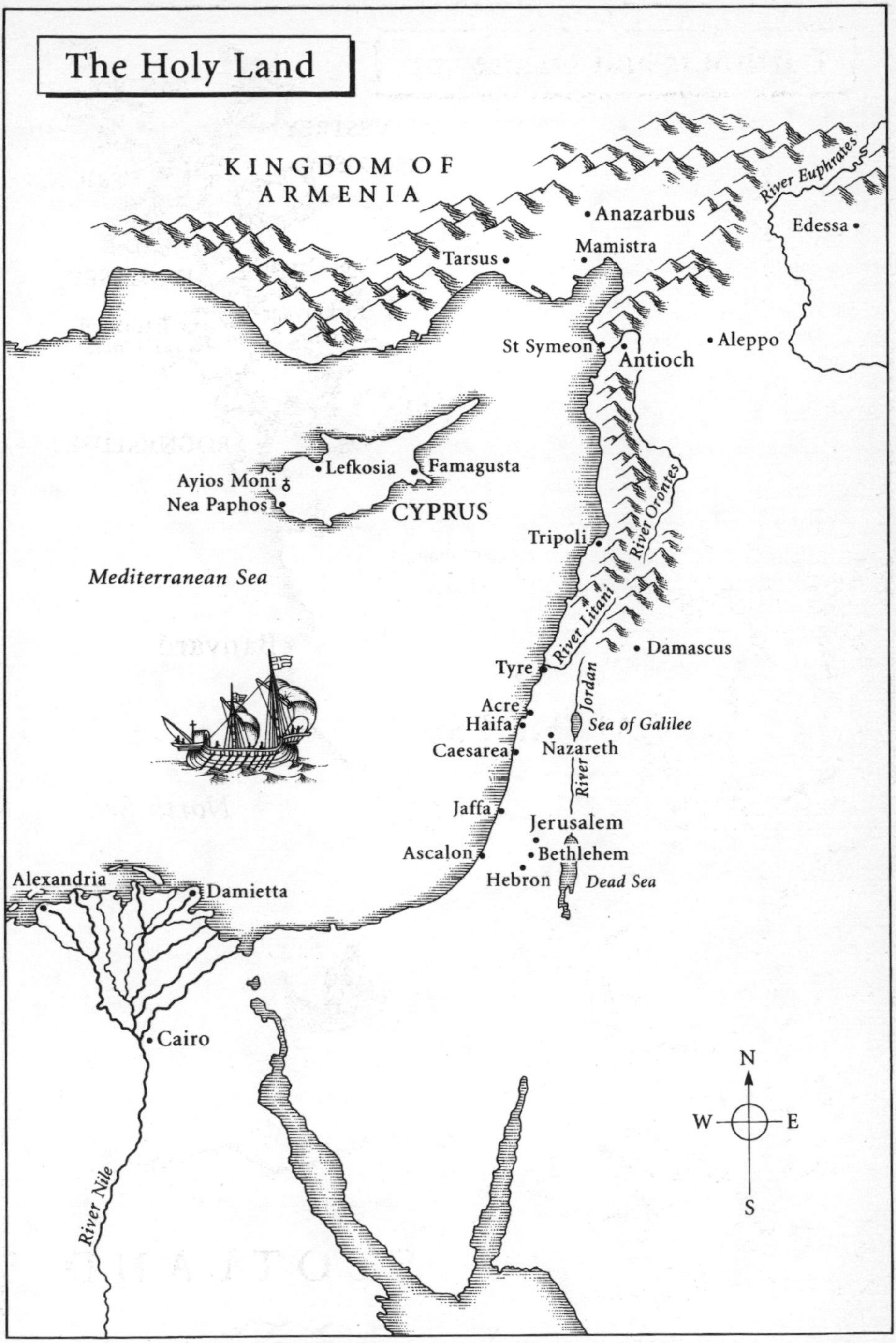

The Holy Land

KINGDOM OF
ARMENIA

• Anazarbus

River Euphrates

Tarsus •

Mamistra

Edessa •

St Symeon •

Antioch

• Aleppo

Ayios Moni •
Nea Paphos •

• Lefkosia

• Famagusta

CYPRUS

River Orontes

Tripoli •

River Litani

Mediterranean Sea

Tyre •

• Damascus

Acre •
Haifa •

Jordan

Sea of Galilee

Caesarea •

Nazareth

River

Jaffa •

Jerusalem

Ascalon •

• Bethlehem

Hebron •

Dead Sea

Alexandria •

• Damietta

• Cairo

River Nile

N
W — E
S

PART I

November 10, 1901: Paphos, Cyprus

The summons came while I was sitting at my desk. The afternoon post had just been delivered – the office boy placing the tidy bundle into my tray – so I thought nothing of it as I slid the paper knife along the pasted seam. It was only upon shaking out the small cream-coloured card that my full attention was engaged. I flipped the card over on the blotter. The single word, '*Tonight*' written in a fine script, brought me upright in my chair.

I felt my stomach tighten as an uncontainable thrill tingled through me. This was followed by an exasperated sigh as I slumped back in my chair, the card thrust at arm's length as if to hold off the inevitable demand of that single, portentous word.

Truth to tell, a fair length of time had passed since the last meeting of the Inner Circle, and I suppose a sort of complacency had set in which resented this sudden and unexpected intrusion into my well-ordered existence. I stared at the offending word, fighting down the urge to pretend I had not seen it. Indeed, I quickly shoved it out of sight into the middle of my sheaf of letters and attempted to forget about it.

Curiosity, and a highly-honed sense of duty, won the struggle. Resigning myself to my fate, I rang for one of the lads and sent him off with a hastily scribbled note of apology to my wife explaining that an engagement of the utmost importance had just arisen and she must soldier on without me for the evening, and please not to wait up as I anticipated being very late. A swift glance in my desk diary revealed that, as luck would have it, the familial household was to be appropriated for a meeting of certain august members of the Ladies' Literacy Institute and Temperance Union, a gaggle of well-meaning old dears whose overabundant maternal energies have been directed to the improvement of society through reading and abstinence from strong drink – except sherry. Worthy goals, to be sure, but unspeakably dull. Instantly, my resentful resignation turned to unbounded elation; I was delighted to have a genuine excuse to forego the dull agonies of an evening which, if past experience was any indicator, could only be described as boredom raised to the level of high art.

Having shed this onerous domestic chore, new vistas of possibility opened before me. I considered dining at the club, but decided on taking an early supper so as to leave plenty of time for the cab journey to the chapel where the members of our clandestine group met on these rare occasions. With a contrite heart made buoyant by a childlike excitement, I contemplated the range of alternatives before me. There were several new restaurants in Hanover Street that I had been meaning to try, with a public house nearby recommended by a junior colleague in the firm; off the leash for the night, I determined my course.

When work finished for the day, I lingered for a time in my office, attending to a few small tasks until I was certain the office boys and junior staff had gone, and I would not be followed, however accidentally. I feel it does no harm to take special precautions on these infrequent occasions; no doubt it is more for my own amusement than anything else, but it makes me feel better all the same. I should not like even the slightest carelessness on my part to compromise the Inner Circle.

After a pint of porter at the Wallace Arms, I proceeded around the corner to Alexander's Chop House, where I dined on a passable roast rabbit in mustard sauce and a glass of first-rate claret before the cab arrived. As the evening was fine and unseasonably balmy, I asked the driver to pull the top of the carriage back and enjoyed a splendid drive through the city and out into the nearby countryside. I arranged with the driver to meet me for the return journey and, when he was well out of sight, walked the last mile or so to the chapel to meet the others.

Upon nearing the place, I saw someone hurrying up the lane ahead of me; I recognized the fellow as De Cardou, but I did not hail him. We never draw attention to one another in public. Even the Brotherhood's lower orders are advised to refrain from acknowledging a fellow member in passing on the street. For them it is a discipline which, faithfully applied, may lead to greater advancement in time; for the Inner Circle, it is an unarguable necessity – now more than ever, if such a thing can be possible.

Admittedly, these arcane concerns seem very far away from the

4

honest simplicity of life on the Greek island where I now find myself. Here in the sun-soaked hills above Paphos, it is easy to forget the storm clouds gathering in the West. But the writing is on the wall for anyone with eyes to see. Even I, the newest recruit to our hallowed and holy order, recognize dangers which did not exist a year or two ago; and in these last days such dangers will only increase. If ever I doubted the importance of the Brotherhood, I doubt it no longer.

Our meeting that night was solemn and sobering. We met in the Star Chamber, hidden beneath the chancel, as it affords a more comfortable setting for discussion. I took my seat at the round table and, after the commencement ritual and prayer, Genotti asked to begin the proceedings with a report on the Brotherhood's interests in South America and the need for urgent intervention in the worsening political climate. 'While the peace treaty concluded in the first months of last year between Chile and Brazil remains in force,' he said, 'efforts to undermine the treaty continue. It has come to my attention that agents in the employ of Caldero, a dangerous anarchistic political faction, are planning an attack on the palace of the Chilean president. This attack will be blamed on Brazil in an effort to draw the two governments back into open conflict.'

Evans, our Number Two, expressed the concern of the group and asked Genotti's recommendation. 'It is my belief that the presidential staff must be warned, of course, so that protective measures may be taken. I also advocate, with the Brotherhood's approval, monies to be advanced to fund the training of an agent to be placed within Caldero and bring about its self-destruction.'

Ordinarily, such a proposal would have engendered a lengthy discussion on the manner and methods of implementing a plan. This time, however, Pemberton rose to his feet and, before debate could begin, thanked Genotti for his industry on the Brotherhood's behalf.

'However,' he said, his voice taking on a sepulchral tone, 'it is becoming increasingly clear that our ventures into the manipulation of political systems cannot continue. It is dangerous, and potentially destructive to the overall aims of the Inner Circle – not least because such meddling in the power structures of sovereign nations possesses a vast and unperceived potential to seduce us away from our prime objectives.'

5

Tall and gaunt in his red robe with the golden cross over the heart, Pemberton looked around the table to ensure that each of us understood him precisely. 'Furthermore, gentlemen, it is increasingly evident that the world has embarked on a new and frightening course. And we cannot hope to remain uncorrupted by the increasingly corrosive powers beginning to assert their influence on the individual populations of this planet. South America is in ferment, Eastern Europe is rapidly sliding towards political anarchy and chaos, the clouds of war are darkening the skies in a dozen places.'

Citing example after undeniable example, our wise leader revealed to us not only the shape and form, but the vast extent of the wickedness about to fall upon an unsuspecting world. 'New threats call for new strategies. In short, gentlemen, we must adapt our methods if we are to survive. We must prepare for a new crusade.'

He went on to lay out for us the battle plan which would shape our future from that night. When he finished, one by one, we of the Sanctus Clarus, Guardians of the True Path, stood to renew our sacred vows, and pledge ourselves to this new crusade.

Our ancient enemy arms itself and its countless minions with new and ever more powerful weapons of mass destruction, so that night we soldiers of the Holy Light likewise armed ourselves for the coming conflict. In the undying spirit of the Célé Dé, we summoned the age-old courage of those dauntless Celtic crusaders who have gone before us and, shoulder-to-shoulder, took our places beside them on the battle line.

The war will come. It is both imminent and inevitable. For the present, however, as I look out on the glimmering Cypriot sea, and smell the heady, blossom-scented breeze, and feel the warmth of the sun and the gentle, abiding love of my good wife, I will savour the last, lingering benevolence of a more humane era which, when it is gone, will not be known again.

Tomorrow's travails will keep until tomorrow. While the sun yet shines I will delight myself in this glorious season, and cherish it against the evil day.

ONE

My Dearest Caitríona,

The worst has happened. As old Pedar would say, 'I am sore becalmed.'

My glorious dream is ashes and dust. It died in the killing heat of a nameless Syrian desert – along with eight thousand good men whose only crime was that of fealty to a stubborn, arrogant boy. I could weep for them, but for the fact that I, no less headstrong and haughty than that misguided boy, will shortly follow them to the grave.

The Saracens insist that I am the esteemed guest of the Caliph of Cairo. In truth, this is nothing more than a polite way of saying I am a captive in his house. They treat me well; indeed, since coming to the Holy Land, I have not known such courtesy, nor such elegance. Nevertheless, I cannot leave the palace until the caliph has seen me. It is for him to decide my fate. I know too well what the outcome will be.

Be that as it may, the great caliph is pursuing enemies in the south and is not expected to return to the city for a goodly while. Thus, I have time enough, and liberty, to set down what can be told about our great and noble purpose so you will know why your father risked all he loved best in life for a single chance to obtain that prize which surpasses all others.

Some of what I shall write is known to you. If this grows tedious, I ask you to bear with me, and remember that this, my last testament, is not for you alone, my heart, but for those who will join us in our labours in days to come. God willing, all will be told before the end.

So now, where to begin? Let us start with the day Torf-Einar came back from the dead.

*   *   *

I was with your grandfather Murdo at the church, helping to oversee the builders working there. The previous summer we had purchased a load of cut stone for the arches and thresholds, and were preparing the site for the arrival of the shipment which was due at any time. Your grandfather and Abbot Emlyn were standing at the table in the yard, studying the drawings which Brother Paulus had made for the building, when one of the monks came running from the fields to say that a boat was putting into the bay.

We quickly assembled a welcome party and went down to meet it. The ship was small – an island runner only – but it was not from Orkneyjar. Nor was it one of King Sigurd's fishing boats as some had assumed. The sailors had rowed the vessel into shallow water and were lifting down a bundle by the time we reached the cove. There were four boatmen in the water and three on deck, and they had a board between them which they were straining to lower. Obviously heavy, they were at pains to keep from dropping their cargo into the cove.

'They are traders from Eíre,' suggested one of the women. 'I wonder what they have brought?'

'It looks like a heap of old rags,' said another.

The sailors muscled their burden over the rail, and waded ashore. As they drew nearer, I saw that the board was really a litter with a body strapped to it. They placed this bundle of cloth and bone before us on the strand, and stepped away – as if mightily glad to have done with an onerous task. I thought it must be the body of some poor seaman, one of their own perhaps, who had died at sea.

No sooner had they put it down, however, than this corpse began to shout and thrash about. 'Unbind me!' it cried, throwing its thin limbs around. 'Let me up!'

Those on the strand gave a start and jumped back. Murdo, however, stepped closer and bent over the heaving mass of tatters. 'Torf?' he said, stooping near. 'Is that you, Torf-Einar?'

To the amazement of everyone looking on, the near-corpse replied, 'And who should it be but myself? Unbind me, I say, and let me up.'

'God in heaven!' cried Murdo. 'Is it true?' Gesturing to some of the men, he said, 'Here, my brother is back from the dead – help me loose him.'

I came forwards along with the abbot and several others, and we untied my long-lost uncle. He had returned from the Holy Land where he had lived since the Great Pilgrimage. The eldest of my father's two brothers, he and the next eldest, Skuli, had joined with Baldwin of Bouillon. In return for their loyal service they were given lands at Edessa where they had remained ever since.

When asked what happened to his brothers, Murdo would always say that they had died chasing their fortunes in the Holy Land. In all the years of my life till then, I had never known it to be otherwise. How not? There never came any word from them – never a letter, or even a greeting sent by way of a returning pilgrim – though opportunities must have been plentiful enough through the years. That is why Murdo said he had come back from the dead. In a way, he had; for no one had ever expected to see Torf-Einar again – either in this world *or* the next.

But now, here he was: to my eyes, little more than gristle and foul temper, but alive still. Of his great fortune, however, there was not so much as the pale glimmer of a silver spoon. The man I saw upon that crude litter had more in common with the sore-ridden beggars that huddle in the shelter of the monastery walls at Kirkjuvágr than a lord of Outremer. Even the lowest swineherd of such a lord would have presented a more impressive spectacle, I swear.

We untied him and thereby learned the reason he had been carried to shore on a plank: his legs were a mass of weeping sores. He could not walk. Indeed, he could barely sit upright. Still, he objected to being bound to his bed and did not cease his thrashing until the cords were loosed and taken away.

'After all these years, why return now?' asked Murdo, sitting back on his heels.

'I have come home to die,' replied Torf-Einar. 'Think you I could abide a grave in that godforsaken land?'

'The Holy Land godforsaken?' wondered Emlyn, shaking his head in amazement.

Torf's wizened face clenched like a fist, and he spat. 'Holy Land,' he sneered. 'The pigsty is more wholesome than that accursed place, and the snake pit is more friendly.'

'What about your lands?' asked Murdo. 'What about your great fortune?'

'Piss on the land!' growled Torf-Einar. 'Piss on the fortune, too! Let the heathen have it. Two-faced demon spawn each and every one. A plague on the swarthy races, I say, and devil take them all.'

He became so agitated that he started thrashing around again. Murdo quickly said, 'Rest easy now, Torf. You are among kinfolk. Nothing will harm you here.'

We carried him to the dún, and tried our best to make the old man comfortable. I call him 'old man' for that was how he appeared to me. In truth, he was only a few years older than my father. The ravages of a life of constant warring and, I think, whoring, had carved the very flesh from him. His skin, blasted dark by the unrelenting Saracen sun, was as cracked and seamed as weathered leather; his faded hair was little more than a handful of grizzled wisps, his eyes were held in a permanent squint and his limbs were so scarred from wounds that they seemed like gnarled stumps. In all, the once-handsome lord looked like a shank bone that had been gnawed close and tossed onto the dungheap.

We brought him into the fortress and laid him in the hall. Murdo arranged for a pallet to be made up and placed in a corner near the hearth; a screen was erected around the pallet to give Torf a little peace from the comings and goings in the hall, but also to shield others from the ragged sight of him, to be sure.

The women scurried around and found food and drink for him, and better clothes – although the latter was not difficult, for the meanest dog mat would have been better than his own foul feathers. My lady mother would have preferred he had a bath before being allowed beneath her roof, but he would have none of it.

When the serving-maid came near with hot water and a little Scottish soap, he cursed her so cruelly she ran away in tears. He called upon heaven to witness his oath, saying that the next time he bathed would be when they put him under the turf. In the end, Murdo declared that he should be left alone, and Ragna had to abide. She would not allow any of the maidens to serve him, however, and said that as he was manifestly unable to make himself agreeable to simple human courtesy, he could receive his care from the stableboy's hands. Even so, I noticed she most often served him herself.

That Torf-Einar had come home to die soon became apparent. His sores oozed constantly, bleeding his small strength away. That first night I happened to pass by the place where he lay on the pallet my father had had prepared for him, and heard what I took to be an animal whimpering. Creeping close, I looked on him to see that he had fallen asleep and one of the hounds was licking the lesions on his exposed leg. The pain made poor Torf moan in his sleep.

Jesu forgive me, I did not have it in me to stay by. I turned away and left him to his wretched dreams.

Over the next few days, I learned much of life in the East. Sick as he was, he did not mind talking to anyone who would listen to his fevered ramblings. Out of pity, I undertook to bring him his evening meal, to give my mother a respite from the tedium of the chore, and sat with him while he ate. Thus, I heard more than most about his life in the County of Edessa. In this way, I also discovered what had befallen poor Skuli.

True to his word, Lord Baldwin had given Torf and Skuli land in return for service. Nor was he ungenerous in his giving. The two brothers had taken adjoining lands so as to form one realm which they then shared between them. 'Our fortress at Khemil was crowned with a palace that had fifty rooms,' he boasted one night as I fed him his pork broth and black bread. His teeth were rotten and pained him, so I had to break the bread into the broth to soften it, and then feed it to him in gobbets he could gum awhile and swallow. 'Fifty rooms, you hear?'

'That is a great many rooms,' I allowed. He was obviously ill and somewhat addled in his thoughts.

'We had sixty-eight menservants and forty serving-maids. Our treasure house had a door as thick as a man's trunk and bound in iron – it took two men just to pull it open. The room itself was big as a granary and hollowed out of solid stone.' He mumbled in his bread for a moment, and then added, 'God's truth, in those first days that room was never less than full to the very top.'

I supposed him to be lying to make his sad story less pathetic than it might have been by dreaming impossible riches for himself, and it disgusted me that he should be so foolish and venal. But, Cait, it was myself who was the fool that night.

Since coming to the East, I have discovered the truth of his tale.

With my own eyes, I have seen palaces which make the one at Khemil seem like wicker cowsheds, and treasure rooms larger than your grandfather Murdo's hall, and filled with such plunder of silver and gold that the devil himself must squirm with envy at such an overabundance of wealth.

That night, however, I believed not a word of his bragging. I fed him his bread, and made small comments when they were required. Mostly, I just sat by his side and listened, trying to keep my eyes from his ravaged and wasted body.

'There was an orchard on our lands – pear trees by the hundreds – and three great olive groves, and one of figs. Aside from the principal fortress at Khemil, we owned the right to rule the two small villages and market within the borders of our realm. Also, since the road from Edessa to Aleppo ran through the southern portion of our lands, we were granted rights to collect the toll. In all, it was a fine place.

'We ruled as kings that first year. Jerusalem had fallen and we shared in the plunder. At Edessa, Count Baldwin was amassing great power, and even more wealth. He made us vassal lords – Skuli and I were Lords of Edessa under Baldwin – along with a score or more just like us. All that first year, we never lifted a blade, nor saddled a horse save to ride to the hunt. We ate the best food, and drank the best wine, and contented ourselves with the improving of our realm.

'Then Skuli died. Fever took him. Mark me, the deserts of the East are breeding grounds for disease and pestilence of all kinds. He lingered six days and gave out on the seventh. The day I buried Skuli – that same day, mind – word came to Edessa that Godfrey was dead. The fever had claimed him, too. Or maybe it was poison ...'

He fell silent, wandering in his thoughts. To lead him gently back, I asked, 'Who was Godfrey?'

He squinted up an eye and regarded me suspiciously. 'Did Murdo never tell you anything?'

'My father has told me much of the Great Pilgrimage,' I replied indignantly.

The old man's mouth squirmed in derision. 'He has told you nothing at all if you do not know Godfrey of Bouillon, first king of Jerusalem.'

I knew of the man. Not from my father, it is true – Murdo rarely spoke of the crusade. Abbot Emlyn, however, talked about it all the time. I remember sitting at his feet while he told of their adventures in the Holy Land. That good monk could tell a tale, as you well know, and I never tired of listening to anything he would say. Thus, I knew a great deal about Lord Godfrey, Defender of the Holy Sepulchre, and his immeasurable folly.

That night, however, I was more interested in what Torf might know, and did not care to reveal my own thoughts, so I said, 'Godfrey was Baldwin's brother, then.'

'He was, and a more courageous man I never met. A very lion on the battlefield; no one could stand against him. Yet, when he was not slaying the infidel, he was on his knees in prayer. For all he was a holy man.' Torf paused, as if remembering the greatness of the man. Then he added, 'Godfrey was an ass.'

After what he'd said, this assessment surprised me. 'Why?' I asked.

Torf gummed some more bread, and then motioned for the bowl; he drained the bowl noisily, put it aside, and lay back. 'Why?' He fixed me with his mocking gaze. 'I suppose you are one of those who think Godfrey a saint now.'

'I think nothing of the kind,' I assured him.

'He was a good enough man, maybe, but he was no saint,' Torf-Einar declared sourly. 'The devil take me, I never saw a man make so many bone-headed mistakes. One after another, and just that quick – as if he feared he could not make them fast enough. Godfrey might have been a sturdy soldier, but he had no brain for kingcraft. He proved that with the Iron Lance.'

His use of that name brought me up short, as you can imagine. I tried to hide my amazement, but he saw I knew, and said, 'Oh, aye – so your father told you something after all did he?'

'He has told me a little,' I replied; although this was not strictly true. Murdo never spoke about the Holy Lance at all. Again, the little I knew of it came from the good abbot.

'Did he tell you how the great imbecile gave it right back to the emperor the instant he got his hands on it?' Torf gave a cruel little laugh, which ended in a gurgling cough.

'No,' I answered, 'my father never told me that.'

'He did! By Christ, I swear he did,' Torf chortled malevolently. 'Only Godfrey could have thrown away something so priceless. The stupid fool. It was his first act as ruler of Jerusalem, too. He got nothing in return for it either, I can tell you.'

Torf then proceeded to tell me how, moments after accepting the throne of Jerusalem, Godfrey had been deceived by the imperial envoy into agreeing to give up the Holy Lance, which the crusaders had discovered in Antioch, and with which the crusaders had conquered the odious Muhammedans. In order to escape the ignominy of surrendering Christendom's most valued possession, Jerusalem's new lord had hit upon the plan to send the sacred relic to Pope Urban for safekeeping.

'It was either that or fight the emperor,' allowed Torf grudgingly, 'and we were no match for the imperial troops. We would have been cut down to a man. It would have been a slaughter. No one crosses blades with the Immortals and lives to tell the tale.'

It seemed to me that Godfrey had been placed in an extremely tight predicament by the Western Lords, and I said so. 'Pah!' spat Torf. 'The Greeks are cunning fiends, and deception is mother's milk to them. Godfrey should have known that he could never outwit a wily Greek with trickery.'

'His plan seemed simple enough to me,' I told him. 'There was little enough trickery in it that I can see. Where did he go wrong?'

'He sent it to Jaffa with only a handful of knights as escort, and the Seljuqs ambushed them. If he'd waited a few days, he could have sent the relic with a proper army – most of the troops were leaving the Holy Land soon – and the Turks would never have taken it.'

'The Turks took it?' I asked.

'Is that not what I'm saying?' he grumbled. 'Of course they took it, the thieving devils.'

'I thought you said Godfrey gave it to the emperor.'

'He *meant* to give it to the emperor,' growled Torf-Einar irritably. 'If you would keep your mouth closed – instead of blathering on endlessly, you might learn something, boy.'

Torf called me boy, even though I had a wife and child of my own. I suppose I seemed very young to him; or, perhaps, very far beneath his regard. I told him I'd try to keep quiet so he could get on with his tale.

'It would be a mercy,' he grumbled testily. 'I said the Seljuqs took the Holy Lance, and if it was up to them, they'd have it to this day.

But Bohemond suspected Godfrey would try some idiot trick, and secretly arranged to follow the relic. When Godfrey's knights left Jerusalem, the Count of Antioch got word of it and gave chase.'

Prince Bohemond of Taranto knew about the lance, too, of course. It was Bohemond who had taken King Magnus into his service to provide warriors for the prince's depleted army. Owing to this friendship, King Magnus had prospered greatly. It was from Magnus that we had our lands in Caithness.

Torf was not unaware of this. He said, 'Godfrey and Baldwin had no love for Bohemond, nor for his vassal Magnus. Still,' he looked around at the well-ordered, expansive hall, 'I can see the king has been good to you. A man must make what friends he can, hey?'

'I suppose.'

'You *suppose!*' He laughed at me. 'I speak the truth, and you know it. In this world, a man must get whatever he can from the chances he's given. You make your bargains and hope for the best. If I had been in Murdo's place, I might have done the same. I bear your father no ill in the matter.'

'I am certain he will leap with joy to hear it,' I muttered.

That was the wrong thing to say, for he swore an oath and told me he was sick of looking at me. I left him in a foul temper, and went to bed that night wondering whether I would ever hear what he knew about the Iron Lance.

TWO

Torf-Einar had indeed come home to die. It soon became apparent that whatever health was left to him, he had spent it on the journey. Despite our care of him, he did not improve. Each day saw a diminution of his swiftly eroding strength.

I fed him the next night in silence. Owing to my discourtesy of the previous evening, he refused to speak to me and I feared he would die before I found out any more about what he knew of the Iron Lance. I spoke to my father about this, but Murdo remained uninterested. He advised me to leave it be. 'It is just stories,' he remarked sourly. 'No doubt he knows a great many such traveller's tales.'

When I insisted that there must be more to it than that, he grew angry and snapped, 'It is all lies and dangerous nonsense, Duncan, God knows. Leave well enough alone.'

Well, how could I? The next evening I found Torf in a better humour, so I said, 'You said Godfrey was a fool for losing the Holy Lance. If he was ambushed by the Turks, I cannot see what he could have done about it.'

'And I suppose you know all about such things now,' he sneered. 'Were you there?' He puffed out his cheeks in derision. 'Had it not been for Bohemond, the thieving Turks would have made off with the prize forever.'

'What did Bohemond do?'

'He pursued the Turks and caught them outside Jaffa,' replied Torf. 'They fought through the night, and when the sun came up the next morning, Bohemond had the Holy Lance.'

'Then it was Bohemond who gave the lance to the emperor,' I replied.

'That he did,' Torf confirmed.

'Forgive me, uncle,' I said, determined not to offend him again. 'But it seems to me that Bohemond was no better than Godfrey.'

Torf frowned at me, and I thought he would not answer. After a moment, he said, 'At least he got himself something for his trouble. In return for the lance, he obtained the support of the emperor – and that was worth the cost of the relic many times over, I can tell you.'

This seemed odd to me. I could not understand why he should hold Godfrey to blame, yet absolve Bohemond whose actions appeared in every way just as suspect, if not more so. Realizing that I would only make him angry again, I refrained from asking any further questions. Still, I turned the matter over in my mind that night, and determined to ask Abbot Emlyn about it the next day.

I found the good abbot at the new church the following morning, and succeeded in arousing his interest with a few well-judged questions. Glancing up from the drawings before him, he said, 'Who have you been talking to, my friend?'

'I am giving Torf-Einar his meals in the evening,' I began.

'And he has told you these tales?'

'Aye, some of them.'

The priest wrinkled his brow and pursed his lips. 'Well, perhaps he knows a little about it.'

Something in Emlyn's tone gave the lie to his words. 'But you do not believe him,' I observed.

'It is not for me to say,' the abbot answered evasively. Now, I had never known the good priest to give me, or anyone else, cause to doubt him, but his answer seemed strange, and I suspected he knew much more than he was telling.

'Who better?' I said, pursuing him gently. 'My father, perhaps?'

Emlyn frowned again. 'Sometimes,' he said slowly, 'it is better to let the dead bury the dead. I think you will get no thanks from Murdo for sticking your nose into the hive.'

'True enough,' I concluded gloomily. 'I already asked him.'

'What did he say?' asked the cleric.

'He said it was all just stories,' I replied. 'Traveller's tales and lies.'

The abbot frowned again, but said nothing. This made me even more determined, for I could plainly see that there was more to the tale than they were telling. I got no more out of Abbot Emlyn that day, however.

Indeed, I might never have got to the heart of the mystery if Torf had died before speaking of the Black Rood.

That very night, his strength failed him. He grew fevered and fell into the sleep of death. Murdo summoned some of the monks from Saint Andrew's Abbey to come and do what they could for the old man, and Emlyn came, too, along with a monk named Padraig.

As it happens, Padraig is Emlyn's nephew – the son of his only sister – a thoughtful, well-meaning monk, despite the fact that he grew up in Eíre. Our good abb has children of his own, of course: two daughters – one of whom lives with her husband's kinfolk south of Caithness, near Inbhir Ness. The other, Niniane, is a priest herself, as gentle and wise as her father, and who, through no fault of her own, has the very great misfortune to be married to my brother, Eirik.

Now then, it is well known that the Célé Dé are wonderfully wise in all things touching the healing arts. They are adept at preparing medicines of surpassing potency and virtue. Brother Padraig set to work at the hearth and in a short while had brewed an elixir which he spooned into the dying man's mouth. This he repeated at intervals through the night, and by morning – wonder of wonders – Torf-Einar was awake once more.

He was still very weak, and it was clear he would not recover. But he was resting much easier now, and the fire had left his eyes. He seemed more at peace as I greeted him. I asked him if there was anything he would like that I could get for him.

'Nay,' he said, his voice hollow and rough, 'unless you can get me a piece of the Black Rood for my confession. Nothing else will do me any good.'

'What is this Black Rood?' I asked. 'If there is any of it nearby, I am certain my father can get it for you.'

This brought a smile to Torf's cracked lips. He shook his head weakly. 'I doubt you will find it,' he croaked. 'There are but four pieces in all the world, and two of those are lost forever.'

This rare thing intrigued me. 'But what is it, and what has it to do with your confession?'

'Never heard of the True Cross?' He regarded me hazily.

'Of course I have heard of *that*,' I told him. 'Everyone has heard of that.'

18

'One and the same, boy, one and the same. The Black Rood is just another name for the True Cross.'

This made no sense to me. 'If that is so, why is it called black?' I asked, suspicious of his explanation. 'And why is it in so many pieces?'

Torf merely smiled, and wet his lips with the tip of his tongue. 'If I am to tell you that,' he replied, 'I must have a drop to wet my throat.'

Turning to Brother Padraig, who had just entered the hall and was approaching the sick man's pallet, I said, 'He is asking for ale. May I give him some?'

'A little ale might do him some good,' replied the monk. 'At least,' he shrugged, 'it will do him no harm.'

While the cleric set about making up some more of his elixir, I went to the kitchen to fetch the ale, returning with a stoup and bowl. Placing the stoup on the floor, I dipped out a bowlful, and gave it to Torf, who guzzled it down greedily. He drank another before he was ready to commence his explanation.

'So,' he said, sinking back onto his pallet, 'why is the rood called black, you ask? And I say because it *is* black – old and black, it is.'

'And why is it in so many pieces?'

'Because Baldwin had it divided up,' replied Torf with a dry chuckle.

I was about to ask him why this Baldwin should have done such a thing, but Abbot Emlyn entered the hall just then to see how the sick man had fared the night. I think he was expecting to see a corpse, and instead found Torf sitting up and talking with me. After a brief word with Padraig, he came and sat down beside the sickbed. 'It seems that God has blessed us with your company a little longer, my friend,' Emlyn said.

'It will not be God,' Torf replied, 'but the devil himself who drags me under.'

'Never say it,' chided Emlyn, shaking his head gently. 'You are not so far from God's blessing, my friend. Of that I am certain.'

Torf's lips curled in a vicious sneer. 'Pah! I am not afraid. I did as I pleased, and I am ready to pay the ferryman what is owed. Get you gone, priest, I won't be shriven.'

'As you say,' allowed Emlyn, 'but know that I will remain near and I will do whatever may be done to ease your passing.'

Torf frowned, and I thought he might send Emlyn away with a curse, so I spoke up quickly, saying, 'My uncle was just about to tell me how the True Cross was cut into pieces.'

'Is this so?' wondered Emlyn.

'Indeed so,' answered Torf.

'Then what I have heard is true;' said the abbot, 'the Holy Cross of Christ has been found.'

'Aye, they found it,' answered Torf, 'and I was there.' I noticed the light come up in his eyes and he seemed to rise to his tale.

'Extraordinary!' murmured Emlyn softly.

'Godfrey it was who found the cross – in the Church of the Holy Sepulchre,' Torf told us. 'He had gone with his chaplain and some priests to pray. It was after the western lords had begun returning home, leaving only Godfrey, Baldwin, and Bohemond in the Holy Land to defend Jerusalem. Well, Bohemond had sailed for Constantinople with the emperor's envoy, bearing the Holy Lance into Greek captivity. Baldwin was preparing to return to Edessa, and we were all eager to go with him, for he had said he would begin apportioning the land he had promised his noblemen.'

'Some of this I know,' mused Emlyn, nodding to himself.

'Aye, well, the night before we were to leave Jerusalem, word came to us that al-Afdal, the Vizier of Egypt, had landed ships at Ascalon, and that fifty thousand Saracens were marching for Jerusalem. Rather than allow them to put the city under siege, Godfrey decided to meet them on the road before they could raise help from the defeated Turks. Taken together, Godfrey's troops and Baldwin's amounted to fewer than seven thousand, and of those only five hundred were knights. The rest were footmen.

'Leaving Baldwin to prepare the troops for battle, Godfrey went to the church to pray a swift and certain victory for us despite the odds against us. While Godfrey was praying, one of the priests fell into a trance and had a vision. I cannot say how it happened, but the way I heard it was that a man in white appeared to him and showed him a curtain. This White Priest told the monk to pull aside the curtain and take up what he found there. When the priest awoke, however, the curtain was gone and he was staring at a white-washed wall only.

'No doubt it would have ended there, except Godfrey came to hear of it, and said, "A wall is sometimes called a curtain." So, he orders the wall to be taken down, and behold! There is the True Cross.'

'God be praised,' gasped Emlyn, clasping his hands reverently.

'It seems,' continued Torf, ignoring the abbot's outburst, 'that when the Saracens first captured the city, those churches they did not destroy, they turned into mosqs. In the Church of the Holy Sepulchre, they found the True Cross hanging above the altar, but even those heathen devils did not dare lay a hand on it, so they walled it up. They mixed a thick mortar and covered over the sacred relic, hiding it from view. Godfrey orders the mortar to be pulled down, and there it is: the True Cross is found. The king declares it to be a sign of God's good pleasure, and orders everyone to kneel before the holy relic and pray for victory in the coming battle.

'This is difficult to do for the church is very small, and there are so many soldiers. So, he orders the cross to be brought out to us, and we all kneel down before it. Skuli and I find ourselves near the front ranks and we see the cross as the priests walk by; two priests, led by Godfrey's chaplain, hold it between them, and two more walk behind carrying censers of burning incense.

'I look up as it passes by, and I see what looks to be a long piece of rough timber, slightly bowed along its length. It is perhaps half a rod long, and thick as a man's thigh. I know it is the True Cross because it is blackened with age, and its surface has been smoothed by the countless hands that have reverenced it through the years.

'The prayers are said, and the monks are returning to the church; as they carry the cross away, someone behind cries out, "Let the cross go before us!" That is all it takes – at once everyone is up and shouting: "Let the cross go before us!"

'Godfrey hears this and calls for order to be restored. He says, "It has pleased God to deliver this most sacred relic into our hands as a sign of his good pleasure in the restoring of his Holy City. As we have kept faith with God, so God has kept faith with us. The enemies of Christ are even now marching against us," cries Godfrey, his voice shaking with righteous rage. "I say this cross – this Black Rood – shall go before us into battle. From this day forth, it shall be the emblem of Jerusalem's defenders, so that those who raise sword against us shall know that Christ himself leads his holy army to victory against the enemies of our faith."

'The monks begin chanting: "Rejoice, O nations, with God's people! For He will avenge the blood of his servants; He will take vengeance on his enemies, and make atonement for his land." And that is how it began . . .' So saying, Torf slumped back, exhausted by the effort.

I stared at him in amazement that he should recall so much of what happened that day long ago. Brother Padraig, who had crept near to hear the tale, motioned to me to fill the bowl again. I poured the ale, and held the bowl to the sick man's lips. Torf drank and revived somewhat.

'Rest now,' suggested Emlyn. 'We will talk again when you are feeling better.'

A bitter smile twisted Torf-Einar's lips. 'I will never feel better than I do now,' he whispered. 'Anyway, there is little more to say. We rode out from Jerusalem the next day, and met the Arabs on the road from Ascalon two days later. They were not expecting us to attack, and had not yet formed a proper invasion force. Two knights carried the cross between them, and Godfrey led the charge. We fell upon al-Afdal's confused army and scattered them to the winds. We routed the infidel, and sent them flying back to their ships.'

Torf drank some more, and pushed the bowl away. 'That was the first time the Black Rood went before us into battle, but it was not the last.' He shook his head, almost sadly. 'Not the last, by God.'

'How did the Holy Cross come to be cut into pieces?' I asked.

He turned his head to look at me, and I saw that the light of life was growing dim in his eyes. 'Godfrey did it. When the troops saw that victory was assured whenever the cross was carried into battle, they refused to fight unless it went before them.' He swallowed and closed his eyes. 'But the Turks and Saracens were relentless and the cross could not be everywhere at once.'

'So, he cut it up,' I surmised.

Torf gave the ghost of a nod. 'What else could he do? I swear that man never looked further ahead than the length of his own two feet. With everyone clamouring for a piece of the relic, Godfrey commanded that it should be cut in half.'

'The priests let him do this?' wondered Emlyn in dismay.

'Aye, the priests helped him do it,' said Torf, his voice growing thin and watery. 'The Patriarch of Jerusalem objected, but Godfrey convinced him in the end.'

'You said they cut it into *four* parts,' I pointed out, remembering what he had told me before.

This brought a flicker of irritation from Torf, who opened an eye and said, 'They sent one half to the church at Antioch to replace the Iron Lance which had been taken by the emperor. This was to be used by the armies in the north. The second half was kept in Jerusalem to be used in southern battles.'

'Over the years those two pieces became four,' surmised the abbot. 'It is not difficult to see how this could happen.'

'You said that only two remain,' I pointed out. 'What happened to the others?'

Torf sighed heavily. The long talk was taxing his failing strength. 'One piece was given to the emperor, and the other two have fallen into the hands of the heathen infidel.' He sighed again, his voice growing softer. 'I cannot say more.'

After awhile he drifted away. I thought he had died, but Brother Padraig pressed an ear to his chest and said, 'He sleeps.' Regarding the dying man, he added, 'I do not think he will wake again soon.'

I rose reluctantly. In the few days I had known Torf-Einar, I had grown to like the crusty old crusader. To be honest, Cait, he had breathed an air of excitement into me. Although I had heard tales of the Great Pilgrimage all my life, it always seemed to me something that happened too long ago and far away to interest me. Torf's unexpected appearance awakened the realization that the crusade continued. In far-off lands men were fighting still; in the Holy Land great deeds were still to be done.

Torf's arrival also awakened questions in my mind. Why did my father regard his brother's appearance with such cool dispassion? I had never known Murdo to be a callous, unfeeling man. Yet, he showed his dying brother scant consideration, or compassion – and not so much as a crumb of curiosity about his life in the East. What had passed between the two of them all those years ago?

Was it fear I heard in his voice when I asked about the Iron Lance? Or, was it something else?

After a brief word with Padraig, Abbot Emlyn rose to leave the hall, and I followed him out into the yard, determined to get some answers to my questions.

23

THREE

'I think your uncle will soon be standing before the Throne of Heaven,' Emlyn said when I caught up with him in the yard. 'I do not expect him to last the night. I should tell your father. He will want to know.'

'It seems to me,' I ventured, 'that my father knows all he wants to of Torf-Einar.'

The little round abbot regarded me with his quick eyes. 'You think he does not care for his brother,' he replied. 'But you are wrong in that, young Duncan. Murdo cares very much.'

'He hides it well, then,' I concluded sourly.

Emlyn stopped in his tracks and faced me. 'There is more to this than you know. Murdo has his reasons for feeling and behaving the way he does. Nor will I tell him how he should feel, or how he should act in this matter.'

The force with which this was said surprised me; it took Emlyn aback, too, I think, for he quickly added in a softer tone: 'The wounds were deep at the time. I think Torf's return has reopened them, and they are painful indeed.'

Accepting his appraisal, I suggested, 'Then maybe it is time those old wounds were healed once and for all. Maybe that is why Torf has come home.'

Abbot Emlyn began walking again. 'You could be right. Perhaps it is time we . . .' His voice drifted off as he turned the matter over in his mind.

I hurried after him. 'What?' I demanded. 'Time for what?'

He waved me off, saying, 'Leave it with me. I will speak to your father.'

'And then?' I called after him.

'And then we shall see what we shall see.'

The abbot hurried away, and I found myself alone for the moment and with nothing to do – a rare enough circumstance for me. I decided to go and see if Rhona was busy, thinking maybe she would like to ride with me down to the sandy cove below the cliffs south of the bay. Rhona and I had been married for seven years, and in that time had produced three children – two boys, and a girl.

Sadly, both boys died in the summer of their first year. Only you, Cait, the smallest and scrawniest infant I ever saw, survived to see your second year. It seems so long ago now, but that day the sun was high and the weather dry, and I still had it in mind to have a son one day. It seemed to me a splendid time to make a bairn, or at least to try.

I found Rhona sitting on a stool outside the storehouse, peeling the outer skins from a bunch of onions. 'To make the dye for Caitríona's new gown,' she announced. Then, seeing my expression, Rhona laughed, and said, 'Did you think I would make you eat them for your supper?'

'If you cooked them, I would eat them,' I replied.

'Oh, you would . . .' she began. Taking the bowl from her lap, I raised her to her feet. 'And what is this you're about?'

'It is a fine day, my love. Come out with me.'

'I thought you had work to do at the church.'

'The stone has not arrived yet, and father can look after the builders. I thought we might ride down to the cove.'

She stepped closer, holding her head to one side. 'And you think I have nothing better to do than go flitting off with you all day?' I saw the hidden smile playing at her lips. 'It is well other people have plenty to do since the young lord of this manor is an idle scapegrace.'

'Well,' I sniffed, 'if you do not wish to go, I suppose I could ask one of the serving-maids. Perhaps the one with the soft brown eyes would not spurn an invitation from Lord Murdo's handsome son.'

'Lord Murdo's handsome son,' she said, her mouth twitching with suppressed laughter. 'I happen to know Bishop Eirik is away to Inbhir Ness on business for the abbey.'

'Lady,' I said, drawing her close to steal a kiss, 'it was myself I was talking about, not my bookish brother.' I made to kiss her then, but she turned her face and I caught her cheek instead.

'Not here in the yard where everyone can see!' she gasped, putting her hands on my chest and pushing me gently away.

'Then come away with me.' I slipped my hands around her slim waist and untied the apron covering her pale green gown. 'The day is beautiful, and so are you. Let us take our pleasure while we may.'

'Someone has been listening to the Maysingers,' she said, drawing the apron over her head. 'Very well, I will go with you, Duncan Murdosson.' She bent and picked up the bowl of onion husks. 'But I must put these away first.'

'I will saddle the horses and meet you at the gate,' I said, stealing another kiss and hurrying away.

The horses were quickly readied and we were soon racing over the gorse- and bracken-covered hills to the south of the estate. The lands of my father's realm are great in extent, but the soil is thin and rocky in most places; also, our vassals are not so numerous as other estates, which means that we must all work the harder to survive. That said, there are good fields and grazing land to the west, and fine fishing in the wide bay between the high, sheltering headlands.

Banvarð has prospered us well enough, and while we may not have possessed the ready wealth of more favoured realms, we nevertheless raised enough in grain and cattle to feed ourselves and our vassals, with plenty left over for gainful trade. From what my mother had told me about her youth in Orkneyjar, it seemed to me that growing up in Caithness was much the same. And, like my father, life in the wild, empty hills suited me.

Not that we had forsaken Orkney forever. Heaven forbid it! We regularly traded at Kirkjuvágr, and Murdo often took part in the councils there. Once a year, the king held court at Orphir, and we always attended. Though we were Lords of Scotland now, in many ways those low-scattered northern islands still held us in their sway. Indeed, on a crisp day, we can see the Dark Isles across the water; like storm clouds spreading along the horizon, or like a bevy of grey seals, the islands raise their sleek heads from the surrounding sea.

On the day that Rhona and I rode out, however, my mind was on other things. With the sun on my back, my lovely lady wife by my side, and a good horse under me, my thoughts were on the sweet joy of life itself. I felt the fresh sea air on my face and smelled the damp earth and the flower-sweet scent of green growing things, and the blood ran strong in me.

We reached the cove, and I tethered the horses at the clifftop where they could get a little grass. Rhona and I climbed down onto the sandy beach where we settled in a sun-warmed hollow in the long sea grass. Rhona untied the bundle she had brought with her and produced a loaf of bread, a lump of cheese, and an apple – all of which I cut up with my knife and shared out between us. After our little meal, we lay back in the hollow and enjoyed the warmth of the sand and sun, and the sound of the lazy waves on the shore. Rhona came readily into my embrace and we abandoned ourselves to our loving, and afterward dozed in one another's arms.

I awoke with my head upon my wife's breast, and the sun lowering in the west. The tide was lapping around the base of the dune; the shadow of the cliffs had reached our once-sunny hollow, and the air was growing cool. I lifted my head and kissed my lady, and she awoke with a shiver. 'We should be getting back,' I suggested, 'before they send the hounds to find us.'

'One more kiss, my love,' said Rhona, pulling me close again.

We dressed quickly, returned to the horses, and rode slowly back to the dún, enjoying the fiery extravagance of a setting sun which set the heavens ablaze with scarlet, purple, and gold.

Even before reaching the road leading up to the fortress, I knew something was amiss.

Lashing our mounts to speed, we hastened up the road, through the open gates and into the empty yard. I dismounted and helped Rhona from her saddle; letting the reins dangle, we started for the hall, and were met by Brother Padraig. I took one look at his face, and said, 'Is it over then?'

'Your uncle died a short while ago,' he answered simply.

I nodded. 'May God have mercy on his soul,' I whispered, and felt Rhona slip her hand into mine.

'The lord and lady are with the body now,' Padraig informed us. 'Abbot Emlyn is saying prayers.'

'Poor soul,' sighed Rhona. 'Was anyone with him when he died?'

'I was at his bedside, my lady,' the monk answered. 'He did not awaken from his sleep. I thought to rouse him at sunset to give him a drink of the potion, but his spirit had flown.'

We went in to find a veritable crowd around the dead man's bed – serving-men and maids mostly, a few vassals, and half a dozen monks in attendance with Emlyn. They were standing with their heads bowed, hands folded, as the good abbot softly intoned the prayers for the soul of the newly departed. Rhona and I came to stand behind the monks, and listened until Emlyn concluded his prayer, whereupon the brothers arranged themselves in order around the dead man's bed, raised it, and began carrying it from the hall.

Moving to my father's side, I said, 'I am sorry he's gone. I cannot help feeling we should have done more for him.'

Murdo shook his head. 'He wanted nothing from us in his life, but to be allowed to die in peace. As he asked, so he was given.' He appeared about to say more, but turned away abruptly, following the monks out into the yard.

My mother laid her hand on my sleeve as she passed by. 'There is an end to all things,' she whispered, giving my arm a comforting squeeze. 'Let this also end.'

I wondered at her words, and would have asked her what she meant, but she moved on quickly, and Rhona came up beside me. 'It is sad,' she sighed.

'Only a few days ago, no one cared whether he was alive or dead,' I reminded her. 'Nothing much has changed.'

Rhona looked sideways at me. 'But *everything* has changed,' she said.

Women, I think, feel these things differently. I do not pretend to understand them.

Torf's body was taken to the nearby monastery where it was washed and wrapped in a shroud of clean linen, and prepared for burial. I had long heard it said – and now know it to be true – that the Roman Church is bereft in the face of death. The rites attending a soul's passing are solemn and severe; the Roman priests make no effort to lighten the burden of grief to be borne by the mourners. It is almost as if they view death as a punishment for the audacity of having accepted the Gifting Giver's boon of life, or as the sorry and inevitable end of sinful flesh.

The Célé Dé, however, see in death a friend whom the All Wise has entrusted with delivering his children from the pain and travail of mortal existence into the eternal paradise of his gracious kingdom. When bodies and hearts become too sick or broken to go on, Brother Death comes to lead the suffering spirit away to its rightful home. Accordingly, this journey is accompanied with laments and dirges for those left behind, but with songs of praise and happiness also for the one who has gone ahead.

While the body was being prepared for burial, Murdo determined that a grave should be dug in the corner of the churchyard. Although, as he said, Torf-Einar had not been one of the Lord's better sheep, he was still a member of the flock. I offered to help with this chore, but my father would not have it any other way but that he should dig the grave himself.

At dusk, the corpse was brought out and borne to the gravesite in the churchyard where most of the settlement's inhabitants had gathered. The sun had set with a fine and radiant brilliance, touching the clouds with fire, and setting the sky alight. In the golden twilight, the linen grave clothes gleamed like rarest samite, and the faces of both monks and mourners glowed. We sang a lament for a departed warrior, and then Abbot Emlyn led us in a Psalm; he said a prayer, following which he invited those closest to the deceased to toss a handful of earth into the grave. Murdo stepped forwards, picked up a fistful of dirt, and let it fall; and I followed his example. I suppose, despite our brief acquaintance, I felt some innate kinship with Torf-Einar. For all his profligate ways, he was still part of the clan, and we did for him what we would do for any family member.

We sang a Psalm while the monks undertook to shovel the dirt into the grave. The deep hole filled up quickly, and a single flat stone with his name scratched onto it was raised upon the mounded earth, whereupon we went back to the hall to drink and eat a meal in Torf's memory. As we reached the hall, I glanced up and saw two stars shining over the steep thatched roof – one for Torf, and one for Skuli, I decided. In the same instant, the monks began singing again, and it seemed to me that the stars shined more brightly. 'Farewell, Torf,' I murmured to myself. 'May it go well with you on your journey hence.'

We feasted in Torf-Einar's memory that night and, after the ale had made several rounds, Murdo rose to his feet and spoke briefly of his brother. He talked about their life together growing up in Orkneyjar, and his father's love and admiration for his first-born son. I could not help noticing, however, that he breathed not a word of their sojourn in the Holy Land. By that I knew the old wound had been reopened in my father's heart.

That night, Rhona and I clung to one another in our bed, exulting in our loving, and celebrating the life running strong in us.

Next day, the mundane chores of the settlement resumed. The awaited ship arrived with its cargo of cut stone, and we began the sweaty task of unloading the ship and dragging the heavy blocks up to the site of the new church. Murdo put as many men to the chore as could be spared from other duties, but it was hard labour still. By day's end we were well exhausted each and every one, and Torf's death and funeral were of no more account than the ripple of a pebble tossed into the sea.

As the weeks passed, however, I found myself thinking about some small thing or other Torf had told me about the Holy Land. Once, I asked Murdo for further explanation, but he just told me that whatever Torf had said was best forgotten. 'The ramblings of a sick man,' he declared flatly. 'He is dead and that is that. I will not speak of it again.'

Of course, this only served to increase my appetite the more. All through the rest of the summer and the harvest season, I fairly itched for some word of the Great Pilgrimage and its many battles, but little enough came my way. No one on the estate or any of the other settlements had taken the cross, or made the journey – save Abbot Emlyn and Murdo. When I asked the good abbot what happened in the Holy Land to make my father so close-mouthed on the subject, he replied, 'One day, perhaps, he will feel like talking about it. No doubt it is for the best.'

Towards the end of harvest that year, Rhona told me that our child-making efforts had borne fruit also: we were to have a baby in the spring. I remember, Cait, looking at you when my lovely lady wife told me the glad news. You were sitting by the hearth stirring a bowl of water with a wooden spoon which your mother had given you so you could cook with her.

'Did you hear, little one?' I shouted. 'You are to have a brother!'

Oh, I was so certain the child would be a boy, and I would have a

30

son at last. We dreamed this happy dream all through the long, cold winter. As Rhona's belly swelled, she often remarked she had never carried a child so large and heavy – a sure sign that a man-child would be born in the spring.

At winter's end, we awaited the appointed time eagerly. One morning, we awakened to the sound of the snow melting from the roof into puddles below the deep, overhanging eaves. I felt Rhona stir beside me and turned to find her watching me. 'Did you sleep well, my heart?' I asked.

'How am I to sleep?' she replied. 'This son of yours gives me no rest at all. He kicks and squirms the whole night through.'

Placing a hand to the bulging dome of her round stomach, I said, 'It is only because he is eager to come out and meet his family.'

'It is because he is his stubborn father's son,' she replied sweetly, stroking my hair with her fingertips.

Little Cait awakened and scampered into bed with us. She snuggled down between us and proceeded to wave her feet in the air while singing a song about a fish. It was a fine and happy moment with my best beloved and I revelled in it. Looking back now, I cherish it all the more – knowing the dark, unendurable days which lay ahead.

FOUR

The birth pangs came on her early the next morning, but Rhona continued with her ordinary chores until midday when the pains grew severe. I ran to alert my lady mother, who came with one of the older women of the settlement who often served as midwife, and one of her serving-maids to help. They took matters in hand, and Ragna sent me off to the church to help Murdo with the building, promising to fetch me as soon as the birth drew near.

I was still there when Ingrid, the serving-maid, came running a short while later. 'Lord Duncan, you must hurry.'

'What,' I said, climbing down from the scaffolding, 'is my son born already?'

'My lady said you were to come as fast as you can,' she replied, wringing her hands in her apron.

I took her by the shoulders to steady her. 'Tell me what has happened.'

'It is your lady wife,' she said. 'Oh, please, come now. Hurry.'

My father heard the commotion below and called down to know what was happening. I explained quickly, and he sent me off, saying he would find Abbot Emlyn and follow as soon as he could.

I raced down the hill to the dún, through the gate, into the yard, and to our house. There were several women standing outside the door; I pushed through them and went in. Ragna met me at the bedside, her face grave and sad. 'There is not much time, my son,' she said softly, taking my hand. 'She wanted to see you.'

I heard the words but could make no sense of what she was saying. 'What is wrong, mother?'

'The birth has torn something inside Rhona,' she replied gently. 'She will not live.'

'B-But –,' I stammered. 'But she will be well. And the child – we were going to –'

'There will be time to speak later,' she said, leading me towards the bed. 'Pluck up your courage, my son, and go to your wife.'

I stepped to the side of the bed and Rhona, her face grey-white with the pallor of death, opened her eyes and smiled weakly. I stared in disbelief. Only a short while ago that same lovely face had been glowing with love and life. How was it possible that such a change could occur so swiftly?

She lifted a finger and motioned me closer. I bent to place my ear near her lips. 'So sorry . . . my soul,' she said, her voice the merest breath of a whisper. 'I tried to get a son for you . . .'

'Shh,' I whispered, trying to soothe. 'Rest now. We will talk about it later.'

'I love you,' she said, her lips barely moving. 'Kiss me.'

I pressed my lips to hers – they were dry as husks, and cold.

'Farewell, my heart . . . ,' she sighed.

A tremor passed through her body. I took her hand and clasped it tight. Her breath went out in a long, slow exhalation, and she lay still.

'Farewell,' I said, my throat closing on the word as the tears came. I raised her hand to my lips and held it there. Then I took her in my arms for the last time. I bent my head and put my face next to hers, and held her close – until I felt my mother's hands on my shoulders, drawing me gently away. I allowed myself to be gathered into my mother's embrace, and we stood for a time, motionless, while she spoke words of comfort and courage to me.

Abbot Emlyn and my father arrived then. The abbot stepped into the room, and discerned instantly what had happened. His round shoulders slumped and his cheerful face dissolved in misery. Murdo rushed to the bedside as if he would command the life back into Rhona's dear body; only when he beheld the stark white skin and her empty upward gaze was he persuaded that there was nothing to be done. He turned to Ragna and me, put his arm on my shoulder.

'Duncan, my son,' he said, drawing me close. 'I am so sorry.'

We three stood there together for a time, our tears flowing freely. Abbot Emlyn stepped forwards and began the rites for the dead. Stretching his hands over the still-warm body, he began chanting –

not in Latin, or Greek, but in the ancient and honorable tongue of the Celts – asking the Swift Sure Hand to enfold the soul of my best beloved, and guide her swiftly to her eternal home. Then he folded Rhona's hands over her breast, straightened her limbs, and told the serving-women to find Rhona's finest clothes.

To me, he said, 'God has called his faithful daughter to join him in paradise. Tonight we will sing a lament for the empty place she leaves behind. Tomorrow we will celebrate her life and rejoice in her receiving her justly-earned reward. Look your last upon her, dear friend, and I will return in a little while to take the body away and prepare it for burial.'

I looked at him in dismay. So soon? I thought. Why does it have to be so soon? But I said nothing, merely nodding my assent instead.

Emlyn left, and I turned once more to the bed. Already she seemed more at ease; the pinched tightness of her features had relaxed, and she appeared to be sleeping peacefully. For a fleeting instant my heart leapt up with joy. I felt like shouting, 'See! It has all been a dreadful mistake! She lives! Rhona is with us still.'

But no. Released from the pains of death, her body was taking on something of its natural calm. Stooping over her, I brushed the damp strands of hair from her face and kissed her forehead. 'Go with God, my soul,' I said, straightening. It was then that I saw the small still form beside her; wrapped in swaddling clothes, looking like little more than a lump in the bed, was the tiny body of my son. Dark-haired, his small face clenched like a fist against a world he would never know, he lay beside his mother.

I beheld the body, and felt my own dear mother beside me. 'The little one did not draw breath,' she told me. 'There was nothing to be done.'

I nodded, and rested my hand on his still chest – my hand almost covered his whole body. 'God bless you, my son. May we meet one day in Blessed Jesu's court.'

We waited with the bodies until the monks came to take them away to the monastery. I could not bring myself to accompany them, nor take part in the preparations. Instead, I went down to the sea and walked along the beach until nightfall, and Emlyn sent Brother Padraig to fetch me back to the hall. 'There is food and drink prepared,' he told me, 'and everyone is waiting.'

'No,' I replied harshly. 'Go back and tell them to eat without me.'

'Master Duncan,' he said gently, so mild and compassionate in his reproof I had not the heart to refuse him again, and so allowed myself to be led back to the hall. Upon entering, I glanced around quickly and Niniane was the first person I happened to see. She stepped swiftly towards me and folded me into her arms. 'Dear, dear, Duncan,' she sighed. 'I am so sorry . . . so very sorry.'

I allowed myself to be consoled for a moment, and then asked, 'How is it you are here?'

'I was on my way to the abbey. I arrived in time to help prepare the – her body.'

Lost in my grief, I had not been aware of the comings or goings around me. 'Is Eirik with you?'

She shook her head. 'There was some trouble in Inbhir Ness. The son of a visiting nobleman accidentally killed a local chieftain's son. The clan has sworn a blood oath and the unlucky boy has taken sanctuary at the monastery. Eirik thought it best to stay on until matters were resolved.'

Niniane regarded me sadly. 'Rhona was a good friend to me, and I will try to be as good a friend to you. I will help in any way I can.'

I thanked her kindly, and escorted her to the table where the food was being served. They had saved a place for me at the board beside my mother, who was holding little Cait in her lap. You, dear heart, unaware of the sombre proceedings, held out your hands to me, and wanted me to play with you. But I could not. I merely sat and gazed glumly at your happy little face, deaf to your childish pleadings.

All I could think was that I would gladly change places with my poor dead wife. It was my fault, after all. If I had not been so insistent on having a son, my beloved Rhona would still be alive. I would be sitting next to her; it would be her face, her bright eyes, I was gazing into now; it would be Rhona's hand reaching to take mine.

There was singing that night, but I remember almost nothing of it. Emlyn sang a lament, as I recall, and some of the women of the settlement likewise sang, and Padraig played the harp. But my mind, like my heart, was with my beloved lying cold and alone on her bier in the church, and I drew no consolation from the kindly expressions of those around me.

A more wretched man there never was than myself, that night.

When at last everyone departed for their beds, I left the hall, too; I thrashed around in my empty bed for a time, and at last, unable to rest, I rose and walked the clifftops above the dark, restless sea until morning.

Following the death service in the old wooden church, we buried Rhona in the new churchyard. She would have approved of her final resting place, I think, as there was a plum thicket growing nearby, and she was always fond of plums. I was the last to leave the yard. I knelt a long time by that mound of stones gathered from the beach, wondering how I could go on living when my light, my life, lay under that heap of earth and rock.

The next days brought no solace. I went about my various chores with dull efficiency, a man bereft of all hope and life, seeing no good thing, hearing no kindly word, taking joy in nothing around me. At night, I roamed the clifftops.

My wretched condition persisted until I could bear it no more. One night, with the moon shining full in the yard, I rose and went out. My feet found the familiar path leading down to the shore. Heartsick, weary with grief, I walked down onto the beach, and out into the sea.

God help me, I could endure the gnawing ache no longer. I felt the cold water surge around my knees, but I kept walking. If I had any thought at all it was that the pain would soon be over and I would be with my beloved forever.

I felt the water rising around me – to my thighs, and then my waist – yet still I walked on, and would have gone on walking. But, as the black water swirled around my chest, I heard a voice call out to me from the shore: 'Duncan, wait!'

I recognized the voice; it was Padraig.

Not to be dissuaded, I paid no heed to the call, but struggled ahead in all determination. In a moment, I heard the splash of footsteps in the water as Padraig pursued me. Not wishing to be caught, or dissuaded from the course before me, I made no answer and pushed deeper into the water.

'Duncan!' he shouted. 'Here, Duncan, I have something for you!'

Ignoring him, I continued on. The water was up to my throat, and the swell of the waves tugged at me, raising me off my feet. He shouted after me again, and then I heard another voice – a child's voice, frightened, crying. Casting a backward glance over my shoulder, I saw him striding after me, holding Caitríona in his arms. So unexpected was the sight of her, I stopped and turned around.

'What do you mean by this?' I shouted. 'Get her away from here.'

He waded nearer and, dearest Cait, your tiny face was twisted in fear and your hands were reaching out to me to help you, to save you – from the water, and the night, and the strangeness of what was happening.

'Come now,' Padraig called. 'Would you leave without saying farewell to your daughter? Better still, why not take her with you?' Stretching his arms, he held the child out to me.

'Take her back to shore, you fool!' I shouted angrily.

He merely shook his head.

I glared at him. 'Have you gone mad?'

'Here,' he said, holding her out to me again. Cait began to shriek as the cold water splashed around her legs. 'Take her now and make an end of it. It will be a kindness.'

'You *are* mad,' I growled.

'Perhaps,' he allowed. 'Still, it would be better, I think, to have died in the arms of your loving father than to lose both parents before you are old enough to remember either of them. As you mean to end your life, so be it. You might as well end her life, too.'

Enraged, I strode forwards and snatched the dear babe from his arms. 'Stupid priest! You know nothing about children.'

'True,' he agreed placidly. 'But I know this water is freezing and night is far gone, and I miss my warm bed. Could we go back now, do you think?'

Cradling my squalling child in my arms, I started towards the shore. We walked back to the dún in silence; Cait had ceased crying by the time we reached the house. Padraig bade me farewell and I went in, wrapped my darling girl in one of her mother's warm mantles and put her in her bed. I sat with her until she was asleep. I slept as well and woke the next morning when I heard voices outside. Thinking Padraig must have told someone what had taken place in the night, I grew embarrassed, and went outside to face the stares of disapproval and reproach. But it was just some women from the settlement coming to bring me and little Caitríona some food. They gave me the baskets and departed, saying how they would be glad to help look after the bairn whenever I needed them.

The women went their way then, but all day long I kept thinking someone would mention the previous night's incident. No one did.

After vespers that evening, I saw Padraig leaving the chapel and went to thank him for not breathing a word to anyone about my shameful behaviour of the night before. He looked at me curiously. 'Behaviour? What shameful behaviour could that be?' he said.

'You know,' I muttered, irritated that he would make me speak it out so bluntly. 'I went walking down by the sea.'

'How very strange,' he said mildly, his face betraying no hint of guile. 'I too went walking in my sleep last night. Now, try as I might, I can remember very little about it.' Leaning close, he said, 'Between ourselves, I would consider it a kindness if you would not tell the abbot. We are not supposed to leave the monastery after prayers.'

'Well,' I told him, 'you can trust me to keep your secret. Only see that it does not happen again.'

'Oh, I have repented of it a hundred times already.' He gave me a look of shrewd appraisal. 'I do not think I will have occasion to sleepwalk again.'

That concluded the matter and nothing else was ever said, either by Padraig or anyone else. Let me tell you, I, also, have repented of that night a hundred times since then. Nevertheless, God is good; out of that disgraceful incident he brought a friendship which is beyond all price. For, from that night Padraig became my dearest companion and spiritual advisor – my *anam cara* as he calls it, my soul friend.

Another result of that night's folly was that I began to consider what I might do to make amends for my cowardly lapse – a self-imposed penance. While some might consider it overly pious, or even rank sanctimony, let them think what they will: I know how close I came to throwing away God's inestimable gift that night. Had I drowned myself, Cait, I would have condemned myself to an eternity of misery. That, I know. Instead, the Gifting Giver has blessed me beyond measure. Though I sit in splendoured captivity awaiting the death decree, I am yet the most grateful of men for having known the love of true friends, and the graceful, happy child that is my daughter, and for having been allowed to dare and do much for the advancement of my saviour's Invisible Kingdom.

Ah, well, make of it what you will. Whatever the workings of the mysterious inner heart, I began to contemplate some mighty work of atonement that I might do. As I pondered on what form this great deed might take, I found release from the shock and sorrow of my Rhona's sad death. My zeal and appetite for life returned and, along with it, a fresh desire for the things of the spirit.

Padraig noticed my newfound devotion. One night after vespers while we talked together over a bowl of ale, he said, 'Beware, Duncan, you will be wanting to become a priest next.'

'What would be wrong with that?' I replied, defiance hardening my voice. 'Do you think it above me? My brother is a priest, remember. I know well enough what would be required. I could –'

'I surrender!' He held up his hands. 'I spoke in jest. You would make a fine priest, of that I have no doubt.'

Despite his words, I heard the reservation in his tone. 'And yet?'

He put out his lip, and regarded me thoughtfully, but made no reply.

'Come now, what is in your mind?'

'Far be it from me to discourage anyone from seeking the priesthood . . .'

'And yet you would discourage me – hey? Well, that is a fine thing.'

'You misunderstand,' he said quickly. 'There are many priests among the Célé Dé, but few noblemen. Our Lord has blessed you richly, Duncan. If you would do something to honour him, let it be in the manner whereby he has created you.'

'As a nobleman, you mean.'

He spread his hands. 'Look at all your father has accomplished for the good of the Célé Dé. Do you imagine it would be half so much if he had been a monk?'

A trifling thing, a few simple words lightly spoken; but it started me thinking in a new way. I thought about what my father had done as a young man – much younger than myself, he was, when he followed the Great Pilgrimage. These thoughts grew to fill my every waking moment, and soon I could think of nothing else. Could it be, I wondered, that I, too, was being called to join the pilgrim way?

Some few nights later, I happened to mention my musings to my father. We were at table for our evening meal; as always in Murdo's hall, there were a number of vassals and friends gathered around the board. Some of the stonemasons working on the new church had been invited to sup with us that night, so the ale and conversation flowed liberally.

Talk turned to Torf-Einar's return, and how he had fared in the Holy Land. Someone said he had heard that Torf left an enormous fortune in the East, and others began speculating on how much this unknown wealth could be, and whether it was in gold or silver. Their ignorance and frivolity vexed me, and I said, 'Perhaps I will go to the Holy Land myself and claim this fortune and become King of Edessa.'

My mother, directing the serving-boys, and listening to the table talk with but half an ear, turned to me as if I had said I meant to burn down the hall with everyone in it. The smile on my father's face vanished in an instant; his head turned slowly towards me. If I had uttered the most obscene blasphemy imaginable, I do not think his expression could have been more aghast. He swallowed the bit of bread he was chewing, forcing down his growing anger. 'That was ill-spoken,' he said, his voice strained and low. 'Idle fancies are the work of the devil.'

I started to object that it was no idle fancy, that I had been considering just such an undertaking, but I glimpsed Lady Ragna desperately trying to warn me off. Their reaction rankled me, truly. Yet, the swiftness and force with which my innocent comment roused my lord's wrath took me aback. I mumbled a vague apology, and begged his pardon.

The tension of the moment melted away, and talk resumed. But nothing more was said about the Holy Land. When the opportunity presented itself, I rose and left the hall. When I arrived at the church the next morning, my father took me aside. 'Your mother thinks I was too quick to judge you last night. She thinks I condemned you out of hand for a comment worth less than the breath to speak it.'

I looked him in the eye. 'What do you think, lord?'

He glanced away. 'I think my good wife is wise and, over the years, I have learned that her opinions in such matters are to be trusted.' He shrugged, and his eyes swung back to me. 'If you tell me she has rightly divined the heart of the thing, and promise me you will never speak of such things again, I will forgive you fully and freely, and say no more about it.'

'Forgive!' I said, my voice harsh with outrage. 'Is it a sin now to speak of the Holy Land? As surely as I am your son, my lord, I will think and speak as I please.'

He glared at me. 'Only a fool jests about things he does not understand. I never knew you for a fool, boy.'

Lest I say something I would later regret, I turned and started away. 'There is another possibility,' I said, looking back over my shoulder.

'And what is that?' he growled after me.

'It was no jest!'

His unreasoning obstinance hardened my determination, I confess. I found myself dwelling on the things Torf-Einar had told me regarding the Holy Land, and imagining what it would be like to go there.

I did not work at the building that day; instead, I spent the day out in a boat beyond the headlands with three of the vassals, catching mackerel for the smokehouse. As the fishing was good, we did not return until it was almost dark, and then spent half the night gutting the fish so they would be ready for the drying racks in the morning. Indeed, I was busy tying the flayed and split mackerel to the birch poles when Abbot Emlyn approached me.

'So, my father has sent you to chastise me,' I said mockingly. 'No doubt he has grown tired of shouldering the burden all by himself.'

The kindly cleric looked at me and sighed. 'You are that much like another young man I once knew,' he said. 'Stubborn as stone.'

'If you are looking for the cause of the trouble,' I told him, 'you come looking in the wrong place. The fault lies not with me, but with my lord.'

'Come,' he said, motioning me to his side, 'walk with me.'

I had it in me to refuse. 'I'm busy,' I told him.

'Come with me, Duncan,' he insisted gently. 'The fish can wait.'

Who can resist the kindly abbot anything? Thus, I found myself falling into step beside him. We walked across the yard and out from the caer; our footsteps found the track down to the sea, and so we followed it, passing the field where some of the vassals were chopping thistles. The breeze was out of the north, and I could smell

41

the clean, wind-washed air faintly tinged with salt – a sign of cool, bright weather to come.

We came onto the pebbled shingle and walked for a time, the sound of our feet crunching in the stones made a hollow sound. Tiny white crabs swarmed the rotting seaweed at the high tide mark, darting out of sight as we passed. At last, the abbot drew a long breath, and said, 'I am disturbed, Duncan.'

I thought I knew what he would say next. I waited for the rebuke and prepared to defend myself against his unjustified disapproval.

'Murdo is not himself.'

This so surprised me, I stopped walking and turned to him. 'What?'

'Your father and I have been friends for many years, but I have never known him to be this contrary and short-tempered.'

'Nor I.'

'For the life of me, I cannot think what has happened to make him so disagreeable.'

'And changeable.'

'Yes,' the abbot agreed. 'Lord Murdo is the steadiest and most resolute of men. It hurts me to see him more miserable by the day.' He looked at me, distress furrowing his forehead. 'What can he be afraid of, do you think?'

'Why afraid?' I said, dismissing the question. 'I have never known my father to be afraid of anything. I think he is just getting set in his ways and resents anyone else having a different opinion.'

Emlyn shook his head gently. 'You know that is not true.'

'I suppose not,' I allowed. 'But why do you say he is afraid?'

'Look deep enough, and you will find that fear is usually at the bottom of all our sins and failings.'

'He is afraid I will go to the Holy Land.'

I had not intended saying that. Indeed, the words were out before I had even considered them. Even so, I knew them to be true the moment I heard them.

Emlyn did not disagree. 'Why should he be afraid of that, do you think?'

'Because,' I began slowly, 'he thinks I will become like Torf-Einar and forsake my family and my birthright.'

'Perhaps it is something like that,' the cleric replied. We resumed walking. The breeze ruffled the waves as they lapped at the stones, making a sound like chuckling.

'Your father never speaks of the Great Pilgrimage,' Emlyn continued after a moment.

'No, he does not.'

'For your father, the Great Pilgrimage brought nothing but hardship and grief. Like many others, Murdo lost nearly everything he cherished in life. Ever since he returned he has worked at replacing all that he lost, and he has succeeded admirably well.'

'Torf-Einar's return reminded him of this,' I mused.

'More than that,' the abbot assured me. 'If Torf had not returned the past would have remained only a memory – painful though it may be.'

I began to see what he was telling me. 'Murdo is afraid I will go to the Holy Land, and he will lose me, too.'

'All things considered, it is not an unreasonable fear.' He looked at me, but I kept my eyes straight ahead so I would not have to meet his gaze.

'I see. So you are united with him in this.'

'It is not like that, Duncan.'

'What if I were to tell you that God was calling me to undertake the pilgrimage myself? How would you counsel me then?'

He did not reply at once, and so I thought I had him at my mercy. I boldly pressed my advantage. 'Well, abbot?' I demanded. 'Obey my father, or obey God – which is it to be?'

When he did not answer, I glanced across at him and saw that he was squinting into the distance as his eyes searched the far-off sea haze on the horizon. 'There is a ship,' he told me. 'Someone is coming.'

'Where?' I quickly scanned the horizon.

'There,' he said, pointing to a patch of bright water out beyond the headland. 'Who could it be, I wonder?'

We watched as the tiny speck grew slowly larger. It was a sizeable ship with red sails, speeding swiftly towards us on the landward breeze. All at once the answer came to me. 'Eirik!'

A moment later we were both hurrying back along the path towards the dún to alert the others that my brother had finally returned.

FIVE

That night we welcomed Eirik home with a modest feast, and sat him in the place of honour at table. He was happy to be back in God's country, he said, and far away from the southern Scots and their interminable squabbles.

'You would think common dignity the rarest, most valuable substance in all the world, the way they ward and worry over it,' he said. 'And if any of them ever get any of the stuff, why he is the most miserable man you ever saw, for he must be on constant guard lest anyone besmirch it with a careless word.'

'Too true,' concurred Emlyn ruefully. 'I once heard of a man from Dunedin who killed a beggar for stepping on his shadow.'

'Are they all so contentious in the south?' said Ragna. 'If that is so, I never want to go there.'

'What say you, Murdo?' asked one of the masons. 'You and Abbot Emlyn have been further south than anyone hereabouts. Are the fellows so bloodthirsty as that?'

Murdo glared at the man for raising the question. 'Worse,' he muttered ominously; and, though the men asked for a story, he bluntly refused to say more.

Eirik marked his father's bad manners, but wisely passed on to other matters. He asked the mason about the new church, which was beginning to resemble something more than just a heap of rubble on bare ground. This proved a durable subject, and we finished the meal with a retelling of the work almost stone by stone.

After supper, Eirik came to me and expressed his sorrow at hearing of Rhona's sad death. I accepted his condolences, and he asked, 'What has happened to father while I was away? A bear with a sore head growls less. Is he feeling well?'

'He is well enough,' I allowed. 'A ghost has returned to haunt him.'

Eirik raised his eyebrows at this, and begged me to say more. I told him about Torf-Einar's untimely return and his lingering death. 'I begin to see now,' replied Eirik. 'The old wounds are reopened.'

'That is exactly what Emlyn says,' I replied. 'Myself, I think the two of them have a secret.'

This intrigued Eirik, and it flattered me to have my elder brother hanging on my every word, so I continued recklessly. 'Indeed,' I said, 'I think something happened while they were on the Great Pilgrimage together – something they have forbidden one another ever to mention aloud.'

Although I was speaking out of utter ignorance, I had struck closer to the truth than anyone could have known.

'Emlyn keep a secret?' wondered Eirik. 'It must be something terrible indeed.'

'Oh, aye,' I said carelessly. 'Whatever dark deed it conceals has reared its head once more, and it has made our father's life a misery ever since.'

'And it was something to do with Torf, you say?' asked Eirik.

'Perhaps,' I replied, 'but that is not what I said. Rather, it was something Torf said.'

'What did he say?'

'Why, he spoke of many things. Mostly, it was to do with his life in the Holy Land – his battles, and treasures, and the like. Father would not listen to him. He called it traveller's tales and dangerous nonsense.'

'Did he, now!'

Eirik pondered this for a moment, then asked, 'Tell me, brother, was Murdo vexed from the first? Or, might there have been a particular moment when his disposition changed?'

'From the very first,' I told him. 'From the moment he clapped eyes to Torf-Einar he was –' I halted as it occurred to me what my brother was really asking. 'No, now that I think about it,' I said, considering the matter more completely, 'it was when Torf began talking about the relics.'

This intrigued Eirik. 'Which relics?' he asked, leaning forwards, his expression keen.

'The Holy Lance, and the Black Rood. It was when I asked our lord about those two relics that he grew angry. He would never listen to anything Torf had to say about them; he said it was all lies, and he refused to hear a word of it. When I asked Emlyn about it, he declined to tell me anything. He told me it was not for him to say.'

'A very mystery,' said Eirik. Already, I could see the plot forming in his mind.

'And likely to remain a mystery. There is no power on earth to make Lord Murdo change his mind.'

'True,' allowed Eirik, pursing his lips and nodding. 'We shall see. We shall see.'

My elder brother is tireless when it comes to achieving the unobtainable. Tell him a thing is impossible, or impractical – better still, impossible *and* impractical – and that is the thing he wants. Nothing else will do. His ceaseless energy knows no impediment, no restraint, no limit. As a boy growing up, I watched him lavish the utmost of his strength and effort on all manner of hopeless enterprises.

Do not think I judge him over-harshly, Cait; he would be the first to admit it. You only have to ask him, and he will tell you. He glories in it! All the more so because every now and then he succeeds – as much to his own amazement as anyone's. One of his impossible achievements was gaining a bishopric at an age when most priests are only beginning to entertain the possibility of becoming an abbot. Another was Niniane. If you want to hear the tale of *that* courtship, Cait, ask your gracious aunt. It is a tale well worth hearing.

Over the next few days, Eirik went to work on the problem. I could see him thinking about it as he attended his priestly duties. He schemed well into the autumn with it; had I not known my brother, I might have imagined he had forgotten about it. Not at all. He was only waiting for the best possible moment to pounce. You see, he was up against a man whose capacity for daring the impossible exceeds even his own: Lord Murdo Ranulfson himself. No doubt Eirik believed that if his chance was squandered, it would surely never come again. True enough, but the Swift Sure Hand was already moving to bring about its own inscrutable purposes, as you shall see.

Just after harvest, Eirik left the abbey and went to make a circuit of the realm. He took four brothers with him, loaded a few supplies and trade goods on a horse, and set off. He was gone but three days, when he returned abruptly saying he had had a vision. Everyone gathered around to hear what had taken place.

'We were camped beside a stream,' he told us, 'and I was tending the fire while the brothers prepared our porridge. I was bending to the flames when I heard someone calling to us from the nearby wood. I looked around and asked the brothers who it could be, for all we were far from any settlement. But they heard nothing.

'I waited a little, and the voice called out again, and yet once more. Did these good brothers hear a sound? No, they never did. Here,' the bishop said, 'ask them – they'll tell you.'

'What did you hear?' demanded one of the vassals.

'We did not hear anything at all,' replied the monks.

'And while I was considering what this might mean, a man came out of the wood. He was dressed all in white, and he called me by name. When I hailed our visitor, and pointed him out to the brothers here, they could not see him.'

'We never did see him,' confessed the clerics. 'We neither saw nor heard anything at all.'

The vassals, agog at this wonder, turned in wide-eyed amazement to one another, and I began to smell a rat.

Strange to say, however, I noticed that Murdo had grown very quiet, and now wore a most thoughtful expression on his face.

'This stranger asked me to walk with him, and truth to tell, I did not want to go,' Eirik said. 'But, he said, "Fear nothing, brother. No harm will come to you." So I said, "Who are you, lord?" For I thought it might be an angel speaking to me.'

'Oh, aye,' murmured the vassals, knowingly – as if they were well used to conversing with angels.

Eirik raised his hands for quiet, and continued. 'The stranger looked at me, and said, "I am a friend, and well known to your family." And I did not know what to say to this. "How can this be?" I ask. "I have never seen you before." This brings a smile to my strange visitor's lips. "Brother Eirik," he says to me, for he knows my name, as I say. "Come, I must be about my business."

'He turned and walked a little away from the camp, and bade me to follow. I did, and he said, "The day is coming when the church your father builds will be my home. Tell Murdo to look for me."

'I agree to deliver the message, and ask, "What name shall I give him?" And this is the strangest part of all, for the stranger merely raised his hand in farewell, and replied, "Tell him the Lord of the Promise is well pleased with his servant."

'And then,' Eirik concluded, 'he disappeared into the wood the way he had come.'

The vassals gabbled in astonishment and, when it was certain the bishop had no more to tell them, they went away shaking their heads in awe of this miraculous occurrence.

'I have delivered the message, father,' Eirik said. 'What does it mean?'

'It was *your* vision,' Murdo replied sharply. 'You tell me.' With that, he turned on his heel and walked quickly away.

The bishop sent his monks along to the abbey, and I walked with Eirik to the hall. 'That was well done,' I told him when we were alone. 'How did you find out about the White Priest?'

He stopped in midstep and turned to me. 'How did you know he was a priest?' he demanded.

'You must have said it just now.'

'I said nothing about that,' he insisted adamantly, and I felt a sudden tingle raise the hairs on my arms.

'*Was* he a priest?' I asked.

'You know very well that he was,' Eirik said. 'But I kept that part of my tale back on purpose. You have had it from someone else.'

'And so have you,' I accused. 'I know what you're trying to do. The vassals may be gulled by your talk of visions in the night, but I am not. I doubt Murdo will be taken in by it, either.'

Eirik regarded me with a look of exasperated pity. 'Duncan, Duncan, what are you saying? Do you think I made up a tale? Is that what you think?'

'Of course you did,' I told him. 'It is nothing to me one way or the other, but –' He rolled his eyes and shook his head. 'What? Are you telling me now it was true?'

'In the name of all that is holy, it is the very truth,' he declared. 'It happened just as I told it. Why would I concoct such a tale?'

'To discover the secret –'

48

The light of understanding broke over my brother just then. 'Murdo and Emlyn's secret – is that what you mean? You believe I made up a story to try to draw them into confession?'

'Yes,' I admitted. 'That is what I thought. And I hope it works, too.'

'Brother,' replied Eirik with a smile, 'you are far more devious than I imagined. I do believe you have the guile of the young Lord Murdo himself about you, and no mistake. But surely as God is my witness,' he vowed earnestly, 'it happened just as I said.'

'Very well,' I allowed, accepting him at his word. 'But will it work, do you think?'

'It might,' replied Eirik, thoughtfully tapping his lower lip with a fingertip. 'We will have to be shrewd about it. Say nothing to either of them. Leave it with me. I think I know a way.'

We parted company then, and he hurried off to the abbey.

'When?' I called after him.

'Soon,' he answered. 'Leave it with me.'

That night at supper, Eirik came to the table, dour-faced and grim of aspect. He said little and stared at his food as if he suspected poison. When anyone spoke to him, all they received was a cheerless nod, or a half-hearted grunt. His doleful humour so permeated the meal that conversation ceased half-way through and people began to speak in furtive whispers so as not to disturb the melancholy cleric.

Murdo, as host of the meal, at first tried to ignore his son's gloomy demeanour. When at last that became impossible, he finally gave in and asked, 'Is it ill you are? You seem to have the weight of the world around your neck.'

Eirik raised his eyes slowly, as if contemplating at the cause of all human misery. 'Take no thought for me, father,' he intoned solemnly. 'The weight I bear is mine alone.'

'Is there nothing we can do for you, my son?' asked Lady Ragna.

'I fear not,' he said with a heavy sigh. 'The vision was given to me, and it sickens inside me ere I discern its meaning. This I will do, though I fear the effort will drive me to madness.'

He rose from the bench and made to depart. 'I am sorry. I should not have come to table tonight. I have spoiled a good meal, and beg your forgiveness, my lord.' He made a bow towards mother. 'My lady. I wish you a good night.'

49

A glance passed between the lady and lord. Ragna urged her husband with her eyes. 'Wait,' said Murdo, calling Eirik back. 'There may be a remedy for your ills. Come back and sit down. Eat something. I will summon the abbot and we will talk when you are feeling better.'

'My lord,' said Eirik resuming his place once more, 'dare I hope that you know something to help put my mind at rest?'

'Perhaps,' allowed Murdo. 'Perhaps. But this is not the place to discuss it. Eat something, son, recover your appetite if you can, and the abbot will be here shortly.'

Murdo dispatched one of the serving-boys to fetch the abbot, and the meal continued in a more convivial spirit than before. Eirik, I noticed, recovered his appetite wonderfully well. By the time Abbot Emlyn arrived, my brother was well into his third barley loaf and second bowl of stew.

The ample abbot settled at the board, declining an offering of meat, but accepting a bowl of brown ale. The other guests, eager to learn the outcome of the curious affair, fell silent and all eyes turned towards the head of the table.

'Good abb,' began Murdo, somewhat uncomfortably, 'it seems our bishop has been suffering for the sake of his extraordinary vision.'

'Indeed?' replied Emlyn, turning sympathetic eyes on the young churchman. 'I would that you had come to me, my friend. What is the matter?'

Eirik explained briefly, whereupon Emlyn turned to Murdo. 'If this is not a sign from our Lord and Saviour, I do not know what it can be.'

'It was my thought, too,' replied Murdo. He stood and called to the serving-boy. 'Bring a jar of ale to my treasure room.' Turning to his other guests, 'I beg you forgive our absence, friends. This matter is best discussed in private. Please, linger as long as you like. My lady wife will see the jars remain filled.'

With that the three of them rose from the board and started from the hall. Those left at table were suddenly stricken with the knowledge that they were to be left out of the discussion and never discover the mystery's resolution. I include myself in that number, for I was not invited to share their private deliberations. I watched them walk away, and felt a mighty disappointment pinch me hard.

50

The meal ended and the guests drifted away. I sat for a time with my mother, glumly watching the fire on the hearth, and feeling as forlorn as a hound banished from my master's side. Haldi, the serving-boy, appeared after awhile with the jars of ale. Ragna called to him as he moved towards the door at the far end of the hall.

'Bring the tray to me, Haldi,' she said. He came and lay the tray on the table. She dismissed him, saying, 'They will be some time at their talk, I think. Help cook in the kitchen and then you can go to bed. I will see to the lord's ale.'

Haldi thanked her and ran off, glad at the prospect of finishing his chores early. Rising then, my mother, yawned and said, 'I have grown tired myself, and believe I will go to bed. Perhaps you would not mind undertaking this duty, Duncan.'

'By all means, my lady,' I replied. 'I am only too happy to oblige.'

She kissed me on the cheek and I bade her good night. Then, so as not to waste another moment, I snatched up the tray and hastened off to the treasure room where the mystery of Eirik's vision was being revealed.

SIX

The treasure room is a small chamber in the centre of the house, with no windows and but a single low door. Its walls are good solid stone and very thick. It was, I believe, the first part of the house to be constructed, and all the rest – the sleeping rooms, stores, workrooms, kitchen and hall – was built around it. Many an Eastern potentate has such a room, I have learned, but few noblemen in the north. The reason is that such wealth as men possess in the wild northlands resides in the land itself – the fields, cattle, grazing land, and the like.

Murdo owns wealth like this in abundance, to be sure. But he also possesses a treasure that would make many a king grow heartsick with envy if the full extent of it were ever known. Murdo has ever been circumspect about his treasure; he never speaks of it, and seldom even visits the room wherein it is housed. Once, as a boy of six or seven summers, I sneaked the great iron key from its hiding place and waited until everyone was about some other chore, and then let myself in to see what I might find.

The room itself was, even to my childish eye, small and low. There was a table in the centre of the room with one chair, and a candletree with half-burnt candles. There were four large oaken chests – one on each wall – and each chest was bound in broad iron bands which were likewise locked. I had no keys for any of the locks, but the discovery of those chests proved almost as exciting as an entire silver hoard. I put my eye to the centre lock of the largest chest and beheld the dusky glimmer of gold within.

Footsteps outside the door prevented me from carrying out similar examinations of the three remaining chests. But that solitary glimpse was enough to fuel my fevered imaginings for many days afterwards.

Ah, but the truth, Cait, is more marvellous by far. One day, you will see for yourself.

That night, however, the treasure was far from my thoughts. I entered the low, candlelit room with the jars of ale, and before anyone remarked on my presence began filling the bowls – as if this were my usual chore. I filled Emlyn's first, then moved on to Eirik's and lastly to Murdo's cup. He thanked me, and then recollected himself and asked what had become of Haldi?

I replied that the lady had sent him to help the cook, and asked me to serve in his stead. 'Since you are here,' Eirik said, 'you might as well stay and hear this.'

The suggestion sat ill with my lord, I could tell. He was on the point of refusing when Abbot Emlyn spoke up. 'Yes, let Duncan stay.'

'Do you think it wise?' asked Murdo doubtfully.

'He must know the truth,' the abbot declared, 'if he is to serve it. Yes, let him stay.'

His words sent a thrill of excitement through me. Was there more to this than I guessed?

Murdo held his frown for a moment longer, and we all waited for him to make up his mind. 'Very well,' he relented at last. 'So be it.' He directed me to close the door and sit down.

I did as he asked and settled atop the great oak chest I had tried to peek into years before. 'We have been speaking of your brother's vision,' my father told me. 'What I am about to say is known only to three other people in all the world. Emlyn, my old friend, is one of them. Your mother is the other.'

He paused then, as if uncertain how to continue. 'Speak it out,' Emlyn exhorted gently. 'It is for the best, I do believe.'

Murdo nodded. Turning to Eirik, he said, 'A long time ago, when I was a young man – little more than a boy – I, too, saw the White Priest . . .'

This surprised me.

'Twice,' he added. 'Once in Antioch, and once in Jerusalem. He appeared to me and asked me to build him a kingdom.' Murdo paused, remembering, and added with a wave of his hand to signify not only the house and caer, but the lands and fields of the settlement beyond. 'This I have tried my best to do.'

'The promise,' said Eirik. 'He said the Lord of the Promise was pleased. He has found favour with your efforts, my lord.'

Murdo nodded thoughtfully. 'Many things happened in the Holy Land, and most of them are best forgotten. Though I have remained true to the vow I made, I had lately begun to think I would not live to see it fulfilled. Indeed, I had not thought to hear from him again.'

'Until today,' said Eirik.

'Until today,' confirmed Murdo.

'Forgive me, lord,' I said. 'But who is this White Priest? Is he a phantom?'

'Perhaps,' replied my father. 'He might be an angel. I cannot say. He told me his name was Andrew, and he appeared in the form of a monk – at least, he looked like one to me.' He paused, remembering, then added, 'Indeed, although I did not know it, I believe he guided me through all that followed – every step of the way from that day to this.'

Murdo went on to explain how he had been deep in the catacombs of the monastery of the Church of Saint Mary outside the walls of Jerusalem when he had his second encounter with the White Priest. 'I was alone for just a moment, waiting for the others to return, and he appeared to me,' Murdo explained, his voice taking on a softer edge as his mind took him back through the years to that portentous meeting.

'We talked, and he asked me to serve him. I asked what he wanted me to do, and he said he wanted me to build him a kingdom where his sheep could safely graze. He said: "Make it far, far away from the ambitions of small-souled men and their ceaseless striving. Make it a kingdom where the True Path can be followed in peace and the Holy Light can shine as a beacon flame in the night." You see,' said Murdo with a slightly embarrassed smile, 'I have remembered every word of it all these years.'

'Was that the first time you heard of the True Path?' I asked.

'Not at all,' replied Murdo, surprised at the question. 'It was Emlyn here who told me. Ronan and Fionn – you remember them; you and Eirik met them once or twice when you were boys – also instructed me. Although, at the time I took little of what they said to heart. I hated priests – and with good reason – as many will tell you.'

'Then this is even more remarkable than I knew,' said Eirik.

'How so?' asked Emlyn. 'The Célé Dé have always been the Guardians of the True Path and Keepers of the Holy Light.'

'And so I truly believe,' replied my brother adamantly. 'But today a man appeared to me in a vision, and told me that he was coming here to live. Why does everyone seem to know about the White Priest but me?'

'I have never spoken of it before now,' said Murdo. 'Nor has Emlyn. Who else could possibly know?'

Eirik put out his hand towards me. 'Duncan knows,' he said, and told them about our conversation earlier that day.

'Is this true, Duncan?' Murdo asked, and I confessed that it was. 'How did you come by this knowledge?'

'Torf-Einar told me before he died,' I answered, and related what he had said about the sacred relics and their mysterious guardian. 'Torf said the White Priest appeared to the pilgrims in Antioch and told them to dig in the church to find the lance of the crucifixion.' Spreading my hands in a profession of innocence, I added, 'I had no way of knowing it was part of any secret.'

Abbot Emlyn had grown very quiet and thoughtful. He regarded Murdo with a look of kindly reproach. My father, becoming increasingly agitated, finally burst out, 'Very well!' Thrusting a hand at the abbot, he said, 'If it will put an end to your pestering, I will tell them everything.'

So saying, he moved to one of the chests, and I thought he meant to unlock it. Instead, he slid one of the iron bands to one side, and withdrew a long rod, with a flattened hook at one end. My curiosity increased as he walked to the centre of the chamber and selected a flagstone on the floor. Slipping the hooked end of the rod into the crack between the stones, he quickly prised it up and lifted it away.

Kneeling down, he reached into a stone-lined cavity and pulled out a long, thin bundle bound in leather which he brought to the table, and began unwrapping. Eirik and I gathered close to see what it could be, and Emlyn stepped to the table, standing with his hands clasped, a look of rapture on his round face.

Beneath the leather was a layer of fine linen, and beneath that, another. My heart beat fast as the last wrap was pulled away to reveal ... a length of old, pitted iron, crooked with age and ruddy-tinted with rust. From the way both Murdo and Emlyn reverenced the object, I could see that it was a very valuable – nay, sacred – thing; but for the life of me I could not imagine what made it so. I beheld the slender rod and my heart sank. This? This is the great secret they had protected these many years?

Eirik, on the other hand, appeared dumbstruck. He gave out a gasp and went down on his knees, raising his hands and closing his eyes. He then lowered his face to the floor and lay there in an attitude of prayer. For his part, Murdo merely gazed on the object in silent wonder.

'What is it?' I asked at last.

My father glanced at Emlyn. The abbot stretched out his hand and held it flat above the thing, and said, 'Behold! The Iron Lance.'

I looked at it again. Less than a span in length, and bowed in the middle, it had an ugly stub of a blade at one end and a small hole at the other. Could this bit of scrap which I had taken for a fragment of broken hearthware – a piece of a spit for roasting meat, say – could it be the selfsame spear which had pierced the Blessed Saviour's side?

'If that is so,' I replied, 'I wonder that the emperor himself is not camped outside our walls at this very moment. Or, that the pope in Rome has not made pilgrimage to pay homage.'

'Watch your tongue, boy,' warned Murdo. 'You stand very close to blasphemy, and I will not hear it.'

Emlyn put out a conciliatory hand, and said, 'You promised to tell them everything.' Turning to me, he said, 'A simple explanation will soon set your mind at ease, Duncan. The reason we are left in peace with this inestimable treasure is that neither the pope nor the emperor – nor anyone else in Christendom – knows we possess the Holy Lance. For all the world knows, the sacred relic resides in the treasury at Constantinople.'

'That is what Torf-Einar believed,' I confirmed. 'He told me that he was there the day Prince Bohemond gave the lance to the emperor's envoy. He said he saw it with his own eyes.'

'Many people were there that day,' the abbot assured me. 'I was one of them. Oh, yes. I was standing on the quay in Jaffa harbour when Bohemond arrived. And I, too, saw him give the Sacred Lance to the emperor's envoy, Dalassenus.'

Murdo allowed himself a small, satisfied smile. 'People do not always see what they *think* they see,' he said and, taking up the jar,

56

he poured out some ale then emptied the bowl. He then explained how this had come to be. That night he revealed his long-kept secret to us – as he will tell you, little Cait, when you are older.

'Why have you never spoken of this till now?' I asked when he finished.

'If you had seen half of what I saw in Jerusalem,' Murdo replied, 'you would not ask.'

'Terrible it was!' cried Abbot Emlyn. 'Like wolves loosed among lambs, they gorged themselves on the blood of the helpless. Their greed knew no restraint – and what they could not carry off, they destroyed.' The good abbot, almost shaking with disgust, bent his head and concluded sorrowfully, 'They broke their vows and disgraced themselves before God and man. They had the chance to show the world the benevolence of true Christians. Instead of presenting themselves the best of men, they behaved as the very worst.'

After a moment, he said, 'This makes the task of the Célé Dé all the more precious and important.'

'Perhaps,' suggested Eirik, 'that is why the White Priest is coming to make this his home.'

'No doubt,' reflected Murdo. 'No doubt you are right about that.'

He placed his hand reverently on the Holy Lance, then picked it up and handed it to me. My fingers closed on the length of old iron; it was cold to the touch, as you might expect, and slightly heavier than it appeared. Beyond that, there was nothing at all remarkable about it. I passed the ancient weapon to Eirik, who bowed his head as he received it, and said a prayer. When he finished, we bound the sacred relic in its linen and leather wrappings, and replaced it in its hiding place beneath the floor.

That night, I could not sleep for thinking about the strangeness of the tale I had heard. All my life I had lived in that house, and never once suspected it concealed one of the holiest objects the world has ever known. What is more, I had touched it and held it in my hands. I thought about the Western noblemen, their greed and wickedness, and the insufferable arrogance of the pope, blithely sending so many thousands to their graves. As I lay sleepless, thinking these thoughts, there kindled in me a righteous rage that such faithless men should hold sway over the poor and humble in their care.

Then, as restless night gave way to placid dawn, I conceived the plan which, for better or worse, has led me to my fate.

SEVEN

I told no one of my plan. I wanted to live with the decision for a time to let it grow, and ripen if it would. On the whole, it is best not to rush headlong into schemes hatched in the dead of night. Daylight so often reveals the cracks that charmed night conceals, and I had no wish to be foolhardy.

Thus, I went about my work in the usual way, and no one was the wiser. Eirik resumed his circuit; Niniane joined the retinue this time, and Abbot Emlyn undertook a journey to Orkneyjar. Murdo threw himself into the building work, making himself and everyone around him busy dawn to dusk. We went about our chores amiably, but never speaking of the things he had revealed that night, or the marvellous treasure hidden in the centre of the house.

The days began to dull, and the nights to lengthen. Work on the new church slowed as, more often than not, the labourers had to finish the day's work by torchlight. Some of the masons would stay on with us through the winter to keep the worst ravages of gale and ice from undoing their efforts; others, however, were growing anxious to return to their homes in the south. They watched the skies and when Orkney's geese started flying, they flew, too.

Murdo had agreed to transport any who wished to leave to Inbhir Ness where they could get ships to take them home to Eoforwik. I went along, mostly to help with the boat on the return; while one man may sail a boat, it is easier with two, and my lord is very particular about his boat.

With Sarn Short-Finger at the tiller, we made good speed down the coast. It had been some time since I was last in Inbhir Ness, and I looked forward to getting any news I could – especially of the Holy Land. Since the weather was fair, and appeared likely to remain that way for a few days, I convinced Sarn to stay a day in the town. He agreed it would be no bad thing and, once we had seen the stone masons settled aboard a ship leaving that night, we walked along the harbour and talked to the sailors.

I found no one who had any word of the Holy Land, but the harbour master said we might pay a call at one of the drinking halls fronting the quayside. This we did, but with no better result. No one knew anything. After our second hall and third bowl of ale, Sarn asked, 'Why do you want to know about the Holy Land?'

'Have you never been curious, Sarn?'

'I was once,' he replied thoughtfully. 'I wanted to know where the badger cub went.' He held out his hand and I saw that his middle finger was shorter than the others. 'I found out, and I was never curious after that.' He was quiet for a moment, then added, 'That is why the sea is better: no badgers.'

We finished our bowls, and walked around the town to clear our heads. I saw an old woman who was making shoes from lambskin and leather; she had a small pair made for a child and adorned with little birds of red and blue thread cleverly sewn. These I bought for my daughter. They kept you warm all winter, Cait, and I think you would be wearing them now if your feet had not grown too big.

There was a baker in the town also, who made little hollow loaves of bread filled with spiced meat and turnips; I bought two of these, and some black bread and sausage, for our supper. We fetched a jar of ale from the hall at the quay before retiring to the boat for the night.

Sarn and I ate our meal and listened to the talk of the sailors around us. Some of them got drunk and started to sing. After awhile, they left off singing and started fighting instead, and three of them ended up in the water. They were fished out by their shipmates and wandered off to find more to drink. Things grew more quiet after that, so Sarn and I rolled ourselves in our cloaks and went to sleep.

We left early the next morning, and were at sea as the sun was rising. On our return to Banvarð, we beached the boat, and staked it down for the winter. Murdo was glad the masons had found swift passage home as it would make them all the more eager to return next year.

This comment, innocent as it undoubtedly was, cast me into a despondent humour. At first I thought I was merely disappointed that my efforts in Inbhir Ness had failed. Although it was not as if I had counted on learning anything of particular significance, still I had hoped. As the days darkened around me, so darkened my mood. I grew irritable, and grumbled when people spoke to me. I lashed out angrily at trifles, and made myself miserable holding grudges for imagined slights.

One night I dreamed of Rhona, and the dream reawakened the grief I imagined was finished. I began feeling her absence more acutely than ever. I spent whole days staring at the fire while the wind whined in the eaves. Other times I walked out along the shore in the snow and sleet until my feet froze and my face turned blue. I would start in my sleep, and awake with the feeling that I was being strangled. The queerness of it frightened me so that I refused to close my eyes when I lay down.

It was then I realized the source of my distress: my plan had come to maturity, but I was unwilling to face it. Having occupied myself with it from the Feast of Saint Brighid to Saint Thomas' Mass, it was time to begin doing something about it. Fearing the opposition my decision was certain to ignite, I hesitated, and this was the source of my misery.

My father would not welcome my decision, this I knew. Nevertheless, I resolved to announce my plan at the Yuletide festivities – imagining that any objection to my scheme would be muted by the general celebration. Having resolved myself, the clouds of gloom lifted for me and I undertook to help with the feast-day preparations, which pleased and gratified my mother greatly.

Yuletide found me in good spirits; some of the vassals remarked that I had finally ceased pining for the loss of my dear wife. Accordingly, I received the kindly attentions of certain daughters whose parents, no doubt, hoped for a noble match. While I enjoyed their blandishments, I did my best not to encourage their hopes. My mind and heart were set on other things, and I would not be dissuaded from my purpose. Still, I did not lack for female companionship, and passed a most pleasant Yule.

I might wish now, my darling Cait, that I had taken one of them to my heart for your sake. To have provided you with a mother ere

I departed would have been a blessing. Alas, the notion occurred to me far too late.

I waited for my chance to reveal my plan. Finally, on the last night of the festivities, when the year had turned, we gathered for the Twelfth Night celebration. Murdo's hall was filled with vassals, monks, and friends from Orkneyjar; the vats were filled with spiced ale, the cauldrons with stewed beef and pork with brown beans, and steaming jars of mulled wine lined the long tables. At the lord's invitation, we took our places at the board and began to eat and drink.

Other dishes were brought and placed before us in their turn: sausages cooked with ale and apples, fish with fennel, and smoked ox-tongue roasted with sour cabbage. On each table were small mountains of special round loaves – the Twelfth Night bread baked specially for the feast. We ate and drank our fill of these delights, and when the first pangs of hunger had receded, Abbot Emlyn rose from his place and called the hall to silence.

'My friends!' said the cleric, lifting his voice above the cheerful rumble. 'On such glad occasions it is good to pause and give thanks to the true Lord of the Feast who has so bounteously provided for his people.' With that, he clasped his hands and bowed his head. His prayer of thanks was simple and sincere, and short – a quality which greatly endeared the abbot to his flock. For when Emlyn prayed, one never got the feeling he was trying to chastise or rebuke his congregation by another means. Nor did he use the opportunity to display his erudition to impress or humble those beneath him – a temptation far too many clerics do not resist. When Emlyn prayed, he merely spoke his mind to his Creator, the Gifting Giver, he so evidently loved.

When he finished, my Lord Murdo rose next. He instructed everyone to fill their cups and bowls, and said, 'We drink to the year now begun! May the God of Goodness and Light bless us richly, and may our realm prosper in every good and worthy thing.' We drank to that, and he said, 'If it shall please our Great Redeemer, this time next year we will gather to consecrate the new church.'

'Amen!' cried Abbot Emlyn. 'So be it.'

We raised our cups again, and then I was on my feet. Every face turned towards me in anticipation.

'Before God and this brave company,' I said, 'I pledge myself to undertake the pilgrimage to Jerusalem for the sake of my soul. If it should please God to reward my journey with success, I will pray for our realm and ask the Good Lord's blessing on us all.'

This unexpected declaration was met with astonishment; gasps and murmurs of surprise filled the hall. Emlyn stood quickly and came to my side. He looked at me inquiringly. 'Are you so resolved?' he asked.

'I am,' I replied.

He gathered me in a strong embrace, saying, 'God bless you, my son! It is the Saviour King himself who has put this into your heart.'

I thanked him, and was suddenly swarmed by others who thronged me to wish me well, and to add their pledges of support to my own. Several of the younger men offered to accompany me, and others to send gifts of provisions or gold to aid the journey. Everyone, it seemed, was delighted with the purpose of my pilgrimage.

Everyone, that is, except the one whose approval I valued the most: Murdo. My lord stood looking at me as if he had taken an arrow through the heart. Then, very slowly, he walked to where I stood. The hard expression on his face soured the mirth and all laughter ceased as an uneasy silence descended over the hall. I could hear the fire crackling in the hearth as he stepped before me, his eyes burning with rage.

'That was ill spoken,' he breathed, his voice soft – as if he struggled mightily to restrain it. My mother, distraught, joined him.

'My lord,' I said, 'it has long been in my mind to do this thing. I believe God has called me to his service.'

'We will speak of this later,' Murdo said stiffly.

'Let us speak now,' I countered recklessly.

'Later,' Murdo insisted. 'This is not the time to pursue a family dispute.'

I made to reply that this was as good a time as any, when I felt my mother's hand on my arm, trying to restrain me. She implored me with a silent shake of her head.

'As you will, lord,' I replied, yielding to Ragna's gentle entreaty. 'We will speak later.'

The feast resumed, but slowly, and I felt like a rowdy cub that had just been slapped down by an annoyed bear. I sat for a while, trying to shrug off my reproof, but it was no use. The rebuke rankled, and I could not easily stifle my resentment. After awhile, I found a chance to slink away and left the hall unnoticed.

I went out into the freezing night and felt the sting of the icy wind on my hot face. What, I asked myself, had I expected? Did I really think Murdo would clap his hands and extol my pilgrimage with high words and praises?

No. What had happened was what I feared would happen, nothing more. The trouble was my own making. If there was any consolation, it was this: at least, I had announced my intention; come what may, my plan was no longer a secret.

All the next day I waited to be summoned to my lord's chamber to receive the reprimand I knew was coming. But it did not come. The day passed and nothing was said; we bade farewell to our guests, and saw them away. Out of consideration for me, no mention was made of my announcement of the previous night. The day turned foul so I stayed in with little Cait, and took supper with my mother in the evening.

'He is that angry with you, Duncan,' she said, pursing her lips in her vexation. 'He has snapped and snarled like a wolf with a toothache all day, and refuses to come to the table.' She stopped ladling the soup into the bowl, and looked at me. 'You must go to him and tell him it was a mistake.'

'How so?' I asked. 'He may not like it, but it was no mistake. I mean to go to Jerusalem just as I said. True, I would go with a better heart if I had his blessing, but with his approval or without it, I *will* go.'

She frowned. 'Duncan, please, you do not know what you are saying.'

'Do I not, my lady?' I said. 'Have I lived so long in this house that I know nothing of such things?'

'That is not what I meant,' she replied, placing the bowl before me. She sat down and, folding her hands, leaned towards me across the board. 'When he returned from the pilgrimage,' she said, 'your father vowed that neither he nor any of his family would ever again journey to the Holy Land. You have gone against him in this, and I fear the outcome.'

'I am sorry, mother,' I replied. 'But I knew nothing of this vow.'

'I wish you had said something, son. I could have told you.' She regarded me with sad eyes. 'Is it so important, this pilgrimage?'

'My lady, it is,' I replied earnestly. 'It is all I have thought about since Rhona died. I believe God has put the desire in my heart, and he alone can take it away.'

'And if you go, it will kill your father,' Ragna pointed out. She frowned again and reached out to squeeze my hand. 'Believe me, Murdo could not stand the torment of your leaving.'

'The torment would be mine,' I said sharply, 'not his.'

Lady Ragna shook her head gently. 'No,' she said, 'because he knows – even if you do not – what lies before you. He has been there, Duncan, and he knows the dangers you will face. He could not live with the hardship and suffering that would befall you.'

'If God has put it in my heart to go, and I do *not* go,' I replied, 'what am I to do then? How am *I* to live with that?'

EIGHT

I left Banvarð without speaking to my father again, and the regret of that bitter leaving pains me still. Believe me, Cait, I would give the world and all its treasures to have departed with a blessing from the one person in the world whose approval alone would have sustained me through the trials I have faced. But Murdo was implacable in his opposition. He refused to speak to me until I repented of my plan. This I could not do.

I have since had many occasions to wonder what he would have said if he had known the *true* purpose of my pilgrimage? Would it have made a difference?

Who can say?

Know this, my soul, and remember it always: I have no fear of death. For me to leave this life is to enter the next in triumph. But the thought that I will die in this foreign land without ever seeing the faces of those I have loved best in life fills me with grief so strong it does take my breath away.

Even so, I bear my lot patiently for your sake, and pray the caliph tarries yet awhile so that I may finish what I have begun.

It is a most curious captivity, I declare. I am given the best of food and drink; my modest needs are met without the humiliation that so often accompanies captivity. I even have a servant to attend me and, in many ways, I am treated as an honoured guest with all courtesy and respect. Even so, I accept all I am given with gratitude, knowing it could so easily be otherwise.

The Muhammedans are a noble people, never doubt it. If peace were ever possible, I think we should find ourselves brothers under the skin. Alas, too much blood has been shed on both sides of the battle line for it to be forgiven. There will never be peace between our peoples until our Lord Christ brings it at his return. This I most heartily believe.

Now I will tell how I came to Marseilles.

On the morning I took the boat, I asked Sarn to accompany me. I did not tell him where I was going. I had made my farewells the night before – not that anyone knew it – and rose at dawn and went down to the bay to rouse Sarn out of his nest of oars and sailcloth. In warm weather he always slept in the hut beneath the cliff on the strand.

I let him think we were going fishing, until we had made the headland, and then I told him to sail for Inbhir Ness. It was then he looked at the pack I had brought aboard. 'Where are you going, lord?' he asked.

'I am going away for a while,' I told him.

'It is the pilgrimage, so?' A sly expression passed over his open, honest features, giving him a look of mild imbecility.

Of course, everyone in the realm knew about my desire to undertake the pilgrimage – *and* my father's unyielding opposition to it. The entire settlement had discussed it at length, and most had taken sides.

'Have you made a wager on me?'

He smiled readily. 'Yes, lord,' he admitted without guile. 'You are your father's son. Some of the others said you would stay, but I knew you would go.'

'Once you have seen me to Inbhir Ness, you can go back and collect your winnings,' I told him.

'The wind is good. We will be there before dusk,' he announced, looking at the sky. Indicating my small bundle of belongings, he said, 'Are you certain you have enough food to see you to Jerusalem? The abbot says it is very far away.'

'I have enough,' I allowed, 'to see me three or four days. After that, I am in God's hands. It is for him to provide.'

'Do you have a sword?' he asked, regarding my sad bundle doubtfully.

'If I need a sword, I will get one,' I told him. 'True pilgrims carry no weapons.'

He frowned at this, but returned to his tiller, and I to the contemplation of the task ahead of me. It was my intention to follow my father's example by going to Inbhir Ness and begging passage as a crewman for any ship sailing south. I did not think it would be more than two or three days before I found a ship to take me on. Certainly, when I bade farewell to Sarn and sent him home, I did not think to see him again.

But, two days later, I was still waiting at the quayside when he returned. I saw the ship as it came into the harbour and recognized it; my heart sank. I imagined my lord had come to take me back. But it was not Murdo he had brought with him, it was Padraig.

'If you have come to talk me out of leaving, you can turn around and go home,' I told him bluntly. 'My mind is made up. I am on pilgrimage.'

The tall, soft-eyed monk regarded me mildly. 'Then I am a pilgrim, too,' he replied.

'What do you mean?' I asked suspiciously. 'Did my father send you to bring me home, or not?'

'Lord Murdo says that if you leave now, you leave forever. You must never think to see your home again, for the dead do not return.'

'He considers me a dead man, is that it?'

'That is what he told me to say.'

'Well, you have said it. You can go back and tell him that I must do what God has given me to do.'

'My uncle said that is what you would say,' Padraig observed placidly. 'Abbot Emlyn said that if you were determined to carry out your plan, then I was to accompany you.'

'Accompany me? All the way to Jerusalem?'

'Yes, lord,' affirmed the monk. 'I am to be your servant and guide.'

'Thank you, Padraig,' I told him. 'But this is my decision. You are free to go home. Tell the abbot I cannot accept responsibility for any life but my own. I thank him for his kindness, however.'

'Sarn will tell him. I am going with you.' He raised his hand and declared, 'Hear me: pilgrimage is a sacred undertaking. We go on faith, or we do not go at all. But if we travel with hope, trusting in our Great Redeemer, we need have no fear, for we shall meet angels along the way who will befriend us.'

'Look you, as much as I would like your company, I cannot allow you to go to Jerusalem with me,' I said. 'You have no provisions, no cloak, no water skin.' Pointing to his bare feet, I added, 'You do not even have shoes.'

68

Padraig smiled. 'My cloak and staff are in the boat. If I have need of anything else, God will supply it out of his matchless bounty.'

Sarn, who had been listening to this exchange from his place at the bow rope, spoke up. 'That is the same thing *you* told *me*, lord,' he chuckled.

'You stay out of this,' I snapped. I glared at them both. Daylight was quickly fading and twilight gathering; if I sent them back now it would be dark before they reached the estuary. 'Very well,' I relented, 'you can stay here with me tonight, but you must leave in the morning.'

Padraig said nothing, but set about making a fire. Sarn tied the boat to a post driven into the earthen bank that served as part of the harbour wall. That finished, he brought out a bundle and began unwrapping it – loaves of bread, dried fish and pork, and other things to make a meal. 'There is ale in the stoup,' he said. 'Lady Ragna thought you might like a last good drink before going to the Holy Land.'

Stepping over the bow and into the ship, I found the jar.

'How did you know I would still be here?'

The seaman shrugged. 'There were no trading ships when I left you. If any came they would not have departed so soon.'

'So now it is Sarn the Shrewd, I suppose?'

He smiled. 'We would have drunk the ale whether you were here or not.'

'See you do not drink too much,' I warned lightly. 'You are leaving in the morning – *both* of you. Together.'

We ate our meal, and night gathered around us. Torches were lit along the bank, and we sat drinking ale and watching the flickering light along the quayside. It was quiet; there were few ships in the harbour, and most of the sailors were at one or the other of the town's inns.

'There are not many ships coming here, I think,' Sarn observed. 'How long will you wait?'

'As long as it takes,' I replied, slightly annoyed by the question. 'I talked with a man yesterday who was at Rouen in the spring. He said the Franks are raising men for the Holy Land.'

'Rouen,' repeated Padraig. 'That is where Lord Ranulf and the northern noblemen joined the crusade.'

'It is,' I confirmed.

'Then maybe we should go there,' suggested the monk.

'Is that not the very thing I plan to do,' I retorted, my irritation growing, 'as soon as I can get a ship?'

'You already have a ship,' Padraig pointed out. 'Sarn could take us.'

I might have resented the idea if it had not struck me as faintly ridiculous. 'He might,' I agreed haughtily, 'if he had a chart and provisions enough for such a trip.'

Sarn brightened, his smile wide in the dark. 'I have these things.'

I stared at him. Had the two of them conspired in this? 'The boat is too small,' I complained. Truly, I had imagined sailing into Jerusalem aboard a Norse longship like the one my father had journeyed in.

'Small, yes,' Sarn conceded amiably, 'but the boat is sound and the weather good. It could easily be done.'

'Where did you get a chart?' I asked.

'The monastery provided the chart,' Padraig replied, and explained how Abbot Emlyn had personally supervised the copying and preparation.

'And you have provisions?'

'These we have also,' confirmed Sarn. 'Enough for three men for several weeks of days – although the abbot does not think it will take so long.'

'We can depart in the morning,' Padraig pointed out. 'If you have no objection, that is.'

'Since you both seem to be determined,' I said, 'then I will allow it. You can accompany me to Rouen, and I shall be glad of the company. Once we reach the port, however,' I continued, raising a finger in warning, 'you will turn around and sail home. Is that understood?'

They both regarded me curiously.

'Is that understood?' I repeated.

'It is a long way to Frankland,' Padraig mused. 'Perhaps it would be best to wait until we see what we find when we get there.'

So, we sailed for Rouen, leaving the next morning as soon as it was light enough to navigate the river estuary. The winds were steady, and the weather stayed fair; we made good speed the first five or six days, keeping the coast in sight by day and night. Sometimes we made camp on land; most often we slept in the boat. We lost sight

70

of land only once when fog stole the coast for a night and part of the next day.

It was only upon crossing the narrows and coming in sight of the Frankish coast that the weather soured, and we were lashed by the tail of a thunderous storm. The wind shrieked and hurled stinging waves over the rails time and again. Padraig clung to the mast and prayed; Sarn and I bailed with cup and water stoup. We stood off the coast until the storm had passed; then, almost shaking with relief and singing psalms of thanksgiving, proceeded south to the sea mouth of the river the Franks call Seine.

The city of Rouen lies a fair way up river, and as there was considerable movement to and fro on along the coast we had no difficulty finding the right channel to take us inland. Indeed, we followed a large Flemish trading vessel and arrived two days later. While Sarn tended the boat, Padraig and I talked to the masters and pilots of other vessels to learn who might be heading south. Padraig's Latin was good, and I was pleased to find that mine sharpened quickly as I regained the rhythms of the speech I'd been taught since boyhood.

It seemed that I had arrived at the right place, for the wharf was very busy. As it happened, I was offered passage on no fewer than three ships in exchange for work. After discussing the matter with Padraig, I decided to accept a place aboard a Danish ship sailing for Genoa – one of the places marked on Sarn's map. Indeed, we were walking along the wharf to inform the ship's master of my decision when two men appeared on the quay. Their arrival caused such a commotion of excitement that Padraig and I turned aside to see what they were about.

Tall and lean, they walked with the confident authority of kings, their dark-bearded faces haughty and lordly as they scanned the waterfront before them. The long swords at their belts were freshly burnished and gleamed; their high boots were new. They wore simple tunics – one brown, the other white. The one in white, I noticed, also had a broad cross of red cloth sewn upon his chest.

A group of sailors sitting on the wharf stood abruptly. I heard one of them murmur a name. I turned to the man, and asked what he had said. He pointed to the red cross on the man's tunic, and said, 'Templars.'

Turning to Padraig, I repeated the word, and added, 'Have you ever heard the name?' He confessed his ignorance, and suggested we join the crowd which was quickly gathering around the two men and see what they had to say.

'Friends!' shouted the man in the white tunic. 'Come closer!' He motioned the people nearer, and when the throng had formed around him, he proclaimed, 'In the name of our Blessed Saviour, I greet you and beg your kind indulgence. My name is Renaud de Bracineaux, and you can see by the cross on my surcoat that I am a knight of the Order of the Poor Fellow-Soldiers of Christ and the Temple of Solomon.'

A flutter of excitement coursed through the crowd. Whatever this Order of Poor Fellow-Soldiers might be, it aroused great interest and enthusiasm among the people, more of whom were running to join the throng.

'I will not detain you from your errands,' the knight continued. 'I merely wish it to be known that our illustrious Grand Master Hugh de Payens has lately arrived from Jerusalem for the purpose of inducing men of noble lineage to join our order, which is dedicated to the aid of Christian pilgrims in the Holy Land and the protection of the True Cross.'

These last words caused my ears to burn. I determined to speak to this knight in private, and was even then calculating how this might be accomplished, when he said, 'I thank you for your courtesy. My sergeant and I will remain in Rouen until dawn tomorrow, if anyone should wish to speak with us further.'

The knight dismissed the crowd with a blessing, and the knot of people slowly dispersed. Several young men wanted to hear more, and followed the two knights as they walked from the quayside. Padraig and I fell in behind, and soon found ourselves before a low wooden house fronted by a wickerwork stall from which a man was selling bread and ale and roast fowl. The sawn stumps of trees topped with planks formed benches on which his patrons might sit to enjoy their meals.

'Friends,' said Renaud, 'it would be a very blessing if you would consent to join Gislebert and myself in our midday repast.'

Of course, we all agreed right readily, whereupon the Templar called to the keeper of the inn to supply us liberally with an assortment of his wares. The merchant and his wife busied themselves at once, producing bowls of frothy brown ale, baskets of bread, and platters of roast fowl. Padraig and I found places on one of the benches. The young men talked excitedly and asked many questions, which the knight answered patiently, explaining what would be required to enter their order – as well as the rich rewards awaiting all who donned the white surcoat.

We drank and ate our fill, and listened carefully to all that was said. I quickly discovered that this Order of the Knights of the Temple was in fact a monastic order made up of noblemen sworn to Christ's service for an agreed period during which they were required to forsake family and possessions, and swear a vow of poverty, chastity, and unswerving loyalty to their brother knights.

In exchange for their vow, the newly-accepted brothers would receive a horse, a fine hauberk of ringed mail, a sword, shield, battle helm, and a fine white surcoat with the distinctive red cross.

'Hear, Padraig?' I whispered. 'They are monks – monks with swords. This is wonderful.'

He nodded, gazing on the knights in amazement. Indeed, who had ever heard of such a thing?

When the young men departed, pledging themselves to return later with the permission of their families to undertake initiation into the order, the Templar turned to me. 'What say you, my friend?' he asked amiably. 'Is there any way I can be of service to you?'

'I thank you most heartily for your generosity,' I replied in my best Latin. 'As I myself am a pilgrim even now bound for the Holy Land, much of what you have said interests me greatly.'

'This is most fortuitous, is it not, Gislebert?' he cried to his companion. 'My friend,' he said to me, 'I ween by your speech that you are a nobleman. Rest assured that should you undertake holy orders, you would be admitted to the highest rank of our brotherhood. Our Lord Christ requires the services of such men to protect his people in the Holy Land from the savage predations of the infidel.'

I granted that, attractive as the opportunity to join the Poor Fellow-Soldiers of Christ undoubtedly was, I had undertaken a separate vow which I could not lightly put off.

'I understand,' Renaud replied sympathetically. 'Still, I would be remiss in my sworn duty if I did not point out that a rare opportunity exists which may be of value to you.'

'What is that?'

'Our illustrious Grand Master has sought and received the commendation of Pope Honorius II to grant full ordination of limited duration to any brother who wishes it.'

'How long would be required?' I asked, intrigued by the notion.

'Whatever God in his wisdom has laid on your heart, my friend,' answered Renaud. 'Speaking strictly for myself, I would think two years to be a sufficient duration to aid the Brotherhood – although, I have known many men to pledge five years, or seven. A few have promised service for only a year, as the spirit leads.'

'I see.'

'I mention this, because,' he said, smiling, his teeth a white flash of lightning against the dark cloud of his beard, 'you seem a most thoughtful and capable man, and one who takes his vows in solemn earnest. Also, since you travel in the company of a monk, I am persuaded that you understand the sanctity of our duty better than most. Tell me, have I misjudged you?'

'In no way, my lord,' I replied.

'Then permit me to suggest that you need not put off your vow at all, merely suspend it for a season.'

I stood and said, 'Be assured I will consider your offer carefully.' I thanked him for his generosity, and wished him farewell.

Rising, the Templar nodded to his sergeant, Gislebert, who went to settle with the proprietor for the ale and food, while he walked a little way with me. 'Tomorrow we must continue on our way,' he said, and went on to explain that his brother knights were likewise searching the towns and cities for men to undertake service in the Holy Land. 'We will come together in Marseilles at summer's end,' he said, 'and sail from there to Otranto, where we will join Bohemond and travel to the Holy Land.'

While he was speaking, a quarrel flared up between the owner of the stall and the Templar sergeant. As my attention was given wholly to Renaud, I did not hear how the altercation began. But suddenly, the owner of the stall was shouting, 'But this is not enough! Sir, you asked for the best and I gave you the best!'

Out of the corner of my eye, I saw the innkeeper holding out his hands in dismay at the few small coins he had been given. 'It is more than enough,' Gislebert told him flatly. 'Be quiet, it is all you get.'

He made to turn away, but the innkeeper put out a hand to stop him. The Templar reacted as if he had been struck a blow from a sword. He spun around, hand upraised, ready to strike. 'Be quiet, you!' he hissed. 'Do you want the whole city to know you are a thief?'

'Is there some trouble, sergeant?' called Renaud, taking an interest at last.

'I asked for ten deniers,' cried the aggrieved merchant. 'It is a fair sum – ask anyone, it is an honest sum.' He thrust out his hand to show the small coins. 'He gives me but seven! Seven only! That is not fair.'

The Templar raised his hand to silence the man. 'Give him what he asks, Gislebert,' he said, adding, 'Let us be more careful where we trade next time.'

'It is a fair price,' the proprietor insisted, accepting the additional coins from the grudging sergeant's hand. 'Ask anyone in the city, they will tell you.'

He appealed to no one; the Templar had already turned back to me and was saying, 'We must be on our way, my friend. But remember, if you should change your mind, you will be most welcome to join us. Only,' he added, 'you must decide very soon. It is a long way to Marseilles.'

Again, I promised to think about all he had said, thanked him for the food and drink, and bade him farewell. 'Pax vobiscum,' called the knight, raising his hand in benediction after us. 'God go with you.'

'Pax vobiscum,' replied Padraig. We walked on in silence, retracing our steps to the quayside where we joined the traders and porters passing to and fro along the wharf with their baskets, kegs, bundles, and chests of goods. Unable to rein in his curiosity any longer, Padraig said, 'Are you truly thinking of joining them?'

'It is tempting,' I confessed. 'But no, my thoughts are otherwise.'

'Then what are you thinking, my lord?'

'I am thinking,' I replied, 'that if a pilgrim were bound for the Holy Land, he could not do better than to travel in the company of God's own knights.'

NINE

We spent the rest of the day, and most of the next, trying to discover more about this Marseilles. For although Padraig professed to know of the place, he had no idea how far it might be, nor by which route it could be found. We showed Sarn's map to the pilots of no fewer than six of the larger ships and asked them if they could show us where it might be. Two of them had never heard of the place; one knew the name and told us it was on the south coast, but had never been there; and three pilots tried to buy Sarn's chart for themselves.

Then, as the sun was going down, a slender young man approached the place where our boat was tied. Sarn and I were sitting on the wharf discussing the problem, and Padraig was stirring among the supplies in preparation of our evening meal. The stranger came to where we stood and bowed low before us. 'Pax vobiscum,' he said, 'I would be most grateful if you could tell me if I am speaking to the men who have been inquiring about Marseilles.'

His speech, although flawless, lacked warmth – as if he were uttering words he was being forced against his will to speak. I regarded him closely. His eyes were large and dark against his sallow skin; his hair was black and thick, and cut close so that the curls were tight to his scalp like a knitted cap. His limbs were thin; the clothing that hung on his bony frame, however, was of the finest cut and cloth, and well made. On his thumb was a huge ring of gold, and a fat purse hung at the wide belt which gathered his long tunic around his too-narrow waist; a large knife with a bone handle protruded from the folds.

'We have been asking about Marseilles,' I replied, and explained that it was our wish to join the Templar fleet travelling to the Holy Land.

His large dark eyes, which had appeared somewhat cloudy or hazy, suddenly brightened at my affirmation. 'This is your boat,' he said, pointing to the sturdy craft behind us.

'It is, yes,' I replied.

'And you are its master, yes?' he asked, almost quivering with excitement.

'The boat belongs to my father,' I told him. 'But I have the use of it.'

'Splendid!' he cried, and I thought he would swoon. When he had calmed himself, he said, 'Please, do not think me brazen, but I would like to hire your boat.'

'I admire your boldness,' I told him, 'but I must disappoint you. My boat is not for hire. You see, we –'

'I have money,' he said quickly. 'I will pay whatever you ask. It is very important that I return to my home in Anazarbus as soon as possible.'

'Again, I fear I must disappoint you,' I replied, and explained that so far as we could understand, it was a very long voyage to our destination, and that we possessed, as anyone could see, only a small vessel. With four passengers it would not only be uncomfortable, but dangerous as well. 'I am very sorry,' I told him. 'Still, this is a busy port. No doubt you will soon find someone else who can take you.'

He frowned as sorrow overtook him, and I thought he would cry. His head dropped forwards and he looked at his feet. Then he drew a deep, steadying breath, and said, 'I have no wish to appear impertinent, but the extremity of my plight makes me persist where others would graciously relent. If I offend you, I beg your forgiveness. It seems to me, however, that you contemplate sailing to Marseilles by sea.'

Sarn smiled. His Latin was good enough to understand most of what the young man was saying. 'Sailing is best done at sea,' he replied dryly.

'Of course,' allowed the stranger, 'a man of your obvious skill would find it so. I merely wish to point out a fact that might have escaped your notice. You see, there is another way.'

'You know this other way?' I asked.

'Indeed, yes.'

'And you would show us?'

'Of course, yes. If I were a passenger in your boat,' he said, 'it would be in my best interest to reach our destination by the fastest way possible.' He smiled, his face suddenly glowing with triumph. 'What do you say, my friend? I will most happily be your guide.'

Now it was Sarn's turn to frown. He leaned near, putting his head close to mine. 'I do not like this fellow,' he said. 'How can we be certain he knows what he is talking about?'

'We will find out more,' I told him. To the thin young man, I said, 'What you say intrigues me, I do confess. Perhaps you would care to have supper with us, and we will sit together and discuss the matter.'

Glancing at Padraig, who was beginning to assemble the various items for our meal, the young man said, 'You are most gracious, lord. I will sup with you, but I must beg you to allow me to contribute something to the meal.'

Despite my assurances that this was not in any way necessary, he hastened away – only to reappear a short while later accompanied by a man carrying a large bundle in one hand, and two good-sized jars in the other. At the young man's direction, the man placed the jars and bundle on the ground and, with a low nod of his head, hurried away.

'Please,' said the young stranger, indicating that we should open the bundle. Sarn obliged, pulling the knot in the cloth, which opened to reveal a veritable feast. There were spit-roasted fowl and fish of several kinds; fresh-baked bread, dried fruit, and sweet-meats; there was a stew of beans and pork in a sauce of savoury herbs; and little cakes made with honey and almonds, and covered in tiny white seeds. There was enough for all of us, and more besides.

Pointing to the two jars, he said, 'I did not know if you preferred ale, or wine – so I brought both.'

Sarn was delighted with the banquet, and grinned happily. 'Perhaps we might listen to what he has to say,' he whispered, and began laying out the food.

I called Padraig to come join us, and bade the young man to sit down. 'I am Duncan Murdosson of Banvarð in Caithness,' I said. 'And this is Sarn Short-Finger my pilot, and Padraig ap Carradoc, my friend and advisor.'

The young man professed himself delighted to make our acquaintance and, bowing low, declared, 'I am Lord Roupen, son of Prince Leo of Armenia.' He sat down on the wharf, removing his shoes and crossing his legs.

Padraig blessed the meal, then handed the bowls and cups around, and we began to eat. The food was excellent, and we were soon licking our fingers and smacking our lips. Our young friend, however, picked at his food as if he found it distasteful or unpalatable. He smiled wanly from time to time as Sarn, unable to help himself, exclaimed over the various dishes.

'Your generosity has won the favour of our pilot, it would seem,' I observed, pouring wine into the young lord's cup. 'But I cannot help noticing that you do not share his enthusiasm for our meal.'

'Alas, it is so,' he sighed. 'Exquisite as it surely is, I cannot eat this fare.'

Sarn heard this, and asked, 'Is it because you are a Jew?'

Roupen smiled sadly. 'I am neither a Jew, nor a Muhammedan – despite what many believe. The Princes of Armenia have been Christians for a thousand years.' He glanced with pensive sadness at the food. 'Alas, my lack of appetite is due to a unknown malady with which I have been inflicted since coming to this country.'

'I am sorry to hear it.'

'You are most kind. Still, I have been far more fortunate than my bodyguard and advisor – they took ill and died of it.' He went on to tell how he had come to Paris as part of a royal delegation hoping to establish formal relations with the Frankish king. There were fifteen men and women altogether, and all had succumbed to the mysterious illness, dying within a few days of one another. 'I, too, was taken seriously ill, and was many weeks under the shadow of death. By God's decree, I alone have survived.'

'That is unfortunate,' I replied, pouring wine into his cup. 'I can well understand your desire to return home as swiftly as possible.' I handed him the cup, which he accepted, bowing his head in gratitude.

We drank together for a moment, and I asked, 'This other way,' I said, 'would I be wrong in thinking it was by river?'

He nodded, raising two fingers. 'There are two rivers with but a short distance between them. Larger ships would find them too narrow and shallow to navigate, but your boat will have no difficulty whatever.'

Sarn put his head near mine and whispered to me. 'My pilot wishes to know if you have navigated these rivers yourself.'

'Do you doubt me, sir?' replied the young man, suddenly irate. 'The route I propose was the same as that by which my companions and myself arrived in Frankland. By all means assure your expert pilot that, aside from a short distance which must be covered by wagon, it is possible to do what I suggest. Otherwise, I would not have mentioned it.'

'Do not misunderstand,' I replied. 'It is not your honesty that concerns him. It is your memory.' I explained quickly about Sarn's map, which the pilot hoped to enlarge by adding the details of our journey.

The young lord smiled thinly. 'Again, I must ask your forgiveness. My many travails in this land have made me unduly suspicious and quick to judge. I beg your indulgence. It will not happen again.'

We drank some more, and he seemed to relax a little. I had already decided that his knowledge of the river route would be invaluable to us, but I did not wish to tell him so without the ready consent of my fellow passengers. So, after the meal, I asked him to allow us a moment to discuss the matter. We spoke our northern tongue so that he would not overhear what we said.

'I think we would be well advised to take this fellow on,' I began. 'A journey by river has much to recommend it over a voyage by sea. I say we take him at his word and let him guide us to our destination.'

Padraig added his approval. 'He is a fellow Christian, and comes seeking our aid. He is obviously unwell. To turn him away would be an offence against Heaven, and one we might regret.'

'It is true our craft is small,' Sarn said. 'But if he helps me with the map, I will be happy to share deck space with him.' He nodded, considering his decision, then added, 'He must control his tongue, though. If he can do that, we will get on well enough.'

'Then we are agreed,' I concluded. 'I will tell him.'

Roupen came close to tears on learning of his good fortune. He took my hands in both of his and pledged his perpetual gratitude and fealty. 'Now then,' he said, recovering himself somewhat, 'we must establish the price of my passage.'

'We have agreed to take you in exchange for showing us the way,' Padraig told him. 'Nothing more is necessary.'

But he would not hear of it. 'The service you do me is invaluable. I will pay for my passage, and gladly. Nor will my father be slow in rewarding you richly for your inestimable assistance.'

Taking the pouch from his belt, he untied it and began shaking gold coins onto his palm. He counted out twenty golden bezants, sorted them into two equal stacks, and passed one of them to me.

'This for my passage to Marseilles,' he said, tipping the gold into my hand. 'And you will receive as much again when we arrive safely.' Raising the second stack, he held it before me. 'This is for the necessary provisions for the journey. I am the son of a prince and accustomed to the best of food and drink wherever I go. Therefore, I expect the boat to be supplied accordingly.'

I accepted the gold gladly and without disagreement – which I could see surprised Padraig somewhat. Truly, it was not a matter of courtesy or generosity. I had come away from Banvarð without so much as the price of a small fish in my purse. I had professed my faith in God to provide for us, and the appearance of young Lord Roupen seemed to be the Gifting Giver's way of answering our need. I was in no wise minded to shun the open hand of the Almighty.

Upon agreeing to the bargain, I said, 'We will depart tomorrow as soon as we have gathered supplies for the journey. Come to us as soon as you are ready. We will await you here.'

He smiled with slight embarrassment. 'If it would not trouble you too much,' he said, 'I would find it agreeable to spend the night aboard the boat. Then you will have no need to wait for me.'

Later, Sarn pointed out that it was not so much a matter of waiting, but of trusting. 'This fellow is afraid we will leave without him,' the pilot said. 'After all, now that we have his gold, we do not need him.'

'Our friend is right to be wary,' I told him. 'Of the four of us, he has the most to lose; I think we can tolerate his distrust until he knows us better.'

'I think you should tell him we are not thieves or cut-throats,' Sarn insisted. 'Otherwise he will wear us out with his watching day and night.'

'*You* tell him,' I said. 'He will thank you for your concern.'

Seeing that I meant it, the pilot approached the young man and, in halting Latin, established the fact that we were Christian pilgrims and not vicious thieves bent on slitting his belly and dumping his corpse in the river at first opportunity. What Roupen made of this assurance, I cannot say. But Sarn certainly seemed pleased to have sworn the innocence of his intentions.

We gave our noble passenger the bottom of the boat for his bed; Sarn slept on the tiller bench, and Padraig and I slept on the wharf. As soon as the port began to stir the next morning, we bought the few things we needed and, with a prayer to speed us on our way, set off up river.

TEN

Sailing on a river is more tedious than navigation by sea. It is not without certain benefits, however. If the wind fails, you can always get out and walk along the bank and, if necessary – when confronted by strong currents, or a contrary wind – you can tow the boat. Also, since a river runs only where it will, there is less chance of losing your way. The Franks called the river Seine, and it was to be our constant companion for a good many days.

Roupen said that the next town we should come to would be Paris, which we would reach in five days. In fact, we reached it in four days. We paused only long enough to gather a few more provisions, and then set off again straightaway, for the merchants of Paris were a haughty, imperious tribe, and over-envious of the gold in our purses.

As we began to adjust to this new way of voyaging, I found the days most pleasant. Sometimes we walked, and sometimes we sailed; occasionally, we towed the boat with ropes tied to the bow. Even going with the current, it was hard work, but there were three of us to spell one another, so no one had to bear the brunt of the labour too long. Still, at the end of a day's towing, we were heartily glad we had only a fishing boat and not a fully laden longship.

The weather remained warm, for the most part, and exceedingly dry, as we slipped further and further into the heart of Frankish land. We passed through many settlements along the way: some large, with fine stone churches; most small – a scattering of huts on a muddy track beside the river, tiny fields, and a cattle enclosure or two. We bought supplies and provisions as required. Often, we bargained with the farmers themselves, or more likely, their wives, who were more canny in their dealings.

In this way, we got fresh eggs, milk, and bread, meat and cheese;

and, as summer passed, fruit: apples, plums of all kinds, pears, and berries. On this honest fare, the sallow young lord began to regain his former health. His colour improved, and his strength increased; he still tired more easily than the rest of us, but undertook such chores as he was able with never a breath of complaint.

As Roupen's stomach could not take heavier meat, we fed him with fish from the river. Sarn grew very adept at catching fine brown trout which we enjoyed almost as much as the mackerel we got at home. Roupen appeared fascinated by Sarn's ability to tease the fish out of the dark water. He watched with such fierce concentration whenever Sarn threw out the line, that the seaman undertook to teach him. By way of exchange, the young man offered to help Sarn with his Latin.

The two of them became good friends. Sarn is of a cautious disposition; he gives away little of himself unless he is satisfied his gift will not be squandered, or belittled. He saw in Roupen someone who would honour his friendship; and the young lord found a steadfast companion who did not demand anything of him save simple kindliness.

Consequently, under Sarn's affable instruction, Roupen began to lose some of the stiff wariness in his demeanour. One day, he startled us all by laughing out loud at something Sarn was attempting to say. He threw back his head, clutched his sides, and shook with mirth, while we looked on in amazement as the veil of melancholy with which he habitually cloaked himself was suddenly ripped away, revealing a young man who, I suspect, had not known a moment's solitary delight in years.

His outburst intrigued me, but I did not like to embarrass him, so I waited until the next day to ask him about it. Sarn and Padraig were towing the boat, I was minding the tiller, and Roupen was braiding a bit of rope Sarn had given him for practice.

'What is it like for you at home?'

He thought for a long moment, and then said, 'It is like living in a church – a very great church, full of priests and penitents and pilgrims. In my father's palace, worship never ceases; indeed, prayers ascend on clouds of incense day and night, and the bells ring continually. From my father the prince, to the least stableboy – everyone says his prayers six times a day.'

'Some would consider that a very paradise,' I remarked.

'Perhaps it would be,' he allowed, 'if the whole world did not seek our destruction. Every hand is against us, and we are continually on guard lest our enemies crush us and scatter our ashes to the four winds.'

When I asked how his people had managed to make so many enemies, he explained that it was ever thus. 'The Latin church does not recognize our faith,' he said mournfully. 'They think us worse than infidels, and Byzantium will not rest until they have brought us under the rule of the emperor. Also, since we are first and foremost Christians, the Muhammedans harass and abuse us at every turn.

'It was for that reason my father sent the delegation to the king of the Franks. It was our hope that we might form an alliance with one or more rulers in the West who could use their authority to prevent the crusaders from attacking us. In return, we would offer to help them maintain the pilgrim roads and keep their pilgrims safe from thieves and Turks.'

'Did the king listen?'

Roupen shook his head sadly. 'The chance never came. We made proper representations to his advisors and courtiers, who accepted our gifts and promised to bring our concerns before the king, but the day of audience was always delayed for one reason or another. When the king finally deigned to see us, the sickness had done its work and there was no one left – except me, and I was too ill to keep my head upright, let alone hold lengthy converse with the king.' He sighed, and his shoulders slumped. 'By the time I was well enough to speak to him, the king had long since gone away with his courtiers to his hunting estates in the north.'

'At least you are alive to try again,' I pointed out. 'No doubt that is why God has spared you – so you can help your people.'

'Perhaps,' he conceded reluctantly. 'Although, I have never understood why God does *anything*. If the Lord of Hosts wanted me to help my people, he might simply have allowed me to speak with the king as we had planned –' he paused thoughtfully, adding, '*and* saved the lives of fourteen people into the bargain.'

'The ways of Heaven are mystery itself,' agreed Padraig. I glanced up to see that the boat was drifting near the bank. Padraig was listening, and offered this observation in all sympathy. 'I will pray

85

that the Great King makes his purpose known to you in a way you will understand.'

We changed places with Sarn and Padraig, slipping our arms into the loops of the tow ropes and, with a long, steady pull to get the boat moving, started off again. The day was fair and the sun hot, and I soon found myself dreaming about what might be happening at home in Scotland.

I thought about you, dearest Cait, and wondered what you were doing at that very moment. I imagined you picking berries with Ragna, or chasing the geese with a willow switch. I thought about Abbot Emlyn, and it gave me some comfort to know that whatever befell us on this journey, he would be praying for us. This put me in mind of the true purpose of my pilgrimage – a thing which I had not shared with a single living soul, not even Padraig. I knew I would have to tell him one day soon, but thought it would not hurt to wait a little longer.

As it happened, that day was a Sabbath, so when we camped for the night, Padraig performed a worship service for us. I sat on the riverbank, listening to his clear, strong voice singing the ancient words in Gaelic while one-by-one the timid stars kindled and took light; I sat there thinking I had never heard anything so beautiful, and wished Rhona was with me to share it.

Although the days seemed to pass in lazy, almost effortless succession, we were all the time growing closer to the most difficult portion of our journey: the portage over the hills leading to the Saône valley.

Upon our arrival at the settlement which marked the end of the navigable stream, we found men who earned their living by hauling boats and passengers and goods from one valley to the other. For a fee, they were prepared to guarantee safe passage overland to the next river. As Roupen had dealt with these men before, he undertook to make the arrangements. Sarn was not content to entrust his boat to rough-handed strangers, so he accompanied the young lord to help him choose an acceptable carrier for our vessel.

They returned a short while later well satisfied with the arrangements they had made. 'The haulier will come with his wagon and oxen tomorrow morning,' Sarn informed us. 'We must have all our goods and belongings stacked on the shore so he can draw the boat out of the water.' He pointed to a place a little way upstream where long pine poles had been laid down side-by-side on a shallow slope of the bank. 'That is where we must wait.'

Next morning, we were ready. By midday we were still waiting; meanwhile, two more boats had arrived and both had been hauled out of the water and carried away, and still there was no sign of our haulier. Twice, I sent Sarn to look for the fellow to no avail. When he finally arrived, the day was hastening from us. 'Here I am,' he called. 'It is Dodu at your service.'

'We were told you would come this morning,' I snapped. 'We have been standing here all day.'

Dodu apologized and explained that on setting out that morning, he noticed one of the axles on his wagon had split and the repair had taken longer than he hoped. He would have sent his boy along to tell us, he said, but the child had injured his foot and stayed at home.

The haulier spoke plainly, his Latin the uncomplicated speech of a child. He smiled and spread his hands. 'Starting off with a broken axle would never do,' he said. 'Such things only get worse, never better.' I agreed with him, and he set about his work, humming cheerfully to himself and calling endearments to his docile pair of brown-and-white spotted oxen.

The wagon was little more than two sets of wheels on heavy axles joined by a strong iron chain which could be adjusted according to the size of the boat to be carried. Once he had pulled the boat from the water, we raised the bow of the craft by way of long poles, and attached the front wheels with ropes. The oxen, straining at their wooden yokes, pulled the craft higher up the bank, and we levered up the stern and attached the rear wheels. We then replaced all the goods and rigging back in the boat, and lashed the mast to the bow and stern. By the time we finished, the sun was well down and we were growing hungry. Nevertheless, I was anxious to get at least a little further along the trail before stopping for the night. So, we made a start.

As it had been dry for many days, the road the boatmen used was high and well-kept. We moved out from the trees which grew along the river, and started up a long, rising slope towards the crest of the first hill. The heat of the day was swiftly fading, and the calls of home-winging birds filled the air.

The oxen moved slowly, sturdy legs stumping, their heavy hooves raising little puffs of dust with every step. The haulier, goad in hand, walked beside them, coaxing them along with whistles and little clucking noises. He was a simple, humble soul – one of those who, not blessed with an overabundance of wit, nevertheless make up the lack with a pleasant, kindly disposition. Dodu was so good-natured, I forgave him his lateness and shortly felt the peace of the evening settle over me. We walked a while, and reached the top of the first hill. I looked back down into the valley the way we had come.

The river was hidden by the trees which formed a dark, ruffled line stretching away into the gathering twilight. The soft night air smelled of dry grass and sage; the scent of wood smoke drifted up from the valley. A stone wall separated the road from a small field. Twilight was deepening around us, so we decided to halt there for the night. Sarn made a fire, and Padraig busied himself cooking a porridge of dried peas and barley, which we ate with hard black bread.

After the meal, Padraig sang a song, and Dodu told us a story about a man from his village who found an image of the Holy Virgin in the moss on the side of his cattle byre. Everyone came to see this wonder, including the lord and the local priest, who declared it a miracle, and commanded that the image be accorded all respect.

The man's wife had gone blind the previous winter, he explained, and when the woman was brought before the cow byre, her eyes began to sting. 'Tears fell in a very flood,' the haulier told us. 'She cried out and wiped her eyes with the hem of her mantle, and when she raised her head, her eyesight was restored.'

Roupen listened, idly stirring the fire with a stick. 'Was anyone else healed by this miraculous image?' he asked, his face illumined by the glowing embers.

'Alas, no,' replied Dodu. 'Word spread far and wide, of course, and the sick and lame began to come in their numbers.'

'What happened?' wondered Sarn.

'It rained, and the image washed away. From that day to this,' he concluded, 'it has never been seen again.'

Sarn nodded sagely, and Padraig smiled to himself; but Roupen made a noise through his nose as if a bug had crawled into his nostril. The haulier turned his head to regard the young lord indignantly.

'What? Do you doubt what I say is true? I can show you the cow byre, and I can show you the woman!'

'I am certain you can,' Roupen said, still stirring the embers. 'I do not doubt you in the least. It merely seemed queer to me that God should trouble himself so with moss and mysterious images. If he wished the woman's sight restored, why did he not simply heal her? Better still, why – if he wanted to help the poor woman – did he allow her to go blind in the first place?'

'Who are you,' demanded Dodu angrily, 'that you know the ways of the Lord God Almighty?'

'I am no one,' replied Roupen, his voice sinking in dejection. 'Please, do not upset yourself over anything I have said. It is merely the buzzing of a gnat in your ear, nothing more.'

With that, he snapped the stick in half and tossed it into the fire. He drew up his knees to his chin, and sat staring into the fire, but said nothing more the rest of the night. Talk dwindled after that, and we fell asleep where we lay – waking at dawn to continue on. We made slow but steady progress throughout the next day, and had the road to ourselves, passing no one in either direction. We camped for the night beside the road as before, only to be awakened just before dawn by the sound of horses coming up the hill.

I heard the faint clop of the hooves and awoke at once. Padraig rose and stood beside me. 'How many?' he asked, peering into the darkness. 'Can you see them?'

'No,' I told him. 'Two or three at least, maybe more.'

The moon had set, and although I could hear the riders coming nearer with every step, I could not see them. 'Wake the others,' I told him. 'There may be trouble.'

The monk had just turned to his task when a voice called out. 'Ho! What have we here?'

The horses stopped. A few muted words were exchanged, and one of the riders came on alone. He emerged out of the night – a big, coarse-looking fellow with a frayed cloak over his broad shoulders. He sat for a moment looking down at us. I could see him taking the measure of our group.

'Hail and welcome,' I said, stepping boldly forwards. 'You are early to the trail.'

The man leaned forwards, patting the neck of his horse. 'It is a sin to waste the day abed,' he replied, grinning easily. 'This way, we also avoid the jostling crowds.'

'Since you are in a hurry,' I replied, 'please do not allow us to delay you. There is the road, and you are welcome to it.'

Still smiling, he looked across to the boat, and the oxen which were tethered nearby. 'That is a heavy chore,' he observed, 'hauling boats over hills. Perhaps we can do you a service.'

'We have no money,' I told him bluntly. 'We could not pay you.'

'Did I say anything about payment?' the man asked, as if aggrieved by my suggestion. 'I am certain we can come to an agreeable arrangement.' He made a motion with his hands, and his comrades came forwards. I heard the cold ring of steel as swords were drawn from hangers, and three more riders appeared, short swords in their fists.

Padraig, having roused the others, came to stand beside me. 'In the name of Christ,' he said softly, 'leave us in peace.'

The foremost rider's smile turned nasty as he drew his sword from beneath his cloak. 'We mean to lighten your load, friends, nothing more. Give us no trouble, and you'll get none. Get up, all of you! Stand over there.' He directed us a few paces away.

Padraig and I obeyed at once. The haulier, groggy with sleep and rubbing his eyes, stumbled forwards complaining. Sarn, glowering and muttering in Norse, came next. Roupen, wary but silent, followed; as he stepped from the road to take his place beside me, I saw his hand twitch at his stomach, and his belt slid free. He dropped it to the ground behind him.

While the leader of the thieves kept watch over us, his men began tossing everything out of the boat. They worked with such deftness and quick purpose, I could see they were well accustomed to their labour.

They made a heap of everything they found, bundled it up, and tied the bundles behind their saddles, while we stood watching, powerless to prevent them. Then, when they turned their attention to the oxen, Dodu started forwards. 'No! No!' he cried. 'Take everything else! Take our food! Take our goods! But leave my beasts!'

'Shut up, you!' warned the thief. 'Get back!'

But the haulier paid him no heed. He rushed forwards, making for the place where the oxen were being untied. The chief bandit wheeled his horse; his arm flashed out and I heard a dull, crunching thud. Dodu moaned and fell sprawling in the dust. Padraig started to his aid.

Swinging around to face us once more, the thief said, 'You there! Stand still, or you'll get the same.'

I pulled Padraig back. 'Just get on with it,' I growled. 'Take it and leave.'

Having secured the oxen, one of the thieves began leading them away. The others returned to their horses and climbed into their saddles. 'You see? We are happy to oblige.' Pointing with the tip of his sword, he indicated Roupen's purse on the ground. 'Now then, if you will kindly hand me that belt and purse, we will be on our way.'

Roupen made no move, but glared stubbornly ahead, his mouth clamped shut in defiance. So, the bandit chief called to one of his men who retrieved the belt, and then searched the young lord roughly from head to foot. Finding nothing else, he passed the belt and purse to his master, who snatched it up. The rogue wheeled his mount and started away. 'Kill them,' he called over his shoulder.

The thug swung towards us, brandishing his sword. I could see him trying to work out which of us to murder first. As Roupen was the nearest, and the weakest, he decided to begin the slaughter with him. I waited until he turned towards the young man, and then simply stretched out my foot and tripped him as he passed. The brute sprawled forwards on his hands and knees, but failed to release his grip on the sword. The blade struck the dirt, and bent near the hilt. Stepping quickly forwards, I stomped down hard on his forearm just above the wrist and heard a crisp snap. The brigand yelped in surprise and pain, as I bent down and snatched the weapon from his unresisting fingers.

'Get up,' I told him. He sat up slowly, scowling at me and rubbing his injured arm.

Sarn ran to the boat and looked inside. 'They have taken everything,' he called, 'even the water skins.'

Meanwhile, Padraig hurried to the haulier's aid, rolled him over and put his face near Dodu's nose and mouth. 'He is alive,' the monk announced. Then, feeling carefully around the injured man's head and neck, he added, 'There is no blood. I think he will live, but we must try to wake him.'

I joined Padraig to help with this task, and gave Sarn and Roupen the chore of tying up the thief. 'Truss him tight,' I told them. 'I want him secure for the next magistrate we meet.'

With Padraig on one side and myself on the other, we gently raised the inert bulk of the unlucky haulier into a sitting position. We were just steadying him when I heard Sarn shout. I looked up to see him rolling on his backside, his legs kicking in the air as the thug made for his horse. With three great bounds he gained the saddle, lashed his mount to speed, and raced after his now-distant comrades, leaving us to ourselves once more.

There was nothing to be done in the dark, so, as Padraig tended the goose-egg on Dodu's head, I built up the fire again and then we all settled down to wait for the dawn. Daylight confirmed that Sarn was right: the bandits had indeed robbed us of everything – except the boat, and that could not be moved without a team of oxen.

'How far is the next settlement?' I asked the haulier.

'Far enough,' he replied sorrowfully. 'Those oxen are my living. Without them I am destitute. Ruined!' He grabbed his head and moaned. 'I am ruined.'

'How far?' I asked again. 'Tell me, Dodu.'

He thought for a moment. 'If this is the first hill . . . ,' he began.

'It is,' I confirmed. 'We passed no others. This was the first.'

'Then there are three more hills before the next settlement – a half day's walk,' he sighed, closing his eyes.

'Half a day ahead, and two behind,' I said. 'I guess we go on.'

'But we will get no help there. It is two farms and a pigsty only. They have nothing – not even a dog.'

'After that?' I said. 'How far to the next?'

'There are no others,' Dodu sighed, 'until you come to the Saône. There is a mill, and the miller keeps oxen to turn the wheel.'

'How far is the mill?'

'Four days,' he moaned. 'And miller Babeau is a very disagreeable man.'

Leaving the haulier to his misery, I rose and went to the boat. I leaned my weight against the stern and gave it a push. The wagon wheels creaked as it rocked forwards slightly.

'What are you thinking?' asked Padraig. 'We cannot pull the boat all the way to the river.'

'We cannot leave it here,' objected Sarn quickly. 'If you do, you leave me behind as well. I will not abandon my boat.'

'Peace!' I told him. 'I am not for abandoning the boat. If we can haul it to the next settlement, you and Roupen can stay there and guard it while we walk to the mill.'

Padraig gazed down the slope before us, and up the long rising incline to the next crest in the distance. 'It grows no shorter for staring at it,' I told him.

'Then we had best get started.'

ELEVEN

Using the ropes with which we had towed the boat on the river, I attached them to the stern. 'Two men on each rope,' I said, handing one of the ends to Padraig. 'We will lower the boat down the hill a step at a time.'

'And the fifth man?' wondered Sarn.

'He will stand ready to place a beam under the wheels to stop the wagon if it begins to roll too fast.'

'Where will we get this beam?' asked Dodu.

I looked at the mast, but it was too long and unwieldy for one person alone. Also, I did not wish to risk damaging it beneath the wheels of the wagon. 'We will use stones until we can find a tree branch large enough.'

Thus, with Padraig and Sarn on one rope, Dodu and me on the other, and Roupen carrying two large stones borrowed from the wall beside the road, we began. At first it appeared we would have an easy time of it. Once we got the wagon onto the road, the slope fell away so gradually that we had only to keep the rope taut to prevent the boat from rolling too fast. Halfway down the hill, the haulier said, 'This is not so bad. Now I know how my team feels in yoke.'

'Wait until we start up the other side before you decide whether you wish to change places with your oxen,' Padraig remarked.

We reached the bottom of the hill and stopped to rest. The sun was moving higher and the day growing warmer. A few wispy clouds trailed across the sky, but they would provide no shade. The air was still, so there would be no cooling breeze. I saw a long, hot, exhausting day stretching out before us – and with no food or water at the end of it to refresh and strengthen us.

The incline of the next hill proved not so steep as it first appeared. Roupen, who had but light work on the way down, more than doubled his labour; he was continually darting from one side of the wagon to the other to place the stones behind the wheels to prevent the boat from rolling backward after each hard pull of the rope had gained us a few precious paces.

By dint of hard work we reached the top of the hill by midday, and stopped for another rest. We looked both ways along the road, but saw no other travellers, nor any signs of habitation anywhere nearby. Padraig found a small spring in a rocky cleft low down at the side of the hill. We all went down to drink our fill, and then climbed the hill once more to sit in the shade of the boat.

We dozed through the heat of the day, and then rose once more to our work, taking up the ropes with stiff hands. Again, the downward slope was gentle, and we made short work of it, reaching the bottom of the hill in less than half the time the ascent required.

The next hill appeared but little steeper than the one we had passed that morning, so I was confident we could reach the top by nightfall. 'We will camp for the night up there,' I said, exhorting my exhausted little band. 'There are some trees for shelter. I think we best move along if we are to finish before dark.'

This brought groans of displeasure as we resumed our places once more. We were well tired now; the day's labour had worn away our strength. Each step was a struggle for but small advance. In the end, my hope of reaching the hilltop by nightfall proved wildly optimistic. The moon rose while we were yet but halfway to the top, and the stars were alight in the clear blue heavens long before we put the stones behind the wheels for the last time and fell sprawling into the long grass beneath the trees. Too tired to talk, we slept where we dropped.

The next day was much like the one before – save that we were stiff and aching from our rough sleep and the previous day's exertions, and the hill rising before us was steeper than either of the two we had conquered. 'The settlement is in the valley beyond,' Dodu said once we gained the top. 'There is a wide meadow and a stream. We will get water and something to eat.'

'Then why are we waiting?' demanded Sarn. 'The sooner we reach the settlement, the sooner we can get something in our stomachs.'

The first part of the ascent went well, but when the incline grew suddenly steeper, and we could no longer move the boat by pulling on the ropes, we were forced to push. The day passed in a haze of sweat and blistering sunlight. The muscles in my shoulders, back, and legs knotted; my throat grew dry and my tongue seemed to swell in my mouth. My feet tangled time and again, so that I had to struggle to stay upright. Each slow, agonizing step became a battle of will and determination as we fought our way to the top where we collapsed in the middle of the road to lay gasping and staring up at the sky, the sweat running from our bodies in rivulets. After a time, I sat up and looked down into the valley. As Dodu had said, the settlement was little more than two clusters of buildings huddled together beside the road with fields on either side; there was a small stone enclosure for pigs, a few hayracks, a raised storehouse, and a stand of trees beyond the fields. It may not have been much, but, God be praised, it was not far, and the slope was not steep.

The end is in sight, I told them; the hard work is over. We have but to ease the wagon down the hill and rest is ours – food and drink as well. 'We will eat and drink tonight,' I said, 'and sleep on straw. Come! Our supper awaits.'

'I wonder if they have any beer?' said Sarn.

'I will gladly settle for bread and water,' remarked Padraig.

'Listen to you now,' said the haulier, still puffing as he climbed laboriously to his feet. 'Down there lives the woman who makes the best ale from the Seine to the Saône – and smoked pork chops, too. I always buy a few whenever I pass.'

'Why have you kept this from us till now?' demanded Sarn. 'You should be telling us this from the first.'

'I did not want to cause you an injury,' replied Dodu. 'Thinking about such things on an empty stomach can cause a man to forget what he is doing.'

Our shadows were long on the hilltop as we rose to take up the ropes for the last time. With groans and moans and much gritting of teeth, we eased the boat-laden wagon down the slope one step at a time. With each step, the farm holding came nearer and I could almost taste the ale in the jar. I was jolted out of this pleasant anticipation when Sarn struck his foot against a stone and fell. I heard him cry out and saw him sprawling in the dust, the rope flying from his hands. Suddenly unbalanced, Dodu stopped and reared back with all his might. Unfortunately, he could not hold the weight by himself, and was jerked off his feet.

Before I knew it, Padraig and I were plummeting down the hill, trying desperately to slow the free-wheeling wagon. Roupen dashed to our aid. He ran up and shoved the tree branch in front of the wheels, but the wagon was already moving too fast. The wheels bumped over the branch and kept on rolling.

There was nothing for it, but to throw off the ropes and save ourselves. Padraig stumbled, still clinging to the rope, and was dragged through the dust. 'Let go, Padraig!' I shouted, releasing my grip.

The boat sped down the slope, rattling and creaking as it bumped over the close-rutted road. Faster and faster it fell, slewing this way and that, gathering pace with astonishing swiftness as it careened down the hill.

Padraig climbed to his feet and brushed himself off. 'Pray God it does not hit the house,' he said.

Even as he spoke, one of the wagon wheels struck the side of the rut. The front wheels bounced and turned, sending the wagon onto a new course – straight for the nearest dwelling. Padraig raced past me, shouting with all his might. 'Danger!' he cried. 'Danger! Get out of the way!'

What anyone might have made of this warning, I cannot say. But suddenly we were all flying down the hill after the runaway boat. Despite our fatigue and aching muscles, we ran like madmen for the settlement, shouting for all we were worth. 'Danger! Get away!'

The on-rushing wagon struck a bump in the road and veered into the long grass growing beside the road; the grass brushed against the hull of the boat and slowed the plummeting wagon somewhat.

A stone wall forming part of the pig enclosure stood beside the house. The wagon ploughed through the grass, scraping the side of the boat against the wall, knocking two or three tiers of stone from the top. This slowed the wagon further – but not enough to prevent the impending collision.

The keel of the boat hit the midden heap, showering dung and debris into the air. The wagon bounded into the air and came down with a terrible crash as it drove into the side of the house.

Padraig was the first to reach the wreckage. He put his head through the hole in the wall and called to see if anyone was hurt. I was next to reach the house. 'I do not think anyone is here,' he said, turning to me.

Sarn, two steps behind me, came running up. 'Is the boat damaged?' He climbed up onto the hull and looked inside.

Roupen, his thin limbs trembling with excitement, came to stand beside me. 'Never in my life have I seen such a thing,' he said, his voice quavering as he gulped down air. 'It was . . .' he paused to find the word he wanted, '. . . magnificent!'

'The hull is unharmed!' announced Sarn, much relieved.

'I wonder where everyone has gone?' said Padraig, moving around the corner of the house to search the yard on the other side.

'Is no one here?' asked Roupen. He put his head in through the collapsed wall, looked quickly, and then said, 'That is a mercy. Someone might have been killed.'

Sarn climbed out of the boat and began examining the place where the hull had scraped against the wall. Padraig reappeared to tell us that there were no animals in the pens, or in the barn, and no one in the fields behind the houses. Then he disappeared again, to search the buildings across the road.

'Is there any ale?' asked Dodu strolling up at last. Red-faced and puffing from the unaccustomed exertion, he sat down on the rim of a wagon wheel and drew his sleeve across his sweating face. 'I am dying.'

'There is no one here,' I informed him.

'Impossible,' replied the haulier. 'In all the years I have been coming this way, there is always someone here.'

'Look for yourself,' I said. 'The house is empty, and so are the fields.'

Padraig returned just then with a wooden bucket in his hands. 'I found the well,' he said, handing the bucket to me. I passed it to Roupen, who put his face in the water and began slurping away.

While the bucket made its slow round, I asked Padraig what else he had discovered. 'There is fodder in the crib,' he said, 'and water in the trough. There is grain in the storehouse. We will have meal and water at least.'

Dodu moaned and shook his head. Sarn stepped around the stern of the boat and said, 'Bad luck. The mast is broken. The end splintered when it struck the house.'

'Can it be repaired?'

'Perhaps,' he said unhappily. 'We will have to see.' He walked away shaking his head.

'What should we do now?' asked Roupen.

'Padraig has found meal and water,' I replied. 'Let us see if we can find anything else to eat.'

While Dodu and Roupen searched the farm houses, Padraig and I set about making a fire in the yard. I took wood from the pile beside the door, and a flint and iron from inside the now-ruined house. While I struggled with lighting the fire, Padraig found a cooking pot and filled it with water from the well. He took a quantity of ground meal from a bag in the storehouse, and added it to the water. He then brought the pot to me and, when the fire was going sufficiently, he placed it on the flames, and sat down to keep watch over it.

Dodu and Roupen emerged from the neighbouring house, the young lord with a small bag in one hand and a bowl in the other. Dodu carried a crock and a wooden cup. 'I knew there would be ale,' he said, placing the crock carefully at his feet. He sat down and began to pour out the sweet brown liquid.

'I found salt,' said Roupen, offering me the bag. From the bowl, he produced two large eggs, and a wedge of hard, milky-white cheese. He handed the eggs to Padraig, saying, 'Maybe we could boil them.'

'I have a better idea,' replied the monk. Taking the bowl from Roupen's hand, he cracked the two eggs against the side and emptied them into the bowl. Then, taking the cheese, he broke off a portion and proceeded to crumble it into the bowl, whereupon he reached in and stirred the eggs and cheese with his fingers very fast until the mixture was a pale yellow colour.

Roupen watched, fascinated. 'Are you a cook in your monastery?'

Padraig smiled. 'The abbey is not large,' he explained, 'so each of us must take his turn with the various chores.' So saying, he up-ended the bowl into the cooking pot with the meal and water, which was beginning to simmer on the flame. He reached for the bag of salt, withdrew a small handful and shook it into the pot as well. 'Now then,' he said, taking up a stick from which he began stripping the bark, 'we wait.'

We passed the ale cup around the circle to occupy ourselves while we waited for the pot to boil. Sarn, having decided that his mast might wait until he had a bite to eat, joined us and demanded his share of the ale, which Dodu reluctantly supplied. After a time, the pot began to boil, and Padraig stirred it with his stick. Sarn went into the house to see if Dodu had overlooked any jars of ale. I lay back and closed my eyes, and listened to the pot burbling away. The smell of the porridge brought the water to my mouth, and my stomach growled. I was just remembering the last meal I had eaten before leaving home, when I felt a touch on my arm.

I opened my eyes, and saw Roupen kneeling over me; his eyes were on the yard behind us. I rolled over and looked where he was staring and saw only the trees of the wood behind the field. 'What do you see?' I asked.

'Someone is there,' he whispered.

Padraig stopped stirring; he placed the stick across the top of the pot, and gazed into the deep-shadowed wood.

'Are you certain?' I asked. The young man nodded. I stood and motioned Padraig to my side. 'We will go have a look. You stay here and guard that pot,' I told Roupen.

Padraig and I walked to the end of the yard, and started across the field, watching the trees for any sign of movement, but could see nothing in the shade. We halted at the edge of the field, and I called into the wood. 'Come out! We have seen you. There is nothing to fear. We need your help. Come out so we can talk to you.'

We waited. No sound or movement came from the wood. I started to shout again, but Padraig said, 'Let me try.' He advanced a few more paces alone, and raised his hands in priestly blessing. 'Pax vobiscum! In the name of our Great Redeemer, I give you good greeting.' He paused and waited for a moment, then added, 'I have made a meal of porridge. Come and share it with us.'

'What are you doing?' I complained. 'There is barely enough for us.'

Ignoring me, Padraig said, 'The porridge is ready. Please, come and eat.'

'We cannot feed the whole countryside!' I complained.

'Hush, Duncan. Be still.'

The over-generous monk repeated his invitation, and we waited some more. Perhaps Roupen was mistaken, I thought; no doubt, hunger had him seeing things. Before I could suggest this to Padraig, however, I heard a rustle in the leaves and out from the forest stepped a wizened old man with a small knife in one hand, and a broken tree branch in the other. His wrinkled face was set in a glare of defiance as he challenged us to do our worst.

TWELVE

'Peace, father,' Padraig said. 'We are pilgrims, and mean no harm.'

The old man came on a pace or two further and then halted. He raised the broken branch in his hand and pointed it at Padraig. 'Are you a priest, truly?' he asked in crude Latin.

'I am,' replied Padraig, still holding out his hands. 'Come, let us break bread together, and you can tell us what happened here.'

The man threw down his rude weapon and gave a nod of approval to the two old women cowering behind him. 'All is well,' he called. 'That one is a priest.'

At this the women ran forwards and fell upon Padraig; they seized his hands and began kissing them, and crying aloud praises to God. The monk allowed himself to be handled for a moment, and then turned and herded his new flock towards the house.

Upon reaching the yard, they went at once to where Roupen was waiting beside the pot of porridge, and stood looking longingly at the steaming, bubbling food. Sarn and Dodu appeared just then, having searched the second house to no avail.

The old people recognized the haulier and ran to him. 'Dodu! Dodu!' they cried and began gabbling at him in a strange language. He patted them on the shoulders and listened, his expression growing sorrowful. Finally, he raised his head and said to us, 'They have been robbed – two days ago. No doubt it was the same bandits we met on the road.'

Dodu listened some more, and then said, 'They took all the pigs – six of them, you know – and the two cows as well. Anna's husband tried to prevent them, and they thumped him on the head.' The old man made a motion with his hand, showing how the blow had struck his friend; his mouth turned down in a frown of sorrow and disgust. 'He died yesterday,' said Dodu. Exchanging a few more words with the old farmer, he added sadly, 'They buried him in the woods beside the stream, where they have been hiding.'

The old women nodded vigorously and pointed to the woods behind them. It seems they had seen us coming down the hill and, fearing another attack, had run into the woods. That had probably saved them from injury when the boat came crashing through their house. I pointed this out, and then led them to the side of the house and showed them the wreckage. They clucked their tongues and muttered to one another, but all-in-all appeared far more interested in the porridge than the ruin of their poor dwelling.

One of the old wives crawled into the house through the hole in the wall, and began rummaging around in the debris. She brought out some wooden bowls, and passed them to her friend. From another corner, she produced a bag and passed that to me. When I opened it, I found hard bread in small loaves. Next she found a wooden ladle, which she carried to the boiling pot and, with a flick of her hand, dismissed Roupen from his post.

Settling herself beside the pot, she dipped in the ladle, blew on the food to cool it, and then tasted. She puckered her lips, and then called a command to the old man, who hurried away at a trot. He went to the storehouse and disappeared inside – emerging a few moments later carrying a brown bundle the size of a baby, which he brought to his wife.

She lay the bundle in her lap, and unwrapped the cloth to reveal a fine side of smoke-cured bacon. Taking a small knife from her sleeve, she began cutting off strips of meat and dropping them into the porridge. Next, the old man produced two onions which she also cut up and stirred into the pot with the ladle.

In a little while, the aroma wafting up from the pot had improved marvellously. The old woman tasted again, then smiled a wide, gap-toothed grin, and we all took up our bowls and gathered around as she ladled out the thick stew. We crumbled the hard bread into the steaming porridge, raised the bowls to our lips and lapped up our first meal in three days.

There was enough to ease the hunger pangs and give us strength to pull the wagon away from the house. We spent the rest of the day helping clean up the wreckage, and moving their few belongings to the other house which, owing to a hole in the roof, they had not been using for several years.

That night the old women made flat bread on the hearthstones, and stewed bacon in ale; they then wrapped the strips of meat in the bread and gave them to us to eat like that. It was simple fare, but good and filling, and we slept that night without the gnawing ache in our stomachs – except for Roupen, whose unsteady stomach could not abide such rough food. He ate with us, but paid the price with pains and bloaty farting which kept him wakeful and miserable all night. Early the next morning, while the others slept, Padraig and I set off for the mill on the Saône.

I had decided that our best hope lay in getting to the river head as soon as possible. If we were lucky, we might persuade one of the hauliers to leave the river and return with us to retrieve our boat. How to pay for this service was a vexing problem, but inasmuch as we had, according to Dodu, at least a three-day walk ahead of us, I was confident we would think of something along the way.

In any event, it was abundantly clear there was no help for us at the settlement. They were poor farmers, made all the poorer by the cruel robbery of their livestock and few pitiful belongings; even to stay with them put that much more strain on their already fragile resources. Indeed, it would be enough of a hardship feeding those who remained behind: Sarn and Dodu, to guard the boat, and Roupen to rest and strengthen himself.

At least Sarn and Dodu would work for their food, for I had promised the farmer while we were away the two men would repair the damage done to their little house. Roupen, however, I advised to take his ease. On the evidence of his indigestion the previous night, it was clear that he was far from fully recovered from the illness that had taken the lives of his friends. What little strength he had gained while on the river had been spent in dragging the boat up and down the hills. I thought a few days' idleness would stand him in good stead.

He had other ideas, however, which I discovered when Padraig and I stopped to rest at midday. The old wives had sent us off with a bag of bread, and two skins of water. After walking briskly through the morning, pausing only once for water, we stopped beside the road for a bite to eat. We were sharing a bit of bread and talking, when

Roupen suddenly came into view on the road behind us. As soon as he came close enough for speech, I stood, and said, 'I thought we agreed you would stay with the others. Is something wrong?'

'No, lord,' he said. 'I thought you might be needing my help.'

I thanked him for the thought, and said, 'As it is, Padraig and I are perfectly capable of dealing with the hauliers. You may as well rest and take your ease for the journey to come.'

'No doubt your powers of persuasion rival those of Great Moses himself,' replied the young lord. 'But unless the hauliers of the Saône are very different from those we have seen so far,' he replied, 'I think it unlikely you will convince them to work for you without pay.'

I allowed that this was true, and pointed out that he had lost his purse to the bandits as well. 'Since you have no money, I cannot see how you mean to help in the matter.'

The thin young man smiled at this, and raised his fist in the air. He came forwards until his hand was before my eyes; then he opened his fingers to reveal the large gold ring he had been wearing on his thumb the night we were robbed.

'I thought they took everything from you,' I said. 'I saw them search you.'

'I hid it in my mouth the moment Padraig wakened me.' He smiled suddenly, and I saw a boldness in him I had not seen before. 'And if they had searched me better, I would have swallowed it.'

It came into my mind that here was a young man who, perhaps for the first time in his life, was truly enjoying himself. Content no longer to be left behind, he had followed us half the day just to take part in whatever would happen next. Sending him back would be a rejection not easily forgiven. Since it obviously meant so much to him, I relented.

'Come along, then,' I said, passing him my waterskin and a piece of bread. 'We will be glad of the company.'

So it was that three of us entered the little mill town on the Saône three days later. The settlement was well placed at a bend in the river, with the mill up river of the town. Above the mill, the stream coursed over the stones of a narrow, rocky ford, too rough and shallow for boats; below the settlement, however, it widened into a navigable stream once more. Looking down into the valley from the hillside, we could see several boats in the water. Although whether these were arriving or departing, we could not tell.

I determined to waste no time, but to get down to the water straightaway and talk to the hauliers to see how matters stood. The road led first to the mill, so we passed by quickly and on towards the settlement. As we hurried past, Roupen halted in the road and turned around.

Padraig and I walked on a few paces before realizing he was no longer with us. I cast a glance over my shoulder and saw him standing stock still, and staring into the field beside the mill where the miller kept his oxen and cattle. The field was small, and surrounded by a low stone wall; two cows and a pair of oxen stood at the end nearest the mill. I called to Roupen, and when he made no answer, Padraig said, 'He has seen something.'

Still anxious to hasten on and speak to the hauliers, I resented having to stop with our destination so near. 'What is it?' I demanded irritably.

Without taking his eyes from the field, he raised a hand and pointed to the cattle. 'Those are Dodu's oxen,' the young lord said.

I looked across at the two big animals standing in the field, and said, 'Let us not judge hastily. After all, one ox looks very much like another.'

'They are,' Roupen insisted. 'I walked behind them long enough to know.' Pointing to the two milk cows, he added, 'And I suspect those cows belong to the farmer.'

I glanced at Padraig, who shrugged unhelpfully, and said, 'Even if what you say is true, I cannot see what we can do about it. We have other –'

Before I could finish, there came a prodigious squealing from somewhere behind the mill. Roupen started towards the sound. 'Someone is being killed,' he said.

'Aye,' agreed Padraig mildly, 'a pig.'

The squeal came again, more frenzied, more terrible. The unfortunate creature was suffering dreadfully, and still its agonies were not cut short.

'For a slaughtering,' I remarked, 'it is poorly done. And unless they do things differently here, it is very early in the year to butcher your pigs.'

'Unless,' added Roupen, 'they are not *your* pigs.'

With that, we started back along the road towards the mill – a huge wooden structure of hewn oak beams in-filled with river stone set in mortar. A great wooden water wheel turned slowly in the stream gushing from the rocky ford. The yard was wide and covered with flagstone so the fully-laden wagons would not become enmired when it rained.

That stone paving, however, was the solitary gesture towards order or cleanliness. As we drew closer the stink of the place hit us full in the face: dung and rancid straw stood in mucky heaps either side of the low barn adjoining the house, filling the air with a sour stench to make the eyes water and the gorge rise. Mounds of human excrement were piled on the ground beneath the upper windows of the millhouse, and dog dirt was scattered over the yard – along with horse manure left where the dray animals had dropped it.

'Our miller is a very earthy fellow,' observed Padraig.

The house itself was in need of repair; the roof had once been handsome red tiles, but many of these were missing – and indeed quite a few lay smashed in the yard – though some had been replaced with ill-fitting chunks of flat stone. The mill wheel was green with moss, which clung in dripping slimy beards from the spokes and paddles.

The door of the barn had fallen off, and was leaning against one wall; and the wall of the ox pen was collapsed, the gap repaired not with the stone, which still lay on the ground, but with tree branches and bits of rope. A pair of bony, thin-shanked brown oxen stood with their heads down, lacking, I expect, the strength to move. Sharing the too-small pen were five fat pigs laying in the dung, their feet bound.

At the far end of the yard lay an enormous round grinding stone which was turned by means of a pole attached to a centre post. If not for the four men standing nearby, I would have thought the mill derelict and abandoned. But I saw the old grindstone and realized that this was what Dodu had been talking about when he said the miller kept oxen: when dry summer turned the stream to a bare trickle no longer capable of turning the great water wheel, the miller hitched his beasts to the grindstone, and kept his customers supplied.

The men were completely engrossed in the activity before them, and took no notice of us as we strolled into the reeking yard. Another sharp pig squeal tore the air with a distressingly human scream, and a sick feeling spread through me as sight confirmed what I had already guessed was taking place.

A young boy – perhaps eight or ten years old – armed with a spear, was making sport of killing the poor pig. Encouraged by those who stood cheering his efforts, the boy was enthusiastically torturing the animal. He had already put out both eyes, and carved a long, bloody slice of hide from the back. Now, he had the spear thrust up the wretched creature's backside, and was jerking the shaft back and forth while the bawling pig, its feet tied so it could not escape, spewed blood from its mouth as it shrieked.

The expression of demented glee on the boy's face filled me with cold rage. That this should be allowed was abhorrent; that it should be encouraged was monstrous. I started forwards, and felt Padraig's hand on my arm, pulling me back. 'Be careful,' he warned. 'There is great evil in this place.'

Shaking off his hand, I said, 'They should be punished for what they are doing.'

'They *will* be punished, never doubt it,' he assured me. 'But you may not be the instrument of that punishment. God, I think, has other plans for you.'

'Then what would you have me do?' I demanded.

'It may be our presence will suffice to shame them,' he said.

'And if not?'

'It is in God's hands, Duncan.' He stared at me. 'Truly.'

'Oh, very well,' I relented. I took a deep breath, and put aside my anger; when I had calmed myself once more, I proceeded towards the men, calling out to let them know we were there. At my greeting, one of the men turned slowly and regarded us with dull malevolence.

'What do you want?' he said, his deep voice sharp with irritation at having been interrupted in his pleasure.

Behind me, I heard Roupen gasp, and whisper to Padraig, 'It is the bandit who robbed us!'

Although I was taken aback quite as much as Roupen, I could not allow the man to see that I recognized him. So I said, 'We have come to ask if you have any oxen we might borrow for a day or two?'

'Ask a haulier,' he grunted, turning away again. 'I grind grain for my pay.'

'You see,' I persisted, moving nearer, 'we have had a slight misfortune on the road. If we could persuade you to lend us two of your oxen, all would be well. We could pay you for your trouble.'

The big man spun around angrily. 'And are you deaf as well as stupid?' he growled, spittle flying from his fleshy lips.

At his shout, two of the men with him turned. One of them bent down and picked up a chunk of wood which was lying beside the grindstone, hefting it like a club.

'I would not ask,' I told the man, 'if need were not great. A few days, no more – and the beasts would be well treated.' I said this last to embarrass him, but he took no notice.

'This is a mill, not a stable!' he roared. 'Get you gone before I set the dogs on you!' He kicked at a lump of dog dirt and sent it flying at me.

The man with the chunk of wood raised it in the air and made as if he would attack. Since there was nothing to be gained by provoking them further, I quickly retreated. I had taken but a step or two when I felt a sharp thump on my back as the wood chunk struck me between the shoulder blades. I did not look back, but straightened and continued on to the sound of the miller and his friends laughing at me.

'Well?' demanded the young lord as I rejoined them. 'Was he the man who robbed us?'

'No,' I told him, 'this man is older and heavier. Even so, the resemblance is too strong to be happenstance.'

Padraig nodded in agreement. 'Brothers then?'

'That is my guess,' I said.

'Be they brothers, sisters, or husband and wife,' snarled Roupen with unusual fury, 'I say those pie-bald oxen belong to Dodu, and the pigs were stolen from the farmer.'

'Peace,' I told him. 'As day follows night, I am certain of it.'

'Then why are we running away?'

'We are not running away,' I replied, starting off once more. 'We are going to find a place to rest.'

'Rest!' he fumed. 'While they laugh at us and torture those animals with impunity?'

'No,' I said. 'While we wait for darkness to befriend us.'

Roupen frowned with dissatisfaction. 'Cowards,' he muttered.

Padraig stepped close. 'He means,' explained the monk, resting his hand on the young man's shoulder, 'that having been as meek as doves, now we will become as shrewd as serpents to bring a measure of justice to bear on the crimes of these wicked men.'

'We gave the brute a chance to treat us courteously and fairly,' I said, 'now we will do business in a way he understands.'

'What are you going to do?' asked Roupen.

'Wait and see,' I told him, striding on.

THIRTEEN

We laid up in a neighbouring field under a rack of drying hay, dozing on and off through the long afternoon. The rest through the heat of the day was welcome, and it was not until the sun began to set that we stirred. I had taken the measure of the millhouse and yard, and knew how I wished to proceed.

My only worry was the dogs the miller had mentioned. Although I had not seen the beasts, I had seen ample sign of them in the lumps of dung scattered across the filth-covered yard. I did not know how many there might be, nor whether they were large and fierce, or small and noisy.

'The oxen will trouble us not at all,' I told my fellow-thieves. 'It is the pigs that will prove difficult. Even if we can avoid rousing the dogs, the pigs will squeal as soon as we go among them.'

We talked about this for a time, and then Padraig said, 'Leave the pigs to me. I will take care of them.' With that he rose and walked out into the field where he lay down on his stomach and stretched out his arms on either side.

'What is he doing?' wondered Roupen.

'Praying,' I said.

'For pigs?'

'For all of us.'

In a little while the last of the daylight faded, and a fine blue twilight descended over us. I lay back and listened as night gathered the little river settlement to its sleep. From the trees along the river came the raucous chatter of rooks in their high nests, and from the surrounding fields the homely sound of cattle lowing as they trailed towards barn and byre; here and there dogs barking, and the rusty clinking of goat bells. When at last darkness grew full, we set to work.

Setting Roupen on the road to watch between the mill and settlement should anyone come along, Padraig and I hurried to the field where Dodu's oxen were being held. It was as I expected: the wall was ill-made and half-falling down, and the animals had not been stabled for the night, nor cared for in any way, but merely left out in the field to browse as they would. We quickly found a weak place in the wall, leaned hard against it, and pushed it down.

We then began shifting the fallen stones to clear a path through the breach. Thus, we had only to remove enough stones to lead the oxen out, and our aim was swiftly accomplished. Hurrying into the field, I loosed the patient beasts' hobbles and led them out while Padraig followed with the milk cows.

Rejoining Roupen on the road, I said, 'We have what we came for, we can leave now and all will be well. If we proceed any further, we may lose everything.' I looked at my fellow-conspirators. 'What is it to be?'

'If you do not free those pigs, I will,' declared Roupen firmly. 'It is not right those rogues should prosper so.'

'The pigs are nothing to us,' Padraig pointed out. 'But they are life or death for the farmer and his wife and sister. I think we should try.'

'Very well,' I said, 'we are agreed. Whatever happens, there will be no looking back in regret.' Turning to the young lord, I said, 'Lead the cattle away. We will join you on the road.'

'I am going with you,' he replied.

'Oxen are slow and easily overtaken,' I told him patiently. 'If we are followed, it would be well if you were out of sight.'

'I am going with you,' Roupen repeated, crossing his arms over his chest.

Before I could object further, Padraig raised his hand. 'Let us go together. If trouble arises, we may have need of another pair of hands.'

Seeing I was outnumbered, I surrendered. Tethering the animals beside the road, we started for the mill. Coming to the edge of the yard, we halted to listen. All was quiet in the holding, save for the slow, creaking scrape of the water wheel as it turned in the stream. No light shone from inside the house. The moon was rising, casting a thin watery light over the empty yard. I could see the ox pen with the starving oxen in it, and the dark shapes of the five remaining pigs.

'I do not see any dogs,' I whispered. 'They must be inside.'

'Or sleeping,' suggested Roupen.

'Either way, we must go quietly so we do not wake them.'

We moved with all stealth across the yard. The stink of the place struck me like a slap in the face. A pile of entrails and offal marked the place where the pig had been killed, and these added their sick-sweet pungence to the heady reek. We made short work of dismantling the decrepit enclosure – indeed, we had to be careful the wall did not collapse of its own and the resulting crash wake the miller and his dogs.

When we had opened a sizeable breach, I turned to Padraig. 'If you know any runes for silencing pigs,' I whispered, 'say them now.'

To my surprise, he said, 'I have already done so.' He then instructed Roupen and me to move well away and remain still.

Then, stepping to the breached wall, the canny monk paused, pressed his hands together and bowed his head. After a moment, he crossed himself and entered the pen. He proceeded to go among the pigs, stooping over them to unbind their feet and moving on, speaking softly to them all the while. He soon had them on their feet, and then, with a gentle urging, led them out into the yard. They followed at his heels like faithful dogs.

He did not stop as he passed us, but walked briskly from the yard and out onto the road – and even then he did not stop, but continued walking back the way we had come. Casting a last glance at the millhouse to see if we had been discovered, I said to Roupen, 'We had best hurry and fetch the cattle, or Padraig and his pigs will leave us behind.'

The moon had risen higher and the road stretched out before us as a softly glowing stream, undulating its way into the hills. By the time we got the cattle moving, Padraig was far ahead. I could see him striding along, surrounded by his little band of swine trotting contentedly with him.

It seems a strange thing to say, but I have known Padraig since he came to the abbey as a stripling youth; and hardly a day has passed since our first meeting when I have not seen or spoken to him. Even so, I was always discovering new and curious things about him. His ability to amaze was, in itself, amazing.

In this respect, he was like his uncle, Abbot Emlyn who, with a word or act, regularly astonished the settlement. It was as if a spring from which one drew water every day continually revealed hidden depths. They were Celts, of course, and this accounted for part of it. The abbey and its teaching was also partly responsible – how much, I had no way of knowing. But, Cait, I was very soon to discover that the Abbey of Saint Andrew was responsible for a great deal more than the peculiarities of a few of its clerics.

Once over the first hill and out of sight of the mill, Padraig stopped and allowed us to catch him. He stood in the road, surrounded by his herd as if by an adoring congregation. 'I would have waited for you,' he said, 'but I did not know how long the rune would hold. I thought it best to keep moving until we were well away from that vile house.'

'How did you do it?' wondered Roupen. 'If they had been mice, they could not have been more quiet.'

'I told them I was taking them home,' the monk explained. 'I asked them to be quiet so that the evil men who lived in the house would not come and stop us.'

'You did well,' I told him. 'No one awoke, and not so much as a snort from a sleeping dog.'

'And yet,' said Padraig looking down the road behind us, 'you *were* followed.'

I turned around, expecting the worst, and saw instead the two forlorn-looking oxen ambling along behind us. I suppose they had wandered through the hole in the pen and, seeing the other cattle, had simply followed the herd. 'What should we do?' asked Roupen.

While I did not relish the possibility of being caught with them – the others were being returned to their rightful owners, after all – I could not bring myself to take them back. 'If they want to follow us, I cannot see how we can prevent them. Anyway, it would be cruelty itself to leave them in that place.'

We walked until almost sunrise, and then began looking for a place to spend the day. I had already decided that the wisest course would be to rest the following day, and travel at night. I reckoned that the miller would discover his stolen livestock missing the next morning and come looking for them. I had seen no horses at the mill, either in the fields or in the barn, but his thieving brother had horses, and if summoned, would quickly overtake us.

At the bottom of one of the next hills, I found what I was looking for: a clump of trees no great distance from the road, yet tucked around the shoulder of the hillside mostly out of sight. So, while Padraig and Roupen led the animals into the wood, I pulled off a few branches from a broom-like bush and, walking back the top of the hill, began sweeping away the animal tracks in the dust.

The sun was rising when I finished and, taking a last look behind me, I ran for the shelter of the grove. It was made up of beech trees mostly, and although the nuts were not yet ripe, we pulled down a few branches for the pigs to chew on, before settling back to rest and wait. 'We will continue on at dusk,' I said, passing the water skin to Roupen. 'We will have to take it in turns to watch the animals so they do not wander away.'

Padraig took the first watch and Roupen the second; I went to sleep and woke around midday to the sound of tapping. After a quick look around, I found Roupen sitting on a rock with a stick in his hand; he was flicking the stick against the side of the rock as he watched the swine rooting for their food. 'Where is Padraig?' I asked.

'He said he heard something, and went to look at the road,' the young lord replied with a yawn. Raising the stick, he pointed out the way.

I ran back through the wood and joined Padraig as he was leaning against a tree. 'See anything?' I asked.

'Two men on horseback passed a little while ago,' he said. I asked if it was anyone we knew. 'It is difficult to say, but I think one of them we have seen before.'

We waited there, and in a little while I heard the steady, rhythmic clop of horses' hooves. The two riders appeared a few moments later, riding easily, heads down, looking for tracks. 'They have followed us this far,' I said, 'let us pray they follow us no further.'

As Padraig had said, one of the riders did indeed have a familiar look about him. Although it was hard to tell from our vantage point, I would have guessed it was the bandit chief himself. The two passed the place where we had gone off the road, slowed, and halted a little way along where the track began to rise to meet the hill. They sat for a time, looking this way and that, while we watched from behind our tree.

In the end, the riders lifted the reins and moved on; we watched until they were out of sight, but remained alert after that. Aside from a shepherd leading a flock of sheep and goats, we saw no one else on the road the rest of the day, and at dusk we gathered our herd and took to the road once more. We walked through the night without encountering anything more troublesome than a foul-tempered badger who thought himself lord of the high way.

Dodu was overjoyed to have his oxen back, and the farmers were astonished to see the pigs and cattle returned. Like most peasants, they were intimately acquainted with hardship, but strangers to good fortune. Consequently, they did not know what to make of the sudden increase in their meagre wealth. They blinked their eyes and shook their heads as they patted the animals with their hands, all the while remarking how they had never witnessed such a miracle. I decided that they should have the extra pair of oxen; once the animals were fattened and their strength restored, they would be useful for pulling and ploughing.

When I told him this, tears came to the old farmer's eyes. Unable to speak, he seized my hand and began kissing it over and over. To Dodu, I said, 'Please tell him the oxen are not a gift. I merely repay the generosity of his hearth, and a modicum of compensation for nearly destroying his house.'

Dodu repeated my words, at which the farmer, embarrassed by my simple praise, bowed his head and shuffled away to look after his new animals. Afterward, Dodu came and told me that the farmers had been using the milk cows to prepare their fields for planting. 'And,' he said, 'when the animals tired, they pulled the plough themselves. Last year they were not able to plant both fields.' He smiled, and added, 'I think you have saved their lives with your gift.'

In the few days we had been away, Sarn had not only repaired the gaping hole in the house, but the broken mast as well. Despite the crudeness of his tools, he declared himself satisfied with the result. 'The mast is shorter now,' he pointed out, 'but it will serve.'

I commended him on his handiwork, and told him what had happened at the mill. 'We will have to be careful on returning.'

'Let them try to make trouble for us,' he muttered. 'I would like to have that thief before me, then he would feel the fury of a true Norseman.'

Next morning we took our leave of the farmer; the women sent us off with little loaves of bread and a fair-sized piece of bacon. This they put in a bag which they pressed into Dodu's hands before scuttling off without a word. They watched us from the doorway of their newly-repaired house.

Three days later we descended the hill overlooking the settlement on the Saône. I considered trying to go around the mill and come to the river by some other way, but there were no other trails. So, we strode out boldly and moved as quickly as possible to the hauliers' landing.

On passing the mill, I allowed myself a sideways glance to see if we were discovered, but the house and yard were quiet; there was no one about. The landing was empty, too, so we wasted not a moment getting the boat back into the water. While Dodu and his oxen practised their trade, Roupen walked into the town to barter with the merchants for needed supplies.

A short while later, the boat was ready and I was anxious to be away lest the miller, or his thieving brother, become aware of our presence in the settlement. But the young lord had still not returned. 'What can be keeping him?' I muttered and, commanding Sarn and Padraig to remain in the boat and be ready to push off as soon as we returned, I went off in search of him.

I had no difficulty finding him. For, as I made my way along the narrow track between the houses of the town, I heard a commotion of angry voices as I entered the bare earth expanse which served as the market square for the settlement. A well stood in the centre of the square, and around it the stalls and wagons of the area's merchants and farmers.

Hurrying into the square, I saw a number of people gathered beside the well; they were shouting at something which was taking place before them. I hurried closer and heard the riffling smack of the lash on flesh, and the groan that followed. Pushing through the crowd, I stepped into the ring and said in a loud voice, 'Unless you wish to suck your supper through broken teeth the rest of your life, I urge you to put down that strap.'

The thug hesitated in mid-stroke and turned slowly. Roupen lay at his feet, cowering, red welts on his arms where he had covered his head. The crowd fell silent as I stepped forwards. Intent only on stopping the beating, I had no wish to fight, nor any weapon with which to back up my rash challenge.

'You,' the ruffian said, recognizing me at once. Though it had been dark on the road that night, I knew him, too. The thief, so cheerful before, was angry now, and all the more dangerous for it. 'Step closer,' he said, 'and I will give you some of what your Jew is having. And then we will discuss the cattle I am missing.'

I made no move. 'Let him go,' I said. 'You can have no quarrel with him. He has done nothing to you.'

Someone from the crowd hollered, 'He's a stinking Jew! He stole a gold ring and tried to sell it.'

'He is not a Jew,' I told the crowd. 'He is a Christian. What is more, he is the son of Leo, Prince of Armenia, whose ring he wears – the very man this town must answer to if you harm his son and heir.' I paused to allow them to consider this, then added, 'Prince Leo commands ten thousand soldiers, while you have none . . . unless you count this brute I see before me.'

A murmur of uncertainty rippled through the crowd – no longer so enthusiastic in their support of the beating as they were only moments before. One or two of the more timid among them crept away quietly.

'And who are you,' demanded the thief, 'to concern yourself with him?'

'I am his protector,' I replied. Ignoring the thug, I moved to Roupen's side and bent over him. 'Can you stand, my lord?' Still cowering, he nodded. 'Very well, let us be about our business.'

The rogue attacked in the same instant. I expected he would strike me then, and I was ready. He charged from the blind side, arms outstretched to seize me in a crushing embrace; I remained crouching and let him come on. At the last instant, I lowered my shoulder and slammed into him with all my weight. I caught him under the ribs, driving the air from his lungs. He fell, sprawling backwards onto the hard-packed dirt.

Not caring to prolong the ordeal, I leapt on him in the same instant, placing my knee on his throat. Unable to breathe, he squirmed and thrashed while the colour of his face slowly deepened from red to blue.

'Do not kill him!' someone shouted.

I raised my head and looked at the crowd. 'You were all for a killing when you thought it was a Jew being murdered. I give this rogue a taste of his own stew, and you cry mercy for him. Would that you had done so for the innocent stranger among you.'

The ruffian ceased struggling beneath me; his eyelids fluttered and his eyes rolled up into his skull and his limbs went slack. Only then did I release my hold on him. I stood slowly. 'Murder!' someone gasped. 'He killed Garbus!'

'This ugly fellow is not dead,' I told them. 'He is merely asleep – although, perhaps it would be better for this town if it were otherwise.'

I stooped down and, tucking my fingers under the brute's belt, lifted upward sharply. This action produced two striking effects: the thief suddenly moaned as the air rushed back into his lungs, and the gold ring slipped from its hiding place beneath the belt and fell out upon the ground – to the astonishment of the townspeople looking on.

I picked up the ring, and handed it to Roupen. 'Come, my lord, the boat is waiting. We will shake the dust of this place from our feet.'

I put my arm around his shoulder and drew him away. 'What about the supplies?' Roupen asked as we walked from the square.

'There will be another settlement down river,' I told him. 'We will buy what we need there. I want nothing more to do with this place.'

Upon returning to the boat, I bade Dodu the haulier farewell. He was sorry to see us go, and said that if he did not have a wife and son waiting for him at home, he would count it a blessing to go on pilgrimage with us to the Holy Land. I told him we would ask for him on our way home. 'After all, I still owe you for hauling the boat.'

'No, no!' he cried. 'You saved my good oxen. I should pay *you*.'

'Nevertheless,' I said, 'I will look forwards to paying this debt. Until then, my friend, I wish you well.'

Some of the more curious townspeople had followed us to the landing. As Sarn pushed the boat out into the slow-moving stream,

Padraig addressed the onlookers. Pointing to Dodu, he said, 'This man is a friend of mine. From now on, you will treat him like a brother. For I will return one day, and if I learn he has been abused in any way by anyone here, I will call down the wrath of God upon this place. Do not think you will escape judgement for your sins.'

The people gaped at us, aghast at this startling pronouncement. The current carried the boat away, and we left them standing on the landing, looking after us in wonder. Roupen, too, was more than a little awe-struck. Once we were safely down stream, he pulled the ring from his finger and offered it to me, saying, 'You saved my life at risk of your own. My father will reward you greatly. Consider this token but a small foretaste of the treasure to come.'

I thanked him for his thoughtfulness, but declined, saying, 'If I take your ring, you will have nothing with which to buy supplies in the next settlement. That is the agreement we made.'

'True,' he agreed, reluctantly slipping on the ring once more. 'Even so, I will remain in your debt until the honour of our family is discharged.'

FOURTEEN

The next settlement was two days down river. We were hungry again by then, but God is good: we arrived at midday on market day, and the market was lively and well-supplied, the merchants eager for trade. In exchange for Roupen's ring, we got two bags of ground meal, a haunch of salt pork, five loaves of bread, half a wheel of hard cheese, a few strips of dried beef, and various other provisions such as eggs, nuts, dried peas, and salt fish. We also bought a cask of cider, which the hardy folk of the region drink almost to the exclusion of all else.

We might have got more for the gold somewhere else – for all it was a very fine ring – but we were already feeling the pinch, and did not know how far the next market might be; also, with space already cramped it would not have helped us to capsize our craft. We bargained hard and were able to come away with our provisions, but nothing left over. While Sarn and Padraig stowed everything aboard the boat, Roupen and I went to inquire of the way ahead. Although the young lord had come up the river, and knew the general route, he could not remember how many days the journey required.

'It is perhaps nine days,' said the merchant I asked. 'This time of year, of course,' he tapped his front teeth with a dirty fingernail, 'when the water is low, I suppose it might take longer.'

We thanked him for this information, and turned to leave. He called us back, saying, 'There is no difficulty, mind. Just keep to the main channel until you come to Lyon, where the river joins with another and changes its name.'

'What does it become?'

'The Rhône,' he said. 'Just keep to the main channel and you will have no difficulty after that. I should know, I have been to Lyon often enough.'

'But we want to go to Marseilles,' I pointed out. 'Is it much further after that?'

'Oh, aye. If I were you I would forget all about Marseilles and go to Lyon instead. It is better in every way. I always enjoy very good trade in Lyon; the people there are very wealthy. Not like here, mind. Still, I make no complaint. The people here are hard-working, and know the value of their goods.'

Again, we thanked him for providing such excellent advice, and made to leave, whereupon he said, 'After Lyon, you are only seven days – or perhaps eight, as I say – from Avignon, and from there it is but a short distance to Marseilles by sea. You should stay a few days if you can. The cathedral is splendid – or will be when it is finished. They have only begun, mind, but already it is a sight worth seeing. Even Paris has not such a grand cathedral.'

Padraig and I walked back to the boat. 'Our young lord Roupen might have warned us it was so far. He doesn't seem to remember anything about the journey at all.'

'Do you regret taking him with us?' asked the priest.

I thought about it for a moment. 'No – at least, not yet,' I replied. 'But we are still a long way from Marseilles.'

It was as the merchant said – we reached Lyon without trouble four days later, and six days after that Avignon – which, I was disappointed to learn, was nowhere near the sea. Our destination was still many days off.

Feeling that time was pressing, we journeyed on without even so much as a glance at the city or its splendid cathedral. It was late in the day when we reached the first shoal south of the city, and decided to camp for the night and begin our exertions afresh in the morning. We stopped at a place where the bull rushes grew tall, forming a high green palisade around us; we pulled the boat up onto the gravel shingle, and Padraig set about making supper with the little that remained of our once-plentiful supplies.

No sooner had we sat down to eat, however, than we were attacked and overwhelmed by dense clouds of biting midges. Despite the smoke from the fire, which usually kept such pests at bay, these fierce flyers swarmed over us, biting each time they alighted. More demon than insect, their constant stinging soon drove us from our food. In order to get some relief, we rolled ourselves in our cloaks, head to foot, and finished our meal in sweltering misery.

We then lay down to sleep, though the air was quite warm, and the sky was still light. All night long I lay with my face covered, scarcely able to breathe, the perpetual buzzing in my ears. We all woke early, ill-rested and itching from a thousand tiny sores which the midges had inflicted. Not wishing to linger even a moment, we did not pause to break fast, but straightaway seized the ropes and began pulling the boat over the gravel shoal, eager to get as far away from that place as quickly as possible.

It was hot work. And stinking, too – owing to the numerous pools of stagnant water lying in the hollows of the sandbars. The ever-present reek of the warm, slime-green water filled our nostrils, driving all thoughts of food from our heads. So, aside from pausing now and then to swallow a few mouthfuls of water, we took no meals. There was little left of our provisions, and the smell and flies took away any desire to eat, so we pushed on and ever on, shouldering the ropes and towing the boat through the heat of the day.

Unfortunately, when the sun began to descend in the west and loosen its grip on the land, then the midges came seeking our blood once more. We spent another endless, insufferable night wrapped in our cloaks. Anyone stumbling upon our camp in the night would have imagined we had all been slain and prepared for burial in our shrouds.

After three days of fighting a losing battle against the vicious midges, we at last entered a deeper channel and, though there was only the slightest, most hesitant breath of a breeze, Sarn raised the sail so that we might leave the plague of pests far behind as swiftly as possible.

Downstream, we stopped long enough to prepare one final, meagre supper with the last of our provisions – a gruel of flaked dried meat and meal which, like starving dogs we devoured instantly; we licked the bowls clean and journeyed on. The channel was good and the moon bright, so we sailed through the night and arrived at Arles late the next day – tired, sore, very hungry, and with no money to buy food.

It was beneath my dignity to beg, although if it came to that, I would so humble myself. Roupen said he would rather starve than beg; and Sarn said that since we were already starving, he did not see that begging made any difference one way or the other. 'Beyond that,' I said, 'I reckon our best hope lies in reaching Marseilles as soon as possible, and beseeching the Templars to take pity on us.'

Padraig, however, had other ideas. 'It may be the Templars will aid us,' he allowed indifferently when I suggested it, 'although I do not see why they should.'

'If you have something better to offer, I am waiting to hear it.' I cupped a hand to my ear and leaned towards him. 'Well, I am still waiting.'

'If you would cease your yammering, you might hear something worthwhile,' he replied testily. 'As it happens, your father stopped here on his way to the Holy Land – or have you forgotten?'

I *had* forgotten. Then again, owing to Murdo's reluctance to speak of his part in the Great Pilgrimage, I knew little about the place to begin with. Most of what I had heard about Arles I owed to Emlyn, who had also told Padraig – apparently far more than he had told me.

'They wintered here,' I said, remembering. 'There is a monastery. We could ask them for food – is that what you are thinking?'

'Come, I will show you what I am thinking.' He started off along the quay and I hurried after, leaving Roupen and Sarn to refresh the water casks and make the boat fast.

Padraig found his way to a market square near the harbour. As in most settlements of any size, there are always a fair number of elder citizens gathered around talking and taking their ease. Padraig greeted them respectfully and, seeing we were strangers, they wanted to know where we were coming from, and where we were going. He told them a little about our pilgrimage to the Holy Land, and they all nodded earnestly. They had heard of the Great Pilgrimage, of course, and several of them said they knew men who had participated, and had stories to tell. We listened and talked like this until they were well satisfied with our integrity, and then Padraig said, 'My uncle wintered here on his way to the Holy Land; he was a priest travelling with some Norsemen. Perhaps some of you remember them.'

The old men shook their heads. No, they did not remember, but they were certain that such things did occur.

'There was also an armourer who lived here. He became friends with this man's father.' Here the priest indicated me, which impressed the choir of idlers enormously. 'I wonder if he is still here.'

Our informants grew very excited. Not only was the fellow still there, they said, he was still doing a brisk business in weapons of all kinds, and only for the noblemen of the region. 'The Templars have been here to see him,' one toothless fellow proclaimed proudly. 'They are fighting priests, you know. Only the best will do for them.'

Upon learning that we were on our way to Marseilles to join the Templar fleet, we were enthusiastically informed that one of the Templar ships had come into the harbour to receive the weapons which had been purchased the previous year. 'They were returning to Marseilles and were to set sail for the Holy Land in three days' time.'

'How many days ago was this?' I asked.

'Four,' replied the old man. 'They will have sailed by now. If it is the Templars you were hoping to find, I fear you have missed them, my friend.'

One of the other men spoke up. 'What are you thinking of, Arnal? It was only two days ago the Templars were here.'

'It was four days,' maintained the one called Arnal. 'I suppose you think I no longer know one day from another, eh?'

'When did you ever know one day from another?' said his friend. 'It was two days ago the Templars were here, I tell you. Charles remembers as well as I.' Turning to a third old fellow, he asked how many days since the Templar ship had sailed. The man leaned forwards on his stick, thought for a moment, opened his mouth, then closed it, thought some more, and then said, 'Three days.'

'There! You see?' cried Arnal triumphantly. 'I told you, it was never two days.'

'Where would we find this armourer?' I asked, breaking into their deliberations. 'Maybe he could tell us more.'

They told us how to find Bezu's forge, and we thanked them for their inestimable help and hurried off in search of the smithy. We passed the priory of Saint Trophime, where, as Padraig remembered, Emlyn and his brother monks had passed many a dreary winter day in fiery debate with the priests of Arles. The day faded around us as we hurried through the narrow streets and pathways and into the old part of the city.

'They said Bezu's forge was once a gatehouse used by the legion,' mused Padraig. Pointing to a high stone wall rising broad and tall above the low rooftops of the houses clustered tight beneath it, he said, 'There it is – and there is the smithy.'

It was a solid stone edifice built into the wall. We could see the place where the old doorway had been closed up with rubble stone. Black smoke issued from a squat chimney, and the clang of hammer on anvil rang out from within. The low, wide door was open, so the canny monk walked directly into the smithy and called to the proprietor, telling him he had visitors who wished to make his acquaintance.

I stepped through the door to see a broad-shouldered man with a thick beard, his face red from the glowing iron in his hand. His shirt was a filthy rag full of tiny burned holes from the sparks and bits of molten metal that flew from his hammer. He regarded us without interest, and went back to his pounding.

I felt a pang of disappointment. 'Are you Bezu?' I asked; but he made no reply.

Instead, my question was answered by a man who suddenly stepped from the darkness of the room behind the forge. This fellow was short, white-haired, plump, and smiling. Clean-shaven, his round face glowing with the heat from the forge fire, he was dressed in a long mantle of fine cloth, with a wide leather belt to which a fine, slender sword was attached. He regarded us with a kindly expression, and said, 'I am Balthazar of Arles, at your service, my friends.'

I begged his pardon, and told him we were looking for the armourer named Bezu.

'My dear friends, of whom I have many, call me Bezu,' he informed me. 'You may do so, if you wish.'

'It is an honour to meet you, Master Bezu,' I told him. 'I am Duncan Murdosson, and this is my friend and companion, Brother Padraig.'

'A man who travels in the company of a priest must either be very devout,' Bezu observed cheerfully, 'or else he is so wicked as to require continual observation and correction.'

'Then again,' I suggested, 'it may be such a man is merely on pilgrimage.'

'Ah, yes, I expect that will be the likeliest explanation.' Bezu laughed, and said, 'You were looking for me? Well, here I am. How can I help you.'

'I have come to meet you, and to thank you,' I replied.

'Have you indeed?' he wondered. 'I am happy to make your acquaintance, sir. But how is it that you should be thanking me?'

'Once, many years ago,' I explained, 'you gave winter refuge to a young man. Like myself, he was from the northern isles and on pilgrimage. His name was Murdo.'

The old armourer's faded eyes grew hazy as his mind raced back over the years. 'You know,' he said, his expression growing thoughtful, 'I believe I did have a young helper by that name. I have not thought about this for many years, but now that you say it, I remember this fellow. Why, he was but a boy.' Bezu regarded me closely, as if trying to decide if he might know me. 'Even so, why should this concern you, my friend?'

I smiled and said, 'That young man you befriended is my father.'

Bezu's eyes grew round; he stared at me and shook his head in amazement. 'Your father, you say!'

'None other.'

I quickly explained that Padraig was the nephew of one of the monks who had been travelling with my father, and that, as we happened to be passing through the city, we could not ignore the chance to thank the armourer for his kindness all those years ago.

'But it was nothing!' Bezu protested. 'He was cold and hungry. I gave him a little food and a place to sleep. He worked. Indeed, I would he had stayed on. He was a good worker, that one, and in those days – when the Great Pilgrimage was just beginning – I had need of a young man or two to help me.'

Bezu grinned, and shook his head again, as if he had been struck a blow which made him dizzy with delight. 'My friends!' he announced suddenly. 'Come, and dine with me tonight. We will have a feast in celebration of this glad meeting. And you will tell me what has become of my hireling since I last laid eyes on him. Come! My house is not far.'

'Nothing would please me more than to break bread with you,

Bezu,' I replied, 'but we are with two others who are waiting for us at the harbour.' I quickly explained how we were even now hastening away to Marseilles to meet the Templar fleet.

'The Templars,' said Bezu. 'But some of them were here, you know. What have you to do with the Soldiers of Christ?'

Not wishing to prolong the tale, I told him we were simply hoping to receive passage to the Holy Land aboard one of their ships. 'They are sailing from Marseilles in the next day or so. We must hurry if we are to join them before they leave.'

The old armourer nodded thoughtfully, then rubbed his hands and declared, 'But this is most fortuitous . . . most fortuitous, indeed. You can help me with a problem which has vexed me greatly.'

'We would be only too glad to aid you in any way we can –' I replied, adding, 'provided, of course, we can still make it to Marseilles before the fleet sails.'

'But that is the very thing,' Bezu told me. 'You see, the Templars were here, as I said, only a day or two ago. They came to collect the weapons bespoken the previous year. I have two other smithies now – did you know? We are kept busy morning to night all the year round. The anvil is never silent.

'Well,' he said, laying his hard hand on my arm confidentially, 'they asked me to make some daggers for them – special knives, these are, for the commanders. Come, I will show you.'

He turned and led us into to a tiny room carved out of the stone of the old Roman wall. Pointing to a bright red rug which concealed an object in the middle of the floor, he directed Padraig to throw aside the covering. The monk bent down and drew off the rug to reveal a small wooden casket bound in iron. 'Open it,' he said. 'It is not locked.'

Padraig opened the box to reveal red silk cloth on which rested six exquisite daggers with blades of inlaid silver, and handles of gold; each had the distinctive Templar cross on the end of the pommel, with a small ruby at the centre.

'They are superb knives,' I said. 'I have never seen any to match them.'

The armourer reached into the box, took up one of the daggers. 'Yes, they are very good,' he said, feeling the heft and balance in his hand before passing it to me. 'I do not do the gold work. I have a friend of many years – a craftsman without equal – a goldsmith; he does the gold and silver, and also engraving. He, like myself, is run off his feet by the demand for his services. He has not been well this year and the knives were not ready when the Templars came.' He smiled quickly. 'I told them I would bring them if they arrived before the fleet sailed. But you are going to Marseilles. If you would consent to deliver the knives for me, it would save me a great deal of trouble. What do you say?'

Padraig glanced at me and nodded, urging me to accept the commission. 'Very well,' I replied, 'we would be honoured to serve you in this way. Leave it to us, and worry no more about it.'

'Ah,' sighed the armourer contentedly, 'I feel better already. I thank you. Now!' he declared, rubbing his hands together. 'To supper! Come with me, and do not worry about your friends. I will send one of my boys to the harbour to fetch them along so they can join us.'

Needless to say, we accepted his invitation with unseemly eagerness, and we all enjoyed a sumptuous meal at Bezu's grand house on the hill overlooking the town and harbour beyond. Night was far gone when we finally pushed away from the table, made our farewells, and returned to the boat; we were therefore late rising the next morning. While we were getting ready to cast off, who should appear but our generous host himself, carrying a large cloth bag.

'Ah! I hoped I would find you here. There was so much left over from last night's feast, I thought you might like to have some of it on your journey,' he said, passing the sack to Sarn, who promptly stowed it in the boat. 'I also brought you this.' He pulled a small purse from beneath his belt and tossed it to me. 'For delivering the knives. I would have had to hire someone anyway, so you might as well have it.'

I was on the point of refusing to accept his money, when Padraig climbed out of the boat and embraced the old man. 'Bless you, my friend,' he said. 'May Heaven's rich light guide you always, and may the Lord of Hosts greet you when you enter his kingdom.' He then made a little bow of respect.

Bezu, discomfited by this unexpected ritual, blushed bright red and, not knowing what to say or do in response, simply pretended that it was a normal occurrence and smiled. We made our farewells then and cast off; the armourer stood on the quayside, watching us away. I waved to him and called a last farewell, and then turned my face towards Marseilles, and hoped we were not already too late.

FIFTEEN

Caitríona, dearest heart of my heart, we must take courage. The day of dread is near. The caliph has returned.

I have been told that he will soon summon me. Wazim Kadi, my amiable Saracen jailer, informs me that I am to prepare myself. Tomorrow, or the day after, I will be called before Caliph al-Hafiz to answer for my crimes.

As I have said before, and say again, the outcome is certain. Death, however, holds no fear for me. My only regret is that I will not see you again, my soul. I had hoped to have time enough to finish this, my final testament; yet it seems that, in his wisdom, our Merciful Redeemer has ordained otherwise.

I search through the pages I have written, and my spirit grieves. There is so much more that I wanted to say to you. I despair to think what you will make of this fragmentary and insubstantial tale. Time was against me from the beginning, I fear, so perhaps I was fortunate to have written even the little you hold in your hands.

Well, no doubt, all is as it was meant to be.

I can but give you what I have left, and that is my everlasting love, and this crude, unfinished document which, if nothing else, will at least bear witness that in my last hours upon this earth, I was thinking of you, my beloved daughter.

Wazim assures me that my letter will be treated with all respect. I have the promise of the caliph that it will find its way to you. I trust in this. The word of the caliph is absolute. Nevertheless, I have instructed faithful Wazim that if any difficulty should arise, the papyri should be given to the Templars who, one way or another, will see that you receive it. Thus, I can rest in peace, assured that you will hear from your loving father again – albeit, from beyond the grave, as it were. For, by the time you receive this, I will be long dead.

So, here, I must leave it. A tale unfinished, but for time. I have prepared a second letter for my father and mother. If, by chance, it fails to arrive with this one, please tell your grandfather Murdo that he was right about everything: the Holy Land is a realm of demons, and only madmen think to conquer it.

Still, I had to try.

Farewell, my love, my light. I pray our Gracious King to send bright angels to surround you all the days of your life. Farewell . . .

PART II

November 11, 1901: Paphos, Cyprus

In the days and weeks following that fateful meeting of the Inner Circle, I determined to educate myself in the crucial events taking place in the world around me. Inspired, not to say alarmed, by the vital importance of the work now before us, I endeavoured to emulate the example of the others by learning all I could of the current social and political climate of Europe and the West, thinking a firm grasp on contemporary affairs would aid me in the coming battle. The Seven had other plans for me, however, as I was to discover one rainy afternoon in early spring.

A wintry gale was blowing cold off the North Sea, lashing the windows and making the lights flutter above my desk. It was nearing closing time, and I was not looking forward to braving the elements on my way home for the evening. I heard footsteps outside my office, shortly accompanied by a rapid knock. 'Enter,' I called, glancing up as the door opened.

To my surprise, it was Pemberton, and with him, Zaccaria. I jumped to my feet at once, for never had a single member of the Brotherhood darkened my door – and now there were two. 'Gentlemen, welcome. Come in,' I said, rushing forth to relieve them of their dripping coats and hats. 'It is beastly out there. Come in, both of you, and sit by the fire. We'll have you dried out in no time.'

'Thank you, Gordon,' said Pemberton genially. 'I hope you will forgive this intrusion.'

'Intrusion? Not at all,' I replied, pushing chairs towards the fireplace where the coals were glowing red and warm in the grate. 'It is, in fact, a welcome break in the monotony that passes for studious industry in a legal firm.'

'You are most kind,' said Zaccaria, settling into the offered chair with a sigh. He patted his face with a folded handkerchief to dry it.

I pulled my own chair from behind the desk and, feeling slightly awkward playing the host, I said, 'May I offer you something to chase the chill – a tot of brandy, perhaps?'

'Splendid,' said Pemberton, rubbing his hands to warm them. 'Just the thing.'

I stepped to the tray of decanters on the sideboard and poured three small snifters of the firm's tolerable brandy, and passed them to my visitors. 'Slàinte!' Pemberton said, raising his glass. We sipped our drinks then, and I took my seat and waited for them to reveal the reason for their visit.

'No doubt you will recall that last time we met mention was made of, shall we say, the *imperatives* before us,' Pemberton said, settling his lean form back in his chair. He cradled the bulbous glass in his long fingers as he swirled the aromatic amber liquid.

'Indeed, yes,' I replied. The dire warnings voiced in that meeting had scarcely been absent from my thoughts.

'You were a classicist at university, I believe?' said Zaccaria suddenly. A small, energetic man of swarthy complexion and sturdy build, he burns with a lively, barely contained intensity many people mistake for giddiness.

'Why, yes,' I allowed, somewhat cautiously, uncertain of the pertinence of this fact, 'now that you mention it, I was. It's been so long since anyone accused me of that, I had all but forgotten.'

'History, too, isn't that correct?'

'I hope you haven't spent too much effort rooting around in the hall of records. I'm afraid my academic career does not make scintillating reading.'

Zaccaria smiled, but did not disagree. 'At least, you showed a distinct affinity for the ancients rarely seen these days. For that, I commend you.'

'You will have studied Latin,' Pemberton said. 'Did you enjoy it?'

'After a fashion. My tutor was a dry old stick, prone to bouts of absentmindedness. He should not shoulder all the blame, however; had I applied myself with a modicum of effort, I might have made a better job of it. Still, Virgil, Cicero, and Julius Caesar have stood by me through thick and thin. Also, being in the legal profession, I have the chance to brush up the odd phrase now and then.'

'What about Greek?'

'Ah, no,' I replied. 'Greek was never my strong suit. After a brief flirtation, I abandoned the enterprise completely. Euripides almost did me in. I managed enough to scrape by, but only just.'

'I suspected as much,' mused Zaccaria; he made it sound as if he had long harboured grave misgivings about my natural parentage and patriotism.

'Then that is where we will begin,' said Pemberton. He tossed down the rest of his drink and set the glass aside. 'We have been thinking it was time you were better acquainted with your heritage, so to speak.'

'My *Greek* heritage?' I said. 'I wasn't aware I had any.'

'Oh, you'd be surprised,' replied Pemberton with a smile. 'Shake a family closet, and you never know what might tumble out.'

'I think it more precise to say your Greek-*speaking* heritage,' Zaccaria said.

'I am intrigued,' I said. 'Please, continue.'

'The Greek islands are pure enchantment. Have you ever been?'

'Only by way of Homer.'

'An excellent introduction to be sure, but not a patch on the real thing, I must say.'

Pemberton leaned forwards earnestly. 'We have a challenge to set before you, Gordon. Would you like to hear it?'

'By all means.' I put aside my glass and gave him my full attention. I imagined this unprecedented visit owed much to the new order anticipated by the Inner Circle and, aware of the seriousness of our endeavour, composed myself with all gravity for what was shortly to be asked of me.

'We want you to learn Greek.'

'Greek!' The suggestion made me laugh out loud. Given the climate of danger into which we were descending, I had anticipated a slightly more noble, if not perilous, undertaking. 'Whatever next? Do you think I am up to it?'

'I think you are more than up to it,' Zaccaria assured me solemnly.

'May I ask why you wish me to learn Greek?'

'That need not concern you at the moment,' Pemberton said, brushing the question aside lightly. 'Let's just say that an opportunity has lately arisen which we are keen to have you exploit to the full. To do that, you will need a good working knowledge of Greek – both antique and modern.'

I looked from one to the other of them. They were quite serious. In fact, Pemberton regarded me with such intensity, I began to suspect there was more to this proposal than I had been told so far. The only way to find out more, I understood, was to accept what had been put before me. Nor was I inclined to turn down my first genuine assignment as a member of the Inner Circle. In any case, I would have agreed just to see what came next.

'Well, why not?' I said at last. 'Yes, of course. I'll do it. With any luck, I'll be speaking like a native in no time at all.'

'That,' said Pemberton dryly, 'is about how long you have to master it.'

'Sorry?'

'You have from now to the end of September,' he said.

'Good heavens!' I counted quickly on my fingertips. 'It's less than six months.'

'If it were up to me, I would give you as much time as you liked. Unfortunately, we no longer have that luxury.'

'I see now why you called it a challenge.'

I had, I suppose, imagined great deeds of high daring to answer the clarion call I had heard so clearly at the last meeting of the Seven. I had allowed myself to believe that when my turn came to serve, it would involve something far more grand and exciting than stuffing my head full of ancient Greek syntax. To tell the truth, I was slightly deflated.

Pemberton astutely read the disappointment in my mood. 'It is important, Gordon,' he said softly, 'vitally so, or I would not have asked you. What is more, you will learn much to your advantage. That I promise.'

'Quite,' agreed Zaccaria. 'Now then,' he reached into his suit pocket and brought out a calling card, 'I have taken the liberty of giving your name to an acquaintance of mine. His name is Rossides, and he is a scholar of the first order.' He handed me the card. 'He lives in Lothian Street near the university.'

I took the card and read the name aloud. 'M. Rossides, D. Phil.' It was written in both Greek and English. 'Do you think he would be inclined to take on a student of my low aptitude and qualification?'

'Oh, indeed,' Zaccaria assured me seriously. 'He has guided

many a floundering Odysseus through the Scylla and Charybdis of aspirated vowels and masculine verb forms. If anyone can get you ready in time, he can.' He reached out and tapped the card in my hand. 'I dare say he'll even get your Latin back in fighting trim.'

'Then I will certainly pay him a visit first chance I get. I'll send him my card and arrange a meeting next week.'

'He is expecting you tomorrow,' Zaccaria informed me. 'Stroke of six. Don't be late. The good professor expects punctuality in his students.'

As if in anticipation of this meeting, the clock in the hallway beyond chimed the hour, and my two guests rose to leave. 'You will want to be getting home, I expect,' said Pemberton. 'Give your lovely Caitlin my best regards, and tell her it might be a good idea to keep the autumn clear in the social diary.' He smiled, enjoying his little mystery. 'I have a feeling you two will be spending some time in sunnier climes.'

SIXTEEN

I have seen the caliph. All praise to our Great Redeemer, I still live – under sentence of imminent death, it is true – nevertheless, it appears I am to be allowed to draw breath in this world another day. For, after the briefest of audiences, I was returned to my rooms to pray for the salvation of my soul.

Since I have every confidence in my redemption, I will use this time to set down a little more of my tale so that you, dear Cait, will have the benefit. That said, I looked over what I wrote yesterday, and would not change a word.

It was as I said it would be: a little after midday, Wazim came to my room. 'Da'ounk,' he said, bowing low, 'the *hour* has come. His Majesty the Khalifa Muhammad Ibn al-Hafiz, Protector of the Faithful and Glorious Potentate of Cairo, has commanded you to be brought before him to answer for your crimes.'

This is how they talk.

'Da'ounk' is the closest semblance to my name my little jailer's Saracen tongue could produce. And this word 'hour' is much liked by the Arab tribes, especially Egyptians; it is less easy to designate, but if you quarter the day from sunrise to sunset, and then divide each quarter into three, you will have cut the daylight into twelve equal parts. Each one of these twelve parts is called an *hour*. There are likewise twelve hours of darkness, too; and all of these have different names, but I do not know them. What is more, Arab philosophers employ various methods of counting these hours throughout the day; and although the reason for this escapes me, it does exercise them greatly.

What Wazim meant, of course, was that my moment of judgement had come. The men with him were dressed in the bold red and yellow of the palace guards – yellow siarcs and trousers, with short red, open-fronted tunics, and large turbans – that is, war helms made of extremely long strips of cloth wound round and round the head in the most cunning fashion imaginable. They carried the distinctive curved sword of the Saracen in the winding cloth that serves the Arab for a belt. They also wielded long, broad-bladed pikes, and curved knives in jewelled sheaths which were fastened to thick gold chains around their necks.

Wazim bowed low as I rose and stepped forwards. I had long ago decided not to argue with my captors, or try to defend my actions in any way, but to accept my portion with good cheer whatever befell me. Since I remained calm and self-possessed, the guards did not lay hand to me, and I was permitted to walk upright and of my own volition into the caliph's presence.

I was taken to a region of the palace I had never visited before. The corridors are wider, the rooms more lavish than any I had seen heretofore, with gold in endless supply gleaming in the furnishings and ornaments, and even the cloth which covered the walls and floors. The rooftrees are polished cedar; the enormous doors are a dark hard wood called ebony, black and shiny as polished jet.

The throne room itself is larger than any banqueting hall known in the West. Wazim told me that once, in observance of the previous caliph's day of birth, fifty men on horseback performed mock battle for the entertainment of scores of spectators. I believe him, for it is an exceedingly spacious hall. And sitting in the centre of it, beneath a live palm tree under which a tent-like canopy had been erected, is the solid gold Throne of Cairo. And on that throne, watching me with eyes as hard as chips of flint, was Hafiz the Resplendent himself.

Surrounded by ranks of servants, aides, scribes, and court officials of various kinds – most of them sitting on the polished marble floor on enormous tufted cushions, the Caliph of Cairo was a much smaller man than I anticipated, very brown, and with the aspect of someone who has spent an active youth beneath the scorching sun of the desert. His skin was deeply creased like well-used leather, and his hair was thick and entirely grey. Like many holy men, his beard was long, and woven into two braids which were drawn up into his turban somehow. And aside from his turban, which was purest white and glistening like sunlight on fresh snow, and bore an enormous blood-red ruby surrounded by the turquoise tips of peacock feathers affixed in gold over his brow, the caliph dressed in the manner of a simple tradesman or farmer. His clothes were spotless and finely made, but of humble, hard-wearing cloth.

He sat on a broad cushion upon his throne with his legs crossed beneath him, as if he were in a tent in a wilderness camp. He frowned when he saw me, and I knew my sentence was sealed.

Still, I bowed low as Wazim presented me and, by way of greeting, I spoke the few words of Arabic which he had taught me. 'Most Excellent and Exalted Khalifa,' I said, 'may the One God who created all men preserve you forever. I am deeply honoured to meet my lord and master, whose kindness and generosity have so long sustained me.'

Although the words were Wazim's, I meant what I said; I was grateful for my benign captivity under his roof. I knew how easily it could have been otherwise.

The great man's frown deepened further, but with consternation. He made no reply, but sat pulling on his long, grey moustache and watching me narrowly.

'As you are an educated man,' he replied in good Latin, 'let us speak directly.'

I was much heartened by this, to be sure; any time an Arab – be he Saracen, Seljuq, Danishman, or Egyptian – deigns to speak to you in your own tongue, number yourself among the few and fortunate. Still, I did not allow my elation to show in my manner or my speech, which would have been disrespectful. 'As you will, lord,' I replied evenly.

He regarded me for a time, and then said, 'You have been sent to me by the Khalifa of Baghdad.'

'That is true, my lord. No doubt he imagined I would be a useful addition to your illustrious court.'

Al-Hafiz grunted at my small attempt at humour. 'What is your name?'

'I am Lord Duncan of Caithness in Scotland. I am on pilgrimage, my lord, and was sojourning in Anazarbus when it was attacked by Amir Ghazi. I was captured and taken prisoner by the Seljuqs.'

'Khalifa al-Mutarshid says that you are a spy and a traitor to Islam. He has condemned you to death.' Then, with a dismissive wave of his hand, he added, 'I see no reason to alter his judgement.' Addressing the guards, he said, 'This one is to be executed at once. Take him away.'

As the guards stepped forwards and grasped me by the arms, al-Hafiz demanded, 'Have you nothing to say?'

Placing myself firmly in the palm of the Swift Sure Hand, I replied, 'No, my lord. All is as the Great King decrees.'

The guards seized me, turned me around, and led me from the hall. Wazim, padding along behind, distraught, muttered platitudes of comfort under his breath. I paid him no heed, for I was gathering my courage to face the headsman's axe.

We reached the great ebony doors and halted while they were opened by two blue-robed porters. From the throne behind us the caliph called, 'Infidel, who did you mean?'

The guards halted, and I was hauled around to face the caliph. 'My lord?'

Lifting his hand from his lap, he motioned the guards to bring me before him once more. 'You spoke of the great king just now. Who did you mean?'

'I meant the Lord God, Ruler of Heaven and Earth, Shaper of Destiny, Architect of the Ages, and Champion of the Faithful.' These last were titles the Muhammedans used for the Almighty, and which any Christian could also espouse in all good faith.

The caliph's dark eyes grew narrow – whether with anger or distrust, I could not tell. 'There is but *one* God,' he declared, thrusting a long finger into the air above his head. 'Allah is One.'

'That is so, my lord,' I said, bowing my head in reverence. 'There is no god but God Alone.'

The frown reappeared upon his dark, wrinkled face. 'What do you know of such things?'

'Very little, my lord. I am but a simple pilgrim –'

'So you have said,' he snapped. 'But not so simple as you make out, I think.' Frowning furiously, he leaned forward, chin in hand, and glared as if trying to decide what to do with me. Finally, he said, 'Do you deny you are a Christian?'

'No, lord,' I answered. 'I am a Christian. With your permission, I would merely point out that I have nothing to do with either Rome or Byzantium. Neither pope nor emperor hold authority over me.'

This surprised him. And, strangely, his surprise gratified him. It was as if he had suspected something curious about me, and now his suspicion was rewarded. The frown vanished instantly, and he regarded me with an expression of wary interest. 'So! You, too, are an Armenian. We know of these Christians.'

'I beg your pardon, Most Excellent Khalifa,' I replied, 'but neither am I an Armenian.'

'Not an Armenian?' he said. 'What are you then, Christian? Tell me quickly.'

'My lord Khalifa, I am of the Célé Dé,' I replied. 'We are an obscure sect – once plentiful, but now vastly diminished in numbers. Where once we ruled the whole of Britain, we are now confined to a small realm in the far north.'

For some reason, this appeared to please him immensely. 'I have heard of this *Pritania*,' he replied. 'It is very far away from Rome and Byzantium, you say?'

'Yes, my lord. As far as east from west with three seas between.'

The caliph squirmed on his cushion impatiently. 'Since you are a Christian of particular devotion,' he said, 'I will grant you a day to make peace with your God before I send you to meet him in judgement.'

'I thank you, my lord,' I replied, bowing in acknowledgement of his generosity.

He gestured to the guards once more, and I was taken from the hall and returned to my rooms, where I now sit and write in contemplation of what has happened. Although I am grateful for even this small reprieve, I cannot think what it might betoken. Still, I have this day. Dare I hope for more?

I pray the hand of the executioner may spare me yet a little longer for your sake, Cait. While I wait, I can think of nothing better than to proceed with my tale. This I will do even now.

Marseilles is a rowdy river town, heaving with rough industry. There are no fewer than five ship yards – all of them clattering to wake the dead from the crack of dawn to after sunset. Half the town and countryside is kept busy serving the shipbuilders, and the other half earns its crust supplying the wharf and harbour with goods and commodities of one kind or another. The harbour is well-protected, wide, and deep; and there we found the last of the Templar ships making ready to set sail.

The larger part of the fleet had already departed – there were forty-two ships in all – but eighteen remained in port, taking on supplies which had not been ready in time. I instructed Sarn to put in close to the Templar ships, and then Padraig and I hurried to find the soldier we had spoken to in Rouen.

'Pax vobiscum,' I said, approaching the first warrior monk we saw. 'God be good to you, my friend. We are looking for one of your brothers.' I explained that we had been instructed to meet a member of his order in this very place. He asked who we were looking for, and I told him.

'It was de Bracineaux?' the man asked, looking us up and down. 'Renaud de Bracineaux, are you certain? If it was Renaud, then you are fortunate indeed. He was to have departed with the first ships, but has been detained. He is still here.'

He told us that Renaud was a commander of the order, and that all the commanders were holding council with the Grand Master over concerns which had arisen while sojourning in the country. 'His return is expected as soon as the council is finished – tomorrow perhaps, or the next day. And then we will sail for Outremer.'

I thanked the brother for his help, and we made our way back to the boat to wait. Roupen had determined to see if he could beg passage from any ship sailing east. Now that he was destitute, he could not afford to pay his way as he had originally planned, and the thought of humbling himself that way cast him into a sour and miserable mood – nor was that all. Although he said nothing against them, anyone could easily discern that he held no fondness for the Templars. I mentioned it to Padraig, who had also noticed how the young lord either grimaced or fidgeted every time the warrior monks were mentioned.

Sarn, too, was unhappy; now that we had reached our destination, he knew he would be sent home and he wanted to continue with us to Jerusalem. This I could not allow. Nor, considering the rigours of the journey, could I in good conscience send him home by himself.

The solution to this quandary remained beyond our grasp the rest of the day – although not for lack of discussion. Sarn could not understand why, having come this far, he should not be permitted to continue the rest of the way. 'You will need strong servants in the Holy Land,' he kept saying.

To which I would reply, 'My father needs strong servants back in Scotland. What is more, he needs his boat.'

'You would send me back alone?' he countered with sullen reproach.

'Believe me, I wish I had a better choice, but it cannot be helped. You must go home as we agreed.'

Next morning, a young Templar came to our mooring and informed us that Renaud de Bracineaux had been apprised of our request and was waiting to see us. Taking up the box containing Bezu's knives, Padraig and I followed the youth to the long double rank of Templar vessels, where we were conducted up the boarding plank and onto the deck of the largest ship I had ever set foot upon in all my life. Renaud was standing by the mast, directing the loading of supplies which were heaped in a small mountain upon the thick deck of the sturdy vessel.

He turned as the young man came before him announcing our presence, and said, 'Here, now! You have found me at last. It is good to see you, my friends.' He put his hands on our shoulders, and said, 'Are you ready to swear the oath and join our order?'

'Nothing would please me more,' I told him. 'As I have said, however, I am foresworn, and cannot undertake another oath.'

He accepted this with good grace. 'I am sorry to hear it. Yet, even knowing this, you have come. Why?'

'We are on pilgrimage to the Holy Land,' I said, indicating Padraig, 'and we had hoped to beg passage aboard one of your ships.'

'I see,' he nodded, his enthusiasm fading, 'I might have guessed. Unfortunately, I fear I must disappoint you. We have room aboard our ships only for fellow Templars, and those who have official business with the order.' He offered us a sad smile. 'Alas, it appears you have travelled a very long way for nothing. I am sorry.'

He turned away from us, saying, 'Now, you must excuse me. As you can see, we are getting ready to sail. I am needed elsewhere.'

Disheartened, I stood for a moment thinking what to do. Padraig held out the box to me. 'You have been most kind,' I told the

Templar commander. 'We will not detain you any longer – only, I am reminded that we have something which belongs to you.'

'That, I heartily doubt,' he replied, already moving away.

'Balthazar of Arles sent it,' I said, raising my voice slightly.

He turned and looked back at me. 'The armourer?' He considered for a moment.

'The same,' I continued. 'You should remember him – you purchased a cargo of weapons from him.'

'We did,' he allowed warily, 'but I cannot see how this could possibly concern you.'

I explained quickly how upon completion of our visit with the armourer, he had given us a box containing six gold-handled daggers. I opened the box to display the knives. 'They were not ready when you came to collect your purchase, and he asked us to deliver them to you.' I passed the box to him. 'We have done what we agreed to do, and now we will leave you in peace.'

The frown reappeared on the Templar's face. Turning, he called to one of his brother knights across the ship; the man joined him and the two held close conversation for a moment, then de Bracineaux said, 'It is true that the knives were missing from the cargo. I owe you my thanks for delivering them, and will pay you for your trouble – for I, also, am an honest man.'

'Bezu has already done that,' I told him. 'You owe us nothing.'

The Templar nodded, regarding Padraig and me with, as I thought, an expression of regret. 'Are you certain we cannot tempt you to join our ranks?'

'I would feel disposed to consider it,' I said, 'if you could provide passage for three pilgrims bound for the Holy Land.'

'Three?' asked de Bracineaux. 'You multiply like weasels, sir. A moment ago there were but two.'

'We have another with us,' I said, and told him about the young Lord Roupen, a nobleman of Armenia.

At the name, his interest reawakened with wonderful swiftness. 'I know only one noble family in Armenia,' he said, 'that of Prince Leo. Could it be the same family?'

'One and the same,' I replied. 'I have undertaken to aid his return to the Holy Land.'

'By all means you must come with us,' de Bracineaux said, making up his mind at once. 'We have room aboard this ship for such as yourselves, and you will be made welcome and enjoy every comfort we can provide. Make whatever preparations you require, we sail tomorrow at dawn.'

I thanked the Templar, whereupon Padraig and I hurried back along the quay to where Sarn and Roupen were waiting. As we walked along, I caught Padraig watching me with a sour expression on his face – as if he had swallowed a bolt of vinegar.

'What?' I demanded, stopping in my tracks. 'Whatever in the world is wrong now?'

'You told the Templar you were foresworn,' he said, 'and could not undertake the Templar vow.'

'Yes,' I agreed. 'So?'

'I know of no such vow.'

'You think I lied to him, is that it?'

'Did you?'

'No. The vow was my own.'

He folded his long arms across his chest and regarded me suspiciously. 'As I am your companion through all things, I think I should know this vow you have taken.'

I started walking again. 'It does not concern you.'

'Duncan!' he said sharply. The gentle priest so rarely raises his voice, I forget he can be quite stubborn when he chooses. 'Everything about this pilgrimage concerns me. I will hear this vow you have made.'

'And I will tell you – but in my own time,' I replied over my shoulder and kept walking so I would not have to speak to him further.

We quickly rejoined Sarn and Roupen, who were waiting to hear how we had fared with the Templars. Roupen was less than overjoyed; he grumbled his thanks and went off to see if he could discover any word of his home from the sailors and merchantmen on the wharf. Sarn, too, grew petulant and quiet. He stared at me balefully, but said nothing; meanwhile, Padraig and I busied ourselves searching for suitable companions to accompany Sarn back to Britain.

Our search was concluded when Padraig discovered a fellow pilgrim named Robert Tookes who, having been sorely wounded

149

in the Holy Land by a Seljuq bandit's arrow, was returning home to Britain with his aged father. The two of them had arrived in Marseilles three days earlier with a Venetian merchant ship from Jaffa, and were now seeking passage to England.

Padraig found them at the small chapel which served the wharf and harbour. He had stopped by to pray at midday, and had passed them as he was leaving. He heard them speaking to one another and, recognizing their speech, had paused to inquire where they were bound. Upon learning their destination, he brought them to the boat.

Although Sarn did his best to discourage them by glaring and frowning as if he were being asked to sail off the edge of the world with the Devil and his brother for passengers, the men were courteous and well-disposed, and we quickly struck a bargain: they would pay for all necessary supplies, and Sarn would take them to Inbhir Ness, where they would easily find a boat going south.

Upon concluding this arrangement, Robert Tookes seized me by the hand in friendship. 'We are both very grateful to you, my father and I,' he told me. 'Have no worry for your man, or your boat; as God is my witness, we will see him safely home.'

We arranged for them to return at first light with their belongings, and they hurried away to secure provisions and prepare for the voyage ahead. All was falling into place at last, and I foresaw only clear and pleasant sailing ahead. Feeling pleased with myself, I settled back and enjoyed a well-deserved nap, despite Sarn's disgruntled huffing and clumping around.

SEVENTEEN

Roupen returned a little after sunset, and we ate our evening meal. 'No one in this fly-blown swamp has even *heard* of Anazarbus,' he complained, disappointed at not discovering any news of his home. Sitting beside the doleful Sarn, the two of them presented a uniformly dismal appearance which Padraig and I did our best to ignore. We talked idly of this and that as night slowly deepened around us. The harbour grew quiet, and we watched the swallows skim the water as the new moon rose in the eastern sky.

I was lying back, and thinking what a fine night it was for star-gazing, when Padraig turned to me, and said, 'I think a prayer before we sleep would see us in good stead for the journey tomorrow.' He stood. 'Come, the chapel is not far.'

'We can say our prayers here just as well,' I pointed out, reluctant to leave the peaceful harbour.

'The chapel would be better,' replied the stubborn monk, climbing quickly from the boat. 'You come, too, Roupen.'

I rose slowly and followed. Roupen declined, saying he would stay with Sarn and help watch the boat. I caught up with the long-legged priest as he started across the all-but-deserted square which fronted the wharf. 'You will like the chapel, Duncan,' he said as I fell into step beside him. 'It has a very unusual carving.'

He led me to a small square building made of stone. A dull glimmer of light shone in the two tiny windows either side of an arched wooden door. An iron latch secured the door, but it lifted easily and Padraig pushed open the door. Two large candles burned either side of a simple wooden altar above which hung the carving Padraig had mentioned.

The candles were poorly made and gave off black smoke which

stank of burning hair. The foul light did little to dispel the gloom, but, as the room was empty, we stepped up to the altar for a closer look at the carving: a mother with an infant child cradled in her arms. A halo of gold surrounded the heads of both mother and the holy child whose figures had been carved from a large piece of very dark wood. Aside from that, it was something one might have seen in any Latin church.

'What do you notice?' asked Padraig.

'The wood carver employed some considerable skill. Beyond that, I find nothing unusual about it.'

'They are black,' said Padraig.

'Well, the wood is black,' I allowed.

'No,' he said. 'Look more closely.'

I did as he directed and put my face near the carving. As I had said, the figures were finely rendered. The child was reaching a tiny hand up towards the mother's solemn face as she gazed with maternal gravity upon the world that would one day revile and crucify her son. Aside from the sombre, almost doleful, expression on the mother's face, I saw nothing at all to remark upon. 'Is there some mystery here that I am supposed to see?' I asked.

'They are black,' Padraig repeated.

'Yes, we have established that. They are black –'

'Not because the wood is black; it is not. They were *painted* black.'

I looked again, more closely, and realized he was right. There were places near the base where scratches in the paint work revealed the lighter colour of the wood beneath. 'How strange,' I remarked, touching the coloured wood lightly with my finger. 'Why would anyone want to paint them black? Is it that they think the mother of Jesu was an Ethiope?'

'She is called the Black Madonna,' announced a voice from the doorway. Roupen had thought better of his decision and joined us after all. He came to the altar and, indicating the mother figure, said, 'Mary she is, but not the mother of Jesu.'

'Then who is she?' I wondered.

'Mary the Magdalene.'

'But that is ridiculous. Why should the Magdalene be cradling the infant Christ? It makes no sense.'

'Indeed.' The monk smiled shrewdly. 'Unless, it is *not* the infant Christ she is holding.'

I waited for one of them to tell me who the infant figure represented. 'Well, am I the only one in all of Frankland who does not know who the infant is supposed to represent?'

'It is Jesu's son,' said Roupen.

His answer so amazed me that it took me a moment to work out all the implications of this extraordinary revelation. 'Christ's *son!*' I exclaimed aloud, staring at the tiny carved figure. 'But that is horrendous!'

Placing a finger to his lips to quiet me, Padraig merely nodded. 'There are those who believe that Jesu and Mary were husband and wife. After all, the scripture speaks often of the disciple Jesu loved. Most scholars assume the appellation betokens John the apostle, but there is no reason why it might not designate another.'

'Besides,' added Roupen, 'it is well known that many women followed Jesu and supported his earthly ministry in various ways – this, too, is well attested in holy scripture.'

'But see here now,' I protested. 'Christ's *son* – think what you are saying.'

'As to that,' the monk replied in the same calm, equivocal tone, 'it was commonplace for a Jewish rabbi to be married. In fact, it would have been remarkable, if not improbable, if it had been otherwise. If, as the church that bears his name believes, Our Lord and Redeemer was subject to the same humanity we all possess, then why should marriage remain beyond Christ's experience? The union of husband and wife is an essential part of God's design for the human family, after all. Should not the author of our faith adhere to the same rigours that are imposed upon his followers?'

'The Magdalene was a prostitute and a demoniac,' I protested. 'Would you have me believe that our Beloved Lord was one flesh with a demon-ridden whore?'

'Again, you speak only hearsay and slanderous supposition. Nowhere in the scripture is it written she was a whore – only that demons were driven from her and she was healed. In all likelihood the designation of prostitute came very much later when it became, let us say, inconvenient for the pope to recognize the rank and position of a powerful and influential woman.' Lifting a hand to the carving, he said, 'However it was, those who hold to this cult believe the union of Jesu and Mary produced a child. After Christ was crucified, and the persecution of the new faith began in Jerusalem, the holy family fled – first to Damascus, and then to Rome. Eventually, however, they settled here.'

'In Marseilles?' I wondered. 'This grows more fantastic with every word.'

'Indeed,' agreed Roupen. 'I have never heard that part of the tale.'

'It was called Marsalla then,' Padraig explained, 'a well-known Roman port. Grain and cattle were shipped from here to the East, and the trade in those days was very good. It was a fine and prosperous city – and far away from the religious intrigues and oppressions of the East. The holy family and their train of followers brought the new faith with them, and they have been revered in this region ever since – as you can see.'

He answered with such assurance, I could not help asking, 'How can you possibly know all this?'

Padraig smiled. 'The cult of the Black Madonna is well known to the Célé Dé. It is heresy, of course, although mild compared to most. Still, it is heresy nonetheless. We came to know of it when it was once laid on the head of Beloved Pelagius, our great teacher and advocate. He defended himself mightily against the charge, answering his accusers in a bold treatise which is preserved and studied by the keepers of the Holy Light.'

Padraig led us briefly in our prayers, and we finished a short while later. Roupen went on ahead, leaving Padraig and me to our talk. 'You knew the Black Madonna was there,' I said. 'Was that why you brought me?'

He shook his head. 'I had no idea it was there until I saw it today when I came in to pray.' He dismissed the carving, saying, 'It is of no account – a curiosity, nothing more.'

'Then why?'

'I wanted to remind you that things are not always as they seem,' he replied. 'And that even the most forthright appearances often hide a deeper meaning for those who know how to look.'

Even in the dim and flickering candlelight, I could see his gaze grow keen, and knew there would be no evading him any longer.

'I brought you here so that you could tell me the true purpose of your pilgrimage.'

I should not have been surprised, but – as I have said, and will say again – the priests of the Célé Dé arc ever full of surprises. I suppose he had worked it out following our brief exchange earlier in the day. Although I would have preferred telling him when we were somewhat closer to our destination, I knew there would be no putting him off now, so I said, 'Very well. It seems this is the night for sharing hidden purposes.'

Padraig smiled knowingly. 'It is that.'

'It is easily told,' I began as we left the chapel, 'and not half so mysterious as the Black Madonna. First, I must ask you whether you have ever heard of the Iron Lance?'

'Of course.' He did not laugh outright, but my question amused him. 'It is the spear of Christ's crucifixion.'

'It is that,' I affirmed. 'And since it seems the priests of the Célé Dé know *everything*, you probably also know that the sacred object resides in my father's treasure room.'

'Now that you bring it up, I seem to recall hearing about that, yes.'

'Have you always known?' I asked, feeling like a fool for ever thinking I might hide anything from him. I stopped walking to look at his reaction.

'No,' he replied. 'Indeed, I learned of it only a day or so before we left.'

'Abbot Emlyn told you, I suppose.'

'He did,' confirmed Padraig. 'But my uncle asked me never to speak of it to anyone – unless, like now, someone else should speak of it first.'

'Have you seen the Sacred Lance?'

'Alas, no. One day, perhaps – who knows?'

'Well,' I told him, resuming our ramble, 'I have seen it and held it in my hands. It was the night my father told me how he had rescued it from the heathen, and from the hands of the iniquitous crusaders who would have made of it a sacrilege. That same night, I vowed within myself that even as my father had rescued the lance, I would rescue the cross.'

'The True Cross,' mused Padraig. I could not tell whether he approved of my plan, or not.

'Torf-Einar told me all about the shameful desecration of that holy treasure before he died,' I said. 'You were there, you heard how they cut the cross of our redemption into pieces – with as little thought as I might chop a kindling stick.'

'I was there, yes. I heard.' He took a slow, deliberate step away, and then turned to face me. 'And this is why you could not swear the oath of the Templars?'

'I did not think it would be right, since I cannot say where or how I shall obtain the pieces of the holy relic. I must remain unencumbered in my search.'

'I can see that.'

'And you approve?'

He did not answer; instead, he asked, 'What will you do with the cross – *if* by some miracle you should obtain it?'

'I will bring it back to Caithness and place it in my father's treasure room alongside the Sacred Lance.'

'I see.'

He was quiet for a time, gazing up into the night-dark sky – as if in search of an answer written in the stars.

'Your plan,' he said at last, 'lacks nothing in audacity. And what it wants in feasibility, it more than makes up in ambition.'

'But do you approve?'

'In truth, I do not,' he declared firmly. 'If this is why you have undertaken pilgrimage to the Holy Land, leaving all you love and hold dearest – then I must tell you as a priest and friend, that I do not approve in the least.'

Deep down in my bones, I suppose I had feared he would say something like this – which is why I had kept it from him. I knew he would not like my plan, but I needed his help.

The wily priest grinned suddenly and spread his hands. 'The Lord moves in mysterious ways his wonders to perform,' he said. 'And, contrary to what you apparently believe, he does not often seek my blessing before he acts.'

'Is this your way of saying you think it is a good idea anyway?'

'No, it is a terrible idea,' Padraig assured me. 'Even so, it may also be inspired.'

'Please, your assurance is breathtaking,' I replied.

'Have you not heard?' wondered Padraig. 'The Good Lord often uses foolishness to humble the wise. If this idea of yours is of God, then the combined might of all the nations on earth cannot stand against it.'

I accepted his judgement, and we walked silently along the darkened street for a time. As we came onto the quayside, I asked, 'You did not tell me, Padraig, why is the Magdalene painted black?'

'That I cannot say. It has been suggested that it was the colour of her cloak when she came to these shores, and that is how she was known to the people: the Black Mary. Others say it is to distinguish her from the mother of Jesu, since they are so often confused one for the other.' He paused thoughtfully, then said, 'Wise Pelagius said that it was to hide a secret which those who revere the Black Mary hold sacred and guard to the death.'

'What is this secret?' I wondered aloud.

'No one outside the cult knows,' said the monk. 'And those inside will never tell.'

EIGHTEEN

The Templars were ready to sail by the time Padraig, Roupen, and I joined the ship the next morning. I wanted to see Sarn safely away before leaving, and although his passengers, the Tookes, were ready, we had to wait for the provisions to be delivered. The merchants appeared just after daybreak, and we quickly loaded the boat, and bade the three returning travellers farewell.

'Take care, Sarn,' I called, pushing the boat from the wharf. 'Give all at home a full and fair account. Ask them to pray for our safe return.' We watched until they were under sail, and then the three of us hurried to board the Templar ship. We were greeted courteously on our arrival, and shortly after climbing onto the deck the order was given to cast off.

We stood at the rail and watched the city of Marseilles pass slowly from view as the ship moved out into the bay. Once in deeper water, the helmsman turned the ship and headed south-west along the coast, and we settled ourselves aboard our new vessel.

I will now describe a Templar ship, for they are very unlike the sort of craft seen in northern waters. Broad of beam and high-sided, they possess several decks, one above another, and a single mast of gigantic proportions. These vessels ride tall in the water and tend to bob awkwardly in the least swell; they are unsteady and woefully difficult to manoeuvre – much, I imagine, like steering a hogshead barrel in a flood. Indeed, for this reason sailors even call them 'round ships'.

For all they are ungainly and largely unsuitable for any purpose save the one for which they were made: the transportation of men and animals across the mild sea of Middle Earth. God forbid that they should ever be caught in one of the storms which scourge the northern isles throughout the winter. I have no doubt the precarious craft would sink like an anvil at first squall. Be that as it may, the Venetians own many of these ships, and the Genoans, and others, too. Our vessel was owned by a merchant from Otranto whose son – a plump, sweet-natured man named Dominic – served as captain.

We were introduced to him shortly after Marseilles disappeared from view. He invited us to break bread with him in his apartment. You see, Cait, how very large these ships can be; there are rooms beneath the uppermost deck, some of them large as chambers in a lordly hall. And this is what the captain had – a chamber with a box bed and a long table with room enough for six men on benches either side.

Thus, Renaud, Padraig and I, and Roupen, as well as other high-ranking Templars were invited to dine with the captain that first night. Roupen excused himself, saying his stomach was unsettled; for all I know, that may have been the truth, and not an excuse to avoid joining the rest of us. However, I think it more likely that he had no stomach for the Templars, never mind the food. Padraig and I eagerly accepted the invitation, and if that meal was in any way typical, I quickly discovered how our captain maintained his rotund form despite his long sea journeys. Of meat and sweet breads, and other fancies, there was no stint: roast fowl and smoked pork, beef, and fish of several kinds, and flat bread made with the oil of olives – which Sicilians especially esteem – and small barley loaves made with honey. Wine was drunk throughout the meal – for the noblemen of Taranto dearly love their wine, and think nothing of serving it *and* drinking it by the tun.

Hoping to keep our wits about us, Padraig and I attempted to dine with some circumspection, as did Commander Renaud. Everyone else, however, behaved as if our supper was a festal meal following a long privation. I was appalled at the amount of food and drink which my fellow diners consumed, shoving bread and meat down their gullets in uncouth chunks and gobbets. Oblivious to any restraint, they guzzled wine until it ran down their beards in crimson streams and pooled about their elbows, which they planted on the table and never removed. My embarrassment for them went unheeded, however, as they blithely ate and drank their way through enough provisions to sustain a dozen farm labourers for a month.

Dominic of Otranto beamed at his guests and bade his serving-boys to keep the wine flagons charged and the cups overflowing. As a consequence, the talk was lively and free, and I learned many things of life in Outremer which were to prove useful in the days to come. For, when they learned that Padraig and I had never been to Jerusalem, or Antioch, or even Constantinople, they eagerly took it upon themselves to educate us in the manner of life we should encounter – not that they were in any way agreed upon the particulars.

Still, I learned that the weather was hot and dry, and that the land was infested with all manner of biting flies and stinging plants which made life a constant misery. Rivers mostly dried up during the summer, and no rain fell from spring until winter, when the fierce wind came to scour the land from top to bottom, and fill every dwelling place with gritty dust.

The people, they said, were poor for the most part, barely scratching a living out of the rocky, unproductive soil – except in the rare river valleys where the streams were sustained by springs in the mountains; *then* the resulting cultivation was a very paradise, bringing forth fruits and vegetables of every kind in almost un-imaginable bounty.

For the most part, however, the language was incomprehensible, the food unpalatable, and the water undrinkable. A more barren land there never was, to be sure. If not for the fact that the Lord High God himself had chosen the place for his own peculiar reasons, surely no one would give it so much as a moment's heed.

As for the people, the women were dried up hags and crones, whose unlovely hides were wrinkled as grapes left too long in the sun. The men were sulky, sly and vengeful, skilled in imagining slights and capable of maintaining heated feuds into the sixth generation. What is more, young or old, they were cunning in all the ways of malice, iniquity, and greed.

'The Arabs are very devils, sir,' one man declared. 'Lies and blasphemies are all they know. Beware.'

'They are born thieves,' agreed another. 'They will steal anything that is not chained down, and stab you the moment your back is turned.'

'Turk or Saracen, they are all alike,' added the first. 'The Greeks, too, are to be trusted only so far as you can spit.'

'But the Greeks are Christians,' Padraig pointed out innocently, 'and therefore allies and fellow soldiers.'

This brought peals of laughter from those gathered around the board. 'If you believe that,' roared the foremost black-bearded Templar, 'then you will wake one night with your throat slit and your balls in your mouth!'

I considered such talk beneath reproach, and made no reply. But my fellow trenchermen followed one vulgarity with another, until I felt justified in remarking on their lack of common decency. 'Life in the Holy Land must be greatly altered indeed,' I observed, 'if such low profanity is cause for mirth rather than shame.'

I fully expected to be reviled for my words. I braced myself as blackbeard's lips drew back in an ugly sneer. But even as he drew breath to decry me, Renaud glanced up sharply. 'Our friends are right to remind us of our manners, brothers,' he said, glaring down along the board as if defying anyone to disagree with him. 'We will each ask forgiveness in our prayers tonight, and examine our hearts in all penitence.'

This quieted the raucous table, and the meal ended in a much more subdued, if not respectful, manner. Afterward, Renaud sought me out on deck where Padraig and I were taking the soft evening air. The commander presented himself with a respectful bow and said, 'Allow me to offer you both apologies for my brother monks' impious behaviour.'

'We are not the ones to receive your apologies,' I replied. 'It was not our table. You owe us nothing.'

'Nevertheless,' the Templar said, 'you were the ones who called us back to our better selves – and were right to do so. My men have been absent from the stringency of the monastery too long and have allowed themselves to grow irreverent.'

'I know what fighting men are like,' I told him. 'Do not think you must explain anything to me.'

He smiled stiffly. 'Even so, please accept my sincere apology for our regrettable lapse. God willing, it will not happen again.'

We began to walk along the rail then, he and I. Padraig padded along unobtrusively behind us, listening, but keeping his thoughts to himself. We came to the stern where some of the sailors were talking and joking among themselves. When we had passed them and could not be overheard, Renaud said, 'I am interested to know how you came to be in the company of Prince Leo's son.'

'We met him in Rouen,' I explained, 'where he was searching for passage home.' I told about how the young lord had survived the illness that had carried off all his travelling party and left him stranded in a strange land with no one to help him.

'Do you know anything of his family?'

'I know his father is a prince in his own country, but nothing more than that,' I answered. Something in the Templar's tone made me wish to defend the young man. 'Whether his people were nobles of the highest rank, or the lowliest of slaves, made not the slightest difference to me. Roupen needed passage home, and we needed someone to guide us to Marseilles. We struck a bargain which was beneficial to both our interests, and he has proven himself a faithful friend.'

Renaud raised his eyebrows at this. 'Are you always so trusting?'

'Until a man shows me otherwise,' I said, bristling slightly at the implication of his question, 'I give him my best regard. It is never a mistake to treat someone as you would wish to be treated if you were in his boots.'

'No,' he allowed quickly, 'of course not. Again, forgive me; I meant no offence. I merely wished to determine what you knew of the circumstances surrounding your young friend's family.'

'As I have said, I know very little of Roupen's family or their circumstances. Is there something I *should* know?'

The Templar pursed his lips thoughtfully. 'Only this,' he said at last. 'Your friend's father, Prince Leo, is an unhappy man in a dangerous position. I fear he is not to be trusted.'

'I am sorry to hear it,' I replied, uncertainly. I could not discern what he intended by telling me this.

As if in reply to my hesitance, Renaud continued, 'Believe me, it gives me no pleasure to say it. I have every sympathy for your friend, Roupen; his situation is grave indeed.'

Looking out over the water to the darkening shoreline – as if gazing at an open and oozing wound – he added, mostly to himself, 'Bohemond's reach does often exceed his grasp.'

Mention of the audacious prince brought to mind my father's dealings, and I said, 'What you say interests me greatly. My father knew Prince Bohemond. They met in Jaffa during the Great Pilgrimage, and my father helped Lord Bohemond secure the aid of the emperor.'

'Truly?' replied the Templar commander, his curiosity instantly piqued.

'Oh, yes,' I assured him, 'and the prince returned the favour. If not for Bohemond's help, my father might never have returned home.'

'Many did not,' agreed the Templar commander. His interest visibly quickened, there was sharp appraisal in his glance as he said, 'But you misunderstand me: I was speaking of young Bohemond, the son of the illustrious prince. Not that it matters overmuch, for the son is that much like his father. Unfortunately, he shares his father's insatiable appetites as well.'

He went on to explain that Bohemond II, son of Prince Bohemond of Taranto, had at last come of age and returned to the Holy Land to claim his inheritance. Not content to receive the County of Antioch in its present condition, he had determined to restore its boundaries to their furthest extent.

'Since coming to the Holy Land four years ago,' Renaud said, 'the young count has waged several successful campaigns and recovered a goodly portion of the land lost since his father had ruled there. He is a restless youth, and a formidable fighter.' De Bracineaux regarded me meaningfully. 'He will not rest until he has won back everything.'

'And this is where the trouble arises,' I surmised.

'Precisely,' the Templar agreed. 'The northern part of the county now belongs to the Armenian principality. At the time young Bohemond's father took it, there was no one to oppose him. The land had been under Seljuq domination for many years, and the Armenian princes had their hands full defending the little that remained to them.'

It was easy to guess what had happened. As the Templar continued the tale, I could almost see the events as movements of the pieces on a game board. Once the Turks had been driven out, Roupen's people immediately reasserted their ownership, expecting, no doubt, that fellow Christians would uphold their rightful claims. In this they had been disappointed, however; their demands for redress were scorned, and their cries for justice unheeded . . . until disaster befell the over-reaching Count of Antioch.

Bohemond ran afoul of Emperor Alexius in the end, and his monstrous ambition was curtailed. After a disastrous battle with the Greeks, the great prince was forced to relinquish the disputed lands which were ceded to the Armenian rulers. Thus, with the emperor's help the Armenian princes had managed to claw back their traditional territory.

'But the peace of these last years will not continue,' Renaud announced bleakly. 'Young Bohemond II is as wilful and stubborn as his father. I fear there will be bloodshed between these two houses very soon.'

He seemed to expect some answer, but I could not imagine why he should be confiding in me, and knew not what to tell him. 'Your candour is both welcome and refreshing,' I said, 'but I would be leading you astray if I permitted you to think I possessed any power in these matters.'

'Of course,' the knight allowed, 'I understand. I merely thought you might derive some benefit from this information – in light of your friendship with Lord Roupen, that is. Naturally, if you were to find yourself in a position to influence the young lord's opinion, you would remember your duty as a Christian.'

This confused me somewhat. I knew full well the Templar was asking me to intervene for him in some way, but I could not understand what he expected me to do. 'Please,' I told him, 'speak plainly. I am unused to the plots and intrigues of the East. If you have a concern, tell me outright. I assure you, I will give it my fullest consideration.'

Renaud nodded, and folded his hands behind his back. 'As Commander of the Antioch Order of the Knights Templar, I am charged by His Holiness Pope Honorius with keeping the peace – not only in the city, but throughout the countryside as well. In addition, I am pledged to support the ruler of the county by whose sufferance we are granted our charter.' He looked at me meaningfully. 'I can put it no more plainly than that.'

At last, I began to see the shape of his dilemma. To uphold the peace, he would have to break faith with Bohemond – an action which would result in the revocation of his charter and the expulsion of the Templars from Antioch.

Although I accepted his assessment of the situation – I had no reason to believe otherwise – I could not help wondering aloud, 'Why do you tell me these things? I am merely a pilgrim on his way to the Holy Land. This is a matter for the rulers involved and would, it seems to me, be better served by a royal council.'

Renaud's smile turned bitter. 'You are right, of course. I will not trouble you further.' He made to walk away.

I caught him by the arm, and held him. 'Speak what is on your mind, man. Where is the harm?'

Glancing at Padraig his mouth drew tight. 'I have said all I care to say.'

'Then go your way,' I replied, releasing him. 'For if you hold the honour and counsel of a priest of the Célé Dé in such low esteem, you deserve all the anguish your silence brings.' Indicating Padraig, I said, 'This man is my friend and advisor, my *anam cara*, the true friend of my soul; he shares my innermost thoughts and is my life's companion and guide. Speak to me, or hold your tongue. That is your choice. But know that any remedy you seek through me will be discussed with my wise counsellor.'

Renaud nodded curtly. He was not used to being addressed in this way, and did not like it, but was man enough to see the sense. He did not dismiss me, or turn me aside harshly, but swallowed his pride once more. 'Forgive me, priest,' he said, bending in a small, but genuine bow of humility. 'I meant no disrespect.'

Padraig inclined his head in acceptance and pardon. 'I forgive you freely. If it would help you to unburden your soul, I will walk a little apart so that the two of you may speak more easily together.'

'No,' said the Templar, making up his mind, 'that is not necessary. I have come this far; let us see the thing to its conclusion.'

He turned and began walking once more, his hands clasped firmly behind him, his eyes downcast. As it was growing dark now, one of the sailors came forwards to light the torches in the iron sconces at the prow and at the base of the mast. We strolled the deck in silence until we were alone once more.

'What I am about to say would be considered treason against my liege lord if it were to reach his ears,' Renaud declared.

I heard the solid weight of his voice and knew he was speaking the dark heart of his fear. I sought to reassure him. 'I give you my word: your confidence will not be betrayed.'

'All this summer, Prince Bohemond has been recruiting men from his former lands in Sicily,' the commander told us. 'He is using ships leased to the Templars to transport them to Antioch.'

I could not think this information treasonous, and told the worried knight as much.

'No,' he replied, 'that much could easily be discerned by one and all. What cannot be perceived is that the bold prince plans a surprise attack on Anazarbus before the summer's end.' He stopped and turned to me. 'There,' he said grimly, 'now you have it. I have entrusted you with knowledge which could defeat my lord on the battlefield, and bring about the ruin of Antioch. Such is the power I bestow. Use it wisely.'

I could feel my very soul shrinking from the terrible responsibility his words had placed upon my unsuspecting shoulders.

The Templar gazed at me, his eyes watchful in the soft glow of the torches. 'You spoke of plots and intrigues just now. Let me give you a word of advice: sooner trust an enemy than a friend.'

'Strange advice.'

'Yes,' the Templar allowed, 'and the difficulty, you will find, is learning to tell the difference between them.'

NINETEEN

Thus, from the very first day aboard ship I was plunged into the labyrinthine schemes of the intrigue-breeding East – and I had not yet set foot in the Holy Land. Over the next many days, I stewed and fretted over every word spoken to me that night. The knowledge festered in me, poisoning my days and nights with dread and the dull apprehension that whatever I did would damn me. For, to save one realm would be to ruin another.

Why had the Templar confided in me? Was it to claim me as an ally, and thus remove me from the young lord's side? Or, did he wish to use my friendship with Roupen in some way? He had hinted as much, but I was at a loss to know what I might do. Try as I might, I could think of no way in which I might serve the common good.

What purpose would it achieve anyway? There was nothing the young lord could do about the planned attack just now, and the knowledge would only bring him misery and pain. Moreover, he might consider himself to be among enemies, and do something precipitous. By holding my tongue, I spared him that at least – although it was at considerable cost to myself.

It was not until we reached Cyprus that I had the opportunity to speak in complete freedom with Padraig about the delicate information the Templar commander had confided. 'What are we to do, Padraig?' I demanded, all the woe rising in a black flood of dread. 'What are we to do?'

We had availed ourselves of the opportunity to walk through the pleasant port and market town of Limasol while the ships took on fresh water and supplies. 'You know as well as I that we cannot just stand by and do nothing.'

'Have I said we should do nothing?'

'What then?' Before he could answer, I said, 'Just remember that hundreds, perhaps thousands of lives are at risk whatever we do. Not to mention –'

Padraig held up his hands. 'Peace, brother! Leave off your pissing and moaning a moment, and let me speak.'

'Speak then!'

'As it happens,' he began, 'you are not the only one to have struggled with this problem. I also have bethought myself what can be done.'

'Yes, yes, get on with it, man!'

'Very well. It comes to this: we must seek out Prince Bohemond at first opportunity and demand that he repent of his decision to attack the Armenians.'

I stared at the priest with envy at his sublime innocence. 'You are a wonder,' I told him. 'Even knowing what you know of princes and their insatiable appetites for wealth and power, you still suggest this? Tell me, what do you think will happen?'

'I expect God will move in Bohemond's heart and the young prince will recognize his error and turn aside before it is too late.'

'Your faith is remarkable, priest,' I told him, 'if you believe the prince will even listen to a single word you say, let alone heed your counsel.'

'That will be his decision,' Padraig replied. 'Our way remains clear: we must do what God would have us do.'

I glared at the monk and knew he meant just what he said; we would have to go before this Prince Bohemond and deliver the judgement: turn aside from your wicked ways, O Mighty Ruler! Repent and seek forgiveness, or suffer divine retribution for your sins.

Yes, and I could just about imagine the reception our call to repentance would receive.

'He will have us flayed alive for our impertinence, and our heads adorning pikes above the city gates,' I grumbled. 'That is what will happen.'

'Perhaps,' granted Padraig with a shrug. 'We cannot refuse what is right and just merely because it may prove painful to us.'

'It will be more than painful,' I countered, 'be assured of that. But supposing – merely for the sake of our discussion – that we escape with our skins intact. What then?'

'Then, if he will not embrace the peace of God, we are free to take a warning to Roupen's people.'

I stared at him. 'And how did you come to that?'

'By reason of the fact that once we have declared our concerns before the prince, his actions will be open for all men to judge. He will repent, or he will not. If Bohemond proceeds with his nefarious plan, he does so in spite of our call to honour God's peace. Thus, there will no longer remain any obstacle to a full and forthright profession of the prince's intentions to any and all concerned.'

I turned this over in my mind for a time. It did seem the only way out of the dilemma Renaud had forced upon us. 'Then it is agreed,' I decided, 'we will make entreaty to the prince the moment we enter the city. But allow *me* to put the case to Bohemond. I will appeal to his honour, not his sin. If de Bracineaux is of the same mind in this matter – and I believe he is, for all his reasons may be his own – then he will support us in our attempt. If the three of us speak with one voice, we may have some chance of escaping the full force of the prince's displeasure.'

'Well said,' concluded Padraig. 'However it falls out with the prince, we must observe the utmost caution. For if Bohemond was to learn the son of his enemy was within his grasp, he would seize the boy and hold him to ransom, or worse. Roupen will have to be told what we intend. His life will be at risk the moment we set foot in Antioch. We cannot keep him in ignorance any longer.'

The next day, when the ships departed on the last leg of the journey to Outremer, we summoned the young lord onto the top deck where we strolled along the rail and watched the rugged brown hills of Cyprus dwindle into the wide, blue distance. When I was certain we would not be overheard by others going about their chores on deck, I informed Roupen of Prince Bohemond's plans to attack the Armenian stronghold at Anazarbus.

'I thank you for telling me,' he said, sinking into himself. 'I know now that you are my true friends. I will impose on you only so far as to see me safely off the ship. Once we make landfall at Saint Symeon, I will leave the company and continue home on my own.'

Although he spoke with a firm resolve, I could tell he was more than a little daunted by the prospect before him. He looked to Padraig as he finished, as if to plead the priest's blessing on his plan.

'Your determination is understandable,' I suggested, 'but there is another way. Come with us to Antioch.'

'Antioch!' he gasped. 'Go among my enemies? I never will.'

'Calm yourself, and listen to me. Padraig and I plan to confront

Bohemond and demand that he turn away from his foolish –' I caught Padraig's glance, 'foolish and sinful plan to attack your people. I have every confidence that Commander de Bracineaux will support us in this.

'Now then, if Bohemond listens to reason, you will have no need to fear him, and you can carry a good report home to your people.'

'And if he does not?' grumbled Roupen dubiously.

'Then you will hasten home with a warning, and we will help you. I cannot speak for the Templars, but I believe we can count on their aid as well.'

'Can we trust them?' he wondered.

'We can,' I told him. 'Renaud knows who you are, and has known since you first came on board this ship. If he had intended ill for you, we would certainly have seen evidence of it by now. He is constrained by his priestly vows, yet I believe he is trying to help you in the only way he can.'

'So we proceed to Antioch – and hide beneath Prince Bohemond's very nose,' Roupen said, little warming to the notion. 'What then?'

'Once we have spoken to Bohemond, we will know how things stand,' Padraig said. 'But understand, whatever comes of this, we will see you safely home.'

Needless to say, our entrance into Antioch a few days later was fraught and uncomfortable with the dread of discovery hanging over us as we passed through the enormous gates and along the palm-lined streets of the great city. How I wish it had been otherwise, for truly, Antioch is a very marvel of a city.

Rising from its rocky roots on the slow Orontes River, the splendid white walls soar upward to a height unequalled by any fortress I have ever seen. Magnificent in the golden sunrise, the city glows like amber. From the water gate at the river's edge to the high citadel nested in the cradling rocks of the stronghold mound, it is a sight to stir the heart with awe.

With our escort of Templars – two hundred strong, on horseback, their red emblems ablaze on white surcoats, spears and helmets gleaming – we descended the low hills and crossed the Orontes valley to join the road leading to the city. We passed over the bridge and in through the central gate, entering the long wide, tree-lined road which formed the city's main thoroughfare. Great houses of wealthy families lined the street, along with ancient basilicas, markets, and churches large and small.

I knew the Iron Lance had been discovered in one of these selfsame churches, and as we rode slowly along I kept turning my head this way and that in the forlorn hope that I might somehow see and recognize the place. If I found it, however, I never learned. For, although I saw several churches, none of them seemed in any way remarkable, and I felt slightly disappointed.

Nor did I have a chance to ask anyone about it, for no sooner had we arrived at the garrison in the lower city, but Prince Bohemond demanded audience of Commander Renaud. The higher-ranking Templars had been given quarters in the citadel itself, and Renaud, having arrived in the city, was evidently expected to go at once to join the prince.

I had confided to the commander my decision to bring a petition before the young prince at the soonest opportunity, and he assented – although he stopped short of assuring me of his complete agreement to the plan. When the Templar commander turned from the prince's messenger, he said, 'You are in luck, my friend. Bohemond deigns to receive me. I will take you and the priest along and we will have this out at once.'

'Now?' I said. 'And with the dust of the road clinging to us?' To avoid the sticky, all-embracing heat of the day we had risen just after midnight and crossed the rough hills before sunrise. The dry days of summer had come, when the sun's rays strike the earth like the blast of an oven, and the slightest footfall on the well-used roads raises a very pall of dust and clouds of biting flies. The further inland we travelled, the hotter and dustier it became. With two hundred mounted Templars, the resulting clouds of grey grit made us appear as if we had spent days at the millstone grinding dry clods into powder.

'The prince arrived in the city four days ago, and is eager to begin planning his campaign,' the commander replied. 'If we hope to dissuade him, this will be our best chance.' He summoned his sergeant. 'Go now, take a moment to wash and refresh yourselves,' he said. 'Gislebert will bring you to the palace when you are ready. I will await you there.'

The sergeant led us through a low door and out into a small courtyard surrounded by long ranks of old Roman-style barracks which were the Templars' quarters. The yard was filled with soldiers welcoming their comrades and seeing them settled in their new surroundings. Gislebert brought us to a fresh-running fountain in the centre of the yard. Roupen, grim and uneasy, stood stiff-legged, glumly watching Padraig and me as we splashed water on our faces from the stone basin

'I will go with you,' he said.

'No,' I said, 'that would not be prudent.'

'I cannot wait here alone. What if someone tells Bohemond I am here?'

'Commander Renaud has given his word,' I replied patiently. 'You are safe in Antioch so long as you remain in the garrison. But you dare not show your face in the palace.'

'I am not afraid,' he announced carelessly. 'I will go and speak to Bohemond myself.'

'You may have opportunity to speak to the prince,' I told him. 'But before we abandon our plan, let us at least determine what manner of man this Prince Bohemond might be.'

'What am I to do while you are away?' he said unhappily, kicking at the base of the fountain.

'Wait patiently,' Padraig said, 'and pray our appeal meets with sincere contrition and repentance.'

'And if it does not?' he snapped angrily. He could not help himself, nor could I blame him. Had I been in his place, I would have behaved in much the same way.

'We can cross but one bridge at a time,' I replied.

'Have faith,' Padraig offered gently. 'Bind courage to your heart, and seek the Good Lord's guiding hand. Trust him, and he will meet you in your need.'

Roupen accepted this with gloomy forbearance and said no more. When we had finished washing and made ourselves as presentable as possible, I turned to the young lord. 'Remain calm, and do not stir from this place. We will return as soon as possible,' I promised, placing my hand on his shoulder. 'God willing, we shall bring you a good report.'

With that, we were led from the courtyard and, following Gislebert, conducted along a dizzying array of narrow streets and stairways up into the heart of the old city to the high citadel and the palace where the Count of Antioch held court.

TWENTY

Bohemond's palace put me in mind of a noble lady fallen into beggary. Undoubtedly, the royal residence had once been a very treasure, but years of indifference and neglect had marred its best features. Costly wooden panels were gouged and scratched; expensive silk rugs were worn threadbare, their fine colours faded and dulled by dirt and indifferent use; once-dazzling painted walls were dingy with the grime of smoke and oily food; polished floors were rutted and dull from too many rough feet, and too few washings. Several of the outer corridors contained filth from discarded slops and excrement which raised a nasty stink in the nose.

In all, the place breathed an atmosphere of forlorn decline and dilapidation. It made me sorry to see it sliding into decay, and I felt myself resenting the thoughtless lord who could allow this to happen. There are far worse things in this world, as well I know, but I glimpsed in the shabby surroundings a malignant disregard which I could not abide. How much of this rot should be laid at the feet of the current inhabitant, I could not tell. But that the prince inhabited these once-splendid halls and did nothing to relieve the distress so evident around him told me something of the man.

His appearance, however, all but dispelled the regrettable impression created by his surroundings. For Prince Bohemond II was a full-blooded, handsome man: broad-shouldered, long-limbed and tall, with a firm jaw and open, pleasant features. His hair was long and fair, and his beard short, cut into the distinctive forked shape favoured by certain Frankish noblemen; his hands were big and strong, and always moving – as if restless when they did not clutch a sword.

Together with Commander Renaud, Padraig and I were conducted into the prince's private chamber by one of his advisors, an old retainer from Antioch who regarded us with the world-weary air of one who has seen too much. The prince was standing over a long table on which a meal of roast fowl and plums had been spread. He had a knife in one hand, poised to strike, and a gold cup in the other.

Glancing up as the door opened to admit us, he exclaimed, 'De Bracineaux! You *are* here! God be praised, man, it is good to see you. They told me you had arrived, and I could not believe my good fortune. I did not expect you for another week.'

Forgetting his rank and place, he leapt forwards to meet us, stepping around the table in quick bounds. He seized the Templar by the arms, and embraced him like a brother. Then, seeing two strangers idling in Renaud's wake, he cried, 'And who is this with you? Come in, sirs! I give you good greeting. Join me, all of you. Food has been prepared, and I was just about to eat.'

'We would be delighted,' replied the Templar. Turning to us, he said, 'May I present: Lord Duncan of Caithness, and Padraig, his chaplain.'

'I am pleased to meet you, gentlemen,' said the prince, inclining his head nicely. He smiled, and despite myself I felt compelled to like him. 'You cannot have been in the city long.'

'We have only just arrived,' I answered.

'Good voyage?'

'Very good indeed, my lord,' I said. 'The Mediterranean is smooth as a highway compared to the rough northern seas around Scotland.'

'I have heard of this Scotland, you know,' Prince Bohemond said. He turned away, indicating that we should follow him to the table. 'They say the men and women there are painted blue.' Smiling, he glanced at Padraig and then at me. 'But you are not painted blue, are you?'

'No, lord, although the Picti are known to daub themselves with woad when they do battle. It is an old custom, but still occasionally to be seen.'

He smiled again, showing neat white teeth. 'I should like to see that.' He speared a roast fowl with his knife. 'Come, my friends, eat!' To his manservant, he said, 'Hemar! Pour some wine for these thirsty fellows. They have come all the way from Scotland.'

Following the prince's invitation, we helped ourselves to the meat and fruit before us. Bohemond and Renaud fell to talking about the voyage and the settling of the troops, and I was glad to have the chance to observe the prince for a while. He was, I decided, somewhat younger than he first appeared. Although his bearing and speech were that of an older, more confident man, I believe he adopted this manner to disguise the fact of his green immaturity. He was little more than a child playing at a game for men, and I felt strangely sorry for him.

As our hosts talked, I considered how best to broach the subject of the prince's plan to attack the Armenians. It would, I considered, be best for all of us if Bohemond would raise the issue himself, giving me a natural opportunity to speak. But he seemed more than content to talk idly of travel and the weather, and it occurred to me that perhaps the prince did not wish to say anything about his plans in front of Padraig and me. So, it was left to us, and if no one else touched on the matter soon, I decided I would raise the issue myself.

I was steeling myself to do just that, when young Bohemond, unable to restrain himself any longer, tapped the table with the hilt of his knife. 'Here now, de Bracineaux, we have beaten the bushes long enough. I want to talk about the campaign. How many men can I count on from you?'

The Templar commander lay aside his cup, and composed himself to answer. 'I have considered your request very carefully,' he answered. 'To put the matter squarely, I must tell you it places me in a very awkward position.'

'Indeed?' wondered Bohemond innocently. 'I am distressed to hear it.' He did not appear dismayed in the least.

'You see, waging open warfare is outside the authority of the Templar Rule. We are pledged to guard the roads and those who travel on them – anything beyond that is a breach of our Rules of Order. In short, my lord, attacking the forces of our Christian allies would be reprehensible and unlawful.'

Bohemond's face tightened with vexation, but he maintained his cheerful demeanour. 'Come now, sir,' he cajoled, 'you know other commanders have joined in battling the common enemy. I am not asking you to do something your brothers would refuse.'

'What others do is a matter for their consciences. For myself, I cannot allow my men to be used as mercenaries.'

'The Grand Master has given me his assurance that there will be no difficulty,' the prince said, somewhat petulantly.

'And there will be none – so long as my men are not required to go against their priestly vows. With all respect, my lord prince, we are defenders, not aggressors.'

'Do you deny that the protection of the borders of my realm is of utmost importance to the safety of pilgrims and citizens within this realm?'

'On the contrary,' replied Renaud, glad to find some area of agreement, 'if the borders of this county should ever fall under enemy threat, you will find the Templars foremost in the fight.'

'I am glad to hear it,' answered Bohemond quickly. 'For a moment I had begun to doubt the wisdom of allowing the Poor Soldiers of Christ to occupy such a large and, I might add, *costly* presence in this city. After all, a lord who cannot trust the courage of his warriors is already captive to his enemies.'

'Never doubt the courage of the Templars,' Renaud said, his voice tightening with suppressed anger. 'Our lives are forsworn before Almighty God, and we will fight to the death rather than dishonour the vow we have taken.'

'Then why this unseemly hesitance?' demanded Bohemond. 'I tell you that so long as the borders of this county are held by Armenians my people are not safe.'

The air fairly bristled between them. Seeing that he had pressed the matter to an impasse with the Templar commander, Bohemond turned his attention to Padraig and me. 'You must excuse us,' he said testily, 'it seems the good commander and myself have opened a subject of disagreement.'

This was my chance to intervene, and I took it. 'Forgive me, lord. I am a stranger to this place, and have no right to speak. But if you would hear me out, I would be much obliged.'

'If you have something sensible to say, I welcome you, sir,' sniffed the prince. 'It would be an agreeable change to listening to the mealy-mouthed excuses of this craven commander.'

Renaud made to object, but thought better of it and held his tongue. Bohemond was young and impetuous; he was hot-headed, and it was difficult to restrain his ambitious impulses. Antagonizing him would only make things worse.

'Although I am newly arrived in Antioch, my family is not without some experience of this part of the world. My grandfather took the cross in the Great Pilgrimage and died in Jerusalem. Moreover, my father once held council with your father – it was in Jaffa, if I remember aright, and my father was about the same age as you are now, my lord. He came away from that meeting with a memory which my family has treasured ever since.'

Padraig frowned and gave me a warning look as if to tell me I was treading too close to our secret for his comfort.

My story pleased young Bohemond immensely and, I thought, favourably disposed him to what I was about to say. 'Indeed, sir!' he cried. 'You see, Renaud! Not everyone in this godforsaken place is as ignorant of their Christian duty as you are. Please, continue.'

'Therefore,' I said, feeling my stomach knot into a hard ball, 'I pray you will not think me reaching too far above my place when I suggest to you that Commander Renaud is right in refusing to support an attack on the Armenians.'

Alas, my words did not strike the young prince as I had hoped. His face clenched and grew dark with anger. 'How dare you!' he muttered. He whirled on the Templar, giving vent to the full force of his anger. 'You worm! You put him up to this! You sneaking coward. Get out of my sight! Everyone get out!'

'Calm yourself, my lord,' I said, attempting to pacify him. 'Renaud is not to blame. My views are my own, and had I never set eyes on the good commander, I would still say the same: it is wrong to attack the Armenians. They are baptized Christians, fellow allies of the Holy Roman Empire, and hold to the same faith as you, my lord.'

'They are filth!' roared Bohemond, his face contorted in hatred. 'What is more, they are scheming filth who have stolen my father's land, and I will have it back.'

He glared around at all of us, angry and frustrated at finding his desires repudiated on all sides.

Padraig rose, and in the gentlest, most gracious tone said, 'In the name of God, I urge you to remember your better self. Put aside your ignoble ambitions, my lord. Repent of your plan and abandon your sinful scheme before –'

Alas, Padraig never finished his exhortation. For the reckless prince picked up his knife from the table and flung it at the priest's head, shouting, 'How dare you! Get out!'

Padraig barely dodged the blade, which struck the wall and fell to the floor. Bohemond jumped up and shoved the table, spilling cups and sending food rolling from the platters. 'All of you, get out! Leave me!' he screamed, his pale face growing scarlet with rage.

As the furious prince reached for another knife, Commander Renaud, already on his feet, moved towards me. 'Go!' he urged. 'Get back to the garrison and wait for me there.'

'We will stay and see it through.'

'Leave us. I will calm him, and follow as soon as I can. Go.' Turning quickly to the prince, he said, 'This is beneath you, sir. Put down that knife, and let us discuss this matter like reasonable men.'

The prince, still shouting and waving the knife, was done with listening. While he raged at the commander, Padraig and I made our way swiftly from the chamber and hurried back through the long, low rooms of the palace, descending by a number of dark and narrow stairways to the former stables below. We passed quickly among the Templars going about their chores, and made for the first door and hurried out into the bright, sunlit street once more.

We hesitated only long enough to locate the street by which we had come up to the citadel, then hastened away again, walking quickly, but not running – nothing rouses citizens of a city as swiftly as the sight of a stranger in full flight. Every now and then I paused to look back and listen, but neither saw nor heard anything to indicate pursuit of any kind.

We retraced our steps down the steeply-angled street to the lower city, gradually easing our pace as we went; the street grew more crowded with people making their way to and from the markets. Our exertions had made us wet with sweat, and I was just thinking of stopping to rest a moment to collect our wits and cool off a little before continuing when Padraig spied the garrison.

Once safely behind the stout garrison walls we allowed ourselves to relax; we crossed to the fountain in the yard and both of us refreshed ourselves with a good long drink before going in to a very distraught Roupen awaiting word of our meeting.

'We failed,' I told him bluntly. 'Bohemond would not listen to reason. Renaud stayed with the prince to try to calm him, but I do not hold out any hope that he will change his mind.'

The young lord nodded grimly. 'Thank you for trying,' he said softly. I could see he was frightened and had allowed himself to place too much hope in our efforts.

'We are not finished yet,' I told him, trying to offer some small comfort. 'When the commander returns we will sit down together and decide what to do.'

Alas, if only it had been that simple.

TWENTY-ONE

We waited uneasily for Commander de Bracineaux to appear. Padraig and I found an opportunity to nap through the heat of the day, taking it in turns to sit with Roupen while the other slept, lest he become fretful and overanxious. The garrison, now full of new arrivals, remained busy with much coming and going – yet peaceful for all that; the warrior monks maintained a cloistered calm amidst the general commotion of military life.

Indeed, the old Roman garrison bore more than a passing resemblance to the monastery: the quiet inner court with a chapel at one end, the long ranks of barracks, which might have been cells; the kitchens, always clattering with activity; the refectory with its long banks of tables and benches, and the Templars themselves – hurrying to and fro on their errands, dressed in the white surcoat of the order – if not for their swords, which they rarely removed, might easily have passed for their peaceable counterpart. A religious order they were, true enough; but these were brothers in arms – a fighting brotherhood first, and a religious fraternity after.

They left us to ourselves for the most part, pressed as they were with accommodating the sudden swelling of their ranks. Now and then we heard one or another of the Templars exclaim as he discovered a countryman among the newly arrived recruits, but otherwise the peace of the churchyard prevailed.

Towards evening I began to worry that something had gone wrong at the citadel. I went in search of the commander's sergeant and found him in the stables inspecting horses which had just arrived from Gaul. I greeted him and told him my concerns. He listened, but I could tell he put no faith in what I was telling him. Gislebert, though he may have been a good soldier, was not a friendly man; we had been shipmates together after all, and yet he treated me with cool, almost callous indifference – as if I had disappointed him in some crucial but inexpressible way, and he was now forced to silently bear the brunt of my grievous inadequacy.

'I can only think that Renaud has suffered some misfortune,' I concluded, after explaining the circumstances of our meeting with the prince. 'Otherwise, he should have returned long since.'

'I am certain it is nothing,' he replied stiffly, dismissing my concern as if it were the trifling qualm of a spoiled and fussy child. 'The business of the garrison sometimes requires more particular attention than one, unused to such matters, may credit.'

I suppose he meant to put me in my place with that. He turned back to his inspection, running his hand down along the foreleg of the horse before him, a fine roan stallion. I decided there was little to be gained by quarrelling with him, and turned to go. 'If he said for you to wait for him, I expect he meant just that,' Gislebert added over his shoulder. As he turned away, I heard him mutter under his breath, 'Only a fool would doubt him.'

I stopped in mid-step and turned around. 'I am no fool, Sergeant Gislebert,' I said sharply, 'contrary to what you seem to think. And I have every confidence in Commander Renaud. Yes, he told us to wait for him here, and all day we have done just that. He also told us that he would soon follow. Clearly, that did not happen. Therefore, in light of the prince's foul mood, I do not think it foolish to inquire after the commander's welfare.'

He straightened slowly, regarding me with rank distaste. 'I leave it with you, Gislebert. It would be the work of a moment to prove me wrong.'

After a moment, he said, 'What would you have me do, my lord?' The words were worms in his mouth.

'Perhaps it would not be too much of an inconvenience to send a message to the Templars at the citadel and ask them to discover what has detained the commander.'

'It will be done,' the sergeant replied grudgingly.

'Good.'

I rejoined Roupen and Padraig, and we waited some more. Twilight was full upon us and the smell from the kitchens was beginning to waft in through the open door. Growing restless, I walked out into the yard and, after strolling around aimlessly for a while, sat down on the edge of the basin beside the fountain. The sky was clear and the night fine; a few bright stars shone overhead, and the moon was already showing above the rooftops. Beyond the garrison walls, I could see smoke drifting up from the houses round about.

I fell to thinking about what you, Cait, might be doing at Banvarð at that moment. I could see you playing on the shore, gathering the glistening shells and holding them out for your grandmother Ragna's inspection. I was immersed in this daydream when I heard someone enter the yard. I looked up to see Gislebert striding quickly towards me.

'It is as you feared,' he said bluntly. Visibly agitated, he grimaced as, forced to his admission, he delivered the bad news. 'Prince Bohemond has confined the commander to the palace.'

'So it is as I thought.'

The sergeant squirmed with embarrassment. 'I was able to inquire after him through the monks in the palace. He is safe and well. He sent a message: you are to leave the city at once. The commander tried to make him see reason, but to no avail. Bohemond has commenced a search. Once they reach the lower city, the garrison will no longer be safe. The commander says you and the young lord must not wait any longer. You must flee.'

'Did he say where we were to go?'

'No, my lord,' answered the sergeant. 'Although, the commander imagines the young lord is anxious to return home as swiftly as possible.'

'He is extremely anxious,' I replied. 'But speak plainly, Gislebert. What does Renaud intend us to do?'

The sturdy soldier regarded me with dull implacability. 'That is all I know, sir.'

I stared back at him, wondering at the cryptic turn the discussion had taken. It came to me that perhaps this was the difficulty the commander had alluded to before – his vows of fealty prevented him from speaking more directly against the wishes of his liege lord. 'Sergeant, did Commander Renaud tell you why we went to see Bohemond?'

'He confides in me from time to time.'

'I believe I understand, Sergeant Gislebert.'

He nodded curtly. 'I take it the matter is concluded.'

'Yes.'

'Then I expect you will be wanting to leave. The city gates are soon closed, and it would not be wise to wait until morning.'

'If there is nothing else . . .' I paused to allow him to say more if he would, 'then we will be on our way, sergeant.'

Padraig and Roupen listened gravely as I told them what the sergeant had discovered. 'Unless we care to risk discovery in the city overnight, we must go before they close the gates.'

I did not like begging provisions from the Templar quarter master, but had no choice. The markets, if any could be found, would be deserted, and we had a long walk ahead of us. Padraig undertook to procure the bare necessities: a few loaves of bread, a little dried meat, and three skins of water – enough to see us to Saint Symeon where we hoped to get a boat. Gislebert might have helped us on our way, but he disappeared and was not seen again until, as we made our way out of the garrison and onto the street, the sergeant caught up with us to add one further complication to what had become a most mysterious flight. 'The commander said that if he was ever forced to flee the city, he would go to Famagusta,' Gislebert said meaningfully.

I had no idea where this might be, nor did Padraig or Roupen.

'It is a port on the island of Cyprus,' the sergeant informed us, 'and home to a man named Yordanus Hippolytus.'

I repeated the name. 'Would it be worthwhile trying to find this fellow, do you think?'

'Perhaps,' Gislebert allowed tentatively. 'He is known to be a very great help to travellers in need.'

With that obscurely significant message, the sergeant hurried back into the garrison; and we proceeded on our way, true pilgrims, carrying nothing but the cloaks on our backs, the waterskins at our sides, and the small bundle of provisions we would share out among us. We flitted through the half-deserted streets and reached the entrance to the city as the guards were preparing to close the gates for the night. Curiously, they were just as wary of travellers trying to leave the city after dark as invaders trying to get in. All gatemen are alike in this regard, I think. They view all who pass through their portals with deepest distrust, never more so than when preparing to bar the doors for the night. They halted us and questioned us closely and inspected us with scowls of disapproval. If not for Padraig, who offered priestly reassurances on our behalf, I do not think they would have let us go.

In the end, we were allowed to pass through the small doors – the larger gates were already shut – and out onto the road by which we had come to Antioch that very morning. The rest we had enjoyed during the latter part of the day stood us in good stead; however, Roupen, worried as he was, had not availed himself of the opportunity provided, and so we were forced to go at a much slower pace and stop more frequently to rest than I would have preferred; but there was nothing to be done about it. The young lord was still not capable of much vigour, and it would not help matters at all to exhaust him, and bring on his illness again.

We allowed ourselves a drink at daybreak and again at midday when we stopped for a meal and a longer rest during the hottest part of the day. As a precaution, we removed ourselves a fair distance from the road and took shelter from the sun beneath some low, blighted olive trees. We ate our food, quickly finishing the last of our scant provisions. I kept watch on the road lest Bohemond's pursuit catch us napping. Even so, I saw no sign of frenzied chase; we had the road and sky and empty hills to ourselves.

A short distance from this scrag of a grove stood a squalid little farm, the crabbed fields of which yielded more stones than corn. A few parched stalks drooped in the oven-hot air, their withered leaves crackling on each fitful breath of wind. That hard labour should be lavished on such hopeless soil would have been pitiable if it were not everywhere the same in that broken desert land.

For, from all that I could see, the Holy Land was but a great hot barren dust heap which everyone continually quarrelled over as if it were a paradise flowing with milk and honey instead of grit and gravel, a wondrous realm of gold and jewels instead of rocks and thorns. That anyone should greatly care who ruled this desert wasteland astounded me; but that anyone should fight and die over the right to do so, gave me to despair. Behold, I thought grimly, the triumph of avarice over sense, of greed over sanity.

While taking our ease, we discussed the plan for reaching our ultimate destination, Anazarbus in Armenia. 'It is a very great distance,' Roupen assured us. 'The wilderness is very rough and barren; there are few roads, and those that exist are not good at all. We will certainly need help to get there, and good horses.'

I asked which direction Armenia lay, and how best to get there. Roupen explained that it was in the low Taurus mountains to the north, and that there were several routes. 'The best way, however, is through Mamistra,' he said. 'We can get there by boat from Famagusta.'

'Mamistra is a sea port?' asked Padraig.

'No, it is inland – on a river. But the water is deep enough for boats and small ships. It serves as the nearest sea port to Anazarbus.'

When the strength of the sun began to wane somewhat, we pushed on again, walking until dusk deepened around us. I remained wary of any pursuit, but saw no one until coming upon a group of Venetian merchants camped beside the road for the night. The merchants, seven in all, had been exploring trading opportunities in Antioch, and were on their way to Ascalon in the south. They greeted us pleasantly and invited us to share their evening meal, and asked how we found life in the Holy Land. Padraig would have talked to them all day long, but I thought it best not to encourage their interest too far, so after wishing them well, I begged to be excused, explaining that we had walked all day and were very tired.

I scraped out a place among the rocks and thorns, lay down, and dozed contentedly until Padraig nudged me awake at daybreak. 'Someone is coming,' he whispered. 'I was just praying and heard horses on the road.'

'Bohemond's men?'

'Maybe. They are still too far away to tell.'

'Then we still have a chance.'

We woke Roupen and crept quietly away from the camp, hiding in a dry ditch of a ravine a few hundred paces from the camp. Shortly, there appeared three riders. They reined up when they came upon the sleeping Venetians. Although we could not hear what was said, I could guess readily enough. The riders roused the merchants with demands and questions; the Venetians looked around, and shrugged as if to say, 'We do not know if they are the men you are looking for. They were here with us last night, but they are gone now. We cannot tell you more.'

The riders did not linger, but rode on quickly – no doubt in the hope of catching us a little further up the road. After they were gone, we waited in the ravine until the merchants departed as well, and then continued on, keeping a sharp watch on the road ahead for the returning soldiers.

We walked until midday, and then stopped for another rest, thinking to move on at dusk and walk through the night so that we could reach the harbour with a good chance of getting a ship before any sailed the next day.

This we did, spending a quiet night out on the road beneath the stars, so that we arrived at the little port town of Saint Symeon just after sunrise. We saw no sign of the soldiers, but two of the roundships were still in the bay, dwarfing the smaller fishing vessels riding peacefully at anchor off shore. We hurried down through the single narrow street to the harbour, where Roupen made a good account of himself by undertaking negotiations with a local fisherman for the hire of his boat to take us across to Famagusta. The sailor knew the place well, and was pleased to have ready payment in silver for his services. He called his son and one of his idle friends to help with the boat and, after providing ourselves with a few loaves of bread, a little wine, and some boiled eggs and hard lumps of goat cheese, we cast off.

As the boat slid out into the bay, I scanned the road and hills for the last time for any sign of our pursuers. There was nothing. I decided that Bohemond had made but a half-hearted attempt at apprehending us; if he had been in deadly earnest, his men would have caught us long since. Thus, I concluded that he had directed his main efforts elsewhere, and relaxed my vigilance. The race, I decided, would not be to outrun pursuers, but to reach Anazarbus first. Towards this end, I dedicated myself.

All that can be said of the voyage is that it was short and blessedly uneventful. We reached the deep-water harbour on the eastern edge of Cyprus on the evening of the second day, and set to work seeking out the fellow named Yordanus. There was little harm in doing so, I thought. If, for some reason, we disliked the man, or determined that making his acquaintance would be of little value to us, we would simply move on and make our way to Anazarbus by ourselves.

That evening, as the moon rose over the quiet harbour, nothing could have been more simple and straightforward. But, as I was learning, nothing was ever simple and straightforward in Outremer. Our search quickly ran aground on the fact that, as night closed in, no one would speak to strangers in the street. In the end, we were forced to take a room from a local wool merchant who put out part of his large house to visitors for a small fee, for which he also provided an excellent meal. We ate heartily, and slept well in soft beds piled deep with fleeces, and rose early next morning to renew our search for Yordanus – with an ever-increasing sense of urgency. For, every day we spent dallying along the trail, Bohemond was that much closer to launching his attack on Anazarbus.

Before leaving the wool merchant's house, we asked if he knew where we might find this Yordanus Hippolytus. Our good-natured host had heard of the fellow. 'Oh, yes,' he assured us. 'He lives in the upper town – the old town. He is a goldsmith – fine man, a very saint, and given to many good works – if he is the man I am thinking of.'

'The man you are thinking of,' said the wool merchant's wife, 'does not live in the old town. He lives in the big house at the end of the road behind the hill.'

The sunny merchant's face clouded. 'How do you know who I am thinking of?' he demanded. 'Be quiet, woman, you will confuse these good men.'

'No more than you have confused them already,' she replied tartly. 'Take my advice and ask someone to show you the way to the house behind the hill.'

'The old town,' the wool man assured us. 'Pay no attention to my wife. She is obviously thinking of someone else.'

Armed with this conflicting information, we began our search in the old town as the merchant suggested. For the price of a seed cake, we hired a young boy at the harbour to show us the way to the old town. He led us to the central market square where many of the artisans and traders had stalls from which they sold their wares. They spoke Greek in Famagusta and, since Padraig's Greek was better than mine, he undertook to find out if anyone knew the man we sought.

'Oh, yes,' said a maker of brass bowls, 'he is well known. He owns many ships. If you wish to find him, you must look down by the harbour, for he is always there tending his fleet.'

'I thank you,' said Padraig, 'but we were given to understand that he was a goldsmith who owned a house in the old town.'

Seeing that strangers had come into the market, several of the more idle traders gathered around to see if we might require anything they could supply.

'Oh, no,' said the man, 'I fear you were told a lie. He owns no house, but sleeps aboard his ship. Look for the biggest ship in the harbour. That is Yordanus' ship.'

'What are you telling these men, Adonis? The man you are talking about died last winter.'

'Impossible!' cried the brass merchant. 'I saw him only two days ago down at the harbour.'

'You saw a ghost perhaps,' said a second man, a potter with large, bare hairy arms covered in dried clay. 'The ships are for sale. Do you wish to buy a ship?' he asked hopefully.

'Not just now,' Padraig said. 'Later, perhaps.'

'Yordanus Hippolytus did you say?' inquired another man, pushing in. His hands were red from the dye he used to stain the leather from which he made sandals and belts. 'I know this man. But he was never a ship owner. He came from Damascus where he grew figs.'

'A fig grower from Damascus?' said the first man. 'There is no such person in all of Famagusta!'

'There is,' replied the sandal maker with admirable confidence. 'He has a daughter who buys in the market. I sold her a pair of sandals once and she said they were the best she had ever seen – better even than Damascus. Perhaps when you are finished here,' he offered helpfully, 'you would like to buy some sandals. Or a belt, maybe.'

'By the beard of Saint Peter!' sighed the potter. 'These men are looking for their friend. They do not want your sandals.'

'I make very good sandals,' insisted the craftsman. 'And belts as well. You should come and see them.'

'Look here, my friend,' said another, 'there is no goldsmith by the name of Yordanus – or a ship owner, either. I have been selling for twenty-three years in this market and I know everyone. There is no one by that name.'

The market traders fell to arguing with one another over the particularities of the man's identity. Turning to us, Padraig said, 'I am thinking the wool merchant's wife was right. Perhaps we should try to find the house behind the hill.'

Again, what should have been a simple task took on unimagined difficulties. No one we asked could tell us where this house might be. As one of our cheerful guides told us, 'The problem is not so much the house, as the hill. There are a great many hills in Cyprus, and most have houses.'

Roupen lost heart and was for returning to the harbour, hiring a boat, and leaving Famagusta behind forever. But, having come this far, and with the day already speeding from us, I was growing more determined than ever to find this Yordanus Hippolytus. Padraig agreed with me. 'If we do not find him today,' I promised Roupen, 'we will be on our way again tomorrow.' So, we tramped around the hills above the port, trying first one house and then another, and came at last to a fine old Roman villa surrounded by a crumbling wall.

In the road ahead I saw a woman carrying a jar in her arms. She turned aside and entered through a low door in the wall. It was hot and we were tired. Thinking merely to ask her for a drink – or at least for directions to a nearby well, I quickened my step and followed her through the doorway and immediately found myself standing in the shaded courtyard of a once-handsome villa. There were large, leafy plants in great earthenware pots around the perimeter of the yard, and a small, finely-formed fig tree growing in the centre beside a rock-rimmed pool. Instantly, the blazing heat of the day vanished, and I felt as if I had entered a haven of peace and calm.

Padraig and Roupen appeared in the doorway behind me, and stepped cautiously into the yard.

'So!' came a voice from the shadows, 'I was right. You *were* following me.'

I turned to see the woman watching us from behind one of the plants, the jar still in her arms.

'Your pardon, good lady,' I said quickly, hoping to reassure her. 'It was never my intention to alarm you.'

'It would take more than the sight of a ragged traveller to alarm me,' she replied, stepping boldly into the courtyard. Tall and willowy, with long dark hair, her simple blue mantle hung in fresh folds, except where she cradled the jar against the fullness of her breasts and the

189

long curve of her hip. 'What do you want here?' she demanded. She spoke Latin, not Greek, but curiously accented, each word taking on a flattened quality.

'Please, we do not mean to intrude –'

'And yet you do intrude.' Her gaze was direct and unsettling.

'Again, I beg your pardon,' I replied, somewhat abashed. I had hardly spoken a dozen words and already I had apologized twice. I returned her gaze, almost daring her to interrupt again before I finished. 'We are looking for the house of a man called Yordanus.'

'Why?'

'We have business with him.'

'Liar!' she said. 'He does not know you.'

'My lady?'

'Be gone with you at once – before I call the servants to send you away.'

Remembering what the sandal maker had said about Yordanus having a daughter, I glanced at her feet and saw sandals the same shade of red as that which stained the merchant's hands. 'Then this *is* his house,' I concluded.

'Yes. But do not think you will see him. He sees no one.'

'We have come a very great distance,' I told her. 'All the way from Antioch. Commander Renaud de Bracineaux sent us.'

A cloud of suspicion passed over her face. She stared at me for a moment. 'And who is this Commander de Bracineaux?' she asked at last.

'I had been told he was a friend of Yordanus Hippolytus.'

'He is *your* friend?'

It was a simple question, but I hesitated. Glancing at Padraig, who merely gazed placidly ahead, I said, 'We know Commander de Bracineaux and respect him – but we are not close friends, no.'

This admission seemed to appease her. 'You can come in,' she said, quickly adding: 'Just one of you. I will ask if my father will receive you.'

'You go, Duncan,' Padraig said. As he and Roupen sat down in the shade, the woman led me across the yard and around the pool to a wide stone-paved walk leading to the entrance to the great house. She did not pause but pushed open the large wooden door, and stepped quickly in, motioning for me to follow.

We entered the cool darkness of a vestibule dressed in marble and tiles. The only light came from a small round window high above the door; it cast a circle of illumination on the blue-tinted tile of the far wall, against which stood a row of statues – some entire human forms, others head-and-shoulders only, and all of them carved in the most wonderful pale, milk-white stone. Although I know nothing of such things, they did appear to me to be very lifelike, which I took to indicate a distinct skill on the part of their maker. That a house should own one such carving was to me a sign of taste and refinement; that this house should boast statues by the rank meant its owner possessed the wealth of a kingdom.

'Wait in there,' instructed Yordanus' daughter, pointing to the chamber beyond, 'and I will see if my father is well enough to receive guests.'

She hurried away and I wandered into the next room – a vast chamber easily more than three times larger than Murdo's great hall back home, and crammed with an assortment of tables, chairs, rugs, cushions, and other costly chattel; ornate jars, ewers, bowls, and platters were stacked carelessly on the tables and floor, and numerous ceremonial spears and halberds with braided tassels and silk bindings stood against the walls.

What I had first taken for tiles on the floor, on closer inspection turned out to be squares of fine polished wood cunningly arranged to form intricate patterns of alternating colours. The two walls at either end of the hall were painted with figures on horseback riding to the hunt of two tusked beasts, accompanied by a pack of enormous hounds. The men in the painting carried spears and small round shields, their clothing loosely flowing and brightly coloured in the manner still favoured by the potentates of the East. The expansive ceiling was tinted the colour of the midday sky.

As I say, the greater portion of the room was given to an accumulation of objects of various kinds: rugs piled in a heap, and others rolled up and tied in bundles resembling cut timber logs; great jars and bowls of bronze and copper; ceremonial weapons – swords, spears, shields, and the like; and baskets of smaller objects – cups and chalices by the score, of horn and onyx and brass. I counted seven enormous banqueting tables, each large enough to seat twenty guests with comfort, and a dozen or more smaller boards; some of these were of gilded wood, and carved with precision. There were chairs, too, some as big as thrones; I saw one or two which the Jarl of Orkneyjar would have boasted to own.

So enthralled was I with the inspection of my surroundings, I failed to discern that I was being watched.

'Take anything,' said a dry, husky voice in formal, precise Latin. 'Take as much as you can carry, just leave us in peace.'

I turned on my heel to see a gaunt, bald-headed man standing in the doorway behind me. He was tall and slope-shouldered; limp hands hung loosely at his sides. Sharp-featured, with a large, beak-like nose and narrow chin, he put me in mind of a fish-eagle. His dark, sad eyes, and the severe downward bend of his damp mouth, however, gave him the unfortunate appearance of an extremely aggrieved fish-eagle.

At first I imagined his doleful aspect resulted from the misapprehension that he had entered his home to confront a thief in the act of robbery – an error I hastened to correct. 'Pax vobiscum,' I told him. 'Pray have no fear, I am not a thief. Your daughter was good enough to admit me, and I merely await her return.'

He sniffed loudly – as if this explanation, so obviously untrue, was far beneath his lofty regard – and continued to watch me with his sad eyes. He was a taller man than he appeared; he carried himself low and hunched over as if bent inward by weight on his neck.

'In truth,' I said, trying to make him understand, 'I have been instructed to wait here.' He made no reply, but continued staring at me. 'You are Yordanus?' I ventured.

'I was,' he answered gravely. He straightened and lifted his head. 'Yordanus Hippolytus is no more.' The flesh of his neck was loose and hung in shapeless wattles, much, I noticed, like the wrinkled skin of his upper arms. 'Who might you be?'

I gave him my name, and told him that my friends and I had come to Cyprus from Antioch, and that we had been told by the commander of the Templars to seek him out and ask his aid. I hoped this would help him feel easier about my presence. I was mistaken.

'I care nothing for your troubles,' he said, turning away abruptly. 'Take whatever you want and go. Leave me in peace.'

He shuffled slowly away, leaving me to gape after him.

TWENTY-TWO

Dearest Caitríona, something has happened which has me shuddering with a ferment of excitement I have not felt in a very long time. An event of uncertain significance, I realize, yet I cannot bring myself to see it as anything other than a sign of great importance. It would not be the first time a lonely prisoner saw in some minute and arbitrary alteration of his bleak life the false gleam of expectation, I know. Still, my mind races and my hands sweat with anticipation.

Early this morning – the sun had not risen, and the palace was dark – the guards came for me. I was roughly roused from sleep so I had no time to prepare my departure; they would not even allow me to seal my missive to you, dear heart. Fortunately, Wazim, wakened by the noise, came padding down the corridor, and I was able to tell him what to do. Thus, I went to face my fate secure in the knowledge that whatever befell me, my labour of love would find its way to you one day.

Accordingly, I was hauled before Caliph al-Hafiz to receive my judgement. All was exactly as before. Indeed, if I had not been aware of the passage of the last few days, I might have imagined that I had left the room, turned around in the corridor and returned to find everything as I had seen it only moments before. The caliph, splendid in his snow-white turban with the peacock feathers, still sat on his golden throne beneath his palm tree, squinting with undisguised animosity as I was brought in.

I was shoved to my knees before him, and made to kiss the polished stone floor, whereupon I was jerked to my feet once more. The caliph twitched his finger, and the guards released me to stand upright in his presence. He sat for a time, gazing at me in a very hostile way and stroking his long, grey moustache, and I gazed back with as much serenity as I could summon.

'So!' he said after a time. 'They tell me you are very busy these days writing in your book.'

'That is true, Most Excellent Khalifa. I try to occupy my time.'

'What is it that you write?'

'I am making an account of my –'

'Captivity,' he said, supplying the word himself.

'Travels, my lord,' I corrected. 'I am making an account of my travels in Outremer.'

He grunted, and pulled on his moustache as he considered this reply. I realized then that the man before me was discontented and oppressed by worry. The eyes that gazed at me were fatigued, and the day was new. 'Who will read this account of your travels?'

'I am making it for my daughter. Although she is still very young, I hope that one day she will want to know what became of her father and she will read it for herself.'

'Tcha!' he cried, as if he had caught me in a lie. 'How do you imagine she will receive this book of yours? Who will take it to her?'

'I cannot say how it will reach her,' I replied readily. 'That is for his Honourable Potentate the Khalifa to decide.'

The answer caught him off guard. 'For *me* to decide?'

'Even so, my lord. It was promised in your name that my last request would be granted. My last request is to have my writings reach my daughter.'

The caliph turned his head and demanded of one of his many advisors, 'Is this so?'

The man, a dark-bearded fellow with a basket of rolled-up parchments beside him, consulted the document before him and nodded. 'It is so, Excellent and Exalted Khalifa. The promise was given in recognition of the prisoner's nobility, according to the custom of Baghdad.'

The caliph's small eyes almost disappeared as his squint deepened. He drew a deep breath through his nostrils and blew it out, then said, 'So shall it be done.'

I bowed courteously. 'I thank you, My Lord Khalifa.'

'You love your daughter, I suppose,' he said stiffly.

'Of course, my lord. She is the jewel of my heart and I cherish her beyond all measure.'

'A parent should love his children,' al-Hafiz declared, as if instructing a stubborn pupil. 'So it is written in the Holy Qur'an.'

'And in the Bible,' I pointed out.

'You are not afraid to die,' he observed.

'No, my lord.'

'Are you so pure of heart and soul that you do not tremble to stand before the Throne of Divine Judgement?'

'How should I tremble, my lord, when even now my righteous advocate intercedes before the throne on my behalf?'

This appeared to interest the caliph. 'This advocate – who is he?'

'He is Jesu, called the Messiah.'

'I know of this Messiah,' said al-Hafiz, with an impatient twitch of dismissal. 'Among the faithful, he is considered a very great prophet.' He frowned, as if daring me to answer, and asked, 'Why should this prophet intercede for you?'

'He intercedes for anyone who trusts in him,' I answered.

Caliph al-Hafiz raised his chin, indicating he was finished with me. 'Then we will see if this advocate has the ear of Allah,' he said. 'At the sixth hour your head will fall to the axe and you will stand before the Throne of Judgement. May your advocate's eloquence open the gates of paradise for you.'

Even though I knew it was coming, hearing the words made me weak in the knees. Somehow, I summoned the strength to bow in humble acceptance of his decision.

'Does this not concern you?' he demanded, apparently rankled by my tranquil demeanour.

'My Lord Khalifa,' I replied, trying to keep my voice steady, 'I love my life as much as any man, but it is in your hands. I am your servant. Judge me how you will.'

'You hope I will pity your insignificant faith and pardon you,' he said, his voice taking on a defiant tone, as if daring me to beg him to spare my life.

I already knew what I would say. 'With all respect, my lord, my hope is in Almighty God, the Merciful Redeemer, who alone holds the power of life and death – in this world *and* the next.'

He stared at me, and I thought I saw doubt creeping into the deeply-creased lines of his face. Suddenly – as if the thought had just occurred to him – he said, 'What do you know of affairs in Cairo?'

The question so surprised me, I could not think how to answer. 'Why, I know nothing of affairs in Cairo,' I replied, when he had repeated it once more. 'I have been a prisoner of the palace since coming here. I see no one, and no one sees me.'

'Just so!' he declared triumphantly, and I understood the question had been a test, but what it was meant to reveal, I could not grasp. Gesturing to the guards, he ordered them to take me back to my cell.

I was swept from his presence and returned to my cell where I spent my last moments praying and preparing myself for the grim ordeal ahead. I do not know how much time passed – it seemed I spent an eternity on my knees – and I heard footsteps outside my door once more. I heard the key in the lock and rose to meet the guards who would conduct me to the place of execution.

It was Wazim who entered, however; and he was alone.

'Da'ounk,' he said, his face beaming like a swarthy sun, 'good tidings! The execution is delayed.'

'Delayed?' Relief flooded through me. 'Why?'

'I was not told the reason,' he answered. 'But I know there is some trouble in the city and the khalifa has sent all the guards to deal with it. He has said that no prisoners are to be executed until peace is regained. Is that not wonderful indeed?'

I agreed that it was wonderful, and asked, 'What is the trouble? Why should the executions be delayed?'

'I do not know what has happened,' Wazim said. 'But if you wish, I will make it my duty to find out. Do you wish it?'

Instantly, I recalled the caliph asking me what I knew of events in Cairo. Inasmuch as I owed my physical well-being to affairs in the city, it made sense to learn more about them if I could. 'Yes,' I told him, 'find out all you can, please.'

'With pleasure, Da'ounk.'

Grinning, Wazim left my cell; I heard him scurrying away, and, after a heartfelt prayer of thanksgiving for my stay of execution, I returned to my table.

After a long time pondering the implications of the unforeseen development in my situation, I picked up my quill once more, and returned to the work at hand.

Leaving the house of Yordanus Hippolytus, I rejoined Roupen and Padraig in the yard. They were sitting beside the little pool, talking quietly. Taking one look at the expression on my face, Padraig said, 'He refused to see you.'

'No, I saw him. He refused to help us.' I quickly explained that I had told him of Commander Renaud's recommendation. 'He said he did not care about our troubles.'

'Then I say we shake the dust off our feet,' Roupen said. 'We have wasted enough time with this already.' He rose abruptly. 'We never should have come here in the first place. We would be half-way to Anazarbus by now if we had not listened to that Templar.'

I was forced to agree with him, and we decided our best course was to return to the harbour and see if we could find a boat to hire; although, considering the little we had left from Bezu's largesse, I reckoned our chances very slender. Nevertheless, we started from the yard and, as I passed through the low gateway, I heard someone calling me and looked back to see Yordanus' daughter hurrying towards us.

I told the others to wait a moment, and turned back.

'Where are you going?' she asked. 'I thought you wanted to see my father.'

'I have seen him,' I replied. 'He did not wish to help us. He said he did not care about our troubles.'

'He says that to everyone,' she sighed. 'I should have warned you.' Her brusque manner had softened somewhat, and I wondered why. 'He can be difficult to understand sometimes.'

'I understood him perfectly well. I am sorry to have troubled you.' I thanked her for her help, and took my leave. 'You will excuse me, my friends are waiting.'

'Don't go.'

The desperation in her voice brought me up short. 'My lady?'

'Please, dine with us tonight. I will speak to my father. He will receive you in a far better mood, I promise you.'

Now it was my turn to frown. 'We have spent all day trying to find this place, only to be told to go away – first by you, and then by your father. Now that we are about to do just that, you say you want us to stay.'

She smiled suddenly – a delicious, winsome flash of fine white teeth against the tawny hue of her skin. For the first time I realized she was of an Eastern race, for her colouring was dark – her hair and eyes were black, and radiantly so, and her flesh glowed with a lustrous sheen the colour of honey mingled with cream.

'Our business is urgent,' I told her. 'We dare not waste time indulging the whims of an old man.'

'Please,' she said, laying a hand on my arm. 'You need to eat somewhere, and it is a long time since we have welcomed guests beneath our roof. Dine with us tonight and let us see what comes of it.'

She was right, the day was rapidly dwindling away, and we would have to find somewhere to stay for the night. We had come this far, I thought, we might as well see it through to the end. 'Very well,' I said. 'I will speak to my friends.'

'Good,' she said, brightening instantly. 'Fetch them back, and I will show you where you can rest and refresh yourselves.'

I hurried out through the gate, and told Padraig and Roupen there had been a change of plan. Upon rejoining Yordanus' daughter in the courtyard, she said, 'As we are to dine together, I must go to the marketplace. It is cool here in the courtyard and there is water in the pool to refresh yourselves. I will return soon.'

I thanked her for her thoughtfulness, but as she made to take her leave, Roupen suddenly demanded, 'Do you mean you would eat with them?'

Before I could reply, he added, 'I will not eat with *Jews*!' With that, he pointed to a bronze disc over the door of the house; it showed the outline of two simple triangles, one inverted and imposed upon the other to form the Star of David, a symbol much employed by the Jews.

'I will not put my feet beneath the same board as a Jew,' Roupen growled angrily. 'Do what you like, I will not break bread with them. I would rather starve first.'

'Then you may do so,' I told him bluntly, aghast at his crude incivility. I had never seen him so irritated and angry.

'They are *Jews*!' he protested unashamedly. 'They cannot be trusted. We do not need them anyway. I am leaving.' With that, he spun on his heel and hastened off down the road. Padraig flew after him, attempting to calm him and bring him back to beg forgiveness.

Mortified by the young lord's discourtesy, I quickly turned to apologize. 'I am sorry, my lady. He is distraught and upset by the urgency of our predicament, but that is no excuse for his uncouth behaviour.'

'And what about you?' she asked sharply. 'Do you also hold Jews in such low regard?'

'I confess I have never known any Jews,' I answered; desperate to make amends, I added: 'Still, if they are even half so kind and generous as you have been, then they are indeed a noble race – and I will fight anyone who says otherwise.'

She gave the remark a dismissive huff and stared at me, her dark eyes searching mine as she pursed her lips in thought. After a moment, she said, 'Do you still wish to eat with us?'

'I would consider it an honour, my lady.'

'Then you may return this evening.'

'With pleasure,' I replied, trying to redeem a bad business. 'In the meantime, I will calm my young friend and teach him better manners.'

'Do so,' the lady replied crisply. 'You may also find it worthwhile to meditate on this: my father and I are *not* Jews.'

'No?'

'We are Copts,' she said, and disappeared into the courtyard, slamming the door behind her.

TWENTY-THREE

We spent what little remained of the day in the market square of the upper town. Under Padraig's ministrations, and mollified by the fact that our host was not a Jew after all, the haughty young lord allowed himself to be persuaded to partake of a meal without further insult.

As a pale yellow moon rose above the surrounding hills, we found ourselves once more standing before the low door in the high wall at the end of the long uphill climb. There was an iron ring hanging from a chain beside the door. Padraig gave the ring a strong pull, and a bell chimed distantly from somewhere inside. We waited for a time, and nothing happened, so he pulled it again, and then once more for good measure. The monk was about to pull the bell yet again when the door flew open and a small brown man poked out his head. He spat a stream of invective which none of us could understand, and then slammed the door again.

'There! You see?' grumbled Roupen, only too ready to abandon what appeared to be an increasingly hopeless enterprise.

'Pull the bell chain,' I directed, refusing to give in.

Again the door flew open, and again the man glared and jabbered fiercely at us. This time, however, I reached in, took hold of his tunic and yanked him out into the street. He sputtered and cursed, and began kicking at us with his bony bare feet.

'Peace!' I said, holding him back. 'We mean you no harm. Stop your fighting. We only want to talk to you.'

He loosed a blistering torrent of angry words at us, all the while kicking, and swinging his fists. I held him at arm's length – as much to keep him from hurting himself as any of us, and was considering what to do next when there appeared in the open doorway a very

200

fat man in a loose-fitting robe. He looked at us with a large, languid unimpressed eye, and said, 'Yes?'

I greeted him politely – still holding off the angry little man – and said, 'Yordanus is pleased to receive us for dinner this evening.'

'So you say,' replied the man, wholly unmoved by my declaration. Reaching out, he tapped the squirming, spitting man squarely on top of the head. Instantly, he stopped fighting; I released him and he scurried away.

'Have you something for me?' asked the fat man when the little porter had gone.

Uncertain how to reply, I glanced at Padraig, who merely shrugged unhelpfully. 'No,' I answered at last. 'Should I have something for you?'

'That is for you to say.'

'I was given nothing for you,' I told him.

'Pity,' he replied. He rolled his eyes lazily from one to the other of us, then sighed and fell silent.

'Is Yordanus at home?' I wondered after an awkward moment.

The fat man yawned, then turned and beckoned us to follow. The three of us stepped through the doorway and crossed the deep-shadowed courtyard. We were led to the door of the villa. 'Wait here,' the man instructed; he pushed open the door and vanished into the darkness within.

In a little while, the small wiry fellow returned. He saw us waiting before the door and instantly flew at us, shouting and waving his hands. He seemed determined to drive us from the house, and might have succeeded, save for the abrupt appearance of Yordanus' daughter. She wore a long white robe and carried a lash of braided leather with which she proceeded to whip the little man.

'Go to, Omer!' she cried, swinging the lash. 'Go to!'

I was about to interpose myself in this attack, when I noticed that most, if not all, the whip strokes struck the earth. The desired effect was achieved, however, and the little mad fellow ran off gibbering.

'You must forgive Omer,' the lady said, recoiling the lash. 'He is not often well.' Stepping to the door, she said, 'Come this way, please.'

The house was in darkness, and we crept like thieves through one passage after another until coming to a room in one of the long wings of the extensive villa. The chamber was ablaze with candlelight and the windows were open to allow the soft evening breezes to waft in – setting candles fluttering on the large candletrees around the room. There were no chairs, but after the fashion of the East, we reclined on large cushions either side of the low table which had been spread with fine, ornately-woven Damascus cloth.

While in the marketplace, Padraig and I had taken the opportunity to have our clothes brushed so as to present a slightly less disagreeable presence at the board. Upon entering the dining chamber, the lady offered a wash basin filled with scented water. Roupen, however, did himself a great dishonour by not only refusing the wash basin, but scowling at everyone and everything as if enduring humiliations to his dignity so intense as to be physically painful.

The lady departed, leaving us to our ablutions. We were alone only a moment when she reappeared. If not for the fact that I had just seen her, I would not have known her as the same person. Having removed the white robe, she now wore a gown of the lightest, most delicate fabric I have ever seen. What is more, the thin stuff shimmered in the candlelight, glistening with a lustre like that of moonbeams on water. It was blue as the midnight sky, and cut low over her bosom, to reveal the graceful swell of her breasts. A wide cloth belt of gold gathered the gown at her slender waist, emphasizing the curve of her hips. Her dark hair hung in loose curls over her bare shoulders.

Unexpectedly, the sight of her slender, shapely arms sent a pang of longing through me of an intensity I had not experienced since my own dear Rhona held me to her heart. It was all I could do not to stare openly at her as she invited us to sit and make ourselves comfortable, saying, 'My father has been informed of your arrival. He will join us when he is ready.'

'Your graciousness, my lady, is exceeded only by your loveliness,' I said, wishing I had something better to offer her than common flattery.

Still, she smiled at the compliment, and it came into my mind that despite her assured and forward manner, she was not as confident as she appeared. Truly, she lived in a madhouse and was likely unaccustomed to common courtesy. 'My name is Sydoni,' she told me.

'I am Duncan of Caithness,' I replied, offering her my hand in greeting. She placed her hand in mine without hesitation and, lifting it, I lightly brushed it with my lips. I then introduced her to Padraig and Roupen; I was explaining who they were and how we came to be together, when Yordanus entered the room.

Grim and tight-lipped, he acknowledged us with chilly, if not hostile, indifference and the meal commenced. Our unhappy host reclined at the head of the table with the peevish and sour disposition of a man being bent into an unbecoming shape. Full of sighs and prickly noises, he fumed and fretted, giving every sign that he wished to be anywhere else in all the world but where he found himself just now. Shameful behaviour in a host, to be sure, and it might have spoiled the evening save for the fact that I only had eyes for Sydoni, and she ignored her father's unpleasantness to the point of invisibility. Clearly, the evening was hers, and she was not about to allow anyone to ruin it.

Once we were all seated, Sydoni presented us with small bowls of peeled pears cooked in a sweet sauce, cooled, and seasoned with a spice I had never tasted before. Tangy, pungent, it gave a warm tingle to the mouth and tongue; when I asked what it was, Sydoni smiled and said, 'It is called cinnamon.'

Roupen grunted at this, as if to say it was a commonplace too drearily familiar to mention. I thought it wonderful, however, and praised it loudly. I praised the next dish also: fish roe and curds of soft new cheese with cream and flavoured with garlic and lemon, all mixed together to form a thick paste into which we dipped strips of flat bread. There was sweet wine, too, and several kinds of bread, and grapes.

When we had eaten our fill of these things, Sydoni brought out the next dish: roast quail stuffed with bread crumbs, pine nuts, and herbs. Glazed with honey, the succulent birds were done to such perfection, even Roupen begrudgingly commended the art of the cook. Before I knew it, I had eaten two of them and was reaching for a third when I saw Sydoni watching me. She smiled the proud, contented smile of a woman well satisfied with herself. It was a look I knew well; Rhona had often worn the same expression when serving me something she knew I enjoyed.

The food and wine worked their age-old magic, and gradually both Roupen and Yordanus began to grow more amiable. As the meal went on, the surly young lord became quite pleasant, and the sour old man grew sweet-tempered and convivial.

'Fill the cups!' he cried at one point, thrusting his beaker into the air. 'I want to drink the health of my new friends.' Happy to oblige, I took up the jar and poured the good red wine. Yordanus then raised his cup high and said, 'I drink to friendship, health, and peace – God's blessing on all his children.' We acclaimed this sentiment with cheers, whereupon our host said, 'May the Lord of the Feast eternally bless us with good food, good wine, and dear friends around the board – for ever and always! Amen!'

Roupen affirmed the benediction, but could not let the comment pass. 'Lord of the Feast?' he said when everyone had drunk. 'That is a title which belongs to Christ, I should have thought.'

Yordanus turned his head and regarded the young man quizzically. 'Yes?'

'Strange words from the mouth of a Copt,' Roupen observed with wine-induced carelessness.

The old man stiffened; the smile hardened on his face and his eyes narrowed.

Roupen, seeing he had offended his host, looked to me for help. But I remained silent and left him to face the consequence of his intolerance. 'I meant nothing more than that,' he offered weakly. 'Why does everyone look at me so?'

'You think Copts unworthy of salvation?' asked Yordanus, quietly bristling.

Roupen red-faced now, raised a hand in defence of his blunder. 'I meant no disresp –'

'You think because I am a Copt, I am less a Christian than you?' Yordanus challenged, growing rigid with indignation.

I made to intercede for the young man, but Padraig prevented me. 'Let him squirm,' the priest whispered. 'It will teach him a lesson.'

Yordanus stared with dull anger at the impudent young lord. 'Once,' he said, his voice growing cold, 'I would not have suffered an insult beneath the roof of my own house. But,' he lifted his bony shoulders in a shrug of heavy resignation, 'I am not the man I used to be.' He extended a long finger towards Roupen. 'It is lucky for you that I am not.'

'Father, *please* –' said Sydoni, reaching across to tug his sleeve.

The old man raised his hands. 'That is all I will say.' Rising to his feet, he threw down his empty cup. 'You must excuse me. I am tired. I am going to bed.'

Roupen, stricken and guilty, stammered, 'Please, sir, I am the one who should leave. And I will do so.' He jumped up from his place. 'Before I go, I will beg your pardon and ask your forgiveness for the offence I have caused. Please accept my deepest apologies.'

He spoke with such contrition that Yordanus, urged by the silent entreaty of his daughter, grudgingly relented. 'Oh, very well,' the old man said. 'Sit down, young man. Sit down. There is no harm done.' He sighed, and forced a sad smile. Flapping a hand at the young lord, he said, 'Come, sit down. We will put this unfortunate misunderstanding behind us.'

Reluctantly, Roupen lowered himself to his place once more. Yordanus gazed at him for a moment. 'For more than thirty generations,' the old man said, thrusting his finger skyward, 'the House of Hippolytus has been a Christian house – before Byzantium, before Rome, before the Gospel of Christ was proclaimed in the streets of Athens, *we* were Christians.'

'An ancestry to glory in,' Padraig remarked. 'If every family could claim such long obedience, this world would not labour under so great a weight of faithlessness and falsehood.'

'Indeed, sir,' said Yordanus proudly. 'When the followers of The Way were thrown out of the High Temple at Jerusalem where they were meeting in those days, my ancestors were there. On the day that the Blessed Stephen was put to death, my ancestors carried his poor, battered corpse to the tomb. When the persecution began, the infant church scattered – north, south, east, west – wherever they hoped to escape the terrible oppression of the mob, and the tyranny of the temple leaders.'

Yordanus raised his cup, and Sydoni emptied the last of the jar into it. He drained the cup and said, 'But all that was a very long time ago. No one wants to hear it now.'

Roupen, duly chastised and anxious to make whatever amends he might, quickly said, 'If you please, sir, I would hear it.'

Certainly, that was the right thing to say, for the old man's eyes rekindled with a spark of his former gladness.

'Well, perhaps I will just say this one thing more – so to improve your understanding,' Yordanus conceded, swiftly overcoming his reluctance. Taking up a small bronze bell from the table, he rang it vigorously several times, and then said, 'Jerusalem became too dangerous, so my people fled south. Since the time of the great patriarch, Abraham, whenever trouble threatened in Palestine, the Jews took refuge in Egypt. This my people did, and in Egypt they stayed. In time, we became Egyptians, and those of us who remained staunch in the faith became known as Copts. My ancestors prospered greatly; they became traders – some with fleets, and some with camels, some with important stalls in the principle markets of the great cities.

'This is the life that was handed down to me. I became a trader, after my own fashion, and my son likewise.' At these words, a shadow passed over the old man's face; his voice faltered. 'My son . . .' he paused, cleared his throat, and finished, saying, 'Once the extent of my interests stretched from the banks of the Nile to the tops of the Tarsus mountains. Now all that is gone . . . gone and finished and dead – like my son. The last hope of my illustrious line.'

Yordanus raised his eyes and smiled sadly. 'I am sorry,' he said, sinking once more into himself, 'my grief is a burden I did not intend forcing upon you. Forgive an old man.'

He paused, during which time the fat man who had met us at the door appeared. 'Gregior,' Yordanus ordered, 'bring us more wine.' The sullen servant turned without a word and lumbered off. 'And try not to drink it all before it reaches the table,' his master called after him.

'I do not believe in keeping slaves,' explained Yordanus. 'But I make an exception for Gregior and Omer. They are hopeless, you must agree. If I turned them out they would soon starve, and I cannot, in good Christian conscience, allow that to happen. So, I keep them for their own good, as no one else would have them.' He smiled weakly and spread his hands. 'I apologize for your sorry reception. Mind you, it would have been no different for anyone else. Be you caliph or king, beggar, leper, or thief, Omer would treat you exactly the same.'

'What language does he speak?' asked Padraig. 'I could not make out a word of it.'

'So far as I know, it is no language at all,' answered our host, chuckling to himself. 'Omer imagines he is speaking Latin, but so long as I have known him, I have never had so much as a single intelligible word out of him in any tongue whatsoever.' He shook his head wearily. 'Hopeless.'

The wine arrived in a great silver jar, and Sydoni poured it into the cups which Yordanus offered to us once more, saying, 'I drink to my friends, old and new! May the High Holy One keep you all in the hollow of his hand. Amen!'

We drank and our host, placing his cup firmly on the table, said, 'Now then, to business. Tell me, why did our Templar friend de Bracineaux send you to old Yordanus?'

TWENTY-FOUR

Yordanus listened with half-closed eyes while I made a brief account of the events which had led us to his door. He nodded and glanced at Padraig as I described how the priest and I had come to be on pilgrimage, and how we had met the Templars and young Lord Roupen in Rouen, and all that had flowed from that meeting – all, that is, save for Bohemond's plan to reclaim the Armenian stronghold at Anazarbus. I thought it best to keep that to myself.

When I finished at last, Yordanus frowned mildly and said, 'A fascinating tale, to be sure. Yet, you have omitted one or two significant details, I think. No doubt you have your reasons, but if I am to help you . . .' He turned his palm up as if offering me a choice.

I hesitated, trying to decide whether to risk telling him more. He saw my reluctance and pressed me further. 'For example,' he continued, 'you have not said why you were forced to flee from Antioch so quickly.' Lifting a hand to Roupen, he added, 'Would I be wrong in thinking your troubles, whatever they may be, began and ended with your young friend here?'

'Not far wrong,' I replied cautiously. Roupen lowered his eyes, but said nothing.

'Come now, my friends, if I am to help you I must know everything about this affair. What have you done? Impugned the prince's virtue? Sullied the patriarch's good name? Stolen the Rood of Antioch?'

At mention of the Holy Cross, my heart clutched in my chest. 'Forgive me, my lord,' I said quickly, 'but I did not care to burden you with our troubles unnecessarily.'

He waved the feeble excuse aside. 'Tell me.'

So, I told him of Prince Bohemond's intention to attack the Armenian stronghold, and how Padraig and I had – out of friendship for Roupen and at the strangely veiled behest of the Templar commander – determined to thwart the impetuous prince's ambition if we could.

'We went to him to ask him to repent of his plan,' I concluded. 'Unfortunately, things got out of hand and de Bracineaux was taken prisoner in the citadel. Padraig, Roupen, and I were forced to flee before Bohemond could capture us as well. The good commander suggested we come to you.'

Yordanus plucked a red plum from a basket and bit off the end. He sucked the juice for a moment, and then observed, 'It seems to me that your path has been prepared from the beginning.'

'Indeed?' I wondered. Padraig nodded, smiling as he regarded the old man with, as I thought, renewed respect and appreciation.

Pushing himself back from the table, the old man beamed expansively. 'Rejoice, my friends!' he declared. 'Yordanus Hippolytus is the one man in the whole world with both power and inclination to speed you to your purpose.' Glancing at the young lord who had yet to exchange his wary, haunted expression for a more mirthful countenance, the ageing trader leaned over and gave him a fatherly pat on the arm. 'Be of good cheer! Your adversaries, though they be legion, have now to deal with me, eh?'

'I did not know we had so many enemies,' Roupen replied, struggling to rise to the occasion.

'For a fact, you do,' Yordanus told him. 'There are many in this part of the world who would love nothing more than to see the Armenian House obliterated by the swiftest means possible. Unsavoury, perhaps, but it is the truth.'

Turning to Padraig and me, he asked, 'Now then, who else knows about your errand?'

'De Bracineaux, of course,' I replied.

'And Bohemond probably, too, by now,' added Padraig.

'No one else?'

'Apart from you and your daughter,' I glanced at Sydoni, who was leaning on her palm and gazing at me, 'no one.'

'Have you spoken to anyone along the way?'

'Not a soul,' I said. Padraig shook his head. Roupen looked glumly ahead.

'Well and good.' Yordanus rose stiffly from his cushion, his mind made up. 'We must work quickly. The necessary arrangements must be made. We begin tonight.'

It was late and I was exhausted; traipsing through the hills all day had taken their toll. 'Tonight?'

'Forgive me. You are tired from your travails. Leave everything to me. Take your rest, and in the morning, God willing, we will be ready to depart.'

He rang the bell and summoned Gregior to lead us to the guest rooms. We bade good-night to our hosts and went to bed in far better spirits than we had enjoyed for many days. Padraig stayed up a little longer saying his prayers, but I lay down and slipped at once into a deep and dreamless sleep – only to be roused some time later by the whispered hush of urgent voices in the courtyard. I listened for a while, but was too sleepy to make anything of it, and soon drifted off again.

The next thing I knew, someone's hands were on me, shaking me awake. I sat up with a start.

'Peace,' said Sydoni, crouching beside me. 'All is well, but it is time to leave.' She rose. 'Gregior has brought you a basin of water. I will leave you to wash and dress. Join us in the great hall as soon as you are ready.'

She left and, as I scraped my scattered thoughts together, I heard her in the next room, waking the young lord with an explanation of our purpose. I stumbled to the steaming basin and washed, praising the Gifting Giver for the luxury of soap. I then dried myself quickly on the linen cloth provided, dressed, and lumbered out the door and down the long, cloistered corridor of the villa to the great hall. The sky was dark, and daybreak still somewhat distant, by my estimation.

Yawning, I joined Yordanus, Sydoni and the others already gathered inside the door of the great hall. Gregior was ambling here and there, lethargically lighting candles and throwing dark glances at his master, who scurried around the enormous room, beckoning us to follow. We caught up with him, pawing through a pile of old maps stacked high on one of the many tables in the room. 'Here! See here – this,' he pointed to a black spot in the centre of the map, 'this is Antioch. The port of Saint Symeon is here, and—' he moved his finger a fair way up a wavy line representing the coast and brought it to rest on a brown spot just below a tiered stretch of jagged sawtooth mountains, '– Anazarbus there.'

Frowning, Roupen bent down and examined the crude representation of his home.

'See here,' Yordanus continued, tracing the route to Antioch with his finger. 'Bohemond must go overland because he has no ships to carry so many men and horses and supplies.'

'Two roundships were still in the harbour at Saint Symeon when we left,' Padraig pointed out.

'It makes no difference,' asserted Yordanus with conviction. He had assumed the aspect of a man very much younger than he had shown himself to be. He became decisive and earnest, and I realized I was seeing a glimpse of the man he had once been. 'Two, you say? Two ships would not even carry enough fodder for the horses. He would need twenty, at least.

'So,' he continued, resuming his reckoning, 'Bohemond's army must go on foot. But it is far faster by way of Marionis on the coast, here.' He placed a long finger on a small spot on the coast north of Antioch. 'From there, Mamistra is easily reached on the river. See it there?' He indicated another black wavy line which was the river to another brown smudge north and a little west of the port. 'From Mamistra, it is horseback the rest of the way. With good luck and God's speed, Anazarbus is but ten days' ride from the river. Even if Prince Bohemond marshalled his troops and marched the same day you fled Antioch, you will reach the city at least four or five days ahead of the prince and his army.'

He glanced up to make certain that we all understood. 'You are frowning again, my friends. Now what is the matter?'

'We have some money with us,' I explained, 'but not enough to buy horses.'

'But I have money enough for anything,' said Yordanus, rubbing his hands enthusiastically, 'and I am going with you. Gregior, run and fetch my box.' The old trader's sudden industry was amazing; it was as if he had shed not only the dull languor and melancholy which had gripped him so tightly, but entire decades of years as well.

The sluggish servant returned with a small chest made of a dark, heavy wood. Yordanus opened the box and withdrew three leather bags, then bethought himself and took three more. 'Here,' he said, thrusting three of the bags at me, 'a man on a journey can never have enough money.'

Thanking my host for his thoughtfulness and generosity, I tied one of the purses to my belt, and gave the other two to Padraig to carry in his monk's satchel. 'With your help, we shall travel like kings,' I told him.

'Ragged kings, at best,' Yordanus said, indicating our clothes. 'Fortunately, I have something for you.' He crossed to a large chest and threw open the lid. Delving into the chest, he began tossing lengths of cloth and various garments onto the floor around him. 'Ah, here! Here!' he said at last, and brought out a long flowing garment like an overlong tunic.

Made of fine, light-weight cloth, it was the colour of the northern sea as night sweeps in from the east. There were trousers of the same cloth and colour, and new boots of soft leather, the sides of which were stitched with coloured thread in a plumed emblem. The tunic's sleeves were long and wide, but close around the wrists. The trousers were secured around the waist with a long cloth belt of woven purple strips to which hundreds of tiny bronze discs had been attached.

In all, it was the raiment of an eastern prince, and although I was impressed, I could not imagine myself wearing such a garment. 'People will think I am pretending to be an Arab,' I said. 'I will feel foolish. It would be better to stay as I am.'

'Nonsense,' said Yordanus, ignoring my objections, 'your clothes are unsuitable for the rigours of the journey ahead. Not only that, they mark you out as a stranger and an outsider. If you wish to travel swiftly without arousing unwanted interest in your affairs, you must not fly the banner of the ignorant foreigner.'

Sydoni agreed with him, and after my initial scepticism, I allowed myself to be convinced. Despite his protests that he was a monk dyed in the wool of his monastery, Padraig, too, came in for the same treatment. In the end, we changed our clothes and marvelled at the difference; I felt cooler and more comfortable instantly, and bade farewell to my tattered homespun in favour of the lighter Eastern stuff.

Only when both Padraig and I were suitably attired did Sydoni allow us to leave the house. 'I will see you as far as the harbour,' she told us.

Leaving the villa, we crossed the darkened courtyard and waited while Gregior unlocked the door, then slipped out onto the deserted road. We hurried down the hill through the new town, and continued on to old Famagusta and the quiet harbour as crimson sunrise broke in the east.

'I will speak to the harbour master directly,' Yordanus told us as we came onto the quay. 'He will know which sailors are available for hire and, of those, who can be trusted.'

'As it happens,' volunteered Padraig, 'we know our way around a ship. Count us among the sailors.'

'Splendid,' said the trader. 'The fewer who know our business, the better.'

Among the vessels riding peacefully at anchor on the tranquil crescent of blue water, there were the usual fishing boats plus a few more substantial craft used by the island traders. There were also four large ships, which I took to be of Venetian or Genoan origin. I was wrong.

Upon arriving at the wharf, Yordanus pointed to the four large ships and said, 'My beauties. Which one do you like the best?'

'The smallest,' I replied, thinking how much work it would be raising sail.

'The fastest,' suggested Padraig. The canny priest was, as usual, closer to the mark.

'That would be *Persephone*,' the old man said, indicating the long, low vessel at the end of the line. Although painted in the Greek style – with a green hull, a slender red mast, and a rail and keel of bright yellow – the ship owed more to the ancient Roman design which had held sway in that part of the world for a thousand years or more. 'Not the smallest, but she fairly flies before the lightest breeze. With God's help and a good wind, we will be in Anazarbus before Bohemond makes the Syrian Gates.'

TWENTY-FIVE

Cait, you will not believe what has taken place. I can scarce believe it myself, and hardly know where to begin to explain. Nor can I say with any certainty whether it is good news for me, or bad. Good, I think. For, if nothing else, it has delayed my execution for another day at least, maybe more. Lord of Hosts in heaven, let it be more!

After dismissing Wazim to learn what he could of matters in the city, I returned to my writing and thought no more about what the caliph had said about the affairs of Cairo. You have been reading the result of my diligence.

This account grows more ungainly by the day, I confess, and my poor hand cramps and burns, and the effort tires me – Cait, sometimes I feel as if I have been wrestling giants from dawn to dusk, though I have not stirred from the chair! Nevertheless I worked through the day and into the night – a common enough practice for me, to be sure; the only difference was that this time no meals were brought to me. I assumed this was because I was soon to die, and the grim assumption spurred me on. Tired as I was, I worked all the more diligently for the knowledge that each page before me might be my last.

It was very late when I again heard rapid footsteps in the corridor. I lay aside my pen, and turned as Wazim burst into the room, excitement making his eyes bulge out. He had gone out to discover what it was that had caused the caliph to suspend the ordered executions; and he had returned with the tale which has caused such alarm throughout the city, and which I shall swiftly relate. First, however, I must explain a detail which is necessary for your understanding.

You will have gathered that the caliph is supreme among Muhammedan rulers. Yet, he is not singular in his authority. Not by any means. He shares the administration of his government with other authorities, chief among them the *wazir* – or vizier, as some say. This he does so that he may undertake more fully his primary duty as the spiritual leader of his people, thus leaving the ordinary charge of temporal matters to the vizier.

As it happens, the Caliph of Cairo, however fortunate in other respects, is cursed with a wayward and unruly son, Hasan. The caliph, upon taking the throne, had struck upon the idea of at once making peace with the stormy youth and bringing him under his control by raising the young man to the rank of vizier. Wazim tells me that, while many counselled against this, the plan nevertheless worked very well at first.

After a time, however, Hasan began to find his office too constricting. He drifted back into his former bad habits. Soon he was once more the bane of his father's life, only this time he was placed where he could work great harm to any and all who opposed him. Although none of this reached my ears, it was well known all along the Nile from Alexandria to Luxor, for the wicked young man ran from one tantrum to the next, plunging the government of Cairo into scandals and skirmishes of every kind.

Matters grew so precarious and unpleasant, and the outcry of aggrieved citizens so loud, that the caliph had lately begun to entertain the suggestions of his advisors who insisted that Vizier Hasan must be deposed. This, I suspect, had been behind al-Hafiz's inquiry into what I knew about affairs in Cairo – but more of that later.

So, there it is. All that remains is for me to say that on the day my execution was to have been effected, Vizier Hasan, on an insane whim, summoned no fewer than forty amirs and atabegs from the city and surrounding region to meet with him that he might receive their heartfelt homage. Once they were assembled, he charged them with plotting against him. Thinking it a crude jest, the noblemen made light of it. Enraged that they should laugh at him, he had them thrown into a *hafir* – a grain house – and then ordered the warriors of his personal bodyguard to slay them all then and there. Without weapons or aid of any kind, there was very little the noblemen could do. The soldiers waded into the hafir, killing all who stood up to them; the rest were butchered one by one as they tried to escape.

I listened with dread amazement at Wazim's gruesome tale. 'When did this happen?' I asked when he finished.

'Da'ounk, at the very moment you stood before the caliph's throne of judgement,' he answered, 'even then this black deed was taking place. Forty amirs – all dead,' he said, shaking his head at the grotesque audacity of it. 'Everyone is most upset.'

'I can see how that would be,' I allowed. 'What has become of the vizier?'

'The khalifa, as you know, was forced to send out the guards. They surrounded the vizier's palace and demanded Hasan to give himself up to them. He refused and there was a small battle.' Wazim paused to gulp down some air, and then hurried on. 'When the vizier's bodyguard saw it was futile to fight against the khalifa's soldiers, they surrendered and delivered Hasan to his father's troops. It is said they have taken the vizier out of the city to a secret fortress where he is to be held until Khalifa al-Hafiz can decide what shall be done with him.'

Now, Cait, that is how the matter sits at the moment. As Padraig so often reminds me: All things work together for the good of him who loves the Lord. Great of Heaven, this is my prayer even now.

Sydoni would not be left behind. While her father discussed suitable crew members with a sleepy harbour master, Sydoni offered to show us around the ship. Taking one of the small boats, Padraig and Roupen rowed us to where the trim *Persephone* was anchored, and we climbed up onto the deck. Once aboard, it quickly became clear that she had no intention of being put off.

When the last of the provisions had been brought aboard and stowed below deck, Yordanus turned to bid farewell to his daughter. 'Save your breath, father,' she said, kissing him lightly on the cheek, 'I am going with you.'

He was against it. There was a brief discussion and, of course, she had her way. The more I saw of Sydoni, the more convinced I became that if she wanted a thing, it was hers already – and no amount of argument would sway her; likewise flattery, threats, or reason. In this, I suspect, she was just like her father, and even he could not compel her against her will.

Thus, with the help of two additional sailors and a pilot, we set off well before midday. *Persephone* was a fine ship; neat and spare in its lines, but able to hold a sizeable cargo with ease. As we had no cargo, the pilot and his two crewmen were able to manage the ship almost entirely on their own. Once under sail, they required only an occasional hand from Padraig and myself, leaving us plenty of time to ourselves.

The first day at sea was a joy. The wind stayed light out of the west, but the ship surged along pleasantly. It felt good to be moving forwards with such efficiency and speed, and with such righteousness of purpose. Very soon our hearts were soaring and our worries seemed to recede like the island behind us. Quietly exhilarated by the inevitable success of our mission, I allowed myself to accept Yordanus' assurances that Bohemond could not possibly outrace us, and that we would reach Anazarbus to deliver our warning long before the greedy prince and his army. Thus, the pressing urgency of our flight began to recede.

Towards evening, dolphins gathered to sport before the prow. Sydoni liked watching them and, drawn by her exuberance, I joined her at the rail to see them leap and dive.

'They say that dolphins are naughty children who taunted Neptune from the safety of the shore,' Sydoni told me. 'In his anger, the god sent a great sea wave to sweep the children off their rock and drown them, but Old Nereus did not have the heart to see them killed, and so gathered them up and changed them into fish, instead.'

'I have never heard that story,' I said. 'But seeing how they play in the waves, I can well believe it.'

We watched the sleek dark shapes dart and glide, splashing in and out of the waves, slicing the wake with their agile fins and weaving trails of bubbles as they rolled and spun in the fire-rimmed water. On the deck behind us, the sailors had lit a small brazier, and the aroma of spit-roasted fish began to steal into the air.

'I love the sea,' Sydoni said lazily, resting her chin on her palm as she leaned on the rail. 'I have spent half my life on ships.'

'And Yordanus?' I asked, because the doughty old trader had gone below deck shortly after we left sight of land, and had not put his head above the boards since.

'He is the worst seaman on any sea,' she observed gleefully. 'The least little ripple in the water and poor Yordanus turns green and goes below.'

'Vexing for a man who must make his living aboard a ship.'

She looked at me for a moment, the setting sun glinting in her dark hair, and turning her dusky skin to warm, glowing bronze. 'Yes,' she agreed softly.

Even as she said it, I knew she had been about to say something else, to confide more personally, but had pulled back at the last instant. Silence fell between us, and I thought she would not say more.

With a last flash of pale underbelly, the dolphins dove down into the darkening water, disappearing in a trail of bubbles, but Sydoni did not seem to notice. She went on staring down at the waves, a pensive look on her face. 'I want to thank you for saving my father.'

I opened my mouth to dispute her claim, but saw that she was in earnest. 'Did he need saving?'

She turned her face towards the far horizon. 'He was dying in that house.' The way she spoke made it sound like a prison. 'He had lost interest in his food, his affairs, life itself – you saw how he was.'

'I see he has changed,' I agreed. 'He has become a very lion on our behalf.'

'Yes, and that is because of you. I am grateful.'

'My lady, I have done nothing. Your father has taken an interest in our troubles for reasons of his own, and has decided to help us. Believe me, I am the one who should be grateful – and I am.'

'I do not expect you to understand,' she said stiffly, and moved away along the rail.

That night we sat on the broad, uncluttered deck and ate flat bread and roast fish basted in olive oil and sprinkled with dried herbs and salt. The moon rose slowly in a clear sky and made the sea bright. Sydoni went below deck as soon as she finished eating, taking a little food for her father. Padraig, Roupen, and I sat and talked to the sailors, all three of whom had travelled to and from the Holy Land many times.

When the others went to bed, I decided to walk around the deck a little before going down to my berth to sleep. I strolled idly, letting the tranquillity of the night seep into my soul. My thoughts turned to prayers and I prayed for the family I had left at home, and for the swift and successful completion of our journey.

218

So occupied by my devotions, I did not notice that I was no longer alone. I heard a soft footfall beside me and glanced around to find Sydoni watching me. 'I am sorry to disturb you,' she said softly; not the least apologetic, she stepped nearer.

'I am finished.'

'A fine night,' she observed, tilting her face towards the heavens. 'I can never sleep when the moon is so bright and the air is so warm. I often sit out alone all night watching the moon and stars.'

'I have been known to do the same at home.'

Still gazing skyward, she asked, 'Is it nice where you live?'

'It is very different from here,' I told her, 'and very different, I would think, from your home in Egypt.'

She smiled, her teeth a glint of whiteness in the dark. 'Not all Copts are born within sight of the Nile. _I_ have never lived in Egypt – nor has my father.'

'But I thought –'

'I grew up in Damascus,' she explained. 'No doubt I would have lived there all my life. It is a glorious city – or used to be. I was very happy there.'

'Why did you leave?'

'We were forced to flee,' she replied, her voice darkening slightly, 'and we were not alone. Three thousand Christians were driven from their homes that day. We were far more fortunate than most. Many lost everything, including their lives. They took most of the ready gold and silver, but we were allowed to bring anything else we could carry.'

'Was it because of the crusade?' I asked.

Sydoni gave a slight shake of her head. 'No, it was the _Fida'in._'

The wondered at the word. 'What is a Fedayeen?'

'_The_ Fida'in,' she corrected. 'Have you never heard of them?'

'No,' I told her, 'but I have not been long in the Holy Land.'

'I wish _I_ had never heard of them. They are vile and hateful murderers,' she replied with disgust. 'Some call them Batinis – those who hold a hidden faith. It is because of them that we were forced to leave Damascus.'

As if fearing she had said too much, she fell silent. I tried to engage her in conversation again, but she said she was tired, and soon went below, leaving me alone once more and gazing at the stars.

The next day, neither she nor her father showed themselves above deck before midday. Padraig and I spent the morning fishing, and caught enough for our dinner that night. I told the priest about what Sydoni had said the night before, and asked if he had ever heard of the Fida'in. He, like myself, professed ignorance, so we asked Roupen.

'Where did you hear about them?' He looked around the bare deck as if he thought they might be hiding behind the mast, ready to leap out on us.

'Sydoni told me,' I replied. 'She said they were the reason she and her father were forced to leave Damascus. She said three thousand Christians fled on the same day.'

The young lord shrugged. 'I am not surprised. Such things happen – especially when the Fida'in are involved.'

'But who are they?' asked Padraig.

'Fida'in means those whose lives are . . . ' he searched for the right word, 'forfeit – like a sacrifice.'

'Sydoni said they held to a hidden faith,' I put in.

Roupen nodded. 'That is why nobody knows much about them. They are very secretive. In fact, I have heard it said they will kill themselves rather than be taken by an enemy. If they die fighting for God, they go instantly to paradise. At least,' he shrugged again, 'that is what they believe.'

Just then, one of the sailors called out that land had been sighted. Yordanus emerged a short while later, and the old trader lurched across the deck to stand squinting in the sunlight and gripping the rail with both hands.

The three of us joined him, and I told Yordanus it was good to see him above deck. 'The air will do you good,' Padraig added.

The old trader gazed across the wide stretch of water at the hazy wrinkle of hills in the blue distance. 'I have not set foot on the mainland since leaving Damascus,' he told us. 'I did not think I ever would again.'

'Sydoni told me about your troubles,' I said.

He turned sad, misty eyes to me. 'Did she?' he asked doubtfully. 'Then I am amazed.' He looked away again. 'That is the first time she has spoken of it to anyone.'

TWENTY-SIX

We reached the mainland after dark and stood off shore during the night, continuing up along the coast the next morning. The sun had but quartered the pale, cloudless sky when the pilot sighted the river mouth and, as the ship made the short run in, Padraig and I quickly became very busy with ropes and sails and suchlike. When I finally had a chance to look up, I saw a wide, shallow-channelled estuary opening out into the sea between two steep banks.

Above the river on the high right bank stood the village of Marionis, its tight clusters of tiny blue-domed houses dazzling white in the bright sun. Seeing that the ship meant to stop, a number of villagers leapt into small boats and rowed out to meet us; the first of these enterprising souls now clamoured for our attention. Yordanus hired two sturdy craft to ferry us to shore, and we soon found ourselves standing in the tiny market square, haggling over the price of mutton.

The old trader rose magnificently to the challenge of bartering for supplies. Truly, he relished the cut and thrust of the exchange with a zeal I had rarely seen in anyone half his age. He conducted the bargaining in Greek and I soon noticed that, although he put on a formidable countenance, he always settled on a price higher than he might have got if he had pressed a little harder.

'They are farmers and goat herders mostly – not wealthy merchants,' he said when I asked him about this later. 'Life is hard in the villages. If I give them a little more, they will go home with joy in their hearts; and tonight when they pray, their prayers will be for me. I am a rich man. I need all the prayers I can get.' He smiled, his pleasure expanding by the moment. 'Besides, you never know when you must come back this way again. Sow a little good will now, who knows what you might reap tomorrow, eh?'

By midday, he had concluded his business and stood with satisfaction before a mound of provisions: big round wheels of bread, several clay jars filled with salted olives, a haunch of fresh mutton, slabs of dried meat and fish, four live chickens bound in pairs by the feet, two bags of flour and jars of oil, round pots of soft goat cheese, and garlanded strands of onions, and bunches of fresh root vegetables of a kind I had never seen before. Also, there was wine – no fewer than five large jars bound in baskets woven of dried river reeds.

At Yordanus' direction, the boys of the village took up the bags and jars and chickens and bread and all the rest and started down to the river. Padraig and I stood atop the bank and watched as the long line of bearers snaked its way from the village square and down the muddy earth track to the water's edge where the various items were loaded into the two boats Yordanus had hired.

Their work completed, the old trader gave each boy a piece of silver, and they raced back to their homes shouting ecstatically. We joined Roupen and Yordanus by the boats. 'Mamistra is two days by river,' Yordanus was saying as we came up, 'maybe three this time of year. It has been a long time since I was there. A man I know trades horses and pack animals, and we will get a good deal – if he is still there.'

'Anazarbus lies ten days beyond that,' Roupen reckoned. 'We will never make it in time.' Since leaving Cyprus, he had grown increasingly anxious. His normally pale aspect was, if possible, even more pallid and strained. I knew he was worried about reaching home to warn his people of Bohemond's attack, and although we had lived with that threat for many days the distress was finally beginning to tell on him.

Yordanus looked up into the bare brown hills beyond the town and tapped his lower lip with a long forefinger. He thought for a moment, and said, 'An army can only travel as fast as its footmen. We have made a fair start; even if they ran all the way they could not overtake us now. We will reach Anazarbus long before Bohemond, never fear.'

Roupen, unconvinced, climbed into the boat and sat down, eager to commence the journey as soon as possible. The rest of the provisions were quickly stowed, and we were ready to cast off. 'Someone is missing,' Padraig said, counting heads. 'Where is Sydoni?'

'She was in the market when we left,' I recalled, and offered to go fetch her. I hurried back up the hill to the village, passed among the houses and once more into the square. She was nowhere to be seen, but three of the boys who had helped carry supplies pointed to a house, and I saw two old women and three or four young girls standing before the house looking in through the open door.

I walked over to the house and looked in, too, and saw a bare room with a freshly-swept floor of beaten-earth and a single table against one wall. Sydoni stood in the centre of the room holding a length of cloth to her body as another woman tucked it up here and there around her. Meanwhile, a third woman, perhaps the mother of the first, sat at a loom in the corner directing this activity; and all three were chattering away at the same time in Greek, oblivious to all else.

Moving into the doorway, I rapped on the doorpost with my knuckles, and Sydoni looked up, saw me, and smiled. It was a smile of recognition and welcome, but also of supreme and unassailable confidence – a woman secure in her domain, completely at ease allowing me a glimpse of it.

'The provisions are loaded, and we are ready to leave,' I told her.

'In a moment,' she said, and resumed her appraisal of the cloth, ignoring me until she had concluded her business. She passed the cloth back to the woman, who folded it carefully, tied it with a length of rag, and placed it on a bare shelf high up on the wall, then handed Sydoni what appeared to be a length of carved willow wrapped in coarse white cloth.

Sydoni then took her leave. The two women followed her out of the house and bade her farewell, each kissing her on both cheeks. We started off across the square, and the elder woman called to one of the young girls outside the house who fell in behind us. 'We are to have an escort,' I said. When Sydoni did not answer, I pointed to the cloth-wrapped stick. 'What have you there?'

'This?' she said almost absently. 'Watch.'

Taking the carved end of the slender rod, she lightly shook out the cloth to reveal a wooden ring which had been hidden in the folds of the cloth. Grasping this ring, she slid it up along the length of the rod; as she did so, the most remarkable thing happened. The thin cloth blossomed out into a large round disc and stretched itself across a cunning latticework of split cane. She fixed the ring somehow and the cloth remained taut.

'What is it?' I said, regarding the strange sail-like object.

Sydoni took one look at my astonished expression and laughed out loud. The sound was magic – a warmly female sound, full of expression and gaiety, gently superior, but lacking any hint of scorn or ridicule. 'Have you never seen a sunshade?' she laughed.

'A sunshade,' I repeated, happy to be the fool if it provoked such a delightful sound. 'Is that what it is?'

Still laughing, she asked, 'What do the women of your land use when they travel about?'

'Nothing,' I replied.

'Then how,' Sydoni demanded in disbelief, 'do they keep the hot sun from wrinkling their skin and making them old before their time?'

'So rarely does the sun shine,' I replied, 'people welcome it rather than hide from it.'

'Are you saying the sun never shines?' She looked at me askance. 'I do not believe you.'

'Truly,' I insisted. 'When the men and women of Scotland see the sun it is a cause for celebration. No one would think of shielding themselves from its warmth and light.'

'Then I hope I never go there,' she replied emphatically. 'It sounds a dark and dismal place.'

Inexplicably, her words were like a stab in the heart; I felt a sharp pang of regret for having spoken of my homeland in such a way as to invite her disdain. 'How is this sun device employed?' I asked.

'Like this,' she said, raising the slender rod and resting it lightly on her shoulder. Her face, neck, and shoulders were now cast into the shadow of the disc-shaped shade. 'See?'

'Clever,' I allowed. 'Why not just wear a hat?'

Since coming to Outremer, I had seen many wide-brimmed hats made of stripped reed or woven straw. They seemed more than able to provide the service of a sunshade. '*Peasants* wear hats,' Sydoni replied. 'Here, try it,' she said, handing the thing to me.

I did as I had seen her do. The sight of a foreign man using a sunshade proved too much for our young escort, who was promptly seized by a fit of giggles and laughed all the way to the boat. I returned the object to Sydoni, who walked merrily beside me, spinning the circle of cloth and humming lightly. For the second time in as many days, I luxuriated in the unexpected intimacy of her cheerful companionship.

Upon arriving at the boat, Sydoni informed her father that she had purchased a mantle to be made by one of the women in the village and instructed him to pay the girl, who would take the money back to her mother. Yordanus counted a few silver coins into the girl's hand. 'And for the sunshade, too,' she said, and he tossed in a few more.

Then, under the watchful eyes of the people of Marionis, we climbed into the boats and began the slow, easy voyage up river to Mamistra. Padraig and I shared the rowing chores with the two men from the village, relieving them when they began to tire. In this way, we worked our way along the winding river course. We spent the first night on a gravel shingle in the middle of the river with nothing overhead but the star-laden sky.

The second night we camped in a grove of fig trees planted beside the river and, as the sun went down on the third day we arrived at Mamistra. Leaving Padraig and Roupen to help the boatmen unload the boats, Yordanus and I went into the town early the next morning to search out his horse-trading acquaintance.

Along the way, we stopped a farmer with a piglet under his arm and asked him if he knew of anyone thereabouts who raised or traded in horses. The farmer squinted his eyes, scratched a bristly jaw, shifted the piglet from one arm to the other, and at last said he might have heard of such a man. When Yordanus presented him with a silver denarius for his trouble, the farmer broke into a wide toothless grin and said, that, yes, he remembered now, the man he was thinking of was called Nurmal.

'Yes! The very fellow I was hoping to find. Where does he live?'

'I cannot say,' answered the farmer. 'If I ever heard where he lived, I do not remember now.'

Yordanus plucked out two more denarii and placed them in the farmer's rough palm. 'Does this help your memory?'

'No, my lord,' replied the farmer, eyeing the silver sadly. 'I still do not know where he lives, but I know where you can find him.'

'Tell me,' said Yordanus, 'and you can keep the silver.'

'There is a mill over there –' the farmer pointed beyond the town to a knoll surmounted by a windmill. 'He buys grain and fodder there on market days.' Hefting his pig, he said, 'Today is the market.'

We thanked the toothless fellow and sent him on his way rejoicing in his unexpected wealth. The mill was further than it first appeared, and it took us some time to walk up the long, rocky slope. Only when we got to the top did we see that there was a road leading up from the other side. Nevertheless, we found a goat track and followed it, arriving at the mill from behind. The miller was a gruff man of few words, but more of Yordanus' silver loosened his tongue and we learned that Nurmal had not been there yet, but was expected some time during the day.

'I will wait here for Nurmal,' Yordanus suggested. 'You go back and tell the others we have found our man. Nurmal and I will join you at the river.'

I did not like leaving him, but as I was walking from the yard, the miller's wife brought him out a bowl of milk to drink. I left him sitting in the shade of the house, sipping cool milk and looking like a man for whom the world held no worries.

Padraig and the boatmen had unloaded the provisions under a tree; the boats were gone now, however, and Padraig was preparing food on a small fire at the river's edge. Sydoni was asleep in the shade of the tree, and Roupen sat on a rock nearby, knees drawn up under his chin, and gazing forlornly into the swirling brown water.

'All is well,' I said, settling on the rock beside him. 'We are making fair speed. We *will* reach Anazarbus before Bohemond and his army, you shall see.'

'It makes no difference,' he muttered without looking up. 'There are not enough soldiers in all of Armenia to repel the crusaders. They will slaughter us like dogs.'

'Roupen,' I said after a moment, 'we will do what we can, and trust God for the rest.' I reached out and put my hand on his shoulder to reassure him. 'Hope and pray.'

'*You* hope,' he snarled, shoving my hand away. '*You* pray.'

I left him to his despair, and went to help Padraig cook the meal. We ate and dozed afterward, and the day grew hot. The sun soared through a sky bleached white with heat haze, and then began its long descent behind the dusty, sage-covered hills beyond Mamistra.

226

Padraig and I were just discussing whether we should go back to the mill and look for Yordanus when we heard a horse whinny and there, coming down along the track leading into the town, was the old trader himself on a milk white stallion, riding beside another man on a black. Behind them rode two more men leading two horses each.

They reined up at the water's edge and while the two men watered the horses, Yordanus presented Nurmal, a smiling, graceful white-haired elder with a skin so brown it looked like polished leather. He wore the silken robes of an Arab potentate, and when he spoke, his long white moustache quivered with excitement.

'What do you think of my horses?' asked Nurmal when everyone had been properly introduced.

'They are wonderful,' I remarked. 'In Scotland, not even kings own such fine horses.'

'I am not surprised. Although they are perhaps more plentiful here,' allowed Nurmal modestly. 'The Arabs place a high value on their animals, and breed the best in the world. Yordanus and I have concluded our bargain. All that remains is for you to choose.' He gestured towards the horses, inviting our inspection.

'I will be more than happy with any of them, I am sure,' I replied casually.

'You are too easily pleased,' he said. 'But that will not do. Any man who must trust life and limb to his mount would be well advised to take a moment's sober reflection over the choice.'

So, I stepped closer and subjected the animals to a more thorough inspection. They stood on long, slender legs, their handsome heads high; their manes and tails were full and long, their necks finely curved and powerful. I ran my hands over their glossy coats, and I could almost feel the surge of those solid shoulders and the earth speeding effortlessly beneath me.

In all, they were magnificent creatures, clearly beyond my own small capacity to judge; aside from the colour of their lustrous coats, there was not a whisker's difference between them that I could see. So, I chose a grey with a speckled rump because it made me think of the mist rising over the moors back home.

The others chose their mounts whereupon Nurmal announced, 'Now then, my friends, we are to ride to my home where you will stay tonight. You will dine with me and tomorrow we will set off for Anazarbus.'

'You mean to go with us?' asked Roupen. I could tell he thought ill of the idea.

'Indeed, yes, my lord. You need a guide and I must look after my horses, no?' Nurmal's smile was broad and handsome.

'Trust this man as you would trust me,' Yordanus said. 'I have already told him of your need for haste and secrecy.'

'That is why it is best for you to stay with me tonight rather than in the town,' Nurmal explained.

Roupen frowned, unconvinced.

'At least it hurries us on our way,' I told him, 'and in a better fashion than we have enjoyed so far.'

Whatever misgivings he might have had about the arrangements were soon swept aside in the exuberance of mounting such excellent horses: spirited, intelligent, compliant without being dull, they were indeed a joy to ride. It had been a fair while since I had been on the back of a horse, but I know I had never sat astride one half so responsive and well-mannered.

We struck off along an old road leading up behind the town and into the quiet hills. The dusky air was cool and heavy with the scent of broom and sage. The sky grew slowly dark, and the moon rose. We rode along, content to remain silent as we passed through the night-dark land, climbing higher into the rough, empty hills until we came to a large walled villa tucked into the fold of a shallow valley and surrounded by stables and yards.

We dismounted in the yard and Nurmal made us welcome, saying, 'Tomorrow we embrace the rigours of the trail. But tonight,' his smile was a glint of white in the moonlight, 'we eat and sleep like kings. Come, the table is prepared. Want for nothing, my friends.'

Thus, we entered a house of such effortless liberality and friendliness that within the space of a simple, wholesome meal we each became monarchs of vast domain, and rose from the table refreshed and renewed for the journey ahead. As we went to our beds, Padraig confided, 'If hospitality was the saving of men, then I have no doubt that when the angels called us to the heavenly banqueting table, we would find Nurmal of Mamistra sitting at God's right hand.'

'Amen,' I replied happily. 'With Nurmal beside him, God could not ask for a more amiable dinner companion.'

TWENTY-SEVEN

It was still dark when we left that homely house. We stopped at sunrise to take the first drink of a long and thirsty day. The night sky grew milky grey, then yellow, and finally blue. Even as we watched the pale fingers of sunlight stretch along the valleys and separate the dark mass of rough hills one from another, we could feel the heat of the day spreading in waves over the land. We mounted up again at once and pushed on so as to get as far as possible along our journey before we were forced to stop and wait for the sun to set.

As I rode along, I thought of all those I had left behind in Scotland – of my mother and father, Abbot Emlyn, and the others – and you, dearest Cait, were foremost among them. I knew Murdo and Ragna were watching over you as well, nay better, than I would if I had been there. Still, I felt a pang of guilt for leaving you, and wished that I might have been a gull or an eagle that I could swoop down and see you and know, if only for an instant, what you were doing at that moment. I held you in my mind, and tried to imagine how you might have grown since I had last seen you. And then, my heart, I held you before the Throne of Grace and asked the High King of Heaven to send three angels to surround you and watch over you day and night until I could return.

Yes, on that rough road into those ragged, dusty, sage-covered hills, my thoughts turned towards going home. And I felt the gnawing agony of what Padraig calls the *hiraeth*, the home-yearning. I felt it like a sharp, clawing ache in my heart, as if a rip had opened up in the fabric of my soul and a blast of cold, bitter wind rushed through. For the first time since leaving Caithness, I wished I was on the homeward trail.

It was after midday before we found a place to water and rest through the long, hot wait until evening. The trees were short and scrubby little thorn-covered oaks large enough for one or two to squat beneath; the flies liked them, too, and worried us incessantly, but at least the dense, leathery leaves kept the sun off our heads. We tethered the horses to graze on whatever they might find to nibble, and then retreated to the shade.

I had not spoken to Yordanus privately for several days, and I had questions on my mind. So, I joined him as he reclined beneath his tree. He welcomed the company and we began to talk. 'There is something I have been wanting to ask you since leaving Famagusta,' I told him.

'An unanswered question is like a toothache that only heals with asking,' he said, turning his face towards me. 'What is vexing you, my friend?'

'Why are you doing this?' At his puzzled glance, I added, 'Ships, supplies, now horses – all this. Why are you helping us?'

'Ah, well,' he replied. 'Cannot a man help a friend in need?'

'Forgive me, Yordanus, but there must be more to it than that.' It came to me then that perhaps *I* was not the friend he meant. 'It is de Bracineaux,' I suggested. 'He sent us to you knowing you would do this. But why? What is between the two of you that you should take such personal interest in this affair?'

He sat with his back to the gnarled little bole, resting his head against the crinkled black bark and staring out across the narrow brown valley shimmering dully in the heat haze. The buzzing of the flies grew loud in the silence. I did not press him, but let him come to it in his own time.

At last he drew a long, low breath and said, in a voice full of mourning and melancholy, 'I am doing it for my son.'

'You mentioned him before,' I said, trying to make it easier for the old man to speak. 'I can see you loved him very much.'

'Julian was his name,' said Nurmal. Having overheard the beginning of our conversation, he had come to join us, bringing a water skin and a wooden cup. 'May I?'

'Please.' Yordanus nodded and patted the ground beside him, and Nurmal sat down. 'Julian was everything a father hopes for in the child who will carry on the family name and lineage,' Yordanus continued, pride edging into his voice. 'He was my hope and my joy.'

The old trader went on to describe the unhappy events of their last days in Damascus. The trouble all began, in his estimation, with the fall of Jerusalem, which shocked the Seljuqs and Saracens beyond all measure. Overnight all previous certainties collapsed and the world was pitched headlong into unimaginable turmoil. Out of the chaos new, and often dangerous, alliances emerged. Everywhere the rulers and potentates of the old order made the best bargains they could with anyone who offered the barest hope of protection from the burgeoning multitude of dangers, perils, and threats arising almost daily.

'It was no different in Damascus,' Yordanus told me. 'Atabeg Tughtigin held out as long as he could. In his prime he had been an able and fair-minded ruler, but in the end his age and health began to tell against him. He made alliance with the Fida'in.'

The word pricked my attention, and I recalled what Sydoni and Roupen had told me about this shadowy sect.

Yordanus saw that I recognized the name and said, 'You have heard of them, I see.'

'Sydoni mentioned them; she called them murderers and said they held a hidden faith, but she did not say what that faith might be.'

'They are Muslims,' Yordanus explained, 'but of a very strict and overzealous stripe. It is their all-consuming desire to unite the Muhammedans in a single observance of the Muslim faith. To do this they are willing to dare all things – even martyrdom.'

'Dangerous men,' I observed.

'Murderous,' Nurmal corrected. 'All the more because of the *hashish*.'

'The hashish?' I had never heard the word before, and asked what it might be.

'Oh, it is a very potent herb that can be used in various ways. The Fida'in eat it, or smoke the dried leaves in pipes. It is a powerful essence, and it makes them foolishly courageous. When they are in the grip of the hashish, they fear nothing,' declared Nurmal. 'For this reason some call them the Hashishin, a name they hate.'

'It is true,' affirmed Yordanus. 'Death holds no terror for them, nor the life hereafter. They sacrifice all to their faith in the belief that they are instruments of God used to bring about divine justice.'

'By murdering their enemies.'

'By slaughtering *anyone* who opposes their schemes,' Yordanus insisted. 'They are everywhere now, and everywhere loathed. Like God, they see and hear every deed and every word; and, like God, they hold all men to judgement.'

'And their judgement is always the same,' added Nurmal. 'Guilty.'

'Sadly, it is so,' agreed Yordanus, nodding sagely.

'You said they came to Damascus,' I suggested, gently prodding the tale back to its beginning.

'Yes, and it was the worst evil ever to befall that admirable city. They were granted refuge in Damascus in return for helping in its defence. Why old Tughtigin ever agreed to this bargain, I will never understand. No doubt he thought it best to have them inside the tent pissing out rather than the other way. I cannot say.

'But as anyone might easily have predicted, the decision was disastrous. Once settled inside the walls, the Fida'in began to worm their way into every corner of the government. Within a few months they had taken control of the wazir's office and were exerting heavy influence over all state affairs. Tughtigin became a ghost in his own palace; unseen, unheard, he roamed the corridors moaning and fretting with remorse over his foolishness. But the damage was done. The Fida'in would not be moved.

'The people endured as best they could. Trade was difficult and unimaginably complicated. For example, if the Fida'in did not like the colour of the cloth you were selling, they declared it unclean, confiscated it, and imposed a heavy fine on you for selling it. If a man stopped in the street to speak to a woman, they fined him. If a woman ventured outside with her head uncovered, she was fined. If they found your turban too tall, or your beard too short, they fined you. If you could not pay these fines, they threw you in prison.

'In no time at all half the population was walking around with debts they could not pay, and the other half was in prison.' Yordanus shook his head ruefully. 'And should you be so unwise as to protest your innocence, you simply disappeared. Sometimes, if you were lucky, someone might find your head nailed to the city gates. Otherwise, you were never seen again.'

'I suppose Christians suffered the worst of it,' I mused.

'So you might think,' Yordanus allowed. 'But no, the perpetrators of this disaster were exceedingly equitable. Oh yes, they favoured all citizens – rich or poor, young or old, Christian, Jew, or Muhammedan – with the same infernal impartiality. Each year it became worse – for the merchants and moneylenders no less than everyone else. Good trade depends not only on a reliable, healthy ebb and flow of goods and services, but a fair expectation of progress and a modest hope for the future. Let these springs dry up, however, and like a river in the desert, all trade swiftly disappears.'

Nurmal poured water into the cup and passed it to Yordanus. 'We endured as best we could for as long as we could,' he said, draining the cup and passing it back. 'In the end it became intolerable.'

'Is that when you decided to leave?' I asked.

'If only it were so,' Yordanus murmured, 'Julian would still be alive.' His mouth twitched in a smile of such sorrowful regret that I could not bear to see it and looked away quickly. 'All is vanity,' he said softly, 'and nothing more so than the heart of man.'

Seeing his friend in such distress, Nurmal quietly moved the conversation onto a less painful subject, and I was left with more questions than when we first began. As soon as the heat of the day began to fade in the desolate hills, we moved on. I thought about what Yordanus had told me, turning the pieces of his tale over in my mind. It seemed to me that Julian and his sorry fate lay at the heart of the mystery and, thinking I would get no more from the father, I decided to ask the sister. But I did not have a chance to speak to her alone that night, nor all the next day. Indeed, it was not until well after dark when we had stopped for the night and everyone else was going to sleep that I was able to get her alone.

'Sydoni,' I said, moving close to where she sat by the dying campfire, 'I would speak to you.'

She looked up at me, the glow of the embers bathing her face like the rosy light of a far-off dawn. 'Sit beside me,' she said, her voice charming and low. Her long hair was upswept to keep it off her shoulders, but small tendrils had escaped and now curled around her ears and along the slender, shapely column of her neck. I wondered what it would be like to wind one of those curls around my finger.

'I asked your father to tell me about what happened in Damascus,' I said, dropping down beside her on the ground.

'And did he?' She regarded me with the same unnerving directness as the first time we met in the villa courtyard. This time, however, there was less defiance in her glance, and more appraisal.

'He told me a little,' I replied. 'He told me about Julian.'

'Then he told you much,' she corrected, turning back to her contemplation of the embers.

'I asked him why he is helping us, and he said he is doing it for his son – for Julian.'

She seemed to consider this, and then rejected it. 'No,' she said thoughtfully, 'whatever the reason it is not Julian.'

'Vanity, then?' I asked. It was the last thing her father had said, and I hoped she might know what he meant.

'Perhaps,' she allowed. 'You see, my father would have been the Governor of Damascus.' She glanced sideways at me. 'I see he did not mention that.'

I shook my head. 'No.'

'It is true. Julian did not approve. He urged father on numerous occasions to leave the city, but Yordanus refused to go because he coveted the exalted position.'

'He blamed the Fida'in,' I pointed out.

'Of course,' she replied as if this was manifestly self-evident. 'None of this would have happened if not for them. *They* were the ones who wanted him to be Governor.'

This made no sense. 'But I thought the Fida'in were Muhammedans,' I pointed out. 'Yordanus said they were ruling the city.'

'Shh,' she hushed, 'keep your voice down, or you'll wake everybody. Be quiet and I will tell you how it was.' Drawing up her long legs, she wrapped her arms around her knees and, staring into the embers as into the still-glowing past, she began to describe their last days in Damascus.

'The atabeg –'

'Tughtigin?'

'The same. He was a sick old man, and getting weaker all the time. The wazir was a vacillating bootlick named al-Mazdaghani, who sided with the Batini – the Fida'in by another name. The day came when the atabeg could no longer rise from his bed. Seeing he was about to die, Tughtigin gave his title to his son, Buri. The amirs were happy to approve the choice because Buri had vowed to rid the city of the hated Fida'in. And that,' Sydoni declared emphatically, 'is when our troubles really began.'

She spoke with quiet candour and I found listening to her a pleasure – and one I had not experienced in a woman's company for a very long time.

'The Fida'in considered themselves the only true Muslims,' she said, 'and in their eyes Buri and the amirs were faithless and unbelieving. As Tughtigin grew weaker, his son took over more and more of his father's power, and began taking steps to eradicate the hated cult. This alarmed the Fida'in, who had imagined they might control the new atabeg as they had controlled his father.

'The more Buri exerted his growing authority, the more the Fida'in feared losing the only place they had ever been welcomed. They soon discovered themselves hunted and harassed at every turn, and in desperation went looking for a protector who could ensure their survival. In secret – the Fida'in are masters of secrecy – they sent an envoy to Edessa –'

At her mention of my uncle Torf's former home in Outremer, Sydoni's recitation suddenly ceased to resemble a tale of long ago, and became immediate and real. 'Baldwin,' I murmured.

'Baldwin the second,' she amended. 'The Fida'in offered to hand over the city to the count, if he would let them have the city of Tyre to rule in return. What prince could resist such a gift? But Baldwin was wary. He sent word back that if the Christians of the city wished his intervention, then they must unite behind a leader who could organize the new regime.

'One night they came to our house.' Sydoni shivered at the memory. 'Six men dressed in black and wearing the curved swords and crossed daggers – they came asking for Yordanus Hippolytus, saying they had an offer for him to consider.

'Julian was not at home, or else he would not have let them in. But my father did not want any trouble, so he agreed to hear them out. That is when they told him that the city would soon be handed over to Baldwin, and that if he agreed to let them leave unhindered, he would be made governor to rule the city under Baldwin.'

'Did he agree to this?'

'Not at first,' Sydoni replied. 'He told them he would pray about it and seek the counsel of the elder Christians in the city. They gave him four days to think it over, and said they would come back for his answer.

'Well, Julian was against it. He did not want to have anything to do with the Batini, but many of my father's friends urged him to accept the offer. They saw it as a chance for the Christians to gain back the power they had lost under the Muslims. Still, my father hesitated.'

'For Julian' sake?'

'He did not like going against Julian, true enough. But he did not think he could trust the Fida'in to keep their part of the bargain. He did not see how he could govern a city where the Muslims far outnumbered the Christians.'

'What changed his mind?' I asked.

'Baldwin sent word that the Templars were ready to back him. The count promised that he would give Damascus a garrison of its own. De Bracineaux was at Edessa then, and he was to have been the Grand Master of the new garrison; he came one night and spoke to my father, and pledged his support. With the Templars at his command, the governorship would be secure. So, my father agreed.'

'What happened?'

'We waited all through the summer, but Baldwin never came,' she replied. 'I do not know why he abandoned us. I heard it said that he marched out with his army and was only waiting for support from the Count of Antioch; by the time he realized Bohemond would not come to his aid, the autumn rains had begun. Baldwin did not care to wage a campaign in the mud and cold, so he marched back to Edessa.'

When it became clear that Baldwin would not attack, she told me, Buri, the new atabeg, decided the time was right to make his move. He gathered some warriors and on the morning the city was to be given over, he marched into the Pavillion of Roses in the palace where the wazir was at prayer. He ordered the wazir to be executed then and there. They hacked the body to pieces with swords and sent the pieces to be hung on the Gate of Iron as a warning to anyone who planned rebellion.

The atabeg decided to expel all the Christians, so any plot they might have made could not succeed. Every last Christian in the city was informed that they had until sunset to gather their belongings and depart; they were allowed to take whatever they could carry with them so long as they left the city before the gates closed. The expulsion was total. Any Christians found in the city after dark would be killed.

They worked like slaves, and Yordanus hired many of his Jewish and Muslim friends as well. He organized an entire caravan and they loaded whole chests of treasure onto donkeys and horses. By sundown they had nearly finished, and Yordanus commanded Julian to begin leading the baggage train out of the city so that it would not be caught when the gates closed.

The danger was real, she said, and I believe her. All of Damascus was in an uproar as never before. They started out, but Julian was fearful of leaving Sydoni and Yordanus behind. So, once he got to the gates, he left the caravan in charge of the hired men and ran back to the house to bring the rest of the family and servants to safety.

Sydoni licked her lips, bracing herself for what came next. 'Once Julian had departed, father changed his mind and abandoned the rest of the packing – what was the use? Instead, we hurried after Julian, but the streets were crowded and it was difficult to get through. We reached the gates only to find the caravan stopped, the hired men scattered, and Julian nowhere to be seen. We searched quickly, asking everyone, but no one would tell us anything.

'At last, we found one of the workmen who said that when Julian could not get through he came back, and the soldiers at the gate challenged him and demanded a second bribe. When Julian refused, the soldiers seized him and dragged him away, threatening the rest of the hired men with violence if they told anyone. The man showed us where the soldiers had taken Julian, and we found his battered body lying in his own blood. The soldiers had beat him and left him to bleed to death behind a dung heap.' Her voice trailed off and we sat listening to the soft tick of the dying coals.

'There was nothing we could do,' she said after a moment. 'Julian was dead, and by then it was growing dark. We had to move on, or face death ourselves. Even so, it was only with great difficulty that I persuaded my father to leave. We paid the workman to take care of the corpse, and made our way to the gate. The greedy soldiers had closed it already, and refused to open it unless father gave them half his silver and gold. In the end, they took more than that, of course, and we were allowed to keep the rest because they were too lazy to unpack the animals.

'It took us nine days to reach Tyre on the coast,' she said, her voice cracking slightly. 'With every step of the way, my father's heart hardened against Baldwin and the other leaders of the Christian principalities that much more. De Bracineaux helped us to reach Cyprus – he even sent soldiers to Sidon and Tripoli to get father's ships back. The merchants there had heard that the Christians had been exiled from Damascus, and they assumed Yordanus had been killed. But it was Julian.'

She turned to me in the soft ember glow, unshed tears gleaming her eyes. 'Now you know,' she said.

I regretted my curiosity; had I known it would cause her such pain, I never would have asked. 'I am sorry, Sydoni,' I murmured, feeling her sorrow as a leaden lump in my heart, and wishing I might have spared her the anguish of those awful days and their retelling. I wanted to put my arm around her shoulders and hold her close, but I did not know whether she would welcome such a gesture of comfort from me.

'That was two years ago and I have not spoken of this to anyone since the day we left Damascus,' she said, pushing the tears away with the heel of her hand. 'I will not speak of it again.'

Nor did I blame her.

TWENTY-EIGHT

Eight days we were on the road, and in that time met only a handful of fellow travellers – a few farmers and shepherds going to or returning from distant markets, four Greek priests, and a company of merchants on their way to seek their fortunes among the Armenians. These last fell in with us and hoped to keep our company until reaching Anazarbus. Otherwise, the journey was forgettable in every way. One rock-strewn hillside is much the same as the next, after all.

We slept and ate and rode on, growing more fretful and peevish, and less companionable, as the days wore away. Yordanus, who had begun with such zeal, began to fade; he was an old man and his strength was not equal to his enthusiasm. Sydoni seemed to retreat into herself, becoming ever more pensive and melancholy. I would see her riding with her sun shade spread above her, and try to engage her in conversation, but the sombre preoccupations of her mind were too potent to quell for very long; she soon slipped back into her distracted reflection. Roupen, anxious and tetchy since leaving Antioch, grew ever more so as his apprehensions mounted. No one could say two words to him without either starting an argument or casting him into a desperate frenzy of morbid self-pity.

Only Padraig and Nurmal remained unaffected by the oppressive sameness – Nurmal, because he loved his horses and found happiness in all circumstances so long as he was sitting in the saddle; and Padraig, because that is the way he is. Priests of the Célé Dé find hardship stimulating and entertaining in an improving way. Indeed, they have been known to fashion misfortune for themselves when supplies of the natural stuff run short.

For myself, I gradually tired of trying to keep the others cheerful, and more often than not found myself deep in brooding meditation on the peculiar twists and turns encountered on life's rocky road – all the more because each twist and turn took me further from my pursuit of the Holy Rood. The urgency and importance of our purpose notwithstanding, I began to resent all the intrusions and irritations, large and small, which kept me from my quest. More and more, I grew anxious to be about my own business, and longed for the day when there would be no one to defend, pamper, or appease, save myself alone.

I was heartily glad when, on the eighth day, we crested a hill and saw the walls of Anazarbus glistering in the heat-sheen. Because of the hills, we had come close upon the city before seeing it, and now there it was, nestled like a clutch of dull ruddy eggs in the protective bends of the curved city walls. Away to the south and east slanted a rough, broken plain through which a river had dug a deep ravine; to the north and west ranged the tumbling, craggy foothills of the high Taurus mountains rising elegantly, if forbiddingly, in the hazy distance.

Once in sight of the city, Roupen, morose and unresponsive at best, now became almost drunk with exuberance. He lifted his head and gave out a shriek which must have been heard in the streets of the city itself. He slapped the reins and urged his good horse to speed. The animal, glad for an excuse to run after so many days of dull plodding, put back its ears, reared, and leapt to a gallop, pulling along the poor pack horse tethered behind.

Following his lead, Nurmal and I gave our horses their heads and let them run, leaving our band of merchants behind. It was as if my heart took wings. Suddenly, the grinding monotony of the road fell away as we thundered down towards the city. Roupen was first to reach the gates, and had already dismounted by the time we arrived. We joined him as he remonstrated with the guards at the gate to let us in.

'Do you not know who it is that demands entrance?' he said, his voice tight with anger, his joy quickly quenched by the obstinate refusal of the gatemen to obey.

'It is Lord Roupen, son of Prince Leo,' offered Nurmal helpfully.

'No one is to enter or leave the city without the lord's leave,' the stolid guard replied; the two soldiers with him nodded and edged nearer.

'But that is absurd!' shouted Roupen. He made to force his way around the guards, who levelled their weapons threateningly.

'Wait!' I said, stepping quickly between Roupen and the gatemen. 'Something is amiss here,' I told him. 'It is useless arguing with them. See if they will agree to take a message to your father.'

Roupen was ill-disposed to take my advice, but saw the sense of it nonetheless. Turning to the porter, he snapped, 'Take a message to your master. Tell him that Lord Roupen waits outside the city walls and begs to be reunited with his family.'

This caused the guards some consternation. The chief among them put out a hand towards the one next to him. 'You heard,' he said, pushing the man away. 'Run!'

The soldier scurried off, disappearing into the gatehouse behind him. 'I beg your pardon, my lord,' the porter muttered. 'We did not know it was you.'

Roupen seemed inclined to take issue with the unhelpful fellow, but Nurmal intervened. 'Save your breath, my friend. The error is soon put right.'

The walls of Anazarbus were curved, as I say, and protected with squat towers along their length, and over the central gate. What is more, despite the peace and calm of the day, soldiers manned the towers and moved along the walls. Upon pointing this out to Nurmal, he replied, 'It was the first thing I noticed. I think they must be expecting someone – but not us.'

Roupen did not hear this, as he was pacing back and forth between us and the guards, growing more and more peevish over the lack of respect shown him. I decided it was best to ignore his ill humour, and sat down on a rock beside the road to wait for the others to join us. Nurmal took up a waterskin, drank, and passed the skin to me. 'It is warm, I fear, but until we get something better ...'

I drank, and then stood, took the skin and poured some into my hand and gave it to my mount. In this way, the thirsty animal finished the little left in the skin, and I was about to fetch some more when Roupen shouted. 'Look! My brothers!'

Out from the gatehouse strode two men – as unlike the young lord as beans from barley. Where he was slender and frail, they were well-muscled, brawny men; where he was long-limbed and languid, they were stocky, broad-shouldered, and vigorous. The only similarity between them that I could see was their thick black hair – a feature they shared with all Armenians.

At the sight of the young man they both shouted a greeting and Roupen ran to meet them. The soldiers, slightly embarrassed that the strict observance of their duty should have inconvenienced the royal household, shrank back, looking both repentant and stubborn as the glad reunion commenced in spite of their earlier efforts to prevent it.

The two men caught the younger and lifted him off his feet in fierce hugs, and pounded him on the back until he winced, all the while speaking in a tongue as rapid as it was unintelligible. They knocked the youth this way and that with the easy abuse of true brothers, and it put me in mind of how Eirik and I had behaved towards one another when we were younger.

Nurmal and I approached and waited to have our presence recognized. Presently, Roupen turned and grinning, said, 'My friends, I give you my brothers!' Indicating the elder of the two, he said, 'This is Thoros.' The man inclined his head politely. Pointing to the second one, he said, 'And this is Constantine.' The man bowed respectfully.

Roupen then introduced me, and explained quickly that if not for me, he would not be standing there now. 'Duncan saved my life,' he said, proudly, 'not once, but twice. He is a true friend.'

The elder brother, Thoros, stepped before me then and seized my hand in both of his. 'We are much indebted to you, sir. Tonight, in your honour, we will hold a feast to celebrate our brother's return.' I accepted his announcement with a modest bow, whereupon he turned at once to Nurmal.

'Here you are! Nurmal, my good friend. I should have known you would have something to do with this.'

'Not at all, my lord,' replied the horse-trader humbly. 'They would have reached Anazarbus on raw determination alone. I merely helped smooth the way a little.'

To me, Thoros said, 'Did you hear that? Never believe it! There is nothing that happens east of the Taurus that does not concern Nurmal of Mamistra.' He laughed then, but Nurmal did not share his patron's jest.

'You exaggerate, Thoros,' the horse-trader protested. 'But no matter. I am happy to serve however I can.'

The rest of our party reined up then, and introductions were made all around. Padraig was made much of; they had never seen a monk who was not dressed in heavy black robes, and refused to believe he was a priest. Yordanus and Sydoni also received especial regard, and I noticed that Thoros lingered over Sydoni's hand as he welcomed her and her father. Then, with good grace and simple sincerity, Thoros thanked everyone for taking care of his brother and helping return him to his home.

'God will honour your charity with the praises of angels,' he said, 'but the Noble House of Anazarbus will fill your pockets will gold!' So saying, he gathered everyone with a great swoop of his arms as if we were children. 'Come now, friends! Let us go in! The prince will want to know his lost son has returned at last.'

Once inside the thick city walls, we were conducted directly to the palace which stood a short distance across a small square directly inside the gates. The palace itself was built in the manner of a church and was flanked by two domed towers, each surmounted with golden crosses.

As we walked across the square, I observed that there were few people about. Nor did there seem to be much activity in the surrounding streets – a few children playing, an old woman carrying a basket of greens, and one or two men pushing carts, but not at all what I might have expected from a city the size of Anazarbus. I was not the only one to notice the absence of the local population. Nurmal, walking easily beside Thoros, said, 'Is everyone in hiding? Where have the people gone?'

'As it happens,' replied Thoros, 'we are under alert. Seljuq raiding parties have been seen in the hills, and it is feared that an attack is imminent.' The big man cast a hasty glance at me behind him. 'Do you mean to say you have seen no sign of them?'

'No, lord. Not so much as a single turban between here and Mamistra,' Nurmal told him.

'Well, they are out there. The scouts say the hills are crawling with them. You are lucky you did not run headlong into Amir Ghazi himself.'

'Ghazi, is it?' mused the horse-trader. 'Why is the old devil sniffing around here? Did you forget to pay your tribute?'

Thoros laughed heartily, and said, 'We have had other things on our minds lately.'

They continued talking in this way, but my attention shifted to what Constantine and Roupen were saying behind me. 'What is the matter with him?' Roupen asked; although he spoke softly, I caught the concern in his tone.

'He is not well,' his brother replied. 'The physicians have done what they can, but no one knows what ails him.'

'How long?'

'Four months,' answered Constantine. 'Maybe a little longer. There is not much hope any more – still, he lingers. The old warrior fights on.' The young man paused, then added, 'He will be glad to know that you are home at last. What happened to everyone else?'

'We were stricken with ague the moment we set foot in Frankland. I escaped, but fever took all the rest.'

'It bodes fair to take the prince as well,' observed Constantine gloomily.

Thus, I pieced together what had caused the closure of the royal city: Prince Leo was gravely ill, and the tribute paid to the Muhammedans had been allowed to lapse. Consequently, their Seljuq overlords were angry; those who should have been their allies and protectors were massing in the hills, gathering the necessary strength to attack. And the Armenians, soon to be forcibly reminded why they paid the tribute in the first place, were about to receive the unhappy news that Bohemond II's army was on its way.

Although not as large or as opulent as the citadel at Antioch, the palace of the Armenian princes was grand without being extravagant. While they obviously shared the same lofty ambitions of all noble families, they at least showed some restraint in the furnishing of the royal residence. Or perhaps their means were not as extensive as some. Then again, they may have had better things to do with their wealth than spend it on over-lavish possessions. Be that as it may, I found the simplicity of my surroundings refreshing.

The walls of the chamber Padraig and I were to share, for example, were painted the deep ruby colour of red wine below a ceiling of dark blue in which small golden discs had been affixed. No trouble had been taken to hide the rooftrees above; indeed, these were painted green. When I lay down that night by candlelight it was as if I looked up through the clustered boughs of a forest into the night sky agleam with stars.

But that was yet to come. For, no sooner were we conducted to our room, than the prince's chamberlain appeared to inform us that Lord Thoros was awaiting us in his receiving chamber. We splashed water on our faces and brushed the dust of the road from our hair and clothes, and then followed the servant. 'You must tell him about Bohemond's attack as soon as possible,' Padraig reminded me. 'They will need time to prepare.'

'Of course,' I agreed.

'At once,' the monk insisted.

'I will, I will.'

We were led through the inner corridors of the palace to a cozy reception chamber somewhere behind the main hall. Thoros was there alone, standing at a table mixing wine with water.

'Come in! Come in!' cried Thoros, pouring the wine into two large gold-rimmed silver bowls. 'I thought a drink might ease the fatigue of the journey,' he said, raising a bowl in each of his hands and extending them to Padraig and myself. After observing the proper greeting and welcome rituals – which he conducted in the Armenian tongue – he invited us to sit with him.

'With pleasure, my lord,' I replied. 'I wanted a word with you before the feast.'

As we stepped into the room, Nurmal appeared behind us. 'Sit with us, my friend! We were just about to share the welcome cup.'

'Nothing would delight me more, my friend,' replied Nurmal, his white moustache bristling with delight. 'It has been far too long since we sat together.'

'Not long enough for me to forget that I owe you a great deal of money,' replied Thoros. He shook his head ruefully. 'I do not need to tell you it has been very difficult here these last two years.' Sorrow dragged down the corners of his mouth as he gazed forlornly into the cup between his huge hands. 'The harvest . . . trade . . .'

'Nonsense!' scoffed Nurmal good-naturedly. 'You have had fine harvests – nay, bounteous harvests! Magnificent harvests! – three years running. And trade has never been better. The coffers of Armenia are bursting!'

Caught in his small lie, Thoros made a shamefaced grin and looked at me from under his heavy brows. 'You see? I told you nothing happened east of the Taurus he does not know.'

'I did not come here to embarrass you into paying me,' Nurmal told him. 'Yet, if it would ease your conscience to lighten the load, I would of course accept any amount you would care to bestow in recognition of our long-forgotten bargain.'

'Ha!' cried Thoros, slapping the table with his hand. 'You are a fine fellow, Nurmal. So I have always said. Never fear, you will not leave Anazarbus empty-handed.'

Lord Thoros, I decided, was like a great shaggy bear, at once fierce and childlike. There was nothing of subtlety or guile in his open features or wide dark eyes. His loyalties could be easily discerned by the expression on his face.

'Yordanus Hippolytus appeared at my door in the company of these good men,' Nurmal volunteered. 'He said he had urgent business in Anazarbus and required horses for himself and his friends. Once I discovered why he needed my horses, what else could I do but see them safely to their destination?'

'Protecting your investment,' said Thoros, wagging his finger knowingly. 'I know you.'

'I will not deny it,' said Nurmal. 'But there is more.' Setting aside his bowl, he looked to me. 'Tell him, Duncan,' he said, his voice taking on a solemn tone.

Thoros sipped his wine and regarded Padraig and me benignly. 'Yes, whatever you have to say, tell it to Thoros. I am in a mood to hear the news of the world.'

I needed no urging from Padraig, silent or otherwise, to speak the message we had all travelled so far and at such great expense to deliver. 'My lord, the news I bring is not good,' I began, and went on to describe how I had learned of Prince Bohemond's desire to restore the County of Antioch to the boundaries established by his father. 'He is on his way here now with his army,' I concluded, 'and means to take the city.'

Thoros received the news remarkably well. 'I know this already,' Thoros said blithely, pouring more wine into the bowls. 'Roupen has told me. Of course, he is known of times to become somewhat . . . overwrought, shall we say? I am happy to have you confirm that this is not the case.' He smiled as if to dismiss the report as an ill-founded and fairly disreputable rumour.

'It is a fact,' Padraig said, speaking up. 'Lord Duncan and I heard it from the lips of Bohemond himself. We called upon him to repent of his plan before God.'

The priest's assertion seemed to impress Thoros, who inquired how this had come to be, so I explained about meeting the Templar Renaud, and how he had given Roupen, Padraig, and myself passage aboard his ship. 'Commander Renaud told me about the prince's plan – although it was by no means a secret. Bohemond had been raising troops for this purpose all summer.'

'But he would not listen to you,' Thoros suggested with a sympathetic shake of the head. 'They rarely do, these Franks.' If these tidings, for which we had endured considerable hardship, caused him the least concern, he hid his distress admirably well.

'We failed to persuade him and had to flee Antioch,' I told him. 'We came here as quickly as we could to warn you. I expect Bohemond wasted no time in gathering his troops. It is entirely possible that he is only a few days' march from here even now.'

Nurmal nodded gravely. Padraig frowned, gazing at the serenely untroubled nobleman as if at a riddle that might be solved by staring long and hard. 'Lord Roupen will no doubt confirm all we have told,' the monk said, watching our host for any sign of dismay or alarm.

Thoros nodded sympathetically. 'You have risked your lives to help my brother and bring this warning to us. For this you shall be rewarded. What is more, I shall order prayers to be sung in your honour tonight.'

'My lord is too kind,' I replied, fighting down a sudden and overwhelming feeling of foolishness. 'We did not come here in anticipation of any reward,' I told him stiffly. 'Indeed, we will be more than satisfied to continue on our way as soon as possible.'

'I will not hear of it,' replied Thoros amiably. 'You have travelled a very great distance. You must rest and take your ease. Allow us to show you the generosity of the noble Armenian race.' He put aside the bowl and rose. 'Please, remain here and refresh yourselves as long as you like. Tonight you will sit with me at the feast. Speaking of which, I have remembered something I must do. I ask you to excuse me.' He bade us farewell, and strolled from the room.

'You should feel proud,' said Nurmal. 'You have done well. The Armenians are a generous people, and will certainly reward you handsomely.'

'We have done only what anyone might do,' I replied, still struggling to shake the feeling that, for all his thanks and praise, Thoros cared more about his wine than the calamity looming over his city. The fate of his people swung in the balance, and his concern was arranging feasts. Moments ago, my chief desire was to see Bohemond and the rulers of Armenia reconciled, and for peace to reign between the two houses. Now, I could think only of leaving the doomed city of Anazarbus before the upstart Bohemond arrived and reduced it to smouldering bricks and ash.

TWENTY-NINE

Padraig and I returned to our room. I was tired, and wanted to rest before the festivities began. I lay down and slept soundly until I was roused by a servant sent by Roupen with fresh clothes for us to wear for the evening's celebration. The young fellow did not speak Latin, but indicated that we were to take the clothes and give him our old ones to be, I thought, cleaned and mended.

By the time we had worked this out and washed and dressed, Roupen was waiting to escort us to the banqueting hall. 'I suppose you will be leaving soon,' he said as we walked across the inner courtyard.

Owing to the nearness of the mountains – whose sun-flamed peaks could be seen rising above the palace roof – the evening air was cool; the play of light and air put me in mind of a summer night at home in Caithness. Before the memory could result in melancholy, I pushed it firmly from me and reminded myself of my vow – now long deferred. 'As soon as may be,' I replied. I no longer cared about anything but returning to the pilgrim trail, and resuming my abandoned quest. 'Tomorrow.'

'You must allow my family to honour you sufficiently,' chided Roupen. 'After all, you two saved the prodigal son and have proven yourselves allies of the Armenian kingdom. It would be ungracious to refuse the homage of my people.'

'I meant no disrespect. I only thought –'

'Peace, my friend,' Roupen replied lightly; I had never seen him so calm and self-composed. 'I spoke in jest. Of course, you will be allowed to leave whenever you like. But let us speak of all that later. Tonight, by Prince Leo's decree, you are to be lauded and praised in the ancient manner.'

'How is your father?' asked Padraig. 'Have you seen him?'

'He is very ill,' Roupen answered. 'But my return has cheered him greatly, and he asked to see me as soon as they told him I was home. Although we talked only for a moment, my mother says he looked in better health than she has seen him for many weeks. The royal physicians are hopeful that he is showing signs of recovery.'

'Good. I am happy to hear it.'

'God willing, my father will be able to thank you himself before you both rush away.'

'We told Thoros about Bohemond's plan to attack Anazarbus,' I said. 'He appeared to take the prospect with astonishing tranquillity. I do not think I could be so placid in the face of the impending destruction of my home and people.'

'That is his way,' Roupen replied. 'Thoros rarely reveals his true disposition to anyone. No one ever knows what he is thinking.'

We reached the entrance to the feast hall then; the doors were flung wide and we were met by the royal steward who bowed low and, in a loud voice, announced to the assembled guests and family members that Lord Roupen and his friends had arrived. We paused to receive the adulation of the gathering, and were then led through the noisy throng, our ears ringing with enthusiastic shouts. Many of the courtiers reached out to clap us on the back; my arms and shoulders were joyfully slapped and pummelled until the flesh stung and I feared my bones would crack.

Padraig and I were brought to the high banquet table where a combed, shaved, and freshly arrayed Yordanus was talking to an ill-at-ease Constantine; Sydoni, immaculate in a thin summer gown of shimmering green silk, was listening to a grey-haired woman with sad dark eyes. At our approach, the older woman held out her arms to Roupen, who kissed and embraced her, and then declared, 'Lord Duncan, Brother Padraig, I present my mother, Princess Elena.'

I bowed dutifully. She offered her hand, and I kissed it. Padraig likewise, whereupon she said, 'Words do not exist to express a mother's gratitude for the return of her lost son.' Her Latin was very formal, and slightly stilted. 'Yet, perhaps you will allow this token to adorn the hair of a lady you love, that when you see it, you will be reminded of one whose prayers you helped to answer.'

So saying, she reached behind and retrieved from the table two small wooden boxes. She gave one to Padraig, and placed the other in my hand and bade me to open it. Inside was a brooch and pin of gold; the brooch was made of a single large blood-red ruby surrounded by a ring of tiny blue sapphires which glittered with frozen starlight. The ruby was carved with a curious symbol – what appeared to be an orb borne between the wings of an eagle; the orb was surmounted by the Greek letter *chi*, forming a cross in the shape of an X.

Padraig had received a band of gold, the ends of which were shaped like two bird's heads – storks, or swans, I think – and between their beaks they clutched a glowing emerald. For size and lustre, the gems were the largest and most brilliant I had ever seen.

'My mother gave these to me, and I wore them on my wedding day. I do not know if priests in your homeland are allowed to marry – I am told that some do not. But I hope you will keep these gifts for the woman who bears you a son as kind and loving as my Roupen.'

'Nothing would give me greater pleasure, my lady,' Padraig said, and thanked her with a blessing in Gaelic.

'And you, Lord Duncan,' she said, tapping the box in my hand with her finger. 'Do you have a wife?'

'Alas, no Lady Elena,' I answered simply. I did not care to disturb the memory of your blessed mother, Cait. 'One day, perhaps, God willing.'

Sydoni, standing behind Princess Elena, caught my glance as I said this; her look of frank appraisal was disconcerting in its intensity.

'Then I will pray the woman you choose will wear it always in love and happiness,' Elena said. Pointing to the symbol carved on the ruby, she said, 'It is the seal of the Royal House of Armenia, our emblem for a thousand years.'

'Your gift is overwhelming, and I thank you, but it is too much,' I demurred, withdrawing from Sydoni's glance with more difficulty than I would have imagined possible. 'I merely accompanied your son along his way.'

The noble woman's expression became condescending. 'Come now, false modesty is as unbecoming as arrogance. Roupen has told me how you twice saved his life, and have been his guardian angel every step of the way.'

I saw that it would do no good to protest further, so I bowed again and, with burning cheeks, accepted my gift as graciously as I could. To my relief, a serving-boy arrived bearing a silver tray with wine in small glass beakers. Constantine took the tray and distributed the cups to our little gathering. Taking up one himself, he said, 'Let us drink to safe journeys and glad homecomings.'

We raised our cups and drank. The wine was sweet and good, and as we drank and talked, I felt myself begin to grow more easy in my manner. Every now and then, one of the other guests would come to the high table to be introduced to Padraig and me and make our acquaintance. Most often, Roupen did the honours; when a name or face failed him, Constantine or Lady Elena obliged. At first, I tried to remember all the names and faces, but there were too many, and not only did they all look alike to me, they seemed to be related to one another in extremely complicated ways so that after awhile it was impossible to tell one from the other.

More people were coming into the hall, and the sound of the crowd soon made speech all but impossible. So, I stood uneasily beside Roupen and his mother, holding my cup and gazing out upon the milling throng. Just when I thought the hall could hold no more, the doors were closed – which made the sound inside even more deafening.

There was a movement in the crowd, and Thoros suddenly appeared, pushing his way through; Nurmal followed in his wake. They proceeded directly to the high table, and greeted the Princess and other members of the royal party waiting there. As they moved from person to person, I noticed that both men were already well into the celebratory spirit. They laughed loudly, kissing everyone and clapping them on the back, their gestures grandiose and exaggerated. In short, they looked for all the world like men who have just won a fortune on a wager, or sailors with silver in their fists who have come into port after a long sea voyage.

I was not the only one to observe their ebullient behaviour. 'The roisterers emerge from their cups at last,' remarked Constantine; he leaned close and all but shouted in my ear. 'Now the festivity can begin for the rest of us.'

This might easily have been the case – too much drink in over-eager celebration makes a man giddy, God knows – and I might have agreed: except for the fact that Padraig and I had been with them before the feast and knew that the drinking had been curtailed. Nurmal, like myself, had returned to his room, and

Thoros had quit the hall before us. Certainly, the two might have met again and resumed their drinking, but I doubted this. The dull sense of dread spreading through me – like dark wine tinting clear water – told me the explanation was never so benign.

Thoros took his seat at the high table, indicating that I should sit at his right hand, and Padraig at his left. Nurmal sat beside me, and the other members of the royal party assumed their places around the board and, the instant they were seated, the entire hall convulsed in a tumultuous commotion as the guests scrambled for places at the other tables. There were far more people than places, and many were forced to stand around the perimeter of the great room looking on, and awaiting their chance to claim a place when someone else finished.

As soon as the hall quieted, an old man dressed in long black robes advanced slowly to the high table and, in a loud voice, called the gathering to prayer. Clasping his hands, he raised them before his face and, in ornately antique Greek, proceeded to entreat the Almighty to bless the realm and the faithful of his flock. My Greek is not so good as my Latin, as I say, but I caught most of it. He prayed for the souls of all gathered within the hall, and prayed for the continuance of divine guidance and protection. He prayed long, often wandering from Greek into the obscure Armenian tongue. When he finished, the doors of the hall were once again thrown open and serving-men appeared bearing platters of food.

The first platters were placed on the high table – huge joints of roast oxen and boar – and instantly the aroma brought the water to my mouth and made me realize how hungry I was. Thoros, acting as Lord of the Feast, thrust his hand into the mounded victuals before him and wrested a gobbet from the mass. 'Eat!' he called expansively. 'Eat, everyone, eat. Enjoy!'

Each hungry guest reached for what was before him, and soon the juices were running down our chins and hands as we devoured the succulent meat. My cup filled itself mysteriously, and bread likewise materialized in my hands. I took no notice of who or what caused this to happen, giving myself entirely to the food, which was excellent in every way.

Indeed, I was so preoccupied, that I did not at first mark the appearance of the black-robed man at Thoros' shoulder. I slowly became aware of the fact that he was speaking earnestly, his demeanour grave and sober – in sharp contrast to the red-faced laughing man seated beneath him. He loomed over Thoros, a dark and threatening eminence, breathing gloom with every word.

I watched as all signs of mirth slowly drained from Lord Thoros' face to be replaced by an expression so wretched and doleful as to stop the laughter in the mouths of all who beheld him. One by one, those at the high table also became aware of the swift alteration in Thoros' jovial mood, and the table fell silent.

'Whatever is the matter with you?' asked Constantine, his voice loud in the sudden hush.

Thoros looked at his brother, and then swung his eyes to his mother, seated beside him. He placed his hands flat on the table and pushed himself upright with, it seemed to me, an enormous effort. He stood there, towering over the feast and, in a deep, hollow voice announced, 'Patriarch Baramistos has just informed me that my father, Prince Leo, is dead.'

THIRTY

Prince Leo's death immediately plunged all the members of the royal family into a multitude of tedious and time-consuming rituals and formalities. The foreign visitors were quickly forgotten; Padraig and I gladly fended for ourselves lest we become a burden to our hosts in their time of distress. Anxious as I was to depart, I would gladly have left the city right then and there, but, in deference to Roupen's feelings, could not bring myself to just sneak away like a thief in the night. Thus, as we had nothing else to do, we took the opportunity to wander around the streets of Anazarbus and see for ourselves how the passing of the noble ruler was marked by the populace.

What I saw was a city sunk in grief over the loss of their much-loved prince. Apparently, Leo had governed his people wisely and well for many years, and the Armenians were genuinely sorry he was gone. Everywhere men and women went about their chores with the mournful countenances of the truly sorrowful, speaking in pensive tones. Scores of small shrines sprang up in the streets – here a painting of the prince, there a carving, or perhaps simply a coin on which Leo's image had been stamped – and each adorned with a palm frond or bit of green foliage, and a candle or lamp. Whenever anyone passed one of these makeshift shrines, he made the sign of the cross on his forehead.

Many of the older men and women wore ashes in their hair, and on their garments; some donned sacking cloth as well. Everyone observed the great prince's passing in a seemly way, and even the younger folk adopted a dutifully subdued and melancholy air.

If ever an entire city grieved, Anazarbus was that place.

The prince himself lay in a gilded casket in the Church of Saint George and Saint Nicholas, the principle church of the city, serving as the cathedral for the Armenian observance. A large, but not imposing building of red stone, it was spare and plain, without much in the way of fussy adornment – much like the chapels the Célé Dé build.

All morning long, Padraig and I strolled about the city, marvelling at the long lines of mourners snaking across the square and into the surrounding streets as the people streamed in and out of the church where Leo's body lay. Every now and then, one of the grieving throng would suddenly throw his hands towards heaven, and let out a heartfelt, wailing cry. Otherwise, the crowds were quiet and respectful.

The monk was keenly fascinated to see how the Armenians conducted their religious services, and was enthralled by the endless ritual. For myself, however, the sorrowing crowds and religious feeling seemed wrong, or at least inappropriate for a city and nation teetering on the precipice of war.

Immersed in mourning, Thoros appeared to have given no further thought to either the Seljuqs lurking in the hills, nor the looming danger of attack by Bohemond and his knights. The beloved Prince Leo's death swept all else aside. Certainly, beyond the posting of a few more soldiers on the walls, there was no other preparation that I could see.

This amazed and troubled me greatly. Why had we risked life and limb to bring a warning that was to remain unheeded? If the rulers of Armenia did not care about their city and the lives of their people, why should we?

Disturbed and distraught, I turned from the gate and started back to the palace, resolved to wait no longer: we would leave at once. I reached the palace forecourt just in time to witness the arrival of a sizeable contingent of Seljuqs. I watched from the inner palace yard as the Turks were conducted with great ceremony into the hall, which had been hastily prepared to receive mourners. Prince Leo's funeral was to begin at dusk and the various services, rituals, and observances would continue through the night, culminating with the burial which would take place at dawn the next morning.

I stood in the shadows and watched as the Seljuq emissaries were met by a delegation of Armenian nobles, and immediately led into the hall where Thoros, his mother, and other members of the royal family were holding court. The extreme civility of their welcome did

256

astonish me, and I must have worn my amazement on my face, for Nurmal, enjoying the fresh air and quiet of the pleasant courtyard, approached, took one look at me, and said, 'What, and have you never seen a Seljuq before?'

'Never,' I replied. 'In truth, I cannot decide which I find the more incredible – that they should wish to honour the prince in this way, or that an avowed enemy should be allowed inside the walls to pay their respects to the mourning family.'

Nurmal chuckled. 'I do not know what it is like in your country, my friend, but here our hostilities are not carved in stone. Our enmities are more fluid – like streams in the desert, continually shifting and changing. The enemy you meet today might be the friend you call upon tomorrow. You must remember that.'

He was speaking a simple truth of the East, and one I had not yet fully grasped. Even so, I heard in the words a foreboding that chilled me to the marrow. I thought: *If enmities are so loosely held, then loyalties are likewise inconstant.*

'Only yesterday, the city was in a state of alarm lest the dreaded Seljuq attack at any moment,' I pointed out.

'True,' Nurmal agreed cheerfully. 'But that was then. Things have changed. What hope would there be for anyone if nothing ever changed?'

With Nurmal's words rolling around in my head, I hurried off to find Yordanus and Sydoni, neither one of whom had I seen since the banquet the night before. I went to the small dining chamber where Thoros had served us wine before the banquet and there found Roupen with his brother Constantine.

They were speaking so earnestly to one another that I thought it best not to intrude. Nevertheless, I could not help overhearing. '– a very dangerous business,' Constantine was saying. 'Even Thoros must see that. If he does not, he is not fit to rule in father's place. I swear to you –'

I came into Roupen's view just then and they ceased their conversation at once – almost guiltily, as it seemed to me. 'My friend,' called Roupen, 'you must forgive us for neglecting you. The demands of royalty are especially onerous at times like this.'

'I understand completely,' I replied, assuring them there was no need to trouble themselves on my account. They hesitated then, anxious to conclude their conversation, so I said, 'Please excuse me, I am looking for Yordanus.'

'We have not seen him,' replied Constantine bluntly. 'No doubt he is still in his chamber.'

'Come to the hall at midday,' Roupen suggested with a tight smile, 'and you will be included in the royal party. I will look for you then.'

I thanked them and moved off, aware of Constantine's pent-up fury. Although it was none of my affair, I could not help wondering what lay behind his agitation. Putting it out of my mind, I found my way to the wing of the palace where Yordanus and Sydoni had been given rooms. The old trader was sitting in a chair, gazing out the open window over the rooftops of the low buildings surrounding the palace.

I greeted him and, not wishing to waste time, explained my deep misgivings over the utter lack of preparation to meet Bohemond's army. I told him that Padraig and I were leaving Anazarbus and, in light of the fact that the city was largely undefended against the imminent attack, suggested that he and his daughter should seriously consider doing the same. 'Of course,' I said, 'we will be happy to escort you and Sydoni to Mamistra.'

He nodded gravely. 'When?'

'As soon as I can arrange horses and provisions – no later than midday.'

'Go then. I will tell Sydoni.'

'Come to the stables as soon as you are ready.'

Next, I hastened to speak to the hostlers about making ready five of Nurmal's horses. I had it in mind that, if Nurmal was agreeable, we might return the horses to Mamistra for him. If need be, I would buy them; the brooch Princess Elena had given me would no doubt purchase a half dozen of his best.

On the way, I found Padraig and told him to hurry and secure enough provisions to see us on our way. 'Get Roupen to help you. He owes us that much, I guess.' So saying, I continued on to the stables, but could find no one who spoke Latin, and with my poor Greek, it took longer than I had hoped to make them understand what I wanted.

I succeeded at last, and then rushed back to the palace to gather my things and take leave of Roupen. Nurmal was in his chamber across the corridor from ours; he was lying on his bed, resting before the evening's ceremonies. I quickly told him my plan, and begged the use of his horses to return to Mamistra. 'Of course, my friend,' he said. 'It was always understood that we would return sooner or later. Go, and with my blessing. But,' he added, 'if you do not mind my asking, why are you in such a hurry? Half the day is almost gone, and you cannot get far before nightfall. Why not wait until tomorrow? Better still, stay a few more days and we will all return together.'

'There is a battle coming, whether anyone in Anazarbus believes it or cares.' I told him I wanted no part of it, that greedy Prince Bohemond's boundary squabble was none of my affair. So far as I was concerned, I had done my duty by Roupen and his people; now it was for them to do what they would. As for myself and Padraig, we would wait no longer; we were leaving the city at once.

Nurmal regarded me with an amused expression. 'There is no hurry, my friend,' he said. 'We can leave whenever we wish.'

'Bohemond and his army could be here at any moment,' I snapped, unable to keep the growing frustration out of my voice. 'He is coming with hundreds of mounted knights and a few thousand footmen. I have no wish to be trapped in a city under siege, much less help defend one.'

'Calm yourself,' Nurmal said. 'Bohemond will never even see the city walls.'

The way he said it – with such careless confidence – sent a warning tingle through me. I stared at him. 'Why? What do you know of this?'

'Amir Ghazi will deal with them,' he said, pushing himself up on an elbow, 'and he has many thousand warriors – all of them mounted, all of them eager to die for the glory of Islam and a martyr's paradise.'

I stared at him, trying to make sense of what he was saying. 'The Seljuqs? Why would they intervene?'

'We have a saying,' Nurmal replied easily. 'My enemy's enemy is my friend. Thoros understands this better than most. He owes Amir Ghazi a very great sum of money. How better to repay his heavy debt than to offer Ghazi the particular honour of, shall we say, delivering Prince Bohemond and his men into Seljuq hands?' He smiled placidly. 'It is a perfect solution: Anazarbus is spared, the invader is defeated, and Ghazi receives the irresistible opportunity to recapture Antioch. Harmony and balance is restored.'

'But this is monstrous!' I protested, stunned by the duplicity of the bargain.

The canny horse-trader shook his head. 'No, it is simple expedience, my friend.'

'If I had imagined such deceit, I would never have left Antioch,' I declared, shaking with fury. 'This is intolerable! Unthinkable! It must be stopped.'

Nurmal frowned with benign pity. 'Peace, Duncan. You will do yourself an injury.' He rose from the bed, and put his hands on my shoulders in a gesture of fatherly advice. 'While I admire your sense of honour, I do not understand your scruples. Why did you come here?'

I did not understand what he was asking. 'You know as well as anyone why we came here.'

'You came to warn the Armenians of Bohemond's attack,' Nurmal said. 'Is this not so?'

'Yes, but –'

'What did you think would happen?'

'I did not think . . .' I began, and faltered, realizing how I had been used. 'My warning has been turned to treachery. I have been made a traitor!'

'Why speak of treachery?' Nurmal demanded, beginning to lose patience with me. 'Where is the betrayal? Where is the treason? Listen to me, my friend. There is no betrayal; there is only fate, and the capricious accidents of war. You learned of the coming attack and flew to prevent a slaughter –'

'Yes! For the love of God, I only thought to prevent it.'

'Well, you have succeeded. It is prevented. Amir Ghazi will see to that, never fear.'

'The slaughter is not prevented;' I growled, my spirit writhing with guilt, 'it is merely diverted.'

Futility and shame descended in heavy waves upon me. I turned on my heel and fled the room. He called after me, but I made no reply. I quickly retrieved my belongings; there was nothing much to gather – my clothes had been taken away for cleaning, and had not been returned.

Very well, I would escape in what I was wearing, I decided, and leave all else behind. I had half a mind to leave the jewelled bauble Princess Elena had given me – I wanted nothing from the Armenians. But practicality got the better of that decision; we would need money if we were to reach Antioch in good time, and the brooch was very valuable. So, I took it from its box, and pinned it to the inside of my mantle next to my skin where it would be safe.

Padraig was waiting with Roupen in the stables. The young lord was unhappy to see us leaving with such unseemly haste. 'I wish it could be otherwise,' I told him. He asked me to reconsider, but I declined. Seeing there was no changing my mind, he gave in with good grace and told me how much he valued our friendship, and that he would pray we concluded our pilgrimage safely.

Yordanus and Sydoni appeared in the doorway then, and Roupen went to bid them farewell and to thank them for their inestimable help in getting him home in time to see his father before he died. While they talked, Padraig and I examined the horses and the packs of provisions; satisfied that all was in order, we led the beasts out into the yard, and bade Roupen a last farewell.

We rode through the gates and out onto the road by which we had come, leaving Anazarbus behind. The sun was high onto midday; the weather was fine and bright, and hot, and we made fair speed with Nurmal's splendid horses. I had chosen the same mounts we had ridden before so they would know us: the speckled grey for me, the roan for Padraig, and the two chestnut mares for Sydoni and Yordanus.

When the city was no longer in sight, we paused briefly for water, and then rode on, at a slightly less frantic pace. Once in the saddle again, I felt slightly less apprehensive. Whatever happened, I thought, it was no longer any of my concern. I had done what I could, and my help had been twisted and perverted in its use. I desired no part of anything so nefarious, and was heartily glad not to have to stay another night in that haven of treachery.

Now, at this remove, Cait, I can but marvel at the innocence of my thoughts and emotions on that day. Nurmal spoke the cold heart of the matter, and he spoke the truth. Bohemond had chosen his course; long before he reached Anazarbus, he had committed his life and the lives of his men to his witless plan.

Why did I imagine anything I might do or say could have changed anything? Did I really think I could sway the balance of heavenly justice?

Who was I, after all, but an ignorant meddler in matters too far above me to even contemplate? How in the name of all that is holy did I hope to prevent that arrogant young prince reaping the harvest of his insatiable ambition?

And why, oh why, did I even try?

The answer, I think, is that I could not in good conscience abide the thought of Christians making war on their Christian brothers, of believers pursuing the hateful waste of God's precious gift of life for the most frivolous and imbecilic of reasons. Blind and arbitrary fortune had placed me in a position to know certain things – the movements of armies, the intentions of rulers – and I had somehow concocted the belief that this knowledge brought with it an obligation to use it wisely and for good.

This is emotion, as I say, not reason. If I had stopped, even for a moment, and reflected on the matter, I would have seen grim futility looming starkly before me. If only I had asked myself one simple question: what did I want?

Now, after endless months of sober reflection, I have come to the conclusion that what I wanted was simply for everyone to sit down across the table and work out their differences in a sane and sensible manner. I believed that fellow Christians, Frank and Armenian, could be united against the common Seljuq enemy. In short, I wanted peace to prevail, and saw no just reason why it should not. I believed that one man of good will could make a difference and that God would honour those who strove to honour him.

In the madness that passes for sanity in the East, this belief was pure delusion. An infinitely sadder and wiser man understands that now.

On that fateful day, however, I raced from the city, eager to distance myself from the insidious deceit of the place and for Padraig and me to resume our pilgrimage. I pressed a swift pace along the rough, uneven road, my heart burning within me, wishing I had never heard of Ghazi, Thoros, or Bohemond.

These thoughts were still in my mind a little while later when, as we crested a steep hill, I saw the land fall away and spread out beneath us in a steeply-angled plain. The plain was a rolling, rock-and-thorn thicket wilderness between the rough foothills of the mountains to the north, and the raised cliffs of a deep-chasmed dry river to the south.

Even as I took this in, I pulled on the reins to halt. For there, where the road passed through the centre of the plain, I saw the sprawling mass of what remained of proud Bohemond's army.

THIRTY-ONE

'Christ have mercy,' Sydoni gasped. Padraig began praying aloud in Gaelic, and Yordanus croaked an incoherent oath.

Across the valley far below, a small brave knot of crusaders were yet fighting for their lives. All but lost amidst the swirling, howling Seljuqs, the Christian commanders were desperately trying to form the battle line. The few mounted knights had grouped themselves into a wedge-shaped complement in the vain hope of blunting the attack – a hopeless attempt, like trying to divide a sea wave with the edge of an oar.

Every time the crusaders made to engage the enemy, the swift Seljuqs melted away, only to assail the exposed flanks. When the crusaders turned to protect the flanks, the Arabs drove in upon them from the front. Indeed, the ceaseless swirling and diving looked like restless waves, and the clash of battle sounded like a distant storm far out on the ocean.

The flat floor of the valley formed a narrow plain between the deeply-eroded ravine of a dry riverbed to the west, and ragged, barren hills to the east. Along this plain, the rest of Bohemond's army lay scattered, fallen, still. From the long, spreading swathe of corpses, I could tell that they had marched up through the valley and into the ambush Ghazi had prepared for them. Pinched between the ravine on one side, and the hills on the other, the hapless crusaders had been cut down as they tried to flee back the way they had come.

Not that there could have been any escape. The barren slopes were covered with mounted Seljuqs from one end of the valley to the other. Some in dark turbans, and some in white, red, yellow, or brown so that they seemed a strangely-mottled sea, they surged onto the plain in a great inundating flood. My heart writhed within me to see the last of the poor doomed Franks throwing down their weapons to lend speed to their flight as the merciless Seljuqs swooped to the kill. I could smell the rich, fetid scent of blood on the breeze.

Once, as a boy, I stood on a rock above one of my father's barley fields and watched the low black clouds of a sudden summer storm sweep across the land. The wind struck first, flattening the tall grain with breathtaking violence. And then, before the golden stalks could rise from beneath the initial onslaught, fierce, wind-driven rain and ripping hail drove the overpowered grain into the ground and battered it to shreds.

What I had witnessed as a boy, I saw again now, and a more terrible harvest could not be imagined. Even from the safe distance of the hilltop, I could see the fearsome gleam of the awful Arab swords as they slashed and slashed and slashed again, like fearful hail falling from on high to pound Bohemond's army into the ground, never to rise again.

Remorse, futility, and anger struggled within me; I did not want to see the final slaughter. 'Come,' I said, wheeling my horse and moving back up the slope.

As I turned from the sight, I caught the glint of gold on the edge of my vision, looked, and saw Bohemond's golden banner gleaming in the hard midday light. And then it was gone. It simply vanished – a fragile light swallowed by the dark-turbaned sea raging all around it. There was but a momentary ripple in the tide, the treacherous flood eddied and swirled, overcame, and then flowed swiftly on.

But wait, suddenly the banner appeared again, streaking across the plain – in the hands of a Seljuq warrior, this time. The enemy rider sped away with the prize, waving it on high, and screaming like the very devil. We could hear him from the hilltop; and long after, his shouts still echoed in my ears.

As we left the killing ground behind us, I raised my eyes towards heaven and prayed for the souls of those poor ignorant soldiers led blindly to the slaughter by the unfettered ambition of their overweening lord. I asked the Great Judge not to hold the stupidity and greed of their leaders against them. 'Demonstrate your immeasurable mercy, Blessed Redeemer,' I prayed, 'and give these unfortunates places in Paradise – if not in Heaven's highest halls, then in the surrounding tents at least.'

We left the battlefield behind and, after a short ride, halted to decide what to do. It seemed to me that our best passage lay on the far side of the dry river, well away from the battlefield. It would take us far out of our way, but keep us well out of sight. Once beyond the battleground, we could rejoin the road and continue on. Padraig and Yordanus agreed.

'There are goat tracks all through these hills,' Yordanus said. 'If we keep the river between us and the valley, we will soon be well away from the fighting.'

Accordingly, I chose a goat track that ran along the back side of the hill, out of sight of the conflict, and led the way; Sydoni came next, then Yordanus, and Padraig last, leading the pack horse. We followed the path a goodly way; when it branched off, I took the new one, always keeping the line of shielding hills to my right.

At one point, the track descended towards the dry riverbed, turning in its descent and passing between two broad outcroppings of broken stone. Much rock had fallen onto the narrow trail from the steep banks on either side, thus making the pass very difficult. It took us some time to pick our way through the jagged stones, and when at last we emerged out onto the dry bed of the river, we paused for a short rest and a drink.

We dismounted in the shade of the overhanging rocks, and Padraig fetched a waterskin from the pack horse, and we passed it among us, each taking a mouthful or two. It was cooler in the shade, and it was a shame to move on, but we had a long way to go to rejoin the road, and wanted to be well away from the battlefield by nightfall.

So, we climbed into our saddles and moved on. The dry stream bed was flat and wide, and sufficiently low to allow us to ride without being seen from the hills where the battle was taking place. I pointed this out to Yordanus, who also thought this would be an easier way to go – at least for a short distance – for, although rocky along the slopes leading to the banks rising steep on either side, at its narrowest the bed was fine sand and still wide enough for two to ride abreast. Sydoni came up beside me as we rode along, and we soon fell into conversation.

We talked about trifling things, nothing of any significance or substance. I think she just wanted to put the massacre out of her mind, and I was happy to oblige. Truth be told, I enjoyed

Sydoni's company; on those few occasions she chose to share it with me, I soon found myself profoundly engrossed. Sydoni's way of expressing herself was unique and, I thought, refreshing. I decided it was her Coptic blood, and her upbringing in Damascus among Muhammedans that made her unlike anyone I had ever known.

Be that as it may, I was paying more attention to her than to the track ahead. 'Peacocks are my favourite,' she was saying, 'especially when they fly. Their tails are so long and graceful. People eat them in Damascus, but I think they are too beautiful. It would be like eating a sunset.'

'What do they taste like?' I asked, glancing at her face. She hesitated, and I saw her eyes go wide. The words died on her tongue.

I looked where she was gazing and saw a party of Seljuq warriors appear around a bend a few hundred paces ahead. They saw us at the same moment.

There were six of them, each in a blood-red turban, black shirts and trousers, and short black cloaks. They were mounted on identical black Arabian steeds, and each carried a small round shield covered in white horse-hide and bearing a sharpened spike in the centre boss. The leader of the group had a single white plume atop his turban; he regarded us with bold severity for a moment, and I held my breath.

Merciful God, cover us with your mighty hand, I prayed.

Then turning to the two warriors on his left, he spoke a rapid command, extending his hand towards us as he did so, and my heart lurched in my breast.

'Fly!' I cried, jerking hard on the reins. The grey responded without so much as a quiver of hesitation, and we were away. The horses leapt into full, racing stride effortlessly and with such swiftness I muttered a heartfelt prayer of thanks to God that Nurmal traded in only the finest animals.

Padraig released the pack horse and led the way with Yordanus right behind; Sydoni and I were last, but only by the length of a tail. I slapped the reins across the noble grey's shoulders and let the horse run, feeling the powerful muscles bunch and flow beneath me as we fled back along the dry stream, the horse's hooves biting deep into the sandy path and flinging grit skyward.

266

In no time at all we reached the bend where the track descended down through the cutting between the steep rock outcroppings. I risked a look over my shoulder to see that we had gained ground on our pursuers. We would have to hurry to get everyone up, but once through the gap we would have a clear path and I doubted the Seljuqs would think it worthwhile to follow.

So, with a prayer on my lips, my heart thudding in my chest, I slowed the pace of the grey enough to allow Sydoni to go ahead. Padraig had already reached the cutting and disappeared up the path; Yordanus followed, holding to the saddle like a child as the horse leapt onto the trail. Sydoni's mount shied. 'Hi!' she shouted, and gave the reluctant animal a sharp kick in the flanks with her heels. The horse darted into the gap after the others.

Then it was my turn. The Seljuqs were almost on me. I slapped the reins hard and urged the animal forwards. The magnificent grey responded without a quiver of complaint, surging up through the cutting and onto the rock-strewn path. I saw Sydoni gain the track on the other side; she paused and looked back. 'Go! Go!' I shouted. 'I'm right behind you!'

She disappeared in a clatter of hooves and I saw clear light through the gap, and an empty trail ahead.

That was the last thing I saw. For the next thing I knew, earth and sky had changed places and the ground was rising up before my face. I was thrown clear of the horse and landed hard against the side of the bank, loose rock pelting down on me.

Dust filled my lungs and eyes; I could not breathe or see. My head felt as if it had been driven down between my shoulder blades. Every bone and joint in my body ached, and my right arm tingled strangely. My hands were scraped raw, and my clothes were torn, the flesh peeled away from my right hip in a wide and nasty gash.

I could not think what had happened. All I knew was that one moment I had been making good my escape, and the next there was a Seljuq standing over me with a sword-point at my throat. I made to rise, but the fellow put his foot on my chest and shoved me firmly back down. I lay back, choking and blinking, trying to drag my shattered senses together.

A second warrior appeared above me, spoke a word, and the two of them reached down and hauled me roughly upright.

I found myself looking into the impassive face of the Seljuq leader.

Now, of course, I know that the Arab chieftain who addressed me was the Atabeg of Albistan. At the time, however, all I knew was that besides the white plume he possessed the natural authority of a respected leader; a single word or the flick of a hand brought unquestioning obedience from his men.

He regarded me with neither rancour nor curiosity, his shrewd dark eyes taking the measure of his prisoner. He must not have been impressed with what he saw before him, for after the briefest scrutiny, he said something to his companion and turned away. He moved towards his horse, and prepared to remount.

The Seljuq warrior beside me tightened his grip, and his comrade with the sword stepped aside – so as to get a better stroke, I thought, bracing myself for the killing blow.

But the man moved away, and I looked to see my own mount thrashing on the ground, trying to rise. Even in my dazed state I could see the poor beast's back was broken, and probably his right foreleg as well. In its eagerness to catch the others, the spirited grey had taken the path too quickly and had stumbled on the loose rock.

The commander spoke another quick burst to the soldier with the sword who bent to examine the injury to the animal. His brief scrutiny completed, he stood; the slow shake of his head confirmed what everyone already knew: there was no hope for the beast.

The commander raised his chin sharply, and the warrior bowed. Two men joined the first; one took the reins, and the other brought out a short throwing spear from its holder beneath his saddle. They made the horse lie on its side, and while one held the reins tightly, the other held the animal's head down, stroking the long jaw and whispering into its ear. The third warrior approached from behind with the spear.

A quick thrust up under the creature's skull, and it was over. The poor beast gave a shuddery kick, wheezed, and lay still. Satisfied that the horse had not suffered, the commander then turned and started back the way they had come.

A loop of rope was passed around my waist, and I was led off down the dry riverbed. I had to run to keep up, but, mercifully, it was no great distance, else I might have collapsed. Even so, my lungs were burning, and dark spots were dancing before my eyes by the time we reached our destination – a low place on the steep bank near where a number of Christian footmen and a few knights had thought to make their escape from the battlefield.

They had been ridden down and killed, and their bodies now lay strewn over the rocks and sand splattered red with their blood. The Seljuq raiding party had been searching for any who might have escaped along the river when we ran into them.

After a quick search of the dead for valuables, they were stripped of weapons and armour, and the Seljuq commander led his men up the low bank and out onto the plain once more, leading me, and three riderless horses behind them.

Most of the dead were amassed in the centre of the plain near the road they had been travelling on when Ghazi sprang his trap. As we approached the road, where the fighting had been fiercest, I began to see corpses heaped one upon another – most of them without armour, and a few even without weapons. I wondered at this and decided that the ambush must have caught them so suddenly that the knights did not have time to arm themselves before the enemy was upon them; they were cut down as they struggled into their helms and hauberks.

The blood of the slain had turned the dust-dry road into a sodden mess, churned to vile mud by the feet of soldiers and Seljuq horses. Already the air was thick with the stink of curdling blood as the white hot sun beat down on the carnage. The sick-sweet stench filled my nostrils bringing the gorge to my mouth; I gasped and gagged as I was pulled along, desperate to keep my feet lest I be dragged through the gore-slick muck.

I tried not to look at the dead, and averted my eyes whenever I could – their slack mouths and lolling tongues, their astonished empty stares, their raw and gaping wounds – lest they be disgraced in my sight. Their piteous plight filled me with an immense and oppressive remorse. I stumbled across the battle-plain staggering over the corpses, bitterness welling anew with every step. An entire army had been cruelly cut down for the ambition of one heedless, headstrong lord. God help me, I cursed Bohemond for the sacrilege of the self-willed arrogance that had blithely squandered so many lives.

My Seljuq captors came to a place a little distance from the road where the victors were gathering. There, under the watchful eyes of their commanders, a vast company of warriors were enthusiastically stripping the dead of their armour, weapons, and clothing. The various items – swords, shields, helmets, spears, mail caps and hauberks, and the like – were brought and tossed onto the swiftly growing heap. Nearby, another, smaller, pile was also increasing; this one contained all the items of silver and gold, or other valuable objects. Bohemond had pressed hard in his effort to reach the Armenian stronghold as quickly as possible, so the crusaders had not pillaged many towns along the way and consequently had little plunder with them.

While I watched this dismal display, a great cry went up from a host of Seljuq warriors massed a short distance away where they were occupied with some great amusement. They waved their curved swords in the air, shouting loudly and enthusiastically. I could not make out what demanded such zealous attention, but more and more warriors were being drawn to the display.

I was still trying to determine what was happening when Amir Ghazi arrived. Surrounded by a bodyguard of fifty warriors on horseback – most of them on milk-white stallions like his own, and all dressed alike in cloaks of deepest blue with crimson turbans – he sat comfortably upon a raised, cushioned saddle of fine polished leather edged in silver. A small, smooth-faced man, he was swathed in shimmering blue samite, and wore a huge red turban surmounted by a peacock plume held in place with a great glittering emerald the size of a duck egg. In his cloak of white samite, he fairly gleamed like a star in the harsh sunlight as he sat in his high saddle and gazed at the still-growing mounds of treasure and weapons with the calm, beatific smile of a cheerful god.

He advanced and reined up before the atabeg and his men. The two addressed one another amiably and fell to discussing, as I imagined, the battle and its aftermath. At one point, the amir turned his attention to me; my captor simply shrugged, as if my presence was of little consequence, and they went back to their conversation.

They were thus occupied when all at once another tremendous shout went up from the nearby host. The amir turned in the saddle and, raising himself in his silver stirrups, attempted to peer over the heads of the close-gathered throng. Failing this, he spoke a command to his men, and a dozen or so warriors wheeled their mounts and rode to the gathering on the plain. Using the butts of their spears, the warriors began prodding them out of the way, clearing a path by which the amir might see what was taking place just beyond them.

As the pathway widened, I saw with sickening dread what it was that so engrossed the watching warriors: the bloody execution of the prisoners. Not all of the crusaders had been slaughtered in the valley; two hundred or so remained alive and had surrendered themselves. These men had been herded together onto the plain, and were now undergoing summary execution by the victors.

This was bad enough; what made it infinitely worse was the way in which the executions were being carried out. Even as I watched, one poor wretch of a foot soldier was pulled screaming from among his companions and hauled to the centre of the plain where he was released. The instant he was freed, two Seljuq riders sped out from the near end of the field – one with a spear and the other brandishing a sword. The two closed rapidly on the fleeing crusader.

Leaning from the saddle, the foremost Arab waved his sword high. There was a glinting flash of steel in the air, and the victim's head flew from his shoulders, spinning bright ribbons of blood into the air. The decapitated corpse stumbled on a step or two and collapsed, jerking and quivering until it lay still. The disembodied head struck the barren ground to roll like a lumpy ball in the dust.

The whole hideous spectacle was greatly and warmly cheered by the ecstatic onlookers, many of whom had struck wagers on the rider's ability. That they should do this appalled me, and rage bubbled up like molten rock inside me. Instantly, I was overcome by a towering fury; my vision darkened and my blood flared like liquid fire in my veins.

Burning with impotent rage, I raised my fist to Heaven and called down fiery judgement to consume the heartless infidel. But the sky remained clear and no flaming thunderbolts descended to scorch the brutal victors' heads. When God withdraws his protective hand, the powers of hell are swift to claim the spoils.

THIRTY-TWO

Cait, my light, I cannot contain myself. For the first time in my captivity, a great fear and uncertainty has descended upon me and I do not know what to do. I pace and pray the night away besieged by a hopeless dread the like of which I have never known.

This very night, two members of the caliph's bodyguard burst into my cell. Although it was late and all the palace was silent, I was hastened directly to the throne room where the exalted caliph had previously received me, as you will remember. The great room was in darkness, save for two torches burning in sconces either side of a door at the far end of the room.

I was led across the empty expanse of floor to that door. It was opened, and one of the soldiers indicated that I was to enter. I did so, the door closed behind me, and I found myself in a small chamber, alone. In the light of a single candletree, I saw a small three-legged stool with a leather seat and a large blue satin cushion of the kind favoured by the caliph. There was a table with a bowl of dates and figs, and a brass bell.

As I stood looking at these things and wondering why I had been brought here in the dead of night, I heard a curious grinding sound – very like that of a mill wheel when it turns; it seemed to come from across the room and, even as I looked, a small seam opened in the corner of the wall. This seam became a low door, which swung outward. A belch of cool air washed over me and I smelled the stale scent of damp, musty earth, and it came to me that the many scattered rooms and buildings of the palace compound were no doubt connected by an elaborate system of passages and tunnels. I heard the slap of a footstep and, an instant later, who should emerge from the hidden passage but Caliph al-Hafiz himself with torch in hand.

He wore no turban, and was dressed only in his nightclothes. His white hair streamed from his head as if he had been tearing at it, and his beard was wild and uncombed. Indeed, he looked like a man driven from his bed by the force of a nightmare that yet bedevilled him.

He started when the door closed behind him and looked around at me. His eyes were baleful, dark, and staring. The grimace with which he beheld me did not bode well, I thought, for the outcome of our meeting.

Nevertheless, I bowed respectfully, and waited for him to begin. He placed the torch in a sconce beside the door and pointed to the stool, indicating that I was to sit. I did so, and he sat, too, cross-legged on the blue cushion facing me. A strange meeting this, I thought – no advisors, counsellors, servants or minions; no impressive array of guards to lend him stature; no lavish and costly appointments of gold and silk and sandalwood – just the two of us, man to man.

He looked at me hard, and I returned his gaze. I saw that he trembled slightly, as old men do when palsy claims them – a quiver of the head, a minute shaking of the hands. Then he began nodding, and intoning a chant in Arabic. After a moment he sighed and then leapt up again, and began striding around the room.

I watched him, mystified by his behaviour, yet moved to pity by the severity of the agitation which gripped him so tightly.

'So!' he cried at last. Then, as if frightened by the violence of his outburst, he repeated it again, but more softly. 'So! It comes to this.'

'My lord,' I replied.

'I am khalifa! Ruler and Protector of Egypt. Armies march at my command! I say what will be and it is. I am the law and the hope of my people, and I answer to Allah alone.' He stared at me as if daring me to defy him.

'Indeed, my lord,' I said.

'Yet,' he thrust a finger into the air, 'it comes to this!'

He seemed content with this statement, and took up his pacing again, legs stumping, arms jerking stiffly. I still could not understand his meaning, and the suspicion that he might be mad was rapidly hardening to certainty. 'You wished to see me, my lord,' I reminded him gently.

'Do not presume!' he shouted, instantly angry. 'I have but to speak a word and your life is forfeit to your impertinence.'

'Forgive me, Most Excellent Khalifa. Your servant awaits your pleasure.'

This seemed to calm him somewhat. He sat down again.

'You are a father,' he said, almost accusingly so it seemed.

'That I am, my lord.'

'You know the love of a father for his children,' he declared, speaking as if it were a celebrated and widely proclaimed fact of my existence.

'I do, yes. God knows.'

He nodded. 'Then you know also the anguish of a father who must chastise his rebellious child.'

'It is a torment that tears at the very soul,' I sympathized.

'Ya'allah! It is true!' he cried. Closing his eyes, he began slowly rocking back and forth, his wrinkled face an image of the pain that was torturing him.

He sat that way for a long time, and I did not intrude on his misery. After awhile, he drew a long breath, and opened his eyes. 'I am the law and the protection of my people,' he said, his voice calm and steady. 'Justice is my decree. It is written: a man who knows the will of Allah and fails to do it shall not escape the everlasting flames of damnation. And again: A believer who departs from the path of righteousness is no better than an infidel; he shall find his reward among the damned.' He regarded me sharply, defiant once more. 'Is this not so?'

'It is so, my lord,' I agreed.

'Yes,' he sighed, his voice soft, almost broken. 'It comes to this: my son is rebellious and unbelieving. He has done great wickedness and the blood of the murdered demands justice. You are a father. You love your child. You know what I am saying.'

Until that moment, I had struggled to understand his anguish, but as he spoke these last few words, the awful import of his summons awakened in me. I knew exactly what he was talking about.

'Eye for eye, tooth for tooth, and life for life. That,' he said, 'is the cold heart of the law.'

I felt my own heart grow cold.

'My son must answer to Allah for his wickedness,' he continued.

'Justice must be satisfied and righteousness upheld. As I am khalifa, it must be.' He looked at me meaningfully, willing me to understand.

The hair on the back of my neck prickled as his purpose broke upon me: *I* was to be that instrument of justice. That was why he had summoned me.

'You are a nobleman and a father,' he said again. 'You understand these things.'

'I understand your predicament, my lord,' I admitted woodenly, wishing with all my heart that I did not.

'I am khalifa!' he snapped suddenly. 'Do not presume!'

'Forgive me, Most Excellent Khalifa. I am unworthy of your regard.'

He stood again quickly. He shouted for the guards, and the door opened at once. Pointing to me, he spoke a rapid command in Arabic, whereupon, they seized me and pulled me away. As I was dragged from the room, al-Hafiz shouted, 'Pray to your God, Christian! Pray as a father that you might live to see your beloved child once more!'

Thus, I was returned to my cell and left to think about what had taken place. The more I pondered the implications of the strange audience, the more extraordinary it became. In his great despair, the Caliph of Egypt had turned to me; he had sought my aid with his wretched son. In some way I had become confessor to the caliph.

Why? I asked myself. Why had he chosen me?

He commanded armies, as he had needlessly reminded me. *The word of the caliph is law . . . justice is my decree . . .* Why confide these things to me, a mere prisoner in his keep?

The old man's reasons remained as dark and inscrutable as the beclouded night itself.

Eye for eye, tooth for tooth, and life for life.

The reasons for the caliph's confidence may have eluded me, but his *purpose* I suspected – and feared. He was asking me to be the instrument of his justice . . . he was asking me to kill his son.

Great King and Saviour, I prayed, inwardly quaking, *may this cup pass from me.*

At the command of the atabeg, I was taken out onto the plain to join the other prisoners awaiting execution. Too exhausted and dispirited to lift their heads, they sat slumped on the ground with eyes downcast, their faces ashen with fatigue, their hearts numb with terror.

Those with presence of mind enough to know their peril were praying fervently; their voices formed a continual low gabble over which the moans and cries of the wounded among them drifted like a mournful dirge.

My Turkish captors untied me and pushed me down with the others. The man next to me raised his head as I settled in beside him. He regarded me dully, his battered face rapidly blackening beneath livid bruises to his cheek, and jaw, and neck; his chin was split to the bone and oozing big drops of blood. 'Are you a priest?' he asked in a ragged voice.

'No,' I replied. He made no reply, but his head sank lower. And then it came to me what he was asking. No man, feeling the cold hand of death on his shoulder, wishes to die unshriven. 'But I will pray with you, if you like,' I offered.

He nodded and, clasping his hands beneath his chin, struggled to his knees before me and began to pray. It was a simple prayer, yet well composed, and at the end of it, he begged the Heavenly Father's forgiveness for his many sins, and asked the Good Lord to remember his mother and his wife, and not to let them sink into beggary now that he was gone.

When he finished, I prayed that Christ the Blessed Redeemer of Men would carry the prayer before the Heavenly Throne, and – 'What is your name?' The man opened his eyes and glanced at me. 'Your name, friend, what is it?'

'Girardus.'

'– carry the prayer before the High Throne of Heaven and that Girardus' last wish for his family will be granted.' I said the *Amen* and signed him with the cross, as I had seen Emlyn and Padraig do when shriving sinners.

Rubbing unshed tears from his eyes, the soldier thanked me, and then, having made peace with his Creator, bent his head to prepare himself for death.

All at once there arose a commotion across the field. I glanced in the direction of the sound and saw a rider streaking towards us, followed by at least a dozen more. They reined in before the resplendent Amir Ghazi, on his milk-white stallion, exchanged a few heated hasty words, and the amir called a command to his men, who were at that moment dragging another screaming wretch out from among the beaten crusaders.

Then, one of the newcomers – a small, dark-skinned Turk with a bristly white beard and a face as flat and scuffed as the bottom of a boot – shouted something, turned his mount and rode out to where we were awaiting execution. This Arab carried no weapons, save a curved gold-handled knife, the pommel of which protruded from his dirty cloth belt. He glared at all around him with a dark and angry countenance, as if furious that we should be reclining while he laboured long in the saddle.

The glittering amir advanced and, smiling pleasantly, addressed the angry Arab in, as I thought, placating tones. The two began to converse, and I supposed the agitated newcomer was being informed of the disposition of the captives.

'He is furious as a tarred ferret,' observed Girardus.

'The amir does not appear overly concerned,' I pointed out.

'He is not the amir,' Girardus informed me. Indicating the small dark angry man, he said, '*That* is Amir Ghazi.'

I looked again at the man I had taken for a lowly scout. Unlike the other Arab chieftains I had seen, the amir was arrayed no better than the lowest soldier in his war host. Instead of flaunting his superiority, he wore the simple black dress of tunic and trousers of a Seljuq warrior, with black boots of soft leather; the only difference that I could see was that where their turbans were black or brown, his was sand-coloured. If Girardus had told me he was a trinket pedlar, I would have believed him. Certainly, the man I saw glaring down at us from the saddle appeared more disposed to selling brass baubles in the street than commanding the combined armies of the mighty Seljuq tribes.

'That is Amir Ghazi?' I said, staring at the dusty, sweating Turk. 'Are you certain?'

'Yes, and he is enraged.'

'Why?'

'He is angry with his commanders for killing so many captives. Noblemen are worth fortunes in ransom, and the rest can be sold as slaves. Ghazi says their thoughtlessness has cost a great deal of money which could have been used to further the war against the Franj.'

I looked at Girardus in amazement. 'How do you know this?'

'I speak Arabic a little,' he said. I professed this to be a very wonder. 'No.' He shook his head. 'It is six years in Antioch.'

'If that is Ghazi,' I said, 'who is the other one?'

'That is Kaisin Tanzuk, Sultan of Jezirah,' my informer replied. 'They say he is wealthier than the Caliph of Baghdad.'

'What is he say –'

'Shh!' Girardus cut me off as he tried to follow the exchange. After a moment, the crusader turned to me, his bruised features forming an expression of pathetic relief. 'The killing is stopped. We are to be taken to Damascus.'

Satisfied that his command was understood, Amir Ghazi returned to his chieftains and began ordering the withdrawal of the army. While I was mightily grateful to be spared a messy and inglorious death, my relief was tempered somewhat by the realization that my rescue would now take longer. I had allowed myself to hope that once Padraig and the others discovered what had happened to me, they would ride to Anazarbus, alert Roupen, and the Armenians would instantly ride to my aid.

In a little while, a number of Turks approached with coils of rope, and began tying the captives together. *It is only for a short while*, I told myself as the Seljuq warrior passed the loop of tough leather rope around my neck. *They will come for me. When they realize what has happened, they will come for me.*

The rope was pulled tight around my throat, looped back to my hands, and secured. When he finished, I was bound to Girardus – who was joined to someone else, and so on – and the warrior gave the rope a final tug and began leading us away. I stumbled forwards into the strange and frightening nightmare world of the war captive.

THIRTY-THREE

So began the most wretched portion of my life. I will spare you the most painful incidents, dearest Caitríona. I could not bear the thought that my distress should cause you grief. Even through my sorest trial, my chief consolation was that you would not know how your father suffered. Thus, you would remain forever blissful in your memories of me – if indeed you should remember me at all. You were so young when I left you, heart of my heart; and for that I am sorry. Believe me, I have repented ten thousand times since then.

Ah, but dull ignorant man that I am, I did not perceive the Swift Sure Hand of God moving mightily in the chaos of those calamitous days. No doubt Padraig would have had the wit to perceive the subtle textures of our Lord's grand design in the intricate warp and weft of time and the myriad actions of men.

'Look here, Duncan,' the good priest might have said, 'see how the cloak is made of many threads – some light, some dark. The pattern is in the interplay of both, and who but the weaver can foresee the design?'

I miss Padraig greatly and pray for him constantly, as I do for you, my soul. Yes, and every day I curse my ignorance and folly. How arrogant I was, imagining I could bring some small order into the chaos of the seething, benighted East. I rue the day I allowed myself to become so deeply mired in affairs that did not concern me, and which only drew me further and further away from the true aim of the pilgrimage.

If we had but waited one more day – half-a-day, even! – the battle would have reached its inevitable conclusion, and I never would have been captured. Had we but waited half-a-day, I would not be here now at the pleasure of the Caliph of Cairo, by whose sufferance I yet draw breath. And yet, as Padraig never tires of pointing out: the

Swift Sure Hand does bend all things to the good of those who love him.

As much as I entrust my hope to this belief, I cannot truly say I perceived the smallest tincture of good in that arduous and harrowing journey to Damascus. If there was a design in that, I confess I never saw it. Perhaps I may be forgiven my dullness of sight, however; most days, I was busy fighting for my life.

Amir Ghazi commanded the massed armies to move south at once. As I think on it now, he must have recognized the priceless opportunity he had won. Having vanquished Antioch's protecting forces, he moved to press his advantage as far as it would go.

So, without a pause to draw breath, much less celebrate their victory, the amir's army was on the move once more. In preparation for this, Seljuq warriors searched through the ranks of crusader captives with swords; anyone with a disabling wound was instantly put to death. Those with lesser injuries were spared, and allowed to continue so long as they could walk. Still, as the days passed, there were times when I reckoned a quick chop in the neck might have been the greatest kindness.

We marched from the plain of battle and into the low hills to the north and east. It was long past dark when we stopped. I spent a cold night on the ground in the company of eight other prisoners. We were tied together in groups to keep us from escaping, and each group separated from the others so that we could not raise rebellion.

Too disheartened to speak, we lay there on the stony ground and slept the sleep of the dead. Indeed, a good few did not rise in the morning; and a fair few more who *did* begin the day's march did not finish.

That day cast the pattern for all the days to follow: our captors roused us at first light, prodding us awake with the butts of their spears. We were bound together two-by-two, each man to another with short cords around the ankles, and a slightly longer one around the neck; our hands were tied behind us. Then we were given a drink of water, and the army moved off, heading south. The main body of the Seljuq warhost rode on ahead; the captives travelled behind with the slower-moving baggage train.

We shuffled along, watching the dull sky brighten, trying to ignore the leather rope chafing our ankles with every step. Soon the sun broke above the surrounding hills and we began to feel the heat of the day to come. As the sun climbed higher in the empty white shell of the sky, the heat mounted and leeched away the little strength the night had restored to us. By midday, some of the worse off had reached their journey's end; they collapsed along the trail.

Our Arab masters were deaf to the cries of the suffering and dying. They pushed mercilessly, pausing only to give us enough water to keep us alive and moving – never enough to satisfy our parched and burning throats.

Hungry, thirsty, aching from our various wounds and injuries, we shuffled over the barren hills, our heads down, our hearts cold hard stone in our chests. Day after infernal day. We did not talk; there was nothing to say.

The sun blazed down on our naked heads with the heat-blast of a forge fire. Sweat streamed from us, stinging our eyes and dissipating our rapidly dwindling strength to the arid desert air. In this way, the decimated Christian army dragged itself across the scorching wastes staggering under the burden of its wounded. Muted curses and muttered Psalms ascended heavenward in equal measure, as the slow torture of heat and thirst began to exact a cruel tariff.

When men fell, the nearest Seljuq guard would ride to see whether any purpose might be served in getting the man back on his feet. If the crusader had life enough in him, those nearby were ordered to carry him. If not, he was simply left where he lay, and the death march moved on. Often those left behind cried out for the knife to end their misery, but these, like all other pleas, went unheeded.

The fourth day was the worst I have ever endured. Around midday, a badly wounded soldier collapsed directly in front of Girardus and myself, pulling down the man bound to him. The Seljuq guard rode up and, without bothering to dismount, commanded the three of us to get the unconscious man on his feet once more.

For this, we required the use of our hands, and so our bonds were loosed, which was a mercy in itself. The three of us were able to raise the wretch, but it was clear he could no longer walk unaided. So, we took it in turn to help him – with two holding him up between us and all-but dragging him along while the third rested. When one of us became weary, the rested one would take his place, and so on.

Meanwhile, our suffering comrade drifted from bad to worse.

After a time, he could no longer move his feet, and so we carried him, taking his entire weight on our shoulders. Damnably awkward it was, and it very quickly exhausted us. Soon it became a trial merely to put one foot before the other and remain upright.

I set my jaw to the task, and trudged on and on through the interminable length of that endless day. After a time, the searing ache in my legs and arms eased as my limbs grew gradually numb. I could no longer feel the uneven ground beneath my feet, and this caused me to stumble over rocks. Each lurch and jostle brought a moan from our unconscious comrade, but his complaints grew gradually weaker and more infrequent.

The land was a barrens of broken rock and thorns; gnarled trees, white with dust and shrivelled by the merciless sun, twisted up from stony crevices. Everything in that godforsaken land was blasted, blighted and deformed. No less easy on the eye than underfoot, the harshness seared itself into the soul. Never did a scrap of green – or any other colour – relieve the limitless sameness.

Seeking refuge from the sun and blight, I turned in my mind to thoughts of Blessed Scotland, and the family waiting there; I brought the image of each face before my mind's eye, and prayed for the soul of every one I could recall. In this way, I withstood the rigours of that inhuman day.

When at last the sun began to fade behind the western hills, the Seljuqs stopped to make camp for the night. The three of us stiffly lowered our wounded comrade to the ground and collapsed beside him. We lay there panting like sun-scalded dogs, unmoving, sweat running in rivulets from our spent bodies to stain the dust beneath us.

The sun was almost down when one of the Seljuqs brought a waterskin and revived us with a few mouthfuls of water. After I drank, I drew myself up on my elbows to rouse our wounded comrade so he could get his share. It was then I discovered he was dead.

When he died, and how long we had carried his lifeless corpse, I cannot say. All I know is that his life passed from him silently, and without so much as a sigh. He lay with his mouth open and eyes closed as if asleep – asleep for ever more.

The guard noted the death with a shrug and turned away. We slept that night tied to a corpse and were only released the next morning when the guard cut us free so we could move on. I prayed I would not die like that wretch, unmourned, unknown, nothing more than an accursed burden to those around me.

We were wakened the next morning to begin another hellish day. My arms and legs felt cast of lead; my head ached and my mouth was coated with scum. Those of us left alive were given a fair ration of water, which we gulped down quickly lest the guards change their minds. I thanked God for every mouthful. Many there were who could not face the day, and refused to get up. The Seljuqs killed two unfortunates where they lay, and the rest, faced with a spear in the gut and an agonizing, lingering death, found the strength to rise once more.

The land grew rough and craggy; the trail degenerated into rugged little goat tracks through dry streams and over shattered hills, making the march yet more strenuous and difficult. Time and again the cry went up for water, food, or rest. We were given none of these things.

I kept myself alive with Psalms and prayers, reciting 'The Lord is my shepherd, I shall not want . . . the Lord is my shepherd, I shall not want . . . he makes me to lie down in pastures green . . . beside the still waters he leads me . . . though I walk through the valley of the Shadow of Death . . . Lord, I walk through the valley of the Shadow of Death, yet I no evil fear . . . no evil fear . . . no evil fear . . .'

Over and over and over again, I spoke these words and the rhythm of their speaking became a litany of life to me. For, as long as I could say them, I knew I would live – at least to the end of the Psalm.

The searing, relentless heat and lack of water began to claw at our numbers. All around me men collapsed and fell, and as the eternal day wore on and on with no end in sight, I began to regard these as the lucky ones.

Mumbling my Psalm, I moved in and out of dreams. I saw Padraig walking before me, and tried to hail him, but my throat was so dry I could not make a sound. When I looked again, it was just another captive crusader. I saw my father, Murdo, sitting on a rock beside the trail. He shook his head in pity as I passed, and I wanted to speak to him, to tell him how sorry I was to leave home without telling him, but he melted into the empty air before I could find voice to speak the words.

I smelled the clean salt air of the sea back home. I smelled the water, and heard the restless sea waves slapping the rocks and tumbling the smooth stones on the shingle. I heard the shrill keen of the seabirds wheeling in the bold blue cloud-dazzled sky – a sky never seen in the desert wilderness of the Holy Land.

The scents and sounds caused me to imagine the faces of those I loved, and I heard the babble of their voices filling my ears. I tried to make out what they said, but in their joy at having me among them once more they spoke over one another so that I could not understand them.

Holding up my hands, I made to speak and forced out a ragged croak, and this made them excited. They rushed to me and I was pulled this way and that, and I realized they were dragging me down to the sea. Stiff-legged, I tried to resist. My strength was gone and I was shoved down to the water.

I felt the blessed wetness lapping around my feet and legs; I heard others splashing in behind me, and turned to see the dusty faces of my fellow pilgrims floundering into the sea. How, I wondered, had they come to be in Scotland? Had they followed me there? Had we walked all the way?

And then people began throwing water over me. The cold shock restored me to my mind. Water! I sank down to my knees and began scooping it up in my hands, throwing it into my mouth and gulping it down, choking on it, and gulping down more.

The water revived me. I raised my eyes and looked around. Gone the cold ocean bay, and gone the prosperous holding snug amongst the dazzling green hills. Before me was a sun-baked settlement shaded by a few scruffy trees and forlorn palms on the bare earth banks of a muddy, but very real lake. The people there were not my beloved friends and family, but Muhammedan shepherds. My heart writhed within me as the dull realization seeped into my sun-dazed awareness: I was alive still, and far, far from home.

We stayed there that night. Revived by the water, and blessed with a moment's respite from the day's heat as evening drew near, the captives began to appraise their chances of survival. And they began to talk.

I soon learned what had happened after Padraig, Roupen, and I had fled Antioch. Commander Renaud had not allowed the Templar garrison to be used to aid Prince Bohemond's ruinous folly. In defiance of the prince, he had refused to send the Poor Soldiers of Christ into battle against other Christians. Opinion among the captives divided sharply over whether this was good or bad.

'If the Templars had been with us, by Christ,' one soldier swore, 'we would not have been defeated.'

'That just shows how stupid you are, Thomas Villery,' growled the man next to him. 'If the Templars had been there they would have been killed along with all the rest.'

'Yes,' agreed another, 'it is for the best. At least this way we have a hope of rescue.'

'What makes you think anyone will rescue us? No one cares,' concluded another gloomily. His head sank onto his chest. 'God has given us over to destruction. His hand is against us. We are dead men – each and every one of us. There is no hope.'

'Has the turd turned philosopher now?' scoffed the soldier called Thomas. 'When the garrison learns that Bohemond's army has been captured, they will ride at once to the rescue.'

'And who is going to tell them, eh?' demanded another soldier, struggling to rise. He had been slashed on the arm, and the wound showing through the blood-crusted rag of his sleeve was grey and watery with pus. 'Idiot! Who is going to ride to Antioch to tell them? Eh?' He glared furiously around the ring of grim faces. 'Gaston is right, we are all dead men.'

'What!' demanded the one called Thomas. 'When they learn the rood has been captured, they will come, by God.'

'Do not speak to me of God, or the rood,' muttered Gaston. 'If the rood goes before us, we cannot lose – so they said. It is God's good pleasure to lead us to victory, they said. Where is the victory now?' He glared around daring anyone to challenge him. 'Damn them! Damn their lies!'

'Forgive me, brother,' I said, breaking into their conversation, 'is it the Holy Cross you mean?'

'Aye,' he agreed dubiously, 'is there any other?'

'The Black Rood,' one of them muttered, 'taken by the cursed heathen Seljuqs.' He spat. 'Much good may it do them. God knows it has done no good for us.'

'Shut your stinking gob, Matthias!' charged Thomas. 'Maybe it is for blasphemers like you that the Almighty gave us up to defeat. Did you ever think of that?'

'How dare you come the high and holy with me!' snarled the offended Matthias. 'I was well and truly shriven ere we left the city – we all were. You'll not go laying the blame for this at *my* feet, so help me –'

'Where is it?' I asked, interrupting their argument.

'The rood? Why, the Turks have taken it,' answered Matthias. 'They will have it with the rest of the plunder. Christ alone knows what they will do with it, the heathens.'

'They'll burn it,' suggested Girardus dolefully. 'By God they will, for they are godless devil worshippers every hell-cursed one.'

The discussion moved on to speculation about what would happen to us when we reached Damascus, but as no one had any notion, I turned instead to pondering what I had learned: the Holy Rood was here . . . somewhere.

I determined then and there that if the High King of Heaven allowed me to remain alive, I would resume my quest: some-how I would find the Holy Rood, and I would save it. This I vowed to do.

THIRTY-FOUR

We stayed four days at Kadiriq, a baked-mud settlement on the banks of the stagnant lake, regaining our strength for the days ahead. I suspect the march from Anazarbus had been made as tortuous as possible to kill off the weak and wounded. The Seljuqs wanted slaves to sell and only those strong enough to survive the ordeal would bring a price worth the trouble of keeping them alive.

I slept nearly all of the first day, and the second I spent lying in the shade of a gnarled little tree beside the lake – I could not bear to be out of sight of the water, and several times went in swimming to cool off. The sight of this white-skinned foreigner thrashing around in the shallows produced great amusement for the children of Kadiriq, who had come out to examine the conquered captives.

That night we were given food for the first time since the battle: flat bread – thin and dry, and tough as parchment – and lentils cooked in beef broth. The second night we were given bread and beans again, and some leathery scraps of goat meat.

On the third day, Amir Ghazi arrived. He travelled in *caravan* – that is to say, with his entire retinue of advisors, liegemen, and a bodyguard of three hundred or more warriors – all mounted, and leading a long train of pack animals, mostly horses. However, moving with a strange, swaying gait, I saw the odd, ungainly desert creatures called camels. With their steep-humped backs, long necks and small, flat heads, they seemed to tower above the surrounding turmoil with lordly sufferance.

The newcomers arrived leading a few dozen more prisoners. Rumours spread among the captives that the main Seljuq army had taken the town of Marash on the border, allowing the amir to enrich himself still further with Christian slaves and plundered treasure.

Ghazi set up his camp on the other side of the lake. I counted over a hundred tents before losing interest. The townspeople were overjoyed to have the honour of hosting the amir, and that night there was a feast in his name. A dozen cows were slaughtered for the spit, and a score of sheep and goats. The festive mood overflowed the town and even spilled out into the captives' camp, to the extent that we were given a humble share of the feast. That night, along with our bread – a soft, thick flat bread flavoured with *anise* – we were also given lamb stewed with figs. It was very good, and there was not a man among us who did not lick the wooden bowl clean. We were also given a drink of fermented goat's milk – slightly salty, with a rancid sour taste which failed to seduce many to its charms.

The next morning, rested, fed, and as hale as I could hope to be in the uncertain days ahead, I determined to try my luck with Amir Ghazi.

The sun was high and the wind hot out of the south. I was bathing in the lake when two of the amir's bodyguard appeared. They spoke to the Seljuq keeping watch on the bank, and I decided the time had come. Hauling myself from the water, I motioned for Girardus to accompany me, and came to stand before them on the bank.

'What are you doing?' he whispered desperately.

'Tell them I demand to see the amir.'

He gaped at me in disbelief, and started to object.

'Tell them.'

The guards glanced at us with haughty contempt, but otherwise ignored us.

'I do not think they speak Arabic,' Girardus concluded quickly. 'Let us go before they make trouble for us.'

'Tell them. Make them understand.'

Rolling his eyes, Girardus spoke up, interrupting the Seljuqs, who were not pleased with our persistence. The guard shouted something, and waved his hands at us to drive us away. 'They say to go away,' Girardus said, much relieved.

'I demand to see the amir,' I said, holding my ground. 'Tell them I *demand* it, Girardus. Use that word. I demand to see him at once.'

After another shouted exchange, Girardus said, 'They say no one can see the amir.'

'Tell them I am a nobleman, and a friend of Lord Thoros of Armenia, and I demand to see Amir Ghazi at once.'

To his credit, Girardus swallowed his fear and spoke up once more. In a halting and trembling voice, he told the guards what I had said. The Seljuq guard started towards us, waving his spear and shouting. But one of the amir's men took him by the arm and pulled him back. He motioned me to him.

Without hesitation, I stepped up. He gazed at me, his dark eyes searching mine. The second guard said something, and flapped a hand at me, but the first guard took me by the arm and turned me around, indicating that I was to walk before them.

'God go with you,' called Girardus.

They marched me around the lake to where the amir had established his camp. Upon arrival, I was brought to stand outside the amir's tent, which was pale blue instead of the deep black-brown of all the others. I was given to understand that I was to remain there – a few score paces before the tent – and my two keepers spoke to a man who appeared briefly at the tent entrance, before retreating to the shade of a small date palm beside the tent where they could watch me. Thus, I stood, waiting for my audience and observing the commerce of the camp.

Amir Ghazi was a very busy man, judging by the comings and goings of the amir's many advisors, and subject lords. Few of the people who entered the tent stayed very long. I expect they were merely paying homage to the amir, or discharging some perfunctory duty. Indeed, the entire Arab race from the highest caliph to the lowest goatherd is hedged about with a veritable wall of duties and obligations, not one brick or block of which can be removed or altered.

Surveying this continuous procession of lords and notables, I marked again how very splendid were these noblemen: arrayed in flowing clothes of the finest cloth and bedecked with gold and jewels, they wore plumes of ostrich and peacock, and carried jewelled weapons. They gleamed and glittered in the bright sun, astride their fine horses, and accompanied by their retinues.

They all came bearing gifts, which they carried in boxes of carved sandalwood. Sometimes – depending, I think, on the rank of the guest – the amir met his visitor at the entrance to his tent, and welcomed him with a kiss. Most often, however, it was one of the amir's servants who, bowing low, directed the guest into the great man's presence.

Not all of the amir's visitors were men. Many of the nobles brought women with them, and these, from what I could see of them, were even more magnificently arrayed than the men – although they hid their splendour under long hooded outer cloaks or gowns which covered them head to toe, and they wore veils across the lower parts of their faces so that between hood and veil, only their eyes were visible. But such eyes! Almond shaped and black as sloe, with long lashes and brows thin and dark and delicately curved.

It put me in mind of Sydoni and I spent a long time happily thinking about her – until I remembered my grave predicament. If I had not been such an impetuous fool I would no doubt be with her now. My thoughts grew so forlorn and pitiable, that I was forced to put them off at last. It does no good to wallow in regret. What might have been is as impossible as what can never be.

After awhile one of my guards fell asleep. As I had been standing in the sun for a goodly while, I sat down. The other guard did not like this; he hissed at me and gestured for me to stand up again, and I obliged. Soon, however, he was fast asleep, too, and so I sat down again and pulled my siarc over my head to keep the sun off me while I waited.

The sun passed midday and began its long slow descent into the west. Still, I sat in my place, dozing now and again, and waiting for the amir, and still people came and went on errands of fealty and homage. As the sun began to stretch my shadow towards the entrance to the tent, I heard horses approaching.

A party of Arab chieftains was riding into camp. I climbed to my feet and, as they dismounted, I darted in among them and started for the entrance to the amir's tent. One of the Arabs called for me to stop. I paid him no heed and kept walking. One of the guardsmen, roused by the shouting, woke up and saw me, however; he rushed upon me and dragged me back to my place where he was joined by two others and all three began shouting and raining blows upon my head.

I do not know whether the disturbance I raised outside his tent drew the attention of the amir, but as I was lying on the ground, trying to protect my head and neck from the fists of the soldiers, a man suddenly appeared in the midst of the commotion.

He barked a single sharp word of command and the men ceased their attack. I looked up to see the Atabeg of Albistan, the same who had captured me days before. He recognized me, too, and bade me rise; he pointed towards the tent and I saw the amir himself standing at the entrance surrounded by advisors and liegemen. He was frowning mightily, none too pleased at the interruption of his affairs.

Rising slowly, I dusted myself off, and prepared for whatever would happen next.

The unhappy amir beckoned his attendant nobleman to him. The atabeg put his hand on my arm and pulled me away from the guards, and I was brought before the amir where I was made to kneel at his feet. This was to humble me, but I did not greatly mind. It is no shame to acknowledge one who is above you, and inasmuch as I was a lowly hostage in his camp, Amir Ghazi was certainly superior in every way.

The black amir scowled down at me. I cannot say what passed in his mind, but I bowed as I had seen the other noblemen do, touching my forehead to the ground, and then, employing my best Greek, said, 'My name is Duncan of Caithness, and I am a friend of Prince Thoros of Armenia.'

He glared, and spoke a word of command and one of his advisors approached on the run. This fellow – an Armenian, I believe, for in manner, dress, and appearance he was very like those I had met at the banquet in Anazarbus – was an ungainly, sallow skinned man, with a large eagle-beaked nose and smooth, hairless jowls like the wattles of a pig, he cast a dour, pitiless black eye over me. 'Who are you?' he asked in Greek, suspicion thickening his reedy voice.

I repeated what I had said before, and added, 'I am a pilgrim from a country in the far north-west, where I am a lord and nobleman. I befriended young Lord Roupen, brother of Prince Thoros, and son of Leo, and became his protector. I was leaving Anazarbus, and blundered upon the battle by mistake.'

I could tell he did not believe me; he looked me up and down as if measuring for a coffin. 'See how I am dressed – are these the clothes of a crusader?' His frown of disbelief deepened. 'Also, we are speaking Greek,' I added.

'Badly,' he sniffed, unimpressed.

'Tell me your name,' I commanded.

The Armenian stiffened slightly at my audacity. But he was well accustomed to taking orders, and replied, 'I am Katib Sahak of Tarawn, advisor to Amir Ghazi.'

I thanked him, and said, 'I ask you now, Katib –'

'Just Sahak only,' he said. '*Katib* is an Arab word. It means scribe.'

'I ask you, Sahak, do the Franks speak Greek?'

At this, the Armenian turned and held close conversation with the amir, whose interest pricked slightly when he heard what Sahak had to say about me. Breathing a fervent prayer, I said, 'I had no part in Bohemond's army, and took no part in the battle. I was a guest of Prince Thoros and was captured by mistake. I was with three others when this man captured me.' Pointing to the atabeg, I said, 'Ask him if this is not so. The others were able to escape. I alone was captured.'

Sahak discussed my story with the atabeg, who nodded, which I took as confirmation that I was telling the truth. 'The Atabeg of Albistan agrees that it happened the way you say,' the scribe confirmed. Ghazi spoke up then, and Sahak added, 'The amir demands proof.'

Looking directly at the amir, I answered, 'Tell him I can prove I have come from the prince's household.' When my words were interpreted for the amir, I said, 'This was given to me by Princess Elena for aiding the return of her son, Roupen.'

So saying, I pulled the neck of my siarc down and twisted it inside out to reveal the brooch I had pinned there the day I left Anazarbus. Sahak's eyes went wide with amazement. 'If you will look closely,' I said, directing their attention to the carved ruby, 'you will see that it bears the royal emblem.'

I showed the gem to each of them in turn. Ghazi and the atabeg exchanged a few words, and the amir issued his command. 'Give me the brooch,' the Armenian translator said.

I refused, saying, 'The amir has said the noblemen are to be ransomed. This,' I held the brooch before them, 'is to be my ransom. What is the word for ransom?' I asked. 'In the amir's tongue, what is the word?'

'*Namus'lu keza*,' replied the advisor.

Tapping the brooch with my finger, I repeated the word. 'Namus'lu keza,' I said, and prayed they understood what I was trying to tell them.

The amir made up his mind. Speaking gruffly, he held out his hand to me.

'Amir Ghazi says you are to give him the jewel.'

I hesitated.

'You have no choice,' Sahak informed me. 'You are to give it to him now. It will be sent to Anazarbus to inform them of your capture.'

With great reluctance, I obeyed, unfastening the brooch and placing it in the amir's palm with a last appeal. 'Namus'lu keza.'

The amir closed his hand over the brooch, turned on his heel and walked away, pausing to toss a word of command to the guards as he retreated to his tent. They took hold of me and I was taken back around the lake to resume my place with the captives.

Girardus was glad at my return to the fold, so to speak. 'I never thought to see you again,' he confided. 'They are saying the amir is holding court, and judgements are being given.'

'It is true,' I told him. Other captives gathered closer to hear. 'The amir is indeed holding court, and he seems to be renewing the loyalties of his vassal lords.' I went on to describe what I had seen of the comings and goings of all the noblemen and women and gifts they brought.

When I finished, Girardus, who had assumed they had taken me away to be tortured or beaten, asked, 'What did they do to you?'

'They kept me waiting all day in the sun,' I answered, 'and then they brought me back here.'

'Did you see the amir?'

'I saw him,' I said glumly. 'I had hoped to persuade him to release me. He was not in a mood to be persuaded.'

'He let you live,' Girardus concluded. 'That is something, at least.'

I remained with the others that night and, wonder of wonders, the guards came for me the next morning and I was brought to stand before the amir's tent. As before, I waited as more, and still more, nobles and dignitaries came to pay homage to Amir Ghazi. I pondered the meaning of this activity, and it came to me that perhaps defeating Bohemond's army was an event of far greater significance for the Seljuqs than I knew.

Ignorant of the forces and powers that held sway in the Holy Land, I could nevertheless imagine that a single great victory could produce a result with far-reaching implications for the man who accomplished it. Certainly, it would not be the first time a shrewd leader, having delivered a decisive conquest, had used it to concentrate his power.

Further, I could well imagine that the hole left in the defences of Antioch had created an opportunity which such a leader might wish to exploit. What the astute amir had in mind, I could not guess, but the activity in the camp gave every indication that he was marshalling his support for an important undertaking.

These thoughts occupied me until a little past midday, when the Atabeg of Albistan, whom I took to be one of the amir's chief advisors, emerged from the tent. He came to stand over me, and I rose quickly to my feet. After a cursory scrutiny, he signalled the guarding warriors, and I was escorted into the amir's tent.

An Arab tent is a wondrous thing. With very little effort the desert folk make them as spacious and comfortable as palaces. The interior is often divided up into smaller rooms for meeting, dining, sleeping, and so forth. Accordingly, Ghazi's tent featured a large outer room where he received his guests before bringing them into his inner chambers, so to speak. This is where I was brought; here also were the gifts which had been heaped upon the amir by those who came to do him honour.

There were many jewelled swords and knives, and ornamental weapons of various sorts – spears, shields, helmets, bows and arrows – and other items of which the Arab artisans excel in making: chalices, bowls, platters, and cunningly carved boxes of pierced wood inlaid with fine yellow gold and precious stones. As I looked over this haphazard mound of wealth, I recognized certain objects and realized there were also many items of plunder which the Seljuq had taken from the defeated crusaders. Indeed, rolled on its wooden pole, I saw Bohemond's golden banner, and a fine new steel hauberk folded atop a chest, a pair of gauntlets with the image of a hawk's head, a silver gorget, and a long Frankish sword.

I saw these things and more, and the thought came to me, *It is here . . . the Holy Rood is here!* Could it be? My heartbeat quickened. Nothing of value escaped the keen appraising eye of the Arab. I stared at the jumbled trove and knew that it must be true. Hidden somewhere amongst all the gifts and plunder lay the greatest prize in Christendom.

After a moment the Armenian scribe, who had served as my interpreter the day before, appeared. 'Do you know why you have been brought here?' Katib Sahak asked; his voice was cold and unforgiving.

'I am hoping the amir has accepted my ransom payment and will now allow me to depart in peace.'

'That is for the amir to decide.' In bearing and tone, Sahak gave every indication of despising me. 'He wishes to ask you some questions. I urge you to tell the truth at all times. Your life depends on it.'

'Be assured I will tell the truth.'

He made a sound in his nose as if he thought such an endeavour unlikely. 'Follow me.'

Stepping to the inner partition, he pulled back a fold of the cloth, indicating that I should enter. The room was simple and spare; there was no furniture of any kind, save cushions; fine silken rugs had been spread thick on the ground to make a soft floor beneath the feet. The mountain of gifts which filled the outer room encroached upon this room as well, but here the heap was smaller, and the objects more costly.

The amir sat in the centre of the room, surrounded by four Seljuqs who, by dress and bearing, I took to be noblemen and advisors – the Atabeg of Albistan among them. Amir Ghazi's expression was stern and challenging. His white beard bristled like hog hair on his flat, wrinkled face; he had put off his buff-coloured turban, and his long grey hair was knotted into a hank, which rested on his shoulder. 'God is great!' he said in Arabic.

Sahak interpreted the amir's words for me, to which I replied, 'Amen!'

Ghazi nodded, and made a flicking motion with his hand. The Armenian bowed, then turned to me and said, 'His Most Excellent Amir Ghazi has considered your claim. He has discussed this with his counsellors and it is the opinion of the amir that you were fleeing the Armenian stronghold or else you would not have been captured. Is this not so?'

'Yes, my lord, it is so,' I answered, gazing full at Ghazi.

'It is the amir's opinion that there are many reasons for a man to flee. The two most common, and therefore most likely reasons – in the Most Excellent Amir's sage opinion – are these: either you have made enemies among the royal family, or you have committed some crime in the royal household. Perhaps the theft of the brooch with which you have attempted to purchase your freedom, yes?'

'Tell my lord the amir that I am not a thief,' I said, trying to remain calm and unruffled. 'I have stolen nothing. Neither have I made enemies among the royal family.'

I might have insisted on recognition of my noble rank, but it serves no purpose to allow one's self-importance to erect obstacles at times like this. As Abbot Emlyn says, martyrs are often burned, not for their beliefs, but for their toplofty pride alone.

Sahak repeated my assertion, and then gave me the amir's terse reply. 'It makes no difference,' he said. 'Amir Ghazi says that you are to remain a captive. You have said your friends escaped. If this is so, those who were with you will send ransom, and then you will be freed. By this he will know the truth, and the matter will be concluded.'

'If no one comes for me?' I hated asking the question, but I had to know.

'You will be sold in the slave market in Damascus with the rest of the captives who have no hope of ransom.'

The amir watched me to see how I would take this news. When I made no outcry or protest, Sahak said, 'Do you understand what I have told you?'

'Completely,' I answered. 'I am more than grateful for the amir's wide forbearance.'

The rancorous scribe's eyes narrowed as he tried to determine whether I was mocking him. Satisfied with my sincerity, he relayed my words to Ghazi, who continued, 'By virtue of the fact that you are a captive of war,' the amir said, speaking through Sahak, 'you stand condemned. Yet, it is written: He who desires mercy shall mercy employ. Therefore, I will show mercy to you, least deserving of men.'

He waited while his words were translated for me, then said, 'You have claimed to be a nobleman and, indeed, I find that you conduct yourself with admirable restraint and courtesy – two of the chief virtues of nobility. Mercy and generosity are two more.'

I could see that Ghazi, for all his sly practicality, nevertheless imagined himself something of a philosopher.

'Therefore,' Sahak continued, 'by the immense mercy and generosity of Lord Ghazi you will be accorded the honour and rank of a nobleman in captivity.'

The pronouncement dismayed me, I will not say otherwise, yet I shouldered the burden of disappointment as manfully as I could. I held my head erect and kept my mouth shut. I tried to preserve my dignity in the circumstance by reminding myself that, at least, by remaining in Ghazi's camp a little while longer, I would be near the Black Rood.

'All noblemen are to be ransomed in Damascus,' Sahak told me with spiteful glee, 'and, should anyone wish to claim you, the amir has decreed a price of ten thousand *dinars* for your release.'

'Please, tell the Excellent and Admirable Amir Ghazi that I am truly overwhelmed by the prodigious magnitude of his mercy and generosity.'

Sahak grimaced. 'Tomorrow we will continue our journey to Damascus. You will travel in the amir's baggage train with the other noble captives. So that you will not offend the Illustrious Atabeg Buri, by arriving empty-handed, the Wise and Benevolent Ghazi will provide you with a gift befitting your rank.'

When the translator was finished, the amir clapped his hands, and a guard entered from the outer room. Ghazi beckoned him near and put his mouth to his servant's ear. The man rose quickly and left. The amir enjoyed a shrewd smile at my expense and I felt a dread apprehension creep over me as the guard returned bearing a large wooden box, which he placed on the floor between myself and the amir.

The box itself was one of the ornately carved variety I had noticed in the anteroom; made of fine wood inlaid with gold tracery, it was costly, certainly, but I reckoned the box itself was not the gift the wily amir had in mind.

'Open it,' commanded Ghazi through his gloating Armenian mouthpiece.

I knelt down and unfastened the simple hasp. Then, taking the top in both hands, I steeled myself and lifted the hinged lid to reveal a severed human head. One brief glimpse of the long yellow hair and the neat forked beard gave me to know it was none other than the golden head of incautious Prince Bohemond.

THIRTY-FIVE

Impetuous no more, Prince Bohemond appeared serene and tranquil, his fine features becalmed, if not beatific – a testimony to the embalmer's art, for even in my fleeting encounter with the hasty Count of Antioch, I could tell that serenity was never part of his nature. Certainly, I had never seen him looking more contented – as if in death, his war with the world now over, he had entered a splendour of peace that had eluded him in life.

The flesh had a waxy texture and a slightly glistening tawny sheen, due to the pitch resin used to preserve the head. Yet, it was lifelike in every other way so that poor Bohemond seemed merely to slumber in the serene tranquility of a golden sunset. Alas, it was a sleep from which there would be no waking, and I might have mourned the life of a brother Christian so brutally cut off – if not for the fact that he had brought this ghastly extremity upon himself.

He had sown destruction, and reaped a bounteous harvest. Those who deserved my grief were the men who had no choice but to follow their vainglorious prince into death's cold and darksome halls.

My Seljuq masters wanted me to feast my gaze upon the grisly prize that I might know the fate awaiting noble traitors. Oh, they took great pleasure in their victory, of which the prince's head was the emblem. Given a choice, I believe Amir Ghazi would rather have had the ransom money – doubtless, the prince would have paid an enormous fortune in treasure for his freedom. Still, the wily amir was not sorry to have annihilated a foe whose continued presence would have been a bane and a curse.

They presented me with the box, and the Armenian katib informed me that I was to carry it – a sort of punishment, I suppose, for causing the amir the aggravation of having to deal with me. Or, maybe it was the scribe's revenge for my subtle mockery of the day before.

Whatever the reason, I carried the head of Bohemond on my back all the way to Damascus. A loathsome labour, I cursed the arrogant young lord every trudging step of the way.

Provided with a length of folded cloth to serve as a strap, I hoisted the bejewelled box onto my back and followed the other servants when, upon striking camp, they set off. The box was heavy, and in a discouragingly short time my shoulders and arms were throbbing with a fiery ache. I eventually worked out that by knotting the ends of the strap and raising the knot to my forehead, the pressure on my shoulders was relieved by taking some of the weight on my hands. It was awkward, and bent me like an old man, but at least I was able to walk like this for long stretches at a time without exhausting myself.

On that first day, I wondered why it was that the amir's caravan made no attempt to keep pace with the troops. After a time, it became apparent that we were travelling by another route. This caused me some concern, and I hoped we would eventually rejoin the rest of the Seljuq army, as I did not like being separated from the other Christian prisoners.

Then, as the day dwindled away towards evening and we stopped to make camp, I was joined by three other captive noblemen bound for ransom in Damascus; all were Franks. One of them had been wounded in the battle, and still suffered from his wounds; the other two were nobles of a more rustic stripe who knew little Latin, and no Greek, which made it difficult to speak with them. Also, because of my dress and speech, they thought me an Armenian and worthy only of contempt; say what I might, I could not disabuse them of this notion. Consequently, they would have nothing to do with me, and I was left to myself for the most part.

In many ways, those servants employed in the keeping of the amir's camp had the best of the travelling. Since much of the treasure and tribute was loaded onto horses, requiring the servants to walk along beside, they stopped regularly for rest and water – much more often than the great mass of the army, which pushed swiftly on. So, when they rested, my fellow prisoners and I rested; and when they drank, we drank.

Those first few days were blessedly shortened, or I do not believe I would have survived. As it was, we walked until the burning sun stretched our shadows long behind us. Then the chief steward, having found a suitable place, would give the command to set up camp. In this chore, I had no part; each servant had his special duties and, as I was given nothing to do – except fetch water for the animals occasionally – I was most often able to rest and watch the hurried proceedings as tents were erected, cooking fires lit, and meals prepared.

Each evening, as the flame-tinted sky flared with the day's last brilliance, the amir and his retinue would arrive and the camp would be ready. The amir ate a simple meal, usually alone, and then received members of his following – sometimes singly, more often in groups of two or three.

Left to myself for the most part, I would find a hollow place among the stones to sleep, and lay on the ground listening to the sound of the Seljuqs' voices, loud in the quiet of the camp. They talked long into the night, their intense discussions frequently interrupted by bursts of rowdy laughter which would cease as abruptly as they began. Then, in the morning, the amir would emerge from his tent, give orders to the chief steward, mount his horse and ride away, leaving us to strike camp and move on to the next stopping place.

After we had been several days on the trail, my presence ceased to be of interest to my erstwhile guards. I was treated no more or less well than a dog or mule belonging to the camp; if no one took any interest in my welfare, neither did they show me cruelty or inflict needless torment. They were not warriors, after all, but servants: inexperienced in keeping prisoners and largely unaware of any pressing need to keep me bound or tethered in any way. Perhaps they reckoned escape unlikely as, with nothing but empty desert wilderness stretching away in every direction, there was no place for me to flee.

This was the unvarying pattern of the next eight or ten days – each day so like the last that I lost count, and simply drifted along until we came in sight of Damascus. I heard one of the Arabs shout, and the others began to chatter excitedly all at once. I raised my head and saw the shimmering dazzle on the far horizon.

It was late in the day, and the low sun set the high, white stone walls glowing like kindled ivory or lustrous alabaster. I wiped the sweat from my eyes, and gazed on the glimmering city with a thrill of mingled excitement and alarm. Ahead lay the fate towards which

I had been slowly moving for many days, and I had no idea what to expect when we reached our destination.

Rather than push on to the city, the chief steward halted the caravan at a nearby well. As the servants scurried to establish the camp, I put down my burden and sat on the mud brick rim of the well to watch while the servants scurried to make ready to receive their lord. I noticed that some greater care attended this evening's chores, and it occurred to me that perhaps the amir was preparing to receive dignitaries from the city.

For, once the amir's tent had been erected beneath the tall date palms, the treasure – which ordinarily remained packed and secured with the animals – was unloaded and brought to the amir's tent. This task finished, the servants hastened to prepare the evening meal, and I took the opportunity to doze awhile in the dying rays of the sun.

The chief steward must have caught sight of me sleeping, and saw the carved box between my feet, for I was roused with a sharp kick in my ribs and I woke to find him standing over me, railing in Arabic. Before he could kick me again, I jumped to my feet, whereupon he snatched up the box and thrust it into my arms. Still shouting, he gestured towards the amir's tent and at last I understood that I was to take the box and put it with the rest of the treasure.

I obeyed. As there was no one to take the box from me – everyone was busy with other chores – and as the entrance flap was open, I entered the tent myself. The treasure had been dumped in a careless, cascading heap. I checked my first impulse to simply pitch the box onto the pile and walk away, but fearing the square casket might come open and spill its grotesque contents, I decided to take a moment and make a secure place for the box to rest.

I carefully pulled a few items from the haphazard hoarding and set them to one side – a golden bowl, a ceremonial quiver containing four gilded arrows, an alabaster chalice rimmed and footed with silver, a pair of beaded silk shoes, and so on. This created a goodly space, but as I bent to retrieve the box a few items from the top of the stack started to slide and I soon found myself pulling things from the heap in order to keep the entire mound from toppling.

One of the objects caught my attention as I picked it up. Black and heavy, it looked like a thick oblong casket made of wood and very old. Less than the length of my forearm, both ends were bound in heavy gold into which a number of rubies had been set; each ruby was ringed with tiny pearls. Curiously, I could see neither hinge nor hasp. Closer examination confirmed that there was no lid or opening of any kind. Further, the wood was deeply grooved, worn smooth and polished by much handling, but dense and heavy still, and hard as iron.

A strange feeling crept over me as I stood holding that short length of age-darkened timber and realized I had found the holiest treasure this side of heaven. I had found the Black Rood. My heart began to beat more quickly, and I was overcome by a powerful urge to kneel down and cradle the strange object to my breast.

Fearful of being discovered, I quickly turned and made my way to the tent opening to see all the servants working away busily. The camp steward was overseeing the preparation of the cooking fires, and there was no one near the tent that I could see. Retreating into the tent once more, I knelt down and picked up the relic and held it for a moment as one might hold an infant child.

Like my father before me, I had discovered the treasure of a lifetime carelessly stowed in an Arab tent. A prize of battle, nothing more, with no more meaning to those who captured it than the price of the gold and gems adorning its surface.

These thoughts were the realization of an instant, and fleeting at that. I knelt and embraced the holy object, and reverenced it with eyes closed and a prayer of thanksgiving in my mouth. Strange to feel such an upwelling of emotion at the ordinary sight of this bulky chunk of old, old wood. Truly, there was no mystery or enchantment in its appearance. Yet, there *was* mystery.

For as I knelt in the fading light of the open entrance, I felt a quickening presence in the tent. The still air suddenly seemed to seethe with an almost oppressive power. My lungs laboured as if trying to breathe water. My hands began to shake uncontrollably; lest I drop the holy object, I placed it on the carpeted floor before me and, to keep my hands from trembling, clasped them tightly together in prayer.

'I am holding fast to God,' I prayed, 'and he is holding fast to me. I am holding fast to Christ, and he is holding fast to me. I am holding fast to the Spirit, and he is holding fast to me. The Great King, Lord of Heaven above and Earth below, holding fast to me!'

I placed my trembling hands on the holy object and prayed, 'Hear your servant, Lord and Master: I stand ready to do your will. Do not let this sacred treasure pass from the world through ignorance or careless disregard. My God and Saviour, let me redeem it from the hands of the unworthy who in their hateful pride and folly have disgraced, defiled, and demeaned your matchless gift.'

The thought that the unclean hands of unbelievers should touch this sacred relic filled me with a great disgust. I took up one of the many rugs which served as a floor for the tent and, reverently and prayerfully, wrapped the holy object in the rug and tied it with a braided cord I pulled from around a large jar containing pungent frankincense.

Then, in all reverence, I carefully replaced the Holy Rood in amongst the other items of plunder, rose, and crept from the tent. Having found the object of my quest, I did not want to allow my Seljuq captors any reason for suspicion. So, I left the tent before I was discovered, and returned to my place beside the well.

That night I lay awake gazing at the stars wheeling slowly overhead, and thinking about the Black Rood. I prayed over and over again that I might be accounted worthy to be the one to rescue it. As I held this prayer in my mind, I sensed the same quickening presence I felt in Ghazi's tent – a curious sensation. I once felt something like it in the woods when I suddenly became aware of someone, or something watching me as I knelt beside a stream for a drink of water. I slowly turned to see a large tufted wildcat crouched in a patch of sunlight a few dozen paces behind me.

Sleek, wild and powerful, muscles twitching, the magnificent creature stood with lowered head, its golden eyes aflame with a fierce intensity as it observed this odd new kind of prey. I had the same feeling now – as if I were being stalked by something of immense power, grace and subtlety; it had drawn near and fixed me in its burning gaze.

I looked across the silent camp to the amir's tent, dark and shadowy against the star-lit sky. Nothing in the camp moved; there was no sound.

The next thing I knew I was on my feet, moving towards the amir's tent. The guards were asleep; no one called out to stop me. And then I was inside. A small lamp, hanging from the central post cast a gently wavering light over the mound of treasure with which the amir impressed his many guests. I could hear the slow ebb and flow of the amir's breathing as he slept on his cushioned bed in the next room; only the cloth partition separated us.

Strangely, I felt no fear of discovery, although it would certainly have brought about immediate execution. On the contrary, I was bathed in a serenity of calm which gave me a feeling of fearless exultation as I set about gently shifting the various items of plunder in the amir's treasure trove in order to uncover the Black Rood. I moved one object and then another, and a few more, and then . . . the priceless relic lay before me.

'Great High King, reveal your glory through your servant,' I whispered. I said the first thing that came to mind only, but as soon as the words touched my lips, wonder of wonders, the tent began to fade around me – as if the fabric walls had become a thin, gauzy stuff allowing me to see, as through a veil, all the camp around me. Yet, it was not the camp I saw, but a busy road leading to the walls of a great city.

As I tried to make sense in what I was seeing, there arose a shout from the direction of the city. I looked towards the towering walls and saw a crowd of people emerging from the wide open gates.

With a cry like that of hounds scenting blood, this dark raging flood poured out from the city almost as swiftly as the dark storm clouds gathering in the dull yellow sky overhead. The blue-black bulging heads and shoulders of mighty clouds boiled in the stifling desert air, and away in the distance I could hear the low grumble of thunder.

There were others nearby, standing beside the road, waiting for the crowd to pass. I quickly joined them to see what was happening. The crowd came closer and soon reached the place where I was standing, and I saw that they were driving some poor wretch before them – prodding and shoving him along. As they drew near, I saw that his arms were tied to a rough-hewn wooden beam, and when he stumbled, they hauled him up by yanking on the ends of the beam and, once on his feet, they drove him on.

The crowd soon reached the place where I stood, but were so intent in the pursuit of their ambition they paid me no heed. They were a murderous rabble, it seemed to me; dirty beggars, street brawlers, and cudgelmen for the most part – although, here and there amidst the bedraggled mob the glint of a gold ring, a silver brooch, or the high, tapering crown of a well-made hat, gave me to know there were men of rank and power among them – and also a handful of soldiers, dressed in Roman armour.

As they hastened by, the prisoner stumbled and went down. Those foremost in the crowd snatched him upright again, and the pain made him gasp with agony, and I saw why: the wretch's back was a sodden expanse of mutilated skin and muscle forming a massive raw, gaping wound. Merciful God, great tattered shreds of flesh hung from his shoulders, ripped from his broad sturdy back by the wicked, iron-tipped Roman lash. Blood coursed freely down his sides, staining his torn robe and spattering the dusty road with each jolting step.

He took but one more step and fell again. They were on him in an instant, kicking at him and shouting for him to get up. Two soldiers shoved into the throng and while one began pushing people away, the other seized the end of the beam and untied the ropes binding the man's arms.

The crowd howled with rage and three more legionaries appeared and waded in, forcing the rabble back with the shafts of their short spears. One of the soldiers turned and seized a man – a huge black Ethiope on his way to the city, and who, like myself, was merely standing alongside the road watching the fearful procession. Too frightened to resist, the poor fellow was yanked into the wild maelstrom, and pressed into service.

Freed from the crushing burden of the beam, the wounded prisoner made to rise; he lifted his head and looked up, his eyes met my gaze, and my heart caught in my throat, for I knew I looked into the battered face of God's own dear son.

THIRTY-SIX

That once-noble visage was bruised and bleeding, the high, handsome brow shattered and the straight, fine nose broken. A circlet cap had been woven of desert briar and the thorns jammed into his scalp. Blood trickled from the wounds, mixing with the dust of the road to form muddy rivulets down his face. His eyes as they beheld mine, although filled with anguish, were yet keen with intelligence and a burning volition.

That was all I had – a single, fleeting look – but I swear all the grief and care of creation was in that pain-riven glance. The crowd, baying like crazed hounds, urged him on. The soldiers gabbed his arms and hauled him upright. He was shoved on his way with the Ethiope following behind, dragging the heavy crossbeam. And the ghastly retinue lurched along once more.

I stood for a moment, too astonished and terrified to move; and then, before I knew it, I was following the crowd, surrounded by a large number of loudly wailing women, and giddy, excited children. We continued down the road towards a curious, hump-shaped hill no great distance from the city walls.

The hill was topped by a rocky outcrop against which a large timberwork frame had been erected. A small contingent of bored-looking legionaries sat waiting on the hillside near the road. By the time I pushed my way to the front of the crowd, I saw the Lord Christ standing with splendid dignity, head erect, struggling to remain upright while the crowd surged and seethed around him.

The soldiers wasted no time. Grabbing the crosspiece from the Ethiope, they dragged it up the hillside a few paces and threw it on the ground. Then, laying hands on the condemned man, they stripped off his clothes and pulled him up to the beam, turned him around, and pushed him down onto his bloody back. He winced with pain, but did not cry out.

One of the waiting legionaries, a burly, muscled hulk in a leather labourer's apron, rose and stepped quickly to the prisoner. Shirtless, his big arms glistening, he gave a nod of command and the prisoner's right arm was stretched out and held down on the timber. Then, kneeling on the condemned man's arm so as to hold it still, he ground a splayed thumb into the hollow of the man's forearm just above the wrist and held it there for a moment.

With his other hand he reached into a pocket of his leather apron and drew out a thick iron spike which he placed where his thumb had been. Then, with quick, practised efficiency he reached behind him and took up a short, heavy blacksmith's hammer. The movement was so swift I did not see what was happening at first.

I saw the soldier's great arm rise with dread purpose and fall with a solid resonating crack. In the same instant the Lord Jesu's head jerked up, eyes bulging, mouth snatched open in a soundless scream of agony as the hard metal smashed through the flesh and tendons and veins of his wrist.

My heart trembled within me, and I wanted to look away – but I could not. I watched, clasping my hands together and murmuring helpless, hopeless prayers.

Bright blood welled up in a sudden crimson gush, and the crowd roared its approval as two more mighty blows drove the cruel spike deep into the stout timber beam – whereupon the soldier rose, stepped over his victim and repeated the procedure on the left arm. Three quick, decisive blows rang like anvil peals, driving the spike between the twin bones of the man's forearm and into the heavy wood.

No sooner had the last blow rung out than the soldiers passed ropes under the timber beam and secured the condemned man's arms at the elbows. They then turned and began hauling the beam up the hill, three soldiers at the end of each rope, dragging their victim with it. The ground was rough and rocky, and Christ's poor wounded back left a bloody swathe in the pale bone-dry dirt.

At the top of the hill, they heaved the ropes over the upper beams of the timber framework. The dangling ends were caught and passed to the legionaries beneath who, with the help of a score or more of the more zealous members of the rabble, eagerly seized the lines and pulled hard. The ropes snapped taut, jerking the suffering Jesu from the ground.

Up, up he soared, rising skyward, the ropes singing over the rough timber until the crosspiece met the upper beam of the framework where it jarred to a stop, leaving him suspended high above the crowd, his arms pinioned to the heavy timber beam. There the Blessed Christ swung, writhing with the violence of his crude ascent.

The crosspiece was quickly lashed to the upper beam of the framework, and there – his gentle, healing hands twisted and deformed into the shape of claws – he hung; high above the ground, he hung, blood coursing in rivulets down his arms and sides, mingling with the muddy sweat of his torment. Stretched between earth and sky, the Holy One of God hung, the weight of his broken body dangling from his strong arms.

Meanwhile, two other unfortunates – thieves caught in the act – were likewise crucified and strung up either side of him. As soon as the two wretches were secured, the soldiers produced a long beam, part of the trunk of a tree, and lashed it tight to the uprights just below the knees of the hanging men. The big Roman then proceeded to drive spikes through the victims' anklebones, fixing them to the lower beam. The two thieves screamed and thrashed in their agony while the mob jeered and applauded.

Unable to bear the torment any longer, Jesu opened his mouth and screamed, 'Elo-i!' The cords stood out on his neck with the force of his shout. 'Elo-i!'

The mob fell back at the fearful power of the cry. They looked at one another and murmured. 'He is calling on Elijah,' someone said. 'No, wait!' said another. 'He is calling on God to save him!'

'He saved others,' scoffed one big brute merrily. 'Now let him save himself!'

'Quiet! He is speaking!' shouted a man near the front. 'I cannot hear what he is saying. Here, give him a drink and maybe he will speak again.'

A sop of wine was raised on the end of a stick and held to his mouth, but Jesu bowed his head and said no more.

A group of elder Jews arrived from the city just then; there were perhaps a dozen or so, some dressed in priestly garb, others in costly red robes with chains of gold around their necks. Gathering up their long cloaks to keep them from the dust, they mounted the side of the hill and pushed their way to the front of the throng.

Their expressions smug and hard, they took their places at the front of the mob and stood, like monuments of self-righteous reprisal, glaring up at the dying man. The Romans, having completed their duties, now turned to other amusements. They had some bread and wine with them and sat down a little apart to eat and drink, while they waited for the execution to reach its fatal and inevitable conclusion.

The crowd continued their crude harangue of the dying men, mocking them, laughing at their misery as they tried to keep the weight of their bodies off their pinioned ankles while, at the same time, relieve the searing torment of their arms. Some of the older youths thought it good sport to pelt the condemned with rocks – which they did with increasing impunity. Indeed, one young thug made a lucky throw, striking one of the thieves full in the face, smashing his cheekbone and knocking out the man's eye; the poor wretch moaned and tossed his head back and forth, the mangled eye dangling and bouncing on his crushed cheek, much to the delight of the jeering throng.

This emboldened the rest, who redoubled their efforts, and I believe the condemned might have been stoned to death on the crosstrees if not for a careless throw which struck the beam and careened into the party of Roman soldiers who, having finished their meal, were now playing at dice for the prisoners' clothes and sandals. The stone struck one of the legionaries on the leg, and up he came; he charged into the boys with drawn sword, walloping one or two of the pluckier ruffians with the flat of his blade. They howled like scalded pups and the whole pack fled.

A strange calm descended on the hump-backed hill then, as the crowd settled down to wait. The sky grew darker, the dreadful yellow turning green-grey like a diseased wound, and the air, already still, became stifling. The only sound to be heard was the desperate wheezing and gasping of the men on the gibbet as they struggled to get air into their lungs; though all three looked as if they were past caring, life clung on and would not abandon them.

The mob quickly grew bored with the tedious display and became restless. Soon the crowd was thinning at the edges as the less fervid, having had their fill, began to creep away quietly, leaving the hardened zealots to their gloating. About this time, a Roman commander arrived on horseback. He sat for a moment, taking in the spectacle, and then called a command to the soldiers lolling on the ground.

I could not make out what was said, for I was on the hillside and the centurion remained on the road. But two of the legionaries jumped to their feet and hastened off to where some of their tools and gear were lying on the ground. One of the soldiers reached for the ladder, and the other a hammer and flat piece of wood which were lying there. Resting the top of the ladder against the upper crossbeam, the first soldier climbed up, while the other, standing below, handed up the hammer and wood. The first soldier then proceeded to nail the wooden placard to the upper beam next to Jesu's head.

There was, so far as I could see, nothing written on the placard, but this oversight was soon corrected, for the commander spoke again, and the legionary on the ground bent down and picked up a stick, broke off one end, and passed it to his friend on the ladder. The soldier took the stick and, holding it to the body of the hanging man, dabbed the broken end in his freely trickling blood. He then proceeded to write in ragged red letters these words: Iesu Nazarethaei Rex Iudae.

Seeing this, the crowd instantly sent up an appalling shriek. The priests and elders standing proudly at the forefront of the crowd flew into a foul rage, wailing and tearing at their clothes and beards. Two of the Jewish leaders hastened down to where the centurion sat on his horse, watching the commotion with a bemused expression.

'Please, hear us, sir,' the senior of the two cried. 'That man is *not* the King of the Jews!'

'We have no king but Caesar!' added the other. Some of those on the hillside took up the reply as a chant. 'We have no king but Caesar!' they shouted half-heartedly.

A white-haired man in priest's robes joined the two. 'The sign is an offence to our people,' he insisted. 'We beg you, lord, take it down.'

The centurion, enjoying the uproar he had provoked with his

innocent order, gazed with unruffled merriment at the three and shook his head slowly.

'My lord,' the old priest pleaded, 'it is an abomination and a stench in the nostrils of God. Please, remove the sign at once.'

Still shaking his head, the commander replied, 'It stays.'

'If it cannot be removed,' one of the other elders suggested, adopting a reasonable tone, 'then perhaps it could be made to read: This Nazarene *claimed* to be King of the Jews.'

At that moment, one of the ruffians in the crowd darted out from among the throng. Before anyone could stop him, he ran to the ladder and climbed up, almost knocking the legionary from his perch as he tried to grab hold of the sign and tear it down.

The centurion lashed his mount forwards up the hill to the ladder and, reaching out, seized the rascal by the leg and pulled him from the ladder. The man rolled on the ground, yelling and fuming, and the priests and elders quickly gathered around pleading with the soldiers to take down the sign and restore the peace. But the Roman commander, growing tired of their sanctimonious bleating, refused to be drawn into the affray. He ordered soldiers to remove the man who had tried to tear down the sign and, as they dragged him aside, the sky gave forth a low, worrisome growl.

A sharp gust of wind sent the dust swirling around the hilltop. The commander raised his eyes skyward, and then, as the first fat drops of rain spattered into the dust, he decided that it was time to disperse the crowds before the situation deteriorated further. Turning to his cohort, he gave the final command: 'Finish it.'

Taking up his hammer once more, the big Roman stepped to the nearest of the victims and with a mighty swing, hurled the flat of the hammer into the man's leg halfway between knee and ankle. The shinbone cracked with a dull sickening crunch – a sound so appalling it even made the blood-lusting crowd wince. The suffering wretch screamed in agony and passed out. The legionary applied the hammer to the other leg, and the unconscious man slumped down hard, the weight of his body tearing his arms from their sockets as his legs folded neatly in half. He gave a strangled sigh, choked on his tongue, and expired.

The executioner moved on to the next thief, who was yet aware enough to know what was about to take place. He began pleading and crying to be spared. But the soldier took no heed, breaking both the man's legs with as many blows of the hammer. The second victim was not so lucky as the first; he did not pass out but screamed and writhed in agony as he kept trying to raise himself up on his ruined legs so as to fill his lungs with air. He jerked and twitched pitifully, the sharp shards of shinbone poking through the flesh of his damaged limbs, each movement bringing fresh torture as the ragged ends of his shattered bones gnashed and splintered like broken teeth.

Turning his attention to the last victim, the big Roman swung his hammer wide, but withheld the blow at the last instant. Looking up into the face of the hanging man, he said, 'This one is dead.'

The watching elders heard this and raised an outcry at once. 'How can it be?' they demanded. 'It is not yet evening!'

'He is not dead!' someone shouted. 'He has only swooned.'

One of the elders, dressed in red robes and wearing a heavy chain of gold around his neck, stepped forwards. 'See here, centurion,' he said in educated Latin, 'the people are right. He has only swooned – revive him, and you will see.'

The executioner heard this and grew angry. 'Do you call me liar?' he snarled.

'By no means!' said the elder, raising his hands as if to fend off a blow. 'But this Jesu was known to be a sorcerer and a magician. He may be using his powers to feign death. Do not be deceived. Rather, do your duty.'

'I know my duty,' growled the big Roman, moving nearer, 'just as I know a dead man when I see one.' Hefting the hammer in his hand, he said, 'Maybe you would like to join him in Hades – or wherever it is you people go.'

The wealthy elder gave a yelp and backed away. The executioner made as if to pursue him into the crowd, but the centurion called him back. 'Longinus! Enough! We will prove it to them,' he said, casting an eye to the gathering storm. 'Then maybe we can get back to the city before we're soaked to the bone.'

The big Roman abandoned his pursuit and returned to the foot of the framework. Taking his spear, he raised it to the Anointed One's side and thrust it up hard beneath his ribs in the centre of his chest. Watery blood burst from the wound, gushing in a pale fountain all at once. There was neither movement nor outcry from the victim, and I knew I looked upon a corpse.

At that moment, there came a great peal of thunder and the storm broke with a force to shake the very earth. A cold wind whirled around the hilltop, whining like an animal in pain, and kicking up prodigious clouds of dust and dirt. Seeing that the condemned men were dead, the crowd retreated, streaming back to the city, throwing their cloaks over their heads as they ran. The Romans quickly gathered up their weapons and followed the throng back to the city, leaving two of their number behind to keep watch.

The rain came hard and fast, pelting down in stinging sheets. I looked around, expecting to find myself alone on the hillside, but was surprised to discover a small, miserable knot of people – women, mostly – standing a little apart. They were weeping and clinging to one another, oblivious to the storm crashing around them.

The wind howled like a wounded animal. Lightning flashed and rolling blasts of thunder shook the ground as if to crack the very walls of Jerusalem. The rain pitched down in great lashing waves – as if the bruised sky had ruptured, spilling out its waters all at once. The dry hillside slowly dissolved into a sticky quagmire.

Despite the savage blast, I waited to see what would happen, and in a little while the storm which had blown up so quickly, passed the same way. The thunder stopped, and the wind calmed. The air, refreshed from the cooling rain, smelled wonderfully of spices and rare desert flowers. The dead men, their corpses washed, hung dripping from their crosspieces, clean now, and ready for burial.

Above the sound of the wailing women, I heard someone calling from the road below; I turned to see a young dark-bearded man in a fine yellow cloak hastening towards the hill and hailing the little knot of mourners as he came. Some distance behind him came a man leading a donkey and cart. I do not know if either of them had been present at the execution, but the young man quickly mounted the hillside and joined the group. They held a brief discussion, whereupon he stepped out from among them and approached the timber frame.

The two soldiers, who had been huddling in the shelter of the rocks, stepped forwards and demanded to know the man's business. He replied, speaking in good Latin, and said that he had come for the body of Jesu. 'It is growing late,' he explained. 'The Sabbath begins at sunset. We must remove the body before the sun sets, for it is against the law to bury a man on the Sabbath. Likewise it is an abomination to leave the dead unburied.'

The young soldier frowned. 'We were told nothing about this. You must get permission from the governor.'

'Please,' the young man said, 'there is no time.' Indicating the bundle under his arm, he said, 'I have brought the shroud, and I will happily take full responsibility for the burial.'

Reaching into his belt he brought out several pieces of silver which he passed to the soldier. 'This is for your trouble. I will need your help to get him down.'

The second soldier looked at the money, and nudged his more reluctant comrade. 'Very well,' the legionary agreed at last. 'You can have all three of them for all I care.'

The young man called to the waiting mourners, still clustered together, sobbing quietly, and two men came out from among them to help. The Romans put up the ladder and one of them ascended with drawn sword, preparing to hack off the hands of the dead man.

'No! Please, no!' cried the young man. 'You must not mutilate the body.'

The legionary grimaced. 'I thought you were in a hurry, friend.' Hefting the broad blade. 'A clean chop – it is the best way.'

'He won't feel a thing,' added the other soldier helpfully. 'He's dead as dung.'

Pointing to the group of women now standing below the body, the young man said, 'Please, for his mother's sake, let us preserve what little dignity remains.'

The soldier shrugged and proceeded to hack at the rope binding the crosspiece to the upper framework. One side gave way and the body slewed sideways. Leaning across the corpse, he cut the other rope, and the body pitched forwards, still attached to the rood piece. Those on the ground caught the blessed body of Our Lord and bore it up while the second legionary raised a massive pair of iron tongs and proceeded to nip the head from the spike through the corpse's ankles.

It was difficult work, and the young Jew continually urged the soldiers to use as much care as possible. Before it was over, all of the mourners were needed to help support the body so as to prevent it breaking off at the feet. But at last the legionary succeeded in freeing the corpse and they laid the inert body of the Lord Jesu gently on the wet ground.

Next, the legionary went to work on the spikes holding the dead man's arms to the crossbeam. Using the huge tongs, he gnawed and worried the beaten heads from the iron nails, and all the while the young man pressed him to hurry as it was growing late. The soldier grew angry. 'Do you want it fast, or do you want it clean?' he demanded. 'Which is it?'

'Joseph,' said one of the women gently. She was younger than the others; long dark hair spilled out from beneath the hood of her cloak. 'Do not anger the man. He is only trying to help.' Her voice was a warm balm of comfort poured out to soothe the cold, cruel hurt of the day.

'Miriam, we must –' He started to object, but she silenced him with a smile of such sweet sadness, it cleft my heart to see it. 'Please, Joseph. It will be all right. There is no hurry anymore.'

'Very well,' the wealthy young man relented. To the legionary, he said, 'Take your time, my friend.'

The soldier, glancing at the woman with something more than benign interest, resumed his work, eventually freeing the right wrist and then the left. The women carefully spread the woven linen shroud on the ground and the body of Heaven's Fairest Son was laid upon it. The men watched while the women carefully arranged the torn limbs and smoothed back the tangled hair, murmuring a low litany of Psalms the while. Then they folded the shroud over the body and secured it with broad bands around the neck, and chest, and feet. Thanking the Roman soldiers, the men took up the body and carried it down the hillside to the cart which was now waiting on the road. They placed the body of the Saviour in the cart and then began the long, slow journey back to the city.

The soldiers divided the money between them and, with a last glance at the two dead thieves, shouldered their spears and departed. 'Who do you think he was?' I heard one of them ask as they started off down the hill.

'It hardly matters,' replied the other. 'One Jew is the same as another. They're all alike, these Jews – zealots, madmen, and murderers.'

They moved off, and I found myself alone on the hillside, staring at the crossbeam which had been left lying on the ground, the headless spikes where the Blessed Saviour's arms had been pierced, the stain of his blood deep in the grain of the rough-hewn wood.

I knelt and placed my hand reverently on the rood, and felt the coarse, unforgiving weight hard beneath my palm. I heard voices behind me and, thinking the legionaries had returned, I glanced quickly over my shoulder and saw myself asleep on the ground beside a well.

Instantly, I was back in Amir Ghazi's camp.

The moon was down and the stars were fading with the first pale hint of dawn showing in the east, and I was in my place beside the well once more.

I rose. The camp was quiet; nothing had changed. Had I crept into the amir's tent? Or, had I fallen asleep and dreamed it? It did not matter. I knew beyond all uncertainty that I had received a vision of rare and special power. My hands and face tingled, and the ground felt thin as water beneath my feet.

My body began to tremble – not with fear or foreboding, but with a ferocious ecstasy. I felt like running and leaping and crying to the star-dusted heavens in praise and thanksgiving to my Generous Creator for the wonderful vision I had been granted.

It was all I could do to keep from laughing out loud and waking all the camp. So, I lay beside the well, exhilarated, shaking with jubilation, joy coursing like liquid fire through my veins, pure elation bubbling up like a wellspring filled not with water, but with sweet, heady wine.

As dawn broke full and glorious in the east, I got up and knelt, raising my face to the sun, and stretching my arms wide, I pledged a solemn vow within my heart that whatever should befall me in the days to come, I would strive above all things to acquit myself with the same humility, strength, and courage I had witnessed in Jesu's death so that I might be worthy of my Redeemer's sacrifice.

PART III

November 17, 1901: Paphos, Cyprus

Professor Manos Rossides lived in the bottom floor of a tiny townhouse. A violin teacher had the upper floors, and there was a violin and cello duet wafting down the stairwell as I stood before the sombre brown door in the semi-darkness waiting for my expectant host to answer the bell.

I yanked the bell-pull again, waited some more, and was just about to give up and go home when I heard a shuffling sound on the other side. Presently a key clicked in the lock and the door opened onto a small dark man with a heavy beetling brow, hooded eyes, and an unruly mass of thick, wavy, dark hair which stood out from his head in all directions; it put me in mind of a storm at sea, and it was all I could do to tear my eyes from the startling sight and say, 'Professor Rossides? I am Gordon Murray. I was given to understand you would be expecting me.'

At the sound of my name the man's sleepy countenance sparked to life. 'Quite right, sir! Right on time!' He smiled and his dark eyes became keen, and his features boyish and winsome. 'Do come in, Mr Murray.' He took my coat and waved me to a chair at a spindle-legged table piled dangerously high with books and papers. A brass lamp with a green glass shade hung over the table, illuminating the stacks of printed matter like upland plateaux in the glare of the summer sun.

'Time is precious,' he announced. 'We begin at once.' With that he began reciting the Greek alphabet, drifting around the room behind me, pounding his fist into the palm of his outstretched hand as he enunciated each letter. After two more recitations, he had me doing it. We worked steadily for ninety minutes, and just as I was beginning to get the feel of the unfamiliar words in my mouth, he called the lesson to a halt.

'Excellent! Excellent!' he cried, beaming at me as if at a prize heifer. 'You are a natural scholar, Mr Murray. Together we will achieve the impossible.'

'I will be content with the merely passable,' I told him.

He laughed, shaking his head. 'Dear me, no. We'll have none of that. You are too able and too clever to settle for second best. No, my friend, when we are finished you will be able to sit in Aphrodite's Taverna on the waterfront in Rhodes and talk politics with the fishermen.'

'Oh?' I said, rising to retrieve my coat. 'Is that all? I rather thought I might indulge in a bit of lecturing on Plato's *Symposium*.'

'Tut, sir,' the professor chided, his eyes wrinkling with mirth. 'I said we should achieve the impossible – not perform miracles!'

Thus began my short, but intensive apprenticeship in conversational Greek. My tutor sent me home with two books that night – one Greek, the other Latin – both of which I was to have read by my next visit the following week. I do not know how he crammed so much expert instruction into our all-too-short sessions. But as the weeks went by, I found my mastery growing by leaps and bounds; nagging little foibles and difficulties that had plagued me since college evaporated in the blistering heat of the professor's searing, searching intellect.

Summer came and went, and as autumn rolled on apace, I began to think ahead to what might await me at the end of September. The answer to this came on my last visit to Professor Rossides' study. Actually, I did not know it was my final visit until my assiduous mentor reached over to the text I was reading, and closed the book. 'Perfect,' he declared. 'Our work together is completed.'

'How can it be finished? I feel as if I have only begun.'

'Oh, indeed. And I congratulate you on a most auspicious beginning. But, my assignment was to enable you to speak and write well enough to make yourself understood, and you have achieved that and more. I shall be making my report to your colleagues shortly. Well done, Mr Murray.'

I bade him farewell, and left feeling slightly saddened by the prospect that I would no longer have the enjoyment of his intensely stimulating lessons. This feeling lasted until the middle of the next week, when I once again received a visit from Pemberton and Zaccaria.

They turned up just before the office closed for the day and, with evident pleasure, pronounced the completion of my assignment satisfactory in every way. 'We knew you would take to your studies,' Zaccaria confided.

'It was a most gratifying experience, I must say. I enjoyed it very much.'

'Be that as it may,' said Pemberton, withdrawing a long white envelope from the inner pocket of his coat. 'I think you will enjoy employing your new skills even more.'

He passed he envelope to me and indicated that I was to open it. I lifted the flap, reached in, and pulled out two steamer tickets – one for my wife, and one for myself – with the destination listed as Paphos, Cyprus. 'As you see, the ship sails two weeks from today,' he said. 'That should give you time enough to arrange your affairs, I should think.'

'Six weeks in Cyprus,' I mused, reading the return portion of the ticket. 'Yes, I think Caitlin and I could do very well with that, thank you very much.'

'I do not anticipate any problems arising from your legal work.' The way he said it, I could not tell if it was a question, or an observation of fact. In any case, I suspected any genuine obstacles would have been foreseen and removed.

'None at all,' I replied. 'As it happens, this time of year is normally very quiet. I can have one of my juniors keep an eye on things while I am gone.'

'Splendid.'

Thus, the arrangements were firmly in place. All I had to do was pack and get myself and the good wife to the steamer on time – a task which somehow expanded to fill every available moment, even as Caitlin filled every available case and trunk. It was not until the ship loosed its moorings and steamed for Cyprus that I realized not a single word had been said about what I would do when I got there.

More mystery was awaiting me on the landing at Paphos harbour in the form of the jovial Mr Melos who stood on the wharf in his best blue suit, holding a card with my last name written on it. His dark hair was oiled and combed, and the lower part of his face was covered by three-day old stubble. He grinned and waved when he saw us, and came bounding across the landing to shake our hands.

'What's this?' wondered Caitlin, charmed by the man's eager-ness to please. 'You didn't tell me we were to be chaperoned, darling.'

'It is non-stop adventure start to finish,' I said.

Our greeter introduced himself and I understood at once why I had sweated and strained through the summer to learn the language: Mr Melos spoke no English. Nevertheless, I was quickly to learn that he was the most expert and knowledgeable guide imaginable. He was an archaeologist who had spent his entire career digging on the island; there was nothing about Cyprus or its history he did not know. He also ran a small, private museum, with a guest house next door, both of which he had filled with mementos from his various digs. 'The more valuable specimens go off to museums around the world,' he said, when he showed us through his rooms one day. 'But the smaller pieces, the duplicates, I keep.'

We spent the first few days in Mr Melos' able care, the sole tenants in his guest house. Caitlin fell instantly in love with the place, and proclaimed that it was high time I had brought her someplace nice, and furthermore, she was never leaving.

That first day we ate a light meal and waited for our luggage to arrive, which it did by donkey cart towards evening. By then, we were already feeling ourselves slipping into what Caitlin called 'Cyprus time' – the pace at which things happened, or didn't, according to the whims and preoccupations of the locals.

The reason for my adventure remained obscure, and I had begun to wonder whether I ought to say something about it, when Mr Melos appeared as we were having breakfast one morning. He presented me with a letter which had arrived some little while previously, I suspect. It was from Zaccaria, and it contained the purpose of my visit. As soon as we were rested from our journey, we were to make our way to a certain monastery in the hills. 'I will take you,' said Melos when I asked him where it was. 'I know this place very well. Leave everything to me; it is all arranged.'

Later that same morning, we gathered our things and proceeded by carriage up into the foothills of the Troodos mountains to the little village of Panayia, where a cottage had been hired for us. We arrived near dusk and Melos took us to our cottage, and introduced us to our housekeeper – a sister of his named Helena, a small, plump woman of mature years who chattered like a mynah bird whether anyone was listening or not. She had a meal ready for us when we arrived, showed us where to find everything, and then left us to eat and sleep in peace.

We spent a wonderful first night in our little cottage, dining by candlelight with the windows open onto the courtyard where late roses were still in bloom. The next morning, our inestimable host collected us and took us to the monastery.

'Ayios Moni is a very ancient place,' he said. 'The monks there maintain a library of many priceless manuscripts.'

It was, of course, these manuscripts that I had come to see – rather, it was one manuscript in particular.

Upon our arrival, we were introduced to the bishop, who conducted us on a tour of the small, but tidy monastery, which was now home to fewer than thirty monks. At the end of the tour, he said, 'I suppose you will be wanting to get started.'

'To tell you the truth,' I replied, silently thanking Rossides for my new-found fluency, 'I would like nothing better. Unfortunately, I do not know precisely why I have come.'

Bald Bishop Naxos laughed, and said, 'You have come to view the Caithness Manuscript.'

'Caithness,' said Caitlin, when I had told her what the bishop had said. 'You mean the Caithness in Scotland?'

'Haven't the foggiest.'

He led us to the library where a few monks were working away, hunched silently over old vellums and parchments. He spoke a few words to the brother in charge of the collection, and the black-robed monk disappeared into the stacks, returning a few moments later with a weighty bundle wrapped in heavy homespun linen.

'Behold,' said Bishop Naxos, 'one of our order's prize possessions.' He directed Brother Nicholas to a nearby table beneath a window, and there the monk opened the parcel. 'The ink is faded, and there are a few water spots – we had a bad storm in the fifteenth century, and the roof leaked. Still, it is in remarkable condition for a document which was written in 1132.'

I translated the priest's words for Caitlin, who marvelled at the age of the venerable manuscript.

He passed his hand lovingly over the bundle of parchment, and fingered the silk cord which bound the bundle together. 'This will be the last time the manuscript is seen in the place where it was created. I think it highly appropriate that you should be the reader.'

He regarded me meaningfully, but the reference was lost on me. 'I do not understand,' I said.

'Next month it is going into a vault at the Ministry of Antiquities in Athens,' he explained, but before I could tell him that this was not what I meant, he added: 'It is felt by my superiors at Khyrsorroyiatissa that our order can no longer protect it adequately.'

'Nonsense!' grumbled Melos sourly.

'We have it for a little while yet.' He smiled sadly, and pulled a chair from the table. 'Please, sit. We would be honoured for you to be our guest for as long as you like.'

Again, I understood that he was according me a special favour, but his meaning remained beyond my comprehension.

I told Caitlin what he had said, and asked if she minded very much amusing herself for awhile. 'Go on with you,' she said, 'and don't be silly. Of course I don't mind. I can well look after myself for a few days.'

So, with the blessing of both bishop and wife, I settled myself into the chair I was to occupy for a good many days. When the others had gone, I loosened the silken cord and turned back the battered old covering.

The script that met my eye was strong and fair. The rich black tone had faded to a pale reddish sepia, but remained clearly legible. I read the first words, and knew why I had been summoned to this task. My heart began to beat with such force I thought I would have to abandon the work before I had even begun. Before me on the table was the account of Murdo's son, Duncan, and, in his own words, a record of his pilgrimage in the Holy Land.

THIRTY-SEVEN

Amir Ghazi's arrival in Damascus was hailed as the triumphal entry of a conquering hero. He massed his army on the wide plain outside the city walls and then proceeded to lead his victorious troops and their wretched captives into the city. The wily amir spared no pomp in making his entrance as impressive as possible. Drummers went before the amir and his bodyguard, pounding out dull thunder; children ran beside the amir's horse, scattering flower petals; trumpeters blew shrill blasts to part the crowds who stood and gaped at the passing spectacle.

We marched through the streets to the citadel where Atabeg Buri and all the officials and dignitaries met the grand cavalcade in the courtyard of the Rose Pavillion. Proud Ghazi made a great show of displaying his prize captives; the prisoners were paraded before a double rank of noble Arabs, some on small cushioned stools and some on thrones, and made to bow before them in a show of subservient humiliation. I, who had carried Bohemond's head on my back, was forced to display the ghastly prize to the Arabs.

Summoned from the fore-ranks of the captives, I was marched before the Seljuqs and Saracens as they sat in festal splendour, enjoying the subjugation of their hated foe. Two guards led me to the foot of the low rise of steps leading up to the perfumed pavilion and, at Ghazi's direction, I was commanded to open the box. The Arab noblemen laughed to see the mighty prince, and bane of their people, disgraced in death.

One of the Arabs, however, did not laugh with the others. Dressed in opulent robes that glowed with the iridescent blues and greens of peacock feathers, and wearing a huge blue turban, he observed the Christian prince's shame with a rapt and thoughtful expression. At the height of the mirth, he beckoned Atabeg Buri nearer and spoke privately to him for some time. Meanwhile, I stood and held the open box for the delight and delectation of the others, hating the display and my part in it.

When the two finished their conversation, Buri invited Amir Ghazi to join them. The amir advanced and was presented to the stranger in the blue turban, whereupon he immediately fell to his knees and pressed the nobleman's hand to his forehead. The Arab potentate endured the fawning servility of the amir with cool aplomb and, to my great chagrin, raised his hand and pointed directly at me.

Ghazi jumped up and, with an ostentatious flourish of his arm, waved me forwards. Accompanied by the guards, I was led to the pavilion steps and there made to kneel, holding the box while the strutting amir presented the resplendent onlooker with the gift of Bohemond's head.

Why he should want the grotesque thing, I could not say. But the bestowing of it filled old flat-faced Ghazi with a rare elation. His rough and weathered visage cracked wide in a grin of exaltation and, in a fit of largesse, he lavished the whole of his trove upon his obviously superior overlord: the objects of gold and silver, the saddles, weapons, and armour, the horses, and all the rest he had accumulated – including the prisoners. Yes, and myself as well.

Although I guessed what was happening at the time, I did not learn until much later that day the identity of the glittering luminary who was to be my new master. It was Sahak, the Armenian scribe and advisor, who told me, and took great delight in the telling. 'You belong to the Caliph of Baghdad now,' he said, unable to suppress a wicked smile at what he imagined would be distressing news to me.

'But that is impossible!' I cried. My reaction gave him great satisfaction, and his hairless jowls jiggled with mirth.

In truth, I was not dismayed in the least. As I say, I had already worked out what had happened, and concluded that it did not greatly matter who held the end of my chain, so to speak, just so long as I remained close to the Black Rood. Still, I had wit enough to adopt a woeful demeanour in order to find out all I could of my new master. For I knew if Sahak thought the information would benefit me in some way, he would doubtless have withheld it out of sheer meanness.

So, making a pretence of consternation, I seized his sleeve and clung to him in desperation. 'What will happen to me?'

'Who can say?' Delighting in his power over me, he said, 'But since you ask, I expect you will be killed.'

'No!' I gasped. 'I have done nothing. My friends,' I said, gripping him harder, 'they will ransom me.'

'So you say.' He shook my hand from his arm. 'But they have not come for you, have they? If I were you, I would forget about being ransomed. Your friends have forgotten you.'

'They would never do that!' I shouted, my agitation increasing his merriment.

'They have given you up,' he maintained, 'or else they would have come for you. If they wanted to ransom you, they would have done so long since.'

'They will come,' I insisted. 'The Caliph of Baghdad, you say? I cannot go with him. You must speak to Amir Ghazi. You must beg him to let me stay in Damascus where my friends can find me. You must tell him, Sahak, you are my only hope.'

'Oh, rest assured, I will do what I can,' he told me, the keen light of treason in his eyes.

'Thank you, Sahak. Thank you,' I said, knowing full well that now I would remain with the caliph and within reach of the Black Rood.

The deceitful katib scuttled away, and I watched him go – a thoroughly detestable fellow, to be sure, but he had his uses. I returned to the corner of my cell and reflected on how even the wicked were not beyond the reach of the Swift Sure Hand, who employed all things as he would to bring about his purposes.

For, following the triumphal entry and Amir Ghazi's rash fit of generosity, my fellow captives and I were taken to the stinking, vermin infested prison of Amir Buri, Damascus' preening potentate, to await the pleasure of our master, the caliph.

In all, it was not so bad for us, and now that I could be assured of remaining near the Holy Rood, I was content. The stench I could tolerate; after endless hot days in the scorching sun, the cool, damp darkness of the dungeons was blessed relief itself. But the rats and mice were a very plague and no one dared fall asleep at night for the instant a body drifted off, the rats would be on him, gnawing at any exposed flesh. Several men lost the tips of fingers and toes before learning to sleep in the day, when the vermin were less active.

Besides the three noblemen, there were other Christians imprisoned with me; those crusaders who had survived the battle and ensuing journey from Anazarbus had also been made to walk in the grand procession in order to enhance the golden lustre of Ghazi's glory. Girardus was among the survivors, but I could not speak to him, for I was held in a cell by myself apart from the others. The reason, I eventually discovered, was that the Christians blamed *me* for Bohemond's defeat.

Word had spread through the prisoner ranks that I was the spy who had betrayed them to the Seljuqs. The loss of their comrades, and their subsequent imprisonment and slavery was my fault, and more than one of them had vowed to kill me the moment the opportunity presented itself. My friend Girardus might have told them otherwise, and perhaps he tried; but if he did, they paid him no heed. I suppose they needed someone to bear the blame for all the hardship. Bohemond was dead – and his closest advisors and commanders with him, and so the surviving captives fastened on me as the source of their troubles.

I suppose I deserved their condemnation – albeit of all those who had a hand in the ill-fated enterprise, I was the only one who had in no way intended for anyone to be killed. But what did that matter? If I had not allowed myself to be drawn into the affair, the massacre would not have happened. Bohemond would have taken Anazarbus and that would have been the end of it. The Armenians would probably have been slaughtered in great numbers, true, but – as I was continually and forcibly reminded – life held but slight value in the East. The destinies of entire nations were bought and sold for a moment's fleeting glory, a few pieces of silver, or the low ambitions of a prince.

Too late I began to understand how Murdo felt about the Holy Land, and why.

Over the next few days, I set about trying to find out what manner of man the Caliph of Baghdad might be. Using the pretence of bargaining to remain in Damascus, the slimy Sahak came and went, enjoying his imagined treachery to the full, while I remained supplied with morsels of worthwhile information.

I learned that aside from being the most powerful ruler in the region, the Caliph of Baghdad was regarded as an able and thoughtful ruler, who valued wisdom and studied the elusive art of philosophy at a school of his own creation. A very religious man, he was a devout Muhammedan, who lectured to students from the Arab holy book, the Qur'an. He was renowned as an authority in the application of the abstruse principles of Islamic justice.

Once I got Sahak talking, I could always count on learning something to my favour; for the small price of enduring his vanity and sneers, I soon gained a fair working knowledge of the caliph's character. This stood me in good stead a few days later, when I was called into his presence.

Having received Ghazi's gift, the caliph had decided to determine its value. Accordingly, he ordered the prisoners to be brought before him. As none of them could speak Arabic, the duty of translating between the caliph and the captives fell to Sahak. I was given no warning. Three Seljuq guards appeared at the door to my cell two days after the amir's grand entry, and I was taken up to the guardroom above the prison cells. There I was given water with which to wash, and a comb for my hair and beard.

Having cleaned myself as well as I could, I was then led by a long and circuitous route through the palace and citadel to the place where the caliph was holding court, and I was instructed by a royal functionary on how to address him, and how to behave in his illustrious presence. Upon receiving my assurance that I understood what was expected of me, I was admitted without ceremony. Sahak was there, ready to speak for me, and for the caliph.

Upon performing the necessary obeisance, I was allowed to stand in his presence and speak freely. A mature man of youthful appearance, he had put off his ceremonial robes and all the glittery trappings of his rank, including the bulbous turban so favoured by the Arab race, and wore a simple dark garment like a long tunic with a silver crescent moon on a chain around his neck. He observed me silently for a moment, tapping his fingers gently on the arms of his chair.

'I am told you are a nobleman,' he said. When I offered my affirmation, he asked, 'What is the country of your birth?'

'My home is in Caithness, Lord Khalifa.' I could tell he had never heard of this place, so I added, 'It is a region in the northern part of the island of Britain.'

The light of understanding came up in his eyes. 'That is very far away, I believe. Why have you come here? Was it to seek your fortune in the pillage of the Arab lands – an enterprise which seems to inflame so many of the Franj?'

'By no means, my lord. I was on pilgrimage,' I said and made certain that Sahak said the right word before continuing, 'and was captured by mistake.'

'That is indeed unfortunate,' he replied without apparent concern. 'Many things happen in war – all of them are unfortunate for someone, you must agree. The amir has set the price of your freedom at ten thousand dinars. That is a large sum of money.' I agreed that it was. 'Do you have any hope of ransom?'

'Assuredly, Most Exalted Khalifa,' I declared with confidence, ignoring Sahak's smirk. 'Even now my friends are hastening to Damascus to purchase my freedom.' As he seemed interested in this, I went on to explain about how we had been staying in Anazarbus when the battle began, and how I had come to be captured.

He listened to all I had to say, and then replied, 'Your fellow hostages denounce you as a traitor and a spy.'

He watched me intently to see how I would respond to this accusation. 'I am aware of their feelings,' I answered reasonably, without hesitation or emotion. 'They are right to feel themselves aggrieved for what has happened to them, but I am not to blame.'

'I see. Yet, this unfortunate indictment persists.'

'As you have said, Wise Khalifa, many unfortunate things happen in war.'

Caliph al-Mutarshid smiled at this. He laced his fingers and looked at me over his fingertips. 'Tell me then, who would you hold to blame? Amir Ghazi? Prince Thoros?'

'No, My Lord Khalifa. These men merely acted according to the circumstances forced upon them. If the prisoners seek to apportion blame, I would look to the Count of Antioch, who led them into such a disastrous trap without provocation, and without sufficient forethought.'

'The count is dead, is he not? I believe I have received his head in a box as a memento of the conflict in which he fell. Therefore, he can no longer be held accountable.'

'That is true.'

'Neither can he affirm or deny the charges made against you.'

'Perhaps not,' I allowed, 'yet, forgive my presumption, Lord Khalifa, but if I am accused of being a traitor by my fellow Christians, then it follows that I have been in service to the Seljuq cause. If you believe this, why am I still a prisoner?'

The caliph's mouth tightened; his eyes narrowed slightly. 'You are not, I think, the innocent you claim to be,' he remarked abruptly. Lifting his hand, he summoned the guards to take me away, saying, 'I will ponder this matter, and we will speak of it further.'

He signalled to the guards and I was returned to my cell. Unable to resist rubbing salt in the wounds he imagined me to be feeling, Sahak came to see me later that day. 'Not wise,' he said, wagging his finger in my face, 'to anger the khalifa. He believes himself a logician and philosopher of great skill and proficiency. It does you no good to better him on the field he has marked as his own.'

'I did not mean to challenge him,' I replied. 'I merely hoped that, as a man of wisdom, he might see the sense of what I said, and take that into account when assessing my position.'

Sahak laughed, and went away shaking his head. That is how I learned of my error, and determined not to make the same mistake again. Alas, the damage was done. The next day the guards came for me and I was once again brought before al-Mutarshid. This time he was delivering his shrewd and perceptive judgements before the assembled counsellors, advisors, and liegemen of his retinue; he wanted his minions to marvel at his renowned sagacity and was in no mood to be amused.

'I have considered all that you have told me,' he announced as I took my place before him, 'and I have concluded that you are a spy of the most dangerous variety: he who is without loyalty, and subject to no lord but himself. Therefore, I have decided that you will remain a prisoner.'

'It was a mistake,' I asserted. 'I should never have been brought here.'

'Yet, here you are,' the caliph said. '*Qismah!* All is as Allah wills it so to be. There is no such thing as a mistake. If you are a captive, it is because that is what Allah intended. Who is wise enough to instruct God?' He gazed around, gathering the admiring glances of his retinue, then said, 'You will remain a prisoner.'

This pronouncement delighted Sahak, my faithless interpreter; it was all he could do to suppress his glee. But the next declaration jolted even Sahak. Regarding me coldly, the caliph said, 'What is more, if no one comes forwards to arrange your ransom in three days' time, you will be executed. In the name of Allah, this is my decree.'

I was in no way prepared for this decision. My thoughts instantly scattered far and wide. I thought of you, Cait, and all I had left back home, of Padraig arriving too late and finding my lifeless body hanging from the city walls, of Sydoni weeping over my grave ... so many strange thoughts raced through my head that it took me a moment to recollect myself.

'My Lord Khalifa,' I said, trying to remain calm in the face of such an illogical and unjust pronouncement. 'I do not know why my friends have not come for me. I can assure you the ransom will be paid; however, three days is not enough time. It is a long way from Anazarbus to Damascus.'

'They could have come for you any time since your capture, but they have not,' the caliph pointed out. 'I suspect they are not coming, that these friends of yours are merely a ruse to prolong your duplicitous existence, and that it is pointless keeping you alive. Three days,' he declared, 'no more.'

The assembled onlookers murmured their approval at the caliph's display of judicial firmness. Steadying my voice to present a brave face, I replied, 'Then, as a nobleman, I beg the Wise Khalifa's indulgence to honour a last request.'

The idea sparked al-Mutarshid's interest. I think he had not expected me to think of that. 'Within reason, of course,' he said. 'What is your last request?'

'I would like to leave a message for my family at home in Scotland, so that they will know what happened to me.'

It was a simple thing, but possessed of a certain nobility, and I could see al-Mutarshid found the idea appealing. 'Very well,' he agreed, 'you shall write your message.' He looked at me with thoughtful curiosity. 'How, in the name of the Prophet, peace be unto him, do you expect this letter of yours to reach your family?'

'Exalted Lord,' I replied, 'it is not beyond your power to command such a thing to be done. Many pilgrims return to the West after their pilgrimage is completed. No doubt one of them would consent to take the message.'

'It will be done,' the caliph said, and the audience was concluded.

Amazed that he should have agreed so easily, I thanked him for his compassion and generosity, and was taken back to my cell. Knowing the Arab mind a little better now, I see I had obligated him with my request and he could not possibly refuse – without appearing a weak and arbitrary ruler in front of his advisors and liegemen. As he had so carefully cultivated himself as a fount of wisdom and learning among his people, he could not allow himself to appear less noble than the insignificant wretch he had just condemned.

Thus, I won the boon I asked. Had I known it would be that easy, Cait, I might have asked for something of greater consequence. Still, I was content.

The guards marched me back to my cell, where I spent the rest of the day and night praying that I might live long enough to fulfil my pilgrimage vow and recover the Black Rood. The next morning, Sahak appeared with a small square of parchment, a pot of ink, and a supply of quills – a gift of the caliph, he said, for my letter.

I was happy to have these things, and I told Sahak to thank the caliph for supplying them. 'He will kill you as he said,' the katib told me unhappily. 'It was no idle threat.'

I told him that no, I did not imagine that the great caliph was in the habit of making idle threats to impress the prisoners with his power. 'I shall be sorry to see you die,' Sahak said.

'Why? You have never liked me. There have been many times when you might have spoken up for me, yet you have not done so – and I, the man who helped save your people from Bohemond's attack.' I let him have the full brunt of my anger and exasperation. 'You might have done it out of charity for a fellow Christian, if nothing else.'

The miserable scribe hung his head. 'It is true,' he simpered. 'But there is more you do not know.'

'Yes?'

He hesitated, drawing his sleeve across damp eyes. 'The brooch . . .'

I stared at him, a sick feeling beginning to spread through me. 'What about it?'

Unable to look me in the eye, he lowered his head still further. 'I did not send it back to Anazarbus,' he muttered. Then, overcome by the enormity of his guilt, he turned and hurried away before I could call down heavenly wrath upon his worthless hide.

I sat down and thought long and hard about what he had told me. After the first storm of fury subsided, I began to survey my position more dispassionately. In the end, I decided that it did not matter whether Sahak returned the brooch as he had promised, or whether, as I suspect, he kept it for himself. Knowing that the Black Rood was among Ghazi's plunder, I wanted to stay close by no matter what. As the amir's captive, I remained close without arousing even the least shade of suspicion.

The Caliph of Baghdad's decree of execution was another matter, but one which was beyond my influence entirely. As I could do nothing to improve my position for the moment, I was content to leave it to the Swift Sure Hand.

Two days passed, but no one came for me, neither did Sahak appear at my door. I wrote my letter, taking time to ponder each and every word before putting it down so I would not have to blot it out. If, in God's eternal plan, I was meant to fall to the headsman's sword, I wanted my last message to be perfect.

The rest of the time, I paced the small confines of my cell, sometimes praying that Padraig would miraculously appear and come striding down the long prison corridor bearing a bag full of silver dinars to buy my release. 'I hope you have not been worrying,' I could hear him say. 'I was delayed a little. Still, all in God's good time. I will have you out of there before you know it.'

Needless to say, Padraig did not arrive.

On the morning of the third day since my last audience with Caliph al-Mutarshid, I awoke to rumbling in the guardroom above the prison cells – the pounding of feet and the clatter of weapons. At first, I thought an attack must be taking place, a raid on the city in reprisal for the destruction of Bohemond's army, perhaps. But then all went very quiet and I, along with the rest of the prisoners, sat waiting throughout the day for some word or sign of what was taking place beyond the prison walls.

Towards evening the guards returned to the guardhouse and our jailer brought our day's ration of food and water. He did not understand us, nor we him, so it was not until Sahak came the next morning that I learned of the arrival of an envoy from the Caliph of Cairo.

At the time, I did not consider this to be an event of much significance. But that is the way of things in the East. Alliances shift like sand on the wind. Loyalties ebb and flow with the tide. The restless wind sifts through the ancient realms and old orders are swept away in the twinkling of an eye. An emissary arrived from Egypt, and the future of the Holy Land changed.

My own predicament altered, too; although at the time I did not perceive, much less understand, the nature of the change, it was no less remarkable in its own way. Indeed, it would be many weeks before I would fully appreciate just how exceptional my circumstances had become – *and* how slender the thread by which my life now swung.

THIRTY-EIGHT

I expected them to come for me in the morning, and they did. I did not expect them to send Sahak, yet it was his face I saw when, at the sound of the bolt being drawn and the iron bar raised, I stood and the door opened. 'Fall on your knees and praise God, my friend,' he proclaimed, and I could see it gave him great pleasure to do so. He had never called me his friend before, and I wondered what lay behind his cheerful greeting. 'It is a very miracle. You have been reprieved.'

Before I could ask how this had come about, he said, 'Hurry. You are to come at once. They want to see you.'

'Why?' I asked, already moving through the open door. Two guards were with him, but neither appeared interested in the proceedings.

'Much has happened in the last two days. There is to be a great celebration.'

We started down the corridor, and I was half-way up the steps to the guardroom when I remembered – 'My letter!'

'Leave it,' Sahak told me. 'There is no time. They are waiting.'

'Let them wait.'

'Yu'allah!' Sahak sighed.

I ran back to the cell and snatched up the folded parchment, stuffing it in my siarc as I rejoined the scribe waiting at the foot of the steps. 'Now tell me, Sahak, who is waiting for me? Is it my friends? Has Padraig come to pay the ransom?'

'Alas, no,' Sahak admitted; he had not thought of that. 'It is that the Caliph of Cairo has sent his personal emissary to Damascus,' he explained meaningfully. 'The man has arrived; he is here in the palace at this very moment.'

'This emissary – he is the one who wants to see me?'

'In a manner of speaking. You are going to Cairo, my friend. Is that not wonderful news? Everything has been arranged. Praise God.'

Any jubilation I might have felt at a stay of execution was swallowed by a new sense of hopelessness. 'If I go to Cairo,' I suggested, 'my friends will never find me.'

'If they look for you in Damascus, they will find you in a traitor's grave,' he countered. 'Is that what you want?'

In truth, rescue was not uppermost in my mind; I was more concerned about becoming separated from the Holy Rood. Even so, there was not much I could do about that; my execution would have effectively separated me from the prize as surely as a sojourn in Cairo, and far more conclusively. Rather than berating Sahak, I decided to be grateful.

We followed the guards up the stone steps and through the empty guardroom, out the open door and across the inner palace yard. Perhaps it was Sahak's excitement making me imagine things, but I did sense a ferment in the air – as that which marks a change in season. Yet, the sun rising above the bulging white domes of the palace was the same, the air hot and dry as ever.

'I thought of this myself,' the scribe declared proudly. 'It troubled me that you should die for helping my people, and I prayed that God would send a way to save you. And then the emissary arrived.' He smiled as if the rest was perfectly obvious.

I thanked him for his skilful intervention on my behalf, and said, 'But I still do not understand why the Caliph of Cairo's emissary should be interested in helping me.'

'Strictly speaking, he does not know he is helping you. He thinks he is merely receiving a gift for his master. But God works in mysterious ways, no?'

'Yes, and so do you, Sahak.'

By the time we reached the Pavillion of Roses where Atabeg Buri was entertaining his two important guests at an early-morning meal following their prayers, I had extracted from Sahak the gist of what had happened, and knew why I had been summoned. The rest took longer to obtain, yet, by dint of perseverance, I gradually unravelled the tangled tale of the stormy relations between the two most powerful caliphates in all the East.

I should pause here and relate the details of my audience with the atabeg and his illustrious visitors; it was, however, of little account at all. They merely wanted to see that I was still alive and hale enough to make the journey to Cairo – along with the rest of the booty to be delivered as gifts to the caliph. You see, Cait, Arabs of all stripes are forever giving gifts to one another. They do it all the time, for any number of reasons: the wealthy do it to belittle their rivals, strengthen ties between noble houses, or win the fealty of those beneath them; the poor do it to curry favour with those above, to secure preferment in business, to demonstrate honour and obedience.

As part of the spoils of war which Ghazi had given to win patronage from Buri, I was brought forwards to bow and scrape before the enthroned Muslim lords, delivered into the hands of a servant of the envoy, and then led away again. I never saw Sahak, al-Mutarshid, Buri, Ghazi, or any of my fellow prisoners again, nor did I ever learn the name of my new master, the envoy. I became once more a commodity of exchange, a vessel of value to be bartered for favour – in this case, the favour of the Caliph of Cairo.

As I say, over the next days, as my depth of understanding grew, so too did the realization of the awful significance of the events Bohemond had set in motion when he decided to attack the Armenians. I watched my new masters closely and observed them in their dealings, and so gained invaluable insight into the complicated affairs of the Arab race – insight which would serve me well in the days to come. I kept my eyes and ears open, and pieced together any scraps of information that came my way, meditating long over them. This is what I learned:

Ghazi's defeat of Bohemond's army greatly relieved and encouraged the Muhammedans; in a single battle the amir had reduced the Christian might in the region and restored Muslim hopes that the hated Franj might yet be pushed out. Antioch was now vulnerable to siege and capture. The Templars could not protect the city by themselves alone; without a swift and abundant supply of fresh troops, the end was a foregone conclusion. For the first time in many, many years the Turks could entertain notions of recapturing that great city. Once Antioch was under Seljuq rule, Jerusalem could not fail to follow.

Shrewd amir that he was, Ghazi was not slow to recognize the rich potential of his victory. That day when he halted the executions on the battlefield, he was already calculating the cost of his next venture: the siege of Antioch.

Aware that he must strike quickly and decisively, Ghazi rushed to Damascus where he knew the Caliph of Baghdad had lately arrived. On the way, he gathered the support for his scheme from those who would help supply the army he hoped to raise. A siege is a lengthy and expensive business, and Ghazi required the aid of more powerful men to mount and supply a force large enough to capture that great city. He also needed the consent of his betters – not only their approval of his military plan, but their sanction of his larger aims as well. Again, the wily amir showed his acuity, for knowing he did not possess the necessary authority, he sought a bargain that would allow him to rule the city once it had been captured.

To this end, he lavished gifts upon his liege lords and vassals alike, demonstrating that he had the discernment and largesse of spirit to rule wisely and well. As I was learning, gift giving among the Arabs is a meticulous arrangement of balances as perilous as it is precise, for each and every gift carries with it an obligation which binds the recipient to the giver in many and various ways. Ghazi gave gifts to his overlords so they would grant him the authority to proceed with his plans of conquest. Caliph al-Mutarshid, commanding the highest power, was given the greatest gifts.

The fortuitous appearance of the Egyptian envoy added another element to the intricate symmetry of powers and obligations which Eastern potentates glory in manipulating. As it happened, the celebration Sahak mentioned was to mark the proposal of a peace treaty between Baghdad and Cairo. It was not until much later that I learned how the two powerful caliphates had been at each other's throats for many years – owing to differences over religious observance, mostly. The fall of Jerusalem had awakened them to the danger of a house divided; the Caliph of Cairo, a more far-thinking ruler than most, had, I would eventually discover, offered his extensive fleet for the use of a combined Arab army united against the common enemy. Together Cairo and Baghdad might drive out the invading foreigners.

This offer had been spurned by the arrogant and pride-bound Baghdad caliphate, which considered itself superior to Cairo in every way. Still, as the years passed and the crusaders established themselves as a continual threat and ever-present thorn in the side of the Arabs, Baghdad began to soften to the idea of uniting against the crusaders. With the fall of Antioch imminent, and the prospect of recapturing Jerusalem a genuine possibility for the first time in many years, the young Caliph al-Mutarshid decided it was time to make peace with Cairo. Towards that end, the Egyptian emissary, who was merely making a routine visit to Damascus, had been summoned and lavished with gifts by way of a peace offering.

The Arabs have long enjoyed a fantastically elaborate game played between two people on a wooden board with dozens of small carved pieces. I once observed this game, and though I failed to grasp any but the most rudimentary principles, it did seem to capture the essence of the intricate convolutions of the Eastern mind. For although the board is marked with fixed squares of alternating colour, red and white, each piece moves entirely at will – but only within certain tightly circumscribed limitations peculiar to its rank. And for each move there is a countermove, each power balanced by an equal and opposite power. A game of infinite possibility, it is nevertheless played out according to rules as immutable as the mountains and invariable as a sunrise.

I had become like one of the lesser pieces in this strange game, and when the emissary departed Damascus two days later, I went with him – and all the rest of the plunder amassed by Ghazi as well, to be given to the Egyptian caliph as tokens of reconciliation between the powerful rulers of Baghdad and Cairo. So, following a five-day march overland from Damascus to the port of Sidon on the coast, I was put aboard one of the sturdy ships of the Egyptian caliph's substantial fleet, and we sailed for Cairo, arriving five days later at Damietta on the wide, spreading, many-fingered delta of the river Nile.

We left the ship at the harbour of Damietta, a foul stink-hole of a town, and proceeded by sailing barge up the wide, muddy river to Cairo. I stood at the low rail and watched the graceful river boats with their single, fin-shaped sails and long steering oars, gliding slowly on the brown water. We passed tiny settlements built on the banks of the river with long, fields of green cultivated grain stretching in wide, generous bands behind. One after another, we passed them, so many that they seemed after awhile to merge into a single, endless strip of villages all the way to Cairo.

I stood on the deck of the barge and watched life along the river unfold like a vast, seamless tapestry unrolled before me to reveal the age-old images of the river realm: three boys riding a donkey piled high with palm branches; a girl with a willow switch in her hand, herding grey geese along the path; two women washing clothes at the riverside; men casting fishing nets from small, bobbing boats; a youth carrying a row of dried fish on a pole over his shoulder; a laughing bevy of girls with water jars on their heads, their mantles knotted around their slender hips; a farmer gathering rushes with a curved scythe, and another leading an ox-drawn cart mounded with yellow melons; naked brown children wading in the cool shallows.

From the moment we entered the river channel, all that had gone before seemed to fade away into the warm, heavy air of the valley lowland. The looming tribulations of the last days dwindled away to piddling insignificance in the face of an immense and all-pervading tranquillity. No mere human event could disturb the prodigious peace of that land; the great tempests of war and ruin that wreak such havoc among men are but fleeting squalls that arise and disappear, swallowed in a serenity as old as the earth. I stood on the deck of the barge, and felt myself being drawn down and down into the limitless depths of the most profound calm I had ever known – as if the timeless sky with its bright spray of stars wheeling through its eternal round proclaimed: *this, too, shall pass.*

From the beginning, I was treated well by those charged with my captivity. Perhaps they were not told the circumstances of my imprisonment. Then again, as my little jailer, Wazim Kadi, told me when I was brought to the caliph's palace, 'The Seljuqs are barbarians. Everyone knows this. They are coarse ruffians from out of Rhum where they live like wandering beasts.'

Of all the many contending races in the turbulent East, the Saracens consider themselves the most civil and refined, with a duty to impart their singular virtues and qualities to those less enlightened than themselves. It may be that when they learned I had been a captive of the Seljuqs, the courtly and cultured Saracens took it upon themselves to demonstrate their courtesy.

Nevertheless, it was with no little trepidation that I disembarked on the wooden quay which serves the impossible sprawl that is *al-Qahirah*, as the Arabs call it – the Victorious, for it overwhelms all would-be conquerors, and vanquishes all with its inexhaustible wealth of seductions.

I looked out from the quay at the dizzying tumult, masses of bodies which seemed to ebb and flow like a mottled flood, shimmering with sweat in the midday swelter, and I quailed before the sight. My *reprieve*, as Sahak called it, merely exchanged one captivity for another. I did not know what manner of reception awaited me with the Saracens; I did not know whether I should be set free, or executed before the day was finished.

The Black Rood, still bound in the rug in which I had wrapped it, went with me. In this only was I content; the holy relic was my strength and my consolation as we made our way up from the river with a train of bearers and handlers hired from the quayside to carry the caliph's treasure. Passing through one squalid settlement after another, we made our slow way towards the massive iron gates that guard the inner city. The poor and wretched of the East have heard that the streets of Cairo are paved with bricks of gold, and the city cannot hold them all; so, they build their hovels between the banks of the Nile and the high city walls, and every spring the floods come and wash these pitiful dwellings away. Many are drowned and their corpses are eaten by crocodiles – ravenous dragon-like river monsters that bedevil the lower marshes of the river.

Another variety of fierce and loathsome creature infests the stinking waste heaps outside the walls, and throng the gates of Cairo, preying on the unwary: beggars. At first I was moved with Christian pity and charity at the appalling sight of them. God have mercy, there were so many – blind and dumb, halt and lame, leprous, maimed, deaf, starving, naked, and sick. My soul quailed before their misery. But the hostile and belligerent bearing of these unfortunates quickly drove out all compassion. Like jackals they prowl the crowds looking for victims, hobbling pathetically or dragging their wizened and mangled bodies along the streets, bleating out their pitiful, and practised, wails of woe. Although I was a prisoner and had nothing at all to give, that did not stop them from descending upon me, grabbing and snatching at my clothes with their withered hands, mewling and bawling their pitiful cries. God forgive me, I

344

soon learned to ignore them and, like the guards, moved quickly through the shabby ranks, pushing aside any who were stubborn enough to stand in the way, turning a deaf ear to their shrieks, and hurrying on.

Anxiety over my impending fate did not survive beyond a few hundred paces inside the gates. For the city was not only larger, noisier, and more crowded than any I had ever seen, it was also more fabulous in every way. Instantly, my sun-dazed senses were overwhelmed and submerged beneath the dizzying inundation of sight and sound – and smell – for the slops and refuse of the street-dwellers are allowed to stew in the sun and infuse the air with noxious and pestilential odours.

While the smells steal the breath away, the sounds buffet and batter: the beggars with their insistent cries, the street merchants with their shrill demands, dogs barking, children screeching, the press of the populace, talking, shouting, calling to one another – a thousand voices clamouring at once. The resulting welter of confusion is dizzying as it is deafening.

And the sights! Cait, in the space of a few dozen paces beyond Cairo's gates you will see more extraordinary things than most people see in their entire lives. Wherever the eye happened to light, some new and startling view presented itself. I saw men and women of wealth swathed head to foot in the most startling robes – the colour of which changed with every movement through all the shifting, radiant hues of the rainbow. I saw copper-domed mosqs covered with gleaming Persian tiles so that they looked as if they had been spun of peacock-coloured glass.

And the people, Cait, were the most unusual to walk under God's wide heaven. The colours of their skin ranged from black as dark as midnight shadow, through browns of every hue from the deep rich tones of walnuts, baked earth, and old leather to the fair pallor of fine parchment. Their shapes and sizes were no less various. I saw men as tall and gaunt and black as ebony pillars, and others small as half-grown children. The fairest of all were the Egyptians themselves. Fine featured, with high noble brows, straight white teeth, and rich black hair that glistens in the sun, they stand erect and move with unhurried grace, gazing upon the world with quiet amusement in their dark, almond-shaped eyes. They say they are descended from gods of old, and you only have to look at them to believe it. A more handsome race you cannot imagine.

To move about the city is to confront wonders on every side. There is more colour, more noise, more *everything* to be found on the streets of Cairo than anywhere else under the sun. Hanging from upper windows I saw gilded cages with birds as big as ravens, but more brightly-coloured than kings, long-tailed and hook-beaked, with feathers scarlet and green, jade blue, white, and yellow. I have no idea what they were or whence they came, but they screeched like the *bhean sidhe* to burst the ear. There were dogs unlike any I have seen before or since: lean and slender, narrow beasts with long, thin faces, hollow haunches and muscled shoulders, almost as big as wolf hounds, but sleek and fine-footed for running in the sand.

Also, though it was a while before I noticed them, cats. Once I began to see them, however, I was astonished at the numbers. There were very multitudes of the creatures, and they were everywhere. Not a shadow in the city, but you did not see the glint of a yellow eye looking back; not a tree, not a market stall, not a doorway, nor window, nor ledge, nor wall, nor rooftop where a cat did not sit, or walk, or stretch itself.

The crooked streets swarmed with every variety of merchant and seller known – some working from stalls, others carrying their wares stacked on their heads, or dangling from their arms – and every last one shouting to make himself heard above the din. Here a candlemaker walked with hundreds of candles attached by their wicks to a long pole; there a butcher shouted for custom with rings of sausage looped round his outstretched arms; next to him, a carpenter balanced four chairs on his back; and over here, an ironmonger jangled examples of the various chains he could make – and more: goldsmiths, gem dealers, slave merchants, and every kind of food vendor ever known.

Any space on the street, large or small, became a veritable marketplace for vendors to tout for business. I saw carts heaped high with hairy coconuts, others with mounds of sweet black dates, and still others with persimmons, or pears, lemons, almonds, or green bitter quinces.

People thronged these impromptu markets, or *bazaars* as they are called, eagerly bargaining with the merchants so that the din was

346

a stupendous uproar. Through the tumult scampered lithe, brown children, darting around the legs of their elders, contributing to the havoc with shrill squeals and shouts. Barefoot ragged youths darted quickly here and there and, more than once as I witnessed with my own eyes, relieved unwary passersby of the burden of any unattended purses or belongings.

Our procession snaked through the throngs, passing one exotic quarter after another – including one filled with tiny houses – the only quiet corner of the entire city, I think, and I soon learned why: the stench arising from this place gave me to know that at very least a great calamity had befallen those who lived there. The powerful odour of death hung like an unseen cloud above the silent streets. Yet, save for a few black-robed men ambling idly around the deserted streets, there was no one about.

'Ah, the city of the dead,' Wazim told me when I asked him. 'Many Egyptians still hold to the old ways, believing they must feed and house their ancestors in the afterlife.'

The caliph's men paid no heed at all to the commotion around them, but passed through it with heads high, looking neither right nor left, as if the riotous tumult was so far beneath them as to be invisible. Because of the crush of people and the narrowness of the streets, it took the better part of the morning to reach our destination: a palace of stone that looked as if it might have been hewn in a single piece from the heart of a mountain.

In the dazzling heat of a midday sun, the pale ochre-coloured stone blazed like faded gold. Flags of red and blue waved fitfully on tall standards as we passed up the long ramp towards the gates which were made of pierced and gilded iron. Four tall black men with spears and the skins of lions on their shoulders guarded the entrance. At the envoy's approach, the gatemen opened the gleaming doors without a word; the baggage train entered the palace precinct, and I passed into my opulent prison.

THIRTY-NINE

Still dazed from the heady journey through the streets of Cairo, our baggage caravan passed through a maze-work of doorways, corridors, walls, and pathways, and arrived at an inner courtyard, there to wait in the sun while the envoy disappeared into one of the many rooms fronting the yard – a pleasant expanse of green grass and small trees of many varieties, all of them meticulously clipped and arranged to show their best features. Peacocks preened in the low branches and paraded in the sunlight, and white doves fluttered around a pool of clear running water. Flowering shrubs, many in gigantic earthenware pots, filled the air with a delightful scent and attracted the lazy hum of bees.

This paradise was bounded by royal residences on three sides; a high, vine-covered wall enclosed the fourth side. Each of the royal apartments and chambers featured a balcony – a roofed, but otherwise open platform affixed to the outer upper floor and surrounded by a wooden railing. These balconies are common in the arid East, for they allow one to escape the heat of the day and enjoy any passing breezes. In the city, I had seen many such balconies, some with elaborate screens of wood; those overlooking the inner courtyard were open, however, so that the residents might enjoy the beauty and calm of the garden below.

As we stood waiting in the sun, I saw a large, very fat man in a golden robe and turban appear at the railing of a nearby balcony; he paused a moment to take in the sight of us, and then ambled away again. A few moments later, I was conducted with the rest of the baggage into a small, wood-panelled hall across the courtyard where this same man was waiting to receive the gifts in the caliph's name.

He balanced his more than ample girth on a stool at a small table with a square of the peculiar thin Egyptian parchment before him, and the bearers brought the items one-by-one to be entered into his account. I watched as both the gold-bound box containing the embalmed head of Prince Bohemond, and the Black Rood, were duly recorded and borne away with the rest of the treasure – where, I could not say.

Then it was my turn. He looked up from his list, passed his eyes over me, and smiled. 'Ah,' he said, and rose to his feet. Speaking first in Greek and then in Latin, he asked which of the two languages I preferred.

'Latin, if you please, my lord.'

'Of course,' he replied. 'My name is Amir Abu Rafidi,' he told me, and explained that he was the caliph's official katib, a position of authority in which, as overseer of the inner palace servants and all the other scribes, counsellors, and courtiers, it had fallen to him to receive the gifts which the Caliph of Baghdad had sent. As I was among these gifts, the amir was obliged to take account of me, and he hoped I did not mind this small formality. 'I am told that you are a nobleman whose chances of ransom have declined to the point of hopelessness,' he said.

'On the contrary,' I replied, 'I am ever hopeful my friends will come for me. I suspect, however, that moving almost continually from one destination to the next since my capture has made the task more difficult.'

'I see,' he replied. 'I am also told that you are a spy who has been condemned to death by the Khalifa of Baghdad. Is this true?'

'Not entirely,' I replied. 'While it is true that the khalifa ordered me to be executed, it is not true that I am a spy.'

He smiled at my reply, his fleshy jowls wobbling. A cheerful man, and easily amused, I could see he bore me no malice. 'It would be a rare man who readily owned such perfidy.'

I agreed, but insisted that it was true nevertheless.

The amir returned to the table and looked at the blank expanse of parchment before him. I could see that he was trying to decide what to write. Gently lowering himself onto the little stool, he folded his arms and rested his chin in his palm, tapping his fingers against his cheek. He looked up into the air, and then down at the table again. Then he rose and walked around the room, hands folded behind him; he looked at me, and said, 'You are a nobleman.'

'I am, indeed.'

'That makes it all more difficult, you see.'

'I am sorry.'

'No, no, think nothing of it.' He quickly reassured me. 'We must all take the rough with the smooth.'

He returned to his place and took up the quill; he dipped it in the ink, and then hesitated, his hand hovering above the parchment. He glanced at me thoughtfully. 'Ah!' he said, as if discovering the solution to a long-vexing problem.

Dipping the pen once more, he began to write, his hand describing an elaborate flourish as he finished. Laying aside the pen, he picked up the parchment – the odd stuff was so thin, the light from the open doorway shone through it and I could see the strange characters he had written on the other side; holding it before his face, he squinted his eyes and grunted with satisfaction. Then, rising and moving to the door, he called out loudly, and returned to his stool.

A few moments later, the call was answered by the appearance of a little brown man in a long, flowing white garment. Fine featured, with skin like a polished nut, he wore a small white cap atop his close-shaved head. Taking a step into the room, he bowed and stepped lively to the table where he stood looking at me with bright interest.

'Khalifa al-Hafiz is away from Cairo for the foreseeable future,' Abu Rafidi told me. He dipped the pen and added a few amendatory strokes to what had been written. 'Only he can decide your fate.' He blew on the wet ink to dry it. 'So until the Khalifa returns, you will be given a room in the palace.'

He lay aside the pen once more and, lifting a hand to the white-robed servant, he said, 'This is Wazim Kadi; he will be your – ah,' he paused, searching for the right word, 'your jailer, let us say. He will attend to your various needs while you reside in the palace.'

'I am to remain a prisoner?' I asked.

'You are to be our . . .' he hesitated, 'our *guest*, let us say. At least, until the khalifa returns.'

'Forgive me for asking, my lord amir,' I said, 'but when is the khalifa's return expected?'

'Only Allah knows,' the katib replied, 'and Allah keeps close counsel.' He smiled pleasantly. 'At least, he does not confide in Rafidi. Come now, Wazim will take you to your room and make you comfortable.'

Thus began my friendship with Wazim, the worthy Saracen jailer who has rendered me invaluable service time and time again in a thousand errands large and small. It was Wazim Kadi who provided me with an endless supply of quills and ink with which to write, and who first introduced to me the queer parchment-like stuff called *papyrus.* The Egyptians make it from the tall puff-topped reeds that grow everywhere along the river's edge; tough, yet light, and with the ability to be rolled up tight, this papyrus is in many ways superior to hide parchment – save in one important way: a slip of the pen cannot be rubbed out. Unlike parchment, where the odd blot or misplaced letter can be carefully scraped away to reveal a fresh layer beneath, any mistakes made on papyrus are there forever.

Despite the differences of race and faith, I could not have asked for a better servant. Unfailingly kind and thoughtful, Wazim Kadi has watched over me like a very angel – much like Padraig, in his own way, and I will miss him.

And now, dearest Caitríona, heart of my heart, I must conclude my long and, I fear, far too indulgent missive. What started as a simple letter of farewell has grown to a book. As I look over the work I have done, it pleases me for the most part. If not for the assurances of the caliph that it will one day find its way to you, I would have despaired long ago. But the Saracens are trustworthy; once honour is invoked, they will dare death and beyond to make good a promise.

The end, whatever that shall be, is near. A short while ago, I began hearing cries and shouts of alarm in the corridors and courtyards of the palace. These have intensified, and just now I caught a faint whiff of smoke through my open window. Wazim, who promised to bring word about what is happening, has not returned and I cannot think that a good sign. If this tale is to be completed, I fear it must be by another hand. I am content.

I will close with a prayer for you, and for all those who come after, that in virtue you will find wisdom ... and in wisdom, peace ... in peace, contentment ... in contentment, joy ... in joy, love ... in love, Jesu ... and in Jesu, God and life eternal. Amen.

Farewell, my Cait, my soul. Until we meet in Paradise.

FORTY

Unable to force open the door, I stood at the window and looked out at the dull red bloom spreading across the night sky. There were fires in the city, and I could hear, like the sighing moan of a fretful wind, the eerie ululation of thousands of voices, shouting, screaming, crying. The smell of smoke was stronger now, and I guessed that, once begun, the flames would quickly race through the narrow, tight-crowded quarters, leaping street to street until the whole city was alight.

I was beginning to think what I might do if the flames should come to the palace, when I heard the scrape of a key in the lock; I turned as the door opened, and Wazim Kadi appeared, his face smudged with dirt and soot; his long tunic was filthy and soaked through with sweat. He was bleeding from a cut on the side of his head, and panting for breath.

'Wazim!' I started towards him. 'What has hap –'

Glancing over his shoulder, he motioned me to silence and then beckoned me to him with a frantic gesture. 'We must hurry, Da'ounk,' he said, his voice a raw, urgent whisper.

Taking up the bundle of papyri I had prepared using one of my siarcs to wrap it, I slipped the loop of a strap over my shoulder, and moved to join him at the door. 'Lead the way.' I left the room without looking back.

He led me quickly along the corridor and then down a flight of steps to another corridor below, along this, and out into the small inner courtyard overlooked by my window. He started away again into the darkness, but I took hold of his arm, and said, 'Wazim, wait! Tell me what is happening. Where are we going?'

'It is very bad,' he said, shaking his head. 'There is no time. We must hurry.'

'Tell me.'

He turned, features dark, eyes glinting in the lurid glow seeping into the sky. 'The people are rioting,' he said. His voice trembled. 'Many have been killed. They have set fire to the great bazaar, and the khalifa has fled to the citadel. We must hurry if we are to escape.'

'The soldiers, Wazim – where are they?'

'Some are protecting the khalifa,' he said. 'Most have been sent to quell the rioting.'

'What about the palace? Are there any soldiers here?'

'A few. Not many.' He pulled on my hands. 'Come, this way. We must hurry to the river. Your friends – they are waiting for you.'

'My friends – you mean Padraig?' After so long a time, I could scarce credit the words. Could it be true at last? 'Padraig is here in Cairo?'

'Yes, him – and the others. Yordanus Hippolytus is with him, and some others. They have a ship. Come, they are waiting.' He made to dart away again, but I held him firmly.

'There is something I must do first.'

'No, please, Da'ounk. There is no time. The soldiers might return at any moment. We must be gone from the palace before they discover I have set you free. I told your friends I would bring you. They are waiting at the quay. We must hurry.'

'I cannot leave yet,' I insisted. 'I need your help, Wazim. Now, listen carefully.' I gripped him by both shoulders and looked into his face. 'On the day I was brought here, some treasures came with me – gifts for the khalifa.'

'Gifts?' he said, growing fearful. 'Do not think about such things. We must go now.'

'You know what I'm talking about,' I replied, trying to maintain a calm and reasonable tone. 'The gifts sent by the Khalifa of Baghdad. What happened to them?'

'They might have been taken to the treasure house,' he allowed, 'but it –'

'Take me there,' I commanded. 'Take me to the treasure house.'

'It is impossible! We cannot go there. It is locked very tight and the caliph only holds the keys. The treasure house cannot be opened.'

'If you will not help me, I will have to find it myself.' I made as if I would go off alone.

'Yordanus paid me to deliver you safely to the ship. How am I to do that if you will not come with me?' He snatched at my sleeve. 'Please, Da'ounk, it is very dangerous to remain here any longer.'

The urgent pleading in his tone warned me. 'Why?'

'They are saying the Fida'in are in the city,' he confessed. 'They may be in the palace even now. If they find us they will kill us. We must leave while we can.'

'Soon. First, the treasure house.'

He rolled his eyes and drew a deep breath, but saw it was no good disagreeing any longer. Muttering dark oaths, he led me across the small courtyard and into another of the facing buildings, along a corridor and out again, into the large garden courtyard I saw when first I arrived at the palace. Quickly, quietly, we proceeded along an unseen pathway in the darkness, skirting one building and another, and coming by furtive means to a very large, many-floored edifice set apart from the main wing of the palace and surrounded by a flowering garden.

We stopped at the edge of the garden and hid beneath a low-growing tree. The garden was planted with night-blooming flowers which filled the air with a sweet and heady fragrance, so strong it got up in my nostrils. I stifled three sneezes, and decided it was time to move along. There was no one about that I could see, and there were no signs of life in any of the buildings surrounding the yard.

'This is the treasure house?' I wondered. Although there were no windows on the ground floor, the upper floors contained wide and generous balconies, most of which were screened, but a few of which were completely open, allowing access to anyone who could make the climb.

'This is the *hareem*,' Wazim replied. 'It is the most protected place in the entire palace, with soldiers keeping watch day and night.' The reason, he explained, was that the hareem, as it was called, was where the female members of the Caliph's family – wives, concubines, and daughters – had their residence.

'I do not see any soldiers,' I pointed out.

'They have taken the royal family and fled to the citadel.'

'Where is the treasure house?'

'It is under the hareem,' Wazim said. 'Below the ground, you know?' As Wazim spoke these words, I recalled my midnight meeting with the Caliph and his unexpected entrance by way of the hidden tunnel.

With admirable efficiency, the treasure house had been constructed beneath the hareem so the same soldiers might guard all the caliph's various treasures at the same time. There were no lights showing in any of the windows, and the huge building was silent. 'This way,' I said, starting towards the entrance.

Although the guards were gone, the door was barred, and the bars were secured with large, iron box-like locks which required the use of keys to open. 'You see,' whispered Wazim, creeping up behind me. 'They are locked. You cannot get in. We will leave now.'

'There must be another way in.'

'There is only this way,' Wazim maintained. 'It is the hareem. There is no other way.'

'Because it *is* the hareem,' I contended, 'there *must* be another way.' Although I knew little of such things, it seemed to me unlikely that the caliph would wish his visits to his various wives to be known by one and all throughout the palace. I reckoned that, as with the private audience chamber behind the throne room, there must be another, less conspicuous entrance to accommodate his visits.

I looked around the square at the surrounding buildings. There were two long ranks of storerooms, one to the left and one behind the hareem; a wing of the palace enclosed the third side, and on the fourth side, a low building with four funnel-topped domes along the roof. 'What is that?' I asked.

'The kitchen and ovens for the hareem.'

I started towards the building. 'You will find nothing there,' Wazim said, scuttling after me.

At first look, it appeared he was right. The long, low room was empty, the large, square hearth bare, the ovens cold. There were a few loaves of bread lying on a table, and some pears in a basket, but I could see nothing else in the dark interior. I went in, and felt along the raised rim of the hearth. 'What are you doing?' said Wazim. 'They will find us. Let us go from here, my friend.'

In a moment, I found what I was looking for: a pile of straw used for kindling to start the fires. I took up a handful and bunched it in my fist, then leaned over and reached out into the centre of the hearth and swept away the top layer of ash to reveal a few glowing coals beneath. Holding the bunch next to the coals, I blew gently on the straw and was soon rewarded with a pale yellow sprout of flame. Soon the rest of the bunch was alight and, holding it up, I quickly searched the room for a candle, finding three; I lit one, stuck one in my belt, and gave the third to Wazim, and told him to stand by the door and keep watch. 'Warn me if anyone comes into the garden,' I said.

By candlelight, I made a thorough search of the kitchen, pausing only to tear one of the loaves in half and cram bits of it into my mouth. It was stale, but edible, and I resumed my search as I chewed. I searched around and between the ovens, and found a small doorway leading outside through which fuel for the hearth and ovens could be brought in. I went outside and found myself in a closed-in area stacked with wood, bundles of twigs, and straw. Cupping my hand around the flame, I moved along behind the row of ovens, and came upon a wooden cover on the ground between two of them. Lifting the cover, I held my candle into the void and saw a short flight of steps leading down.

I removed the cover quietly and set it aside, then fetched Wazim. He took one look at what I had found and said, 'It is the ash traps – for cleaning the ovens. There is nothing here.'

Ignoring him, I moved down the steps and found that he was right. A brick rampart ran along the back of a dressed stone wall, forming a large box to catch the ash falling through the oven grates above. A walkway in front of the rampart allowed the cleaners to remove the ash; at one end of the walkway was a small opening for air to feed the fires from beneath, and at the other end of the walkway, a door.

I called Wazim to follow me, and proceeded to the door. Lifting the latch, I opened the door and stepped through into the cool, damp darkness of a great, cavernous room. I heard the liquid drip of water splash in the distance. 'It is the cistern for the hareem,' Wazim announced upon joining me. His voice echoed from unseen walls. 'Come, there is nothing here.'

'But there is,' I told him. 'Look.' Raising my candle, I held it close to the wall to reveal a torch in an iron sconce beside the door. I took it up, lit it from the candle, and the resulting flame revealed a short walkway forming a ledge alongside the basin of the cistern. At the end of this walkway there was another door. 'This way.'

The door opened onto a small room which served to connect two corridors, one to the left, and one to the right. As we were now beneath the hareem, I imagined one corridor or the other must lead to the treasure house. While thinking which to try first, a sharp tapping sound came from some distance away down the corridor on the right-hand side: three taps, followed by a short silence, and then three more.

Wazim heard them, too, and pulled on my sleeve. 'Someone is down here,' he whispered desperately. 'They will find us if we stay any longer.'

'Stay close,' I said, and started down the corridor. It was a low, vaulted passage of brick and stone; I held the torch before me and crept quietly along, listening to the rhythmic tapping which grew louder the further we advanced. A line of small openings ran along the top portion of the tunnel; no larger than a man's hand, I could feel cool air moving through these openings as I crept past.

The passage ended a few score paces along, joining another, larger tunnel, which angled sharply down. The tapping sound was louder here, and I could hear something else – it sounded like voices, but too muffled and indistinct to make out what they were saying. Drawn on by these sounds, I descended the passageway, Wazim trembling behind me, tugging insistently at my sleeve and urging me away with every step.

We soon arrived at another juncture; I could see it for the faint flickering of torchlight on the brickwork several score paces directly ahead of me. The rhythmic tapping had become a steady thudding pound, punctuated by grunts and mutterings.

'Stay here,' I said. Handing the torch to Wazim, I slipped the strap on the bundle of papyri from my shoulder and handed that to him as well. 'I will see what is ahead.'

He made to object, but I waved him to silence, and pointed to the spot on the ground where he was to plant himself, and then crept forwards alone. As I neared the end, I could see that a heavy iron grate sealed the opening. I lay down and squirmed forwards the last few paces on my stomach and, looking between the thick bars of the grate, peered around the corner and into the adjoining corridor beyond.

By the smudgy light of half a dozen torches scattered around them on the ground, two men with short axes were hacking at a timber door. The door, however, was bound with thick iron bands and was resisting their best efforts. The men were Arabs, dressed in black with dark brown turbans, and were unlike any I had ever seen among the caliph's soldiers or bodyguard. Their determined expressions and relentless hammering gave me to know that I had indeed found the treasure house.

I edged back from the grate and was about to withdraw until I could devise a plan for getting rid of my unwanted fellow thieves, when someone called out. The two stopped working and for a moment the passage became silent. Curious, I crawled back to the grating. The two had downed their axes and were talking to someone who had joined them. The third man remained out of sight beyond the edge of the corridor, and although I could not see who it might be, something about the sound of the voice held me.

From the way the thieves were complaining and gesturing to the door with their inadequate axes, I guessed they were bemoaning their lack of success to an impatient superior – who apparently had little sympathy for their troubles. For, as I lay watching, one of the black-turbaned thieves offered his axe to the newcomer, indicating that he should try the door himself.

The proffered tool hung between them, and for an instant I thought the other would decline, but then a hand reached out and took the axe. The newcomer stepped into view and proceeded to try his hand at the unyielding door. The blade clattered against the wood – once, twice, and again, whereupon he stopped, and handed the axe back to its owner. He turned, and my breath caught in my throat as his face was revealed in the fluttering torchlight: the Templar Renaud de Bracineaux.

FORTY-ONE

De Bracineaux returned the axe to the Arab, and the two stood discussing the matter. My first thought was to call out to him, to let him know that I was here – but the sight of the Templar commander instructing Arab thieves in their own tongue was too strange and, as it seemed to me, sinister. I hesitated, watching silently.

I was still trying to decide what to do when I felt Wazim creep up beside me. Raising a finger to my lips, I cautioned him to silence, and then allowed him to peer around the corner. The instant he put his face to the grate, a strange thing happened: he sniffed once, and again, then froze, his eyes going wide with terror. He backed away at once and retreated down the passage. I went after him, pausing to retrieve the torch he had dropped. By the time I caught up with him at the junction, the pounding had begun again.

Grabbing hold of his elbow as he entered the adjoining corridor, I arrested his flight. 'Who are they?' I demanded. 'The Arabs – you knew them. Who are they?'

'Fida'in!' Wazim gasped.

'Are you certain?'

He nodded, his eyes still wide with fright. 'The smell,' he said. 'Did you not smell it?'

Now that he said it, I did recall a sweet pungency. 'I thought it was from the torches.'

'It is hashish. We must get away from here. If the Fida'in find us, they will kill us.'

Templars and Fida'in together? Were these not the fanatical sect that had caused the death of Yordanus' son, and the reason he had to flee Damascus? Any other time I might have doubted such an unlikely alliance. As extraordinary as it seemed, however, I knew Wazim was right.

What were they after in the caliph's treasure house? Not, I thought, his gold and silver – at least not entirely. The presence of Renaud de Bracineaux put the thought in my head that they, too, sought the Black Rood. The amount of plunder gleaned from the massacre was not great, but de Bracineaux would know that the capture of the Holy Rood was a greater calamity than the destruction of Bohemond and his troops.

The more my thoughts raced along this path, the more convinced I became that de Bracineaux's quest and my own were one and the same. If the Templars found the rood first, I would lose it forever.

'Please, Da'ounk, let us go. All the treasure in the world will do you no good if you are dead.'

'I care nothing for the caliph's gold.' I decided it was time to trust Wazim with the truth. 'Listen to me, my friend, there is something you must know.' I told him about the remnant of the Sacred Cross even now residing in the caliph's treasure house.

'By all that is holy . . .' breathed Wazim Kadi, lapsing into an astonished silence.

His reaction surprised me. I had not expected the Saracen to hold such reverence for a Christian relic. But there was no time to wonder about it now. 'That is why the Templars are here. They know Bohemond lost it, and they are here to get it back.'

'Then they will surely succeed,' concluded Wazim gloomily. 'We cannot subdue the Templars or the Fida'in, and we cannot fight them together.'

'I do not intend to fight them for it,' I told him. 'Neither will I stand aside and watch them grab it away again.' So saying, I slung the bundle of papyri over my shoulder and started off along the passage again, this time in the opposite direction, and with a heavy heart. I counted de Bracineaux a friend; in any other circumstances I would have hailed him and embraced him as a brother. But cruel fate, aided by Bohemond's folly, had placed us in sharp contention for the prize. If I got hold of the Black Rood first, I would not be giving it back to the Templars, or anyone else. I had made a sacred vow, and it was not in me to betray it.

'Please, can we leave now?' said Wazim, padding dutifully after me.

'Not until we find another way into the treasure house.'

'But there *is* no other way. It is a treasure house; there is only one way in.'

'That is what you said about the hareem.'

We hurried back to the first junction where the passage divided to the right and left. The left-hand side led back to the cistern, so I took the passage to the right. 'This way.'

Almost immediately, we came to an opening with steps leading up – into the hareem, I supposed. There was an unlit torch in a sconce beside the steps and, taking this, I handed it to Wazim, and continued on. After a few hundred paces, the passage narrowed and began to bend downward. There were two more openings off the main passage, one to the right, and one to the left. The one on the left was half the height of a man, and the one on the right was not much larger.

As we passed the opening on the right, a faint rush of air fluttered the torch flame; the air was warm and I could smell the scent of flowers. I put the torch into the opening, but could see little save a downward angled shaft and another vertical shaft directly above. Leaning into the shaft, I looked up into the connecting vent and saw stars in the square opening above.

There seemed no point in lingering, so we moved quickly on. The downward angle of the slope increased sharply; every few paces a step appeared, and then two, and then three at a time. No more junctions or openings appeared, however; nor did this tunnel of a passageway divide or branch off.

After a while, I lost heart and began to think Wazim was right after all. I came to a long flight of steps, the end of which I could not see in the feeble light of the torch, and there we paused.

'Why are we stopping?' asked Wazim a little breathlessly.

'Listen.'

Down the passageway – some distance ahead, by the sound of it – I heard the ripple and splash of moving water – an aqueduct, perhaps, supplying water to the palace.

'It sounds like a stream. We have left the palace behind. It might be the Nile.'

'Perhaps,' I allowed, and started off again. The steps led down and down, and soon I could smell the water and feel the cool dampness on my skin.

The last few steps disappeared beneath the surface of the water, dropping away so quickly I was almost in the stream before I caught myself. A rusted iron ring protruded from the step on which I stood, and there was a rope tied to the ring. Bending down, I pulled on the rope, but it was secured to something heavy which remained out of sight beyond the small circle of light. Handing the torch to Wazim, I took the rope in both hands and pulled harder; there was a rippling sound and a boat came gliding into view.

Wazim took one look at the boat and said, 'This is the canal of Khalifa al-Hakim. It leads to the river.'

'You know this?'

He shrugged. 'I have heard of it. The canal was built many years ago – a hundred years or more. Al-Hakim was despised. He built many great things – the palace, the hareem, and the citadel . . . many things – but he taxed the people hard to pay for all these buildings and there were many riots in those days. They say he built this secret canal so that he could escape if the people ever revolted against him.' Indicating the channel, Wazim added, 'You hear many such things in the palace. Until now, I never believed all these stories.'

Time slipped away; every moment we wasted, the Templars' quest advanced unhindered, and mine faltered. Back we raced, taking the steps two at a time as they came, arriving breathless at the top of the passage. A few more steps brought us to where the two smaller openings joined the tunnel, and I decided to try the low one on the right-hand side first.

Once more, I gave Wazim the bundle of papyri and bade him wait for me. Going on hands and knees, I entered the opening; it was dry and dusty, and ended after only a few dozen paces. Unable to turn around, I backed up. 'It is closed up with brick,' I said upon rejoining Wazim. 'We will try the other one.'

Stepping across the passage, I entered the second opening. The roof of the tunnel was higher than the last one, though not so high that a man might walk upright, and it was narrow; after a few steps I was forced to turn sideways. A few more steps and I had to slide along with my back to the wall – difficult to do as I could not fully stand.

In this slow way, I proceeded along until I came to a tight, sharply-angled bend, beyond which all was darkness and I could see nothing. If not for the fact that I could feel cool air moving on my face, I would have turned back. Instead, I called Wazim to follow with the light, and, taking a deep breath, squeezed through the opening and waited for him on the other side.

The moving air made a faint but steady breeze which guttered the low-burning torch. 'It will go out soon,' Wazim observed.

'Give it to me,' I told him, 'and keep the other one ready.'

Once past the angled bend, the passageway opened out once more. We moved on and came to a small, three-cornered room, one side of which opened onto a steep flight of stone steps. The steps were set in a spiral which ended in a room identical to the one below, and with a narrow tunnel leading on in the opposite direction. We paused a moment to light the second torch; I retrieved from him my precious bundle and then moved along.

Just ahead, this new passage ended in a short downward flight of steps, and the shattered remains of a wooden door. The door had been barred, but the timber was old and rotten; someone had kicked their way through the lower half of the door, the fractured pieces of which were scattered over the floor inside.

Holding the torch before me, I squatted down, ducked through the opening, crawled over the broken bits of timber, and found myself in a small vaulted room containing stacks of slowly mouldering papyrus scrolls tied in braided cords. Moving quickly on, I proceeded through the arched doorway at the end of the room and entered a much larger room, this one filled with ceremonial saddles, bridles, and other such tack for horses and camels – row upon row of high-backed saddles trimmed in silver and gold, some displayed on standards, some merely heaped on the floor. There were scores of lances, too, most with cloth pennons and flags attached to their blunted ends; and in one corner, I saw four chariots, resting on their axles, their painted wheels stacked and leaning against a pillar.

'We have found the treasure house, Wazim,' I said softly. 'Now to find the rood.'

I had expected to find a single, hall-like room filled with the caliph's wealth and riches – a great jumble of objects, boxes, and caskets filled with coin and plate, bowls and cups, rings and jewelled ornaments, and the like. It was instead a very house: room gave way to room, with connecting galleries and corridors, halls, chambers, and storerooms. We passed quickly through the first two chambers and came to a long, double-vaulted gallery with a central row of pillars and low doorways on either side.

Upon entering this gallery, the pounding sound – which had been absent for some time – commenced anew; this time the blows were sharper, harder, more measured. I suspected that either newer, fresher troops had been assigned to the duty, or better tools had been found – perhaps both. I did not know how long the iron-bound timber could withstand such battering, but reckoned that we had little time to make our discovery and escape. There were many rooms to explore, but only one torch, and that would not last long. So, without an instant's hesitation, we started the search – beginning with the nearest rooms.

The first two chambers contained jars of various kinds; as the dust on the floor revealed no recent footprints, I did not bother looking further than the doorway. The third room contained rugs, rolled up or tied in bundles; the fourth room was full of caskets of many sizes, and at first I thought I might find some of the treasure that had come to Cairo with me, but again, the dust had not been disturbed in a very long time, so we quickly moved on.

Meanwhile, the crashing on the wooden door grew steadily louder, the blows falling harder and more rapidly, as if those on the other side were becoming more determined. We had searched but four rooms, and twice that many remained. At the pace we were making, the torch would burn out before we finished – if the Templars did not break through first. 'There must be an easier way,' I grumbled, darting towards the doorway of the next room.

And then it came to me . . . the dust on the floors – of course!

Abandoning the search of the chambers at the end of the gallery, I made directly for the rooms nearest the entrance. Holding the torch low, I saw that the chamber on the right-hand side had not been recently used. I cautioned Wazim to silence, and moved quickly to the other side of the gallery, passing the door which was now shuddering under the violence of the attack; I could hear the wood splintering as the axes thudded, and the grunt of the men as they hewed at the solid timber.

At the doorway to the last room, I paused and held the torch to the floor – holding my breath at the same time. And I saw it: a trail in the dust of the chamber floor caused by the passing of many feet. 'This way,' I whispered. I stepped into the chamber, and my heart sank.

It was not a chamber at all, but another gallery, and larger than the one we had just searched. The torch was already flickering as it burned the last of its fuel, and from the sound of the shuddering door, the Templars would soon be through. There was nothing for it, but to go on and hope for the best.

Holding the torch low, I moved as quickly as I could, following the trail in the dust. Once inside the gallery, however, the trail quickly dissolved as footprints scattered everywhere across the floor. It seemed to me that most of them tended towards the rooms on the left-hand side of the long, double-vaulted room, so that is where we began.

The first chamber contained a quantity of small wooden caskets – many carved and inlaid with mother-of-pearl; a swift inspection revealed the boxes contained cups, bowls, and ornamental bells. 'Hold this,' I said, giving the torch to Wazim. And, taking up one of the caskets, I dumped out the cup and carried the empty box back out into the gallery where I smashed it against a pillar. The wood was old and dry, and splintered easily into pieces. I instructed Wazim to break up the pieces still further, and hurried back for another. I did this with three more of the boxes, then heaped the broken fragments against the base of the pillar and, using a wad of cloth from the inside of one of the caskets, set the heap on fire with the torch.

'Stay here and keep the fire going,' I instructed Wazim. Taking up the torch, I hurried on.

The second room contained earthenware jars filled with perfumed oil, and in the third rolls and bundles of cloth of gold, and silver, and multi-coloured, richly patterned Damascus cloth. I looked in three more – each with similar items, but there was nothing I recognized as having come from Amir Ghazi's hoard.

As I rushed on to the next rooms, a great crash sounded from the main gallery. The sound seemed to fill the treasure house, resounding and echoing through the underground corridors. This mighty clash was followed by a long silence, after which the pounding of the axes resumed in earnest.

I quickly completed the search of the last three rooms – one was little more than a narrow alcove and contained nothing but a few pottery jars and, high up on the end wall, a large, square vent covered by a partially open iron-work grate. The other two rooms were each filled with items of ceremonial armour: stacks of painted wooden shields, bundles of tasselled halberds, sheaves of curved swords standing upright in wooden barrels, helmets ranged around the walls and floor in ranks. Upon examining the last room, I dashed across and started in on the opposite side of the gallery.

Feeling the grip of desperation tightening around me, I prayed, 'Great King, if you care about the honour of your name, help me to restore it now.'

In truth, I do not know what I meant by this; the words came to me and I spoke them out. The reply was immediate – if from an unexpected source.

'Da'ounk!' Wazim Kadi shouted behind me. I turned to see the little Saracen standing beside the pillar, the fire at its base burning brightly in the gloom of the gallery. He was pointing across to a chamber on the other side of the entrance. 'Look!'

I glanced where he indicated and saw the glow of a torch as it passed from view into the chamber.

'Did you see who it was?' I called, already running for the doorway.

'It was a father,' he replied.

At least, that is what I thought he said; it did not make sense to me, but there was no time to ask questions. I sped to the chamber and looked in. It was a large room with several columns forming aisles, between several of the columns someone had heaped up mounds of objects. There was no sign of the torch-bearing man Wazim had seen. Was it a trick of the light? Had we imagined it? Then I saw the gold-trimmed box containing Bohemond's head, and all questions vanished. Having carried that grotesque trophy all the way from Kadiriq to Damascus, I would have recognized its gleaming tracery and metal-bound edges in my sleep.

I started for the heap, just as another tremendous crash resounded from the main gallery – this one accompanied by a slow, creaking, cracking sound and a second clatter. I guessed part of the door had given way. It would not be long before the Templars and their Fida'in allies gained entrance.

I dived into the mound and, tossing the torch to the floor, began pulling things from the heap and throwing them aside. Many were objects I recognized, and this encouraged me greatly. But as the pile diminished, my hopes began to fade.

There came another enormous, walloping crash, followed by a long, groaning crack as another portion of the iron-clad door gave way. An instant later, the low-burning torch gave a last sputtering spurt and sizzled out. I raced back to the doorway, and called for Wazim to bring a piece of wood from the fire.

'They are getting very close now,' he said, handing the burning brand to me.

'So are we,' I replied. 'The relic is in this room somewhere.'

There came another tremendous crack on the door. I could hear the timber splintering as sections were ripped away.

'What would you have me do, Da'ounk?'

'Pray, Wazim.'

To my surprise the little jailer folded his hands, closed his eyes, and began chanting then and there. Leaving him to his prayers, I took the burning chunk of wood and, kneeling beside the casket containing Prince Bohemond's head, I unfastened the clasp and opened it.

The flickering light playing over the embalmed prince's frozen features made it seem as if he was trying to awaken from his serene and perpetual sleep. 'May God forgive me for what I am about to do,' I said, and touched the burning wood to the prince's stiff hair.

The resulting flame was much brighter and larger than I expected; due to the pitch resin in the embalming mixture, the waxen flesh burned readily. I watched for a moment as the flames licked across the contours of his face, singeing off eyelashes and brows, and painting his becalmed expression with a liquid glaze of shimmering flame. Satisfied that the flame would not go out, I picked up the box and carried it quickly along the colonnade to the next mound of plunder. There, by the light of Bohemond's flaming head, I began pawing through the trove – this time to Wazim's rapidly muttered prayers, which he interrupted long enough to urge me to hurry faster.

Two more booming crashes trembled the walls of the treasure house before I reached the bottom of the heap, only to come up empty handed. My frustration was eased by the thought that there was only one mound left and the rood must be there.

The casket containing the burning head was on fire now and too hot to pick up, so I shoved it with my foot to the next hoarded heap and waded in, scattering valuable objects right and left.

Crack! The door in the main gallery splintered and groaned.

'Hurry!' shouted Wazim. He was standing at the chamber doorway. 'They have made a hole in the door. I can see them now.'

'Over here!' I called. 'It has to be in this heap somewhere. Help me find it.'

Wazim hastened to my side and together we ploughed into the mound of objects. Heedless, I strewed costly objects everywhere; I tossed aside jewelled daggers, carelessly threw away a fine bow and quiver of golden arrows, and sent silver bowls and chalices clattering across the floor. And then, I found it: the rug in which I had wrapped the holy relic. I fell upon it at once and pulled it to me.

Even as my hand closed on the rolled rug, however, I knew my hope was disappointed. The roll was empty. The Black Rood was gone. Beneath the rug, I saw one of the gem-encrusted, gold bands that had capped the ends of the piece; the other gold band lay beside it, mangled and flattened by the bearer's clumsy feet. My poor heart rending with dismay, I stooped and retrieved the flattened band. There, in the dying light of Bohemond's burning skull, tears welled up in my eyes as my failure overwhelmed me.

All that time I had spent in captivity, nursing the hope, however tenuous, that I might rescue the sacred relic. But the Black Rood was gone.

'Da'ounk?' said Wazim. 'What is wrong?'

'It is gone,' I replied, letting the gold bands slip from my hands. 'We are finished.'

From the main gallery there came a final thunderous crash and the sound of splintered timber careening across the floor. A cheer went up from the soldiers on the other side. With that, the last of the flames gave out; the box broke into embers and the skull rolled onto the floor, empty eye sockets staring at me, lipless mouth grinning in grim mockery. The burned bone glowed red for a moment, and then that, too, disappeared in the darkness.

Wazim called me again. I made no reply.

There was nothing to say. The soldiers would be on us at any moment, and that would be the end of it.

I heard Wazim moving in the darkness, and felt a touch on my arm. I thought he meant to move me along. 'I am sorry, Wazim,' I said. 'It was all for nothing.'

Out in the main gallery, the last remnant of the door gave way and, with shouts of triumph, the Templars stormed into the treasure house.

FORTY-TWO

I stood in the darkness, listening to the whoops and shouts of the Templars and Fida'in resounding through the main gallery and echoing in the chambers and passages, as the light from their torches flickered dimly on the walls – a phantom army swarming up from the netherworld to plunder the caliph's treasure.

And they would have it, too. There was no one to stop them. *Templars and Fida'in together*, I thought. *On what unholy day had that alliance been forged?*

I listened to the sounds of their hurried footsteps as they raced to the plunder . . . a race I had hoped to win.

I had failed – a truth made more brutal for the fact that I had allowed myself to believe that God was with me, leading me each step of the way, that my trials had been for a purpose, that my suffering had meaning.

But it was all a lie. I knew it now, and the knowledge made my heart writhe like a snake in hot ashes. I could have wept for the futility of it, if not for the knot of hard, hot anger coiling in my gut.

Wazim whispered my name again, gently pulling me from my miserable reverie. 'Look!' he said in a voice half-stifled with awe. 'The holy father is here!'

I turned my head towards the sound of his voice and saw a faint glimmer of golden light reflecting on the surface of one of the stone pillars behind us. It vanished again before I could determine the source. Nevertheless, I moved towards the place and discovered that the pillar stood before the alcove I had examined a few moments ago. The light appeared to emanate from within this narrow, crypt-like room.

Stepping quickly to the low entrance, I saw a man dressed all in white holding a torch in his left hand. His robe was that of a cleric – a priest of an Eastern order, so I thought – and his bearing both lordly and humble, that of a venerated patriarch. I understood at once why Wazim had called him a holy father. Yet, in face and form he was youthful still, his beard and hair black, the glance of his dark eyes keen.

He beckoned me to him, but astonished as I was, I made no move to join him. For, although he held a torch, it was not the torch which shed the light, it was the whole of his being.

Raising his hand, he beckoned me again, more insistently, and said, 'Come quickly, Duncan, time grows short.'

At the sound of my name, I edged forwards a step or two. 'Who are you, lord, that you know me?'

'Duncan,' he said in a tone of gentle reproof. 'Does not the master know his servants? How should I forget one who has served me so well?'

'The White Priest,' I whispered. Wazim Kadi sank to his knees beside me, bowed his head and shut his eyes tight.

'Call me Brother Andrew,' he replied lightly. 'As I once asked your father, so I now ask you: what do you want?'

It seemed a strange question – with soldiers clattering through the main gallery behind us, rushing eagerly to the plunder, what difference did it make what I wanted? Strange, too, his question instantly brought to mind the cool clean breeze of the northern Scottish coast, and I saw the dark waves driven white upon the hard rock shingle of Caithness bay, and standing on the high headland gazing out to sea, two figures: one tall and gaunt, one small, cherubic, her long hair blowing in the wind – Murdo, my father, with little Caitríona by his side – and they were searching the wide, wave-worried sea.

At that moment, I wanted nothing more than to be sailing into that bay, and to hold those people in my arms. 'I want to go home,' I murmured, feeling the tears rising to my eyes.

'So did your father,' replied the White Priest, 'but he was proud and would not admit it.'

'Perhaps he was made of sterner stuff than his unfortunate son.'

'Why unfortunate?' asked the mysterious monk. 'You have the

Holy Light to guide your steps along the True Path. Murdo paid dearly to learn what you already know.'

There came a shout at the door of the chamber behind us. Wazim, on his knees beside me, clasping his hands and muttering fervent prayers, jumped to his feet, turned and ran to the alcove entrance.

'I know nothing,' I said, feeling my failure afresh. 'And unless you help us, I will not live to see another morning in this land.'.

'O, man of little faith. I will tell you what I told your father the first time we met.'

'What is that?'

'Take heart. You are closer than you know.'

At that moment, Wazim called from the doorway. 'Da'ounk!' he whispered urgently. 'They are coming this way!'

I glanced towards Wazim as he spoke, and as I did so the light in the alcove began to fade. 'What if –' I said, turning once more towards the White Priest. He was gone, leaving only a gently fading glow where he had been standing. But in that shimmering light, I saw that he was right.

'What are we going to do?' Wazim rasped in desperation. 'They are almost here!'

'Peace, Wazim,' I whispered. 'Come away from there.' Taking his arm, I pulled him away from the alcove entrance. 'Brother Andrew has led us to the treasure.'

He glanced around the near-empty room, and then turned frightened eyes on me. 'Where?' he asked.

'There,' I told him, pointing to the vent shaft where an old length of timber was propping open the iron grate. 'He has also shown us our way out.'

As darkness closed around us, I reached up and caught the edge of the shaft opening. I jumped, and Wazim took hold of my legs and boosted me up into the opening, whereupon I scrambled into the shaft. Once inside, I reached down and pulled Wazim up after me. Then, carefully, reverently, I took hold of the short wooden beam and, with Wazim's help, gently eased the heavy iron grate shut. It closed with a dull clank, as two Templars entered the chamber behind us.

They searched the room, sweeping the corners with torchlight and, finding nothing, swiftly moved on. I allowed myself a low sigh of relief, and sat back a moment to catch my breath and reflect on how best to make our retreat. 'Now we go,' I whispered to Wazim.

'What about the Holy Cross?' he asked.

'The search is over,' I told him. 'Here – give me your hand.'

In the darkness, I found his hand and guided it to the scarred length of timber cradled in my arms. Like a blind man, his fingers traced the deep-grooved lines and ridges of the ancient wood, and tears formed in his eyes, and mine, as, each in our own way, we honoured the sacred relic.

The voices of the Templars and Fida'in echoed in the chamber below, and my thoughts turned once again to escape. Of the few courses open to me, I determined that the vent shaft offered the best chance of evading discovery and capture. The ascent was steep, but not impossibly so. I soon found that I could crawl up the incline slowly on hands and knees, pushing the rood before me.

This I did, and a short time later Wazim and I had reached the secret passage above. Although it was as dark as the deepest cavern, I smelled the night-blooming flowers in the breeze from the vertical shaft and knew without a doubt where we were. Standing with my back to the shaft, the tunnel opened out to the right and left. The passage to the right led back to the cistern and the ash-traps below the kitchens; the left-hand passage led to the underground canal.

The canal would take us to the river, thereby avoiding not only the palace and any lurking Templars or Fida'in, but also the overcrowded streets with their rioting throngs. This, I decided, was the way we would go.

Hefting the rood piece onto my shoulder, we started off – one blind man following the other. Wazim walked before me with my bundle of rolled papyrus scrolls slung across his chest, and I followed, keeping my left hand outstretched, my fingertips brushing his back – more for comfort than need, since the passage led in only one direction, without divisions, branches, or turnings; there was no chance of becoming lost.

Thus, we made our way to the secret stream, stumbling now and then, but proceeding with good speed. The sacred relic was heavy and unwieldy, but after carrying Bohemond's head all that time, I had learned how to bear a burden without tiring myself unduly. And, after a time, I found I did not greatly mind the darkness; although I was blind as a stone, I knew the canal lay just ahead, and that there was a boat waiting to take us to the Nile, where at long last I would be reunited with Padraig and the others.

In a little while, the downward trend of the passage increased and we came to the first of the series of low steps – first one, and then two, and so on, until I could hear the ripple and splash of the stream ahead. We checked our pace, and continued with greater caution, arriving at the water's edge at last. Passing the rood to Wazim, I knelt down on the last step and felt along the edge of the wall for the ring to which the boat was tethered. After much fumbling, I found the ring and then set about untying the rope.

It was knotted tight and there was no loosening it. The braided cord, however, was old, and scuffing it against the brickwork of the passage it soon frayed to the place where, using all my strength, I was able to pull it apart.

Wrapping the end of the rope around my hand, I pulled the boat to the steps and instructed Wazim to lay the rood down on the path behind me, and get into the small craft. 'I will steady it for you,' I told him. 'When you are ready, I will hand you the rood.'

Slowly, and with exaggerated care, we settled Wazim in the boat, and I handed him the rood, telling him to hold it upright and clenched between his knees, keeping one hand on it at all times. Then it was my turn; I was able to get in without capsizing our vessel, and allowing the stream to turn us, I released my hold, pushing away as the bow came around.

The flow of water was not fast and the boat glided away slowly. It was strange, floating along in utter darkness. But for the gentle stirring of air on our faces, we might have been sitting completely still in the water. From time to time, I dipped my hand in the stream to test that we were indeed moving along with the flow. Once we bumped against the side of the canal – which startled both of us, and caused Wazim to cry out in alarm. I was able to push away without incident and from then on kept one hand out so as to fend off another collision.

Unfortunately, the damage was already done. The boat was old, the wood rotten, and the impact, though mild, had loosened part of the hull and caused a seam to open, allowing water to seep into the boat. The first I knew of it was when I felt my feet getting wet; I put down my hand and realized the bottom of the boat was awash.

'Stay very still,' I warned Wazim. 'The leak is slight, and we may yet reach our destination before the hull fills with water.'

That was not to be, however. Soon water was sloshing over our ankles. Bailing was futile. Although I tried for a while, cupping my hands and flipping it out by the handful, I could not keep pace with the rising water. 'Can you swim, Wazim?' I asked.

'No, master,' he replied, his voice taking on a quaver of concern.

I assured him that I could swim well enough for both of us and that there was nothing to worry about. I was still offering this assurance when the boat struck the canal wall again and the seam opened wider. I felt the water rising, and said, 'Listen carefully, Wazim. I am going to get out of the boat and into the water. Stay just as you are, and do not move. I will hold to the side of the boat and all will be well.'

This was far too optimistic, however; the darkness complicated everything – even simple movements became manoeuvres fraught with difficulty. In the end, I succeeded in sliding over the side without overturning our fragile craft. The water was not overly cold, and I reckoned that by removing my weight from the boat, we just might make it to the river before the vessel sank.

We struck the side two more times in quick succession, and the second bump spun the boat around. Despite being in the water, I was able to keep the vessel from overturning, and perhaps we would have made it to our destination intact if the current had not picked up markedly at the same time. I could not see what caused the stream to move more quickly, but thought it must be that the walls of the canal had narrowed.

And then, in the distance, I heard the rushing splash of falling water. Not wishing to alarm Wazim, I said, 'I think it would be a good idea to join me now.'

'I am happy to remain in the boat, Da'ounk,' he replied, his voice trembling in the darkness.

'I think you may have no choice, Wazim. I want you to hand the rood to me first, and then ease over the side. We can hold to the rail. The boat will float a long time yet, even with water in it.'

I could feel the stream beginning to swirl around me as the current strengthened. The rushing sound grew louder. In the dark, it would be impossible to judge the severity of the drop, or even to know how far ahead it lay. I kept this to myself, however, as I did not wish to frighten Wazim the more. 'Here,' I said, tapping the rail with my hand, 'let me take the rood, and then I will help you over the side.'

Muttering in some incomprehensible tongue, he passed the holy relic to me, and then prepared to ease himself over the side. Gripping the side of the boat, he made to stand and at that moment I felt the bow veer sharply away; the boat struck the wall of the canal and poor anxious Wazim was thrown off balance. He gave out a terrified yelp and released my hand as he fell back into the boat.

I heard the dry crack of rotten wood. There was a shuddering splash and the fragile craft began to break apart. Grappling with chunks of wreckage, I shouted for Wazim and made for the sound of his thrashing and coughing.

All at once the water surged around me. I felt the floor come up sharply beneath my feet, and floundered for a foothold. Chunks of stone scraped my knees and shins as I was dragged forwards by the force of the water. I shouted for Wazim to keep his head up, and then felt a rising swell like that of the open sea as I was swept over the falls.

Holding tight to the rood, I plunged sideways and struck a jumble of stone blocks on the bottom of the stream bed. I was tumbled along beneath the surface of the water, pummelled by pieces of wreckage as the ruined boat came sliding over the falls. The Black Rood slipped from my hands as I was rolled over again and again by the force of the water.

All was darkness and turmoil. I could not tell where I was, nor which way to the surface. I flailed underwater, desperate to rise, but the stream went on and on. My lungs felt like they were on fire. My chest ached. I must soon breathe, or burst.

And then I collided with something hard – a dense and solid mass, moving with me in the water. Even blind and confused, I knew it was the rood. I threw my arms around it and let it guide me to the surface.

I clung to the Holy Rood, gasping, gulping down air, and thanking the Swift Sure Hand for his timely deliverance.

I felt something squirming in the water as it slid past; I snaked out a hand and snagged the edge of Wazim's robe, and pulled him up. He spluttered and coughed, and thrashed around wildly.

'Peace, Wazim!' I shouted. 'I have you now. Be still. You will not drown.'

I had to repeat this several times before he ceased struggling; but eventually the fight went out of him and he allowed me to bear him up.

Holding to the rood with one hand, and to Wazim with the other – while at the same time trying to keep my head above water – I could do little more than drift with the current, and this I did, until the stream began to lose some of its force and turbulence. We bobbed along for a time, until I struck the side of the canal with my foot. Releasing Wazim for a moment, I fumbled in the darkness for a handhold on the rough stonework. 'Here, Wazim,' I said, dragging him to the wall. 'We are saved. Grab hold and hang on.'

We were saved, indeed. Pushing the holy relic before me, I worked my way along the wall, feeling for each handhold and talking to Wazim all the while, soothing him with words of encouragement. We edged along this way for untold ages. It is strange, but in the darkness, with nothing to mark either passage or progress, time seemed to stop; we floated in a timeless eternity with neither beginning nor end, only a very wet and endless present.

As I say, I do not know how long we continued this way, but there came a place where I reached for a handhold and instead of stone, my fingers touched wet moss or slime, and slipped; my head sank below the surface. I kicked my legs to right myself and touched something soft underfoot – not once only, but twice, and then again. It took me a moment to realize that it was mud.

The bottom of the canal was covered with soft, mushy silt. A short time later, I found I could stand and keep my head above water. 'See here, Wazim,' I said encouragingly, 'the water is growing more shallow. Get your feet under you and stand.'

We moved on a little further, and the level of the stream continued to drop as the channel grew wider; soon we were sloshing through waist-high water. I pushed the floating rood along beside me, and a short time after that, I noticed a watery grey dimness seeping into the air. After so long a time in the inky blackness of utter darkness, I did not trust my eyesight. But the wan gloaming held and strengthened,

376

and after a time I could deny it no longer. Wazim noticed it, too. 'I think it is getting lighter, praise God's Almighty Christ,' he said, crossing himself in the Eastern manner.

'You surprise me, Wazim.'

'Why? Did you think you were the only Christian in all of Egypt?' He gave me a wry smile. 'The Copts may not be numbered among the mightiest, but what we lack in strength, we make up in stealth.'

'You knew – all this time you knew *I* was a Christian, yet you never said anything, you never let on. Why? Why did you not tell me, give me a sign or something?'

'A Christian in the khalifa's court must be very careful if he cares to keep his head on his shoulders.'

The water level continued to fall as the walls of the canal stretched further apart; I noticed that the roof had become bare rock, instead of brick, and soon we were slogging through water just over our knees. I picked up the rood and carried it on my shoulder.

We walked on and the light grew steadily brighter. It came to me that this was because it was growing lighter outside. While we toiled below ground, night had passed in the wider world and dawn was breaking; people were rising to begin their daily tasks, and I . . . *I* was free and on my way home with the prize I had set out to rescue.

The satisfaction I felt in this achievement was sharply diminished a few steps later when I realized I had lost my sheaf of papyri.

'Wazim, the bundle I gave you – where is it?'

He stopped and patted himself about the chest and back. 'I do not know, my friend.' He turned and looked into the solid black recesses of the tunnel behind us. 'I think the strap must have come loose when I fell out of the boat.' He turned mournful eyes to me. 'I am sorry, Da'ounk.'

'No matter,' I replied weakly, feeling the loss. All the time I had spent in that singular labour . . . gone. How absurd to bemoan such a trivial thing, I thought. The letter was merely a meagre attempt at consolation for my failure to return home and, all things considered, it was far better to have survived in the flesh. Still, foolish as it was, I regretted losing something that had occupied so much of my thought and care these many months. I felt as if a part of my life had been carelessly lopped off and discarded.

'See there, Da'ounk,' Wazim said, drawing me from my thoughts.

I looked where he was pointing and saw sunlight on a pale grey wall of stone a few hundred paces further ahead; a short time later we rounded a bend in the canal and reached our destination.

A massive iron portcullis covered the canal entrance, but this was so old and rusted there were gaps showing in the ironwork and it was but the chore of a moment to force a hole wide enough to squeeze through. A few more steps, following the stream around the base of a massive shoulder of fallen rock loosed from the overhanging cliffs above, and we were standing in the reed-fringed shallows, peering with dazzled eyes at a golden sunrise shimmering on the Nile.

FORTY-THREE

Our underground journey had taken us to a place on the river below the city walls which rose sheer from the pale ochre cliffs above us. The sun was just rising in a glare of golden fire, and the air was already warm and heavy. The tall reeds and river grass bent in a light breeze, and I could hear the buzzing thrum of flies overhead as we stood in a sandy shoal, feeling the life-giving sunlight play over our faces.

Across the river, the low mud-brick huts of craftsmen and farmers glistened like pale gold in the early-morning light. A man and a boy led an ox along the bank, scaring two snow-white egrets into flight. Out on the water, a graceful low-hulled Egyptian ship was raising sail to begin the voyage north. All was so peaceful, bright, and calm, our tribulations of the previous night seemed small and insignificant, and very far away.

I looked up and down the riverbank, green-fringed with the stately plumes of river grass as far as the eye could see. While I was standing there, I felt something bump against my leg. I looked down to see a piece of wood from the wrecked boat floating out from the canal and, tangled by its broken strap, my bundle of parchments.

'Good news, my friend,' crowed Wazim cheerily. 'God has returned your writings to you!'

'I wish he had taken better care of them,' I replied, lifting the soggy bundle from the stream. Ink tinted water leaked from the corner of the bag. The pages inside would be a black-stained mushy mess. I had neither the heart to open the bundle, nor to throw it away; so I knotted the strap and slung the sodden load over my shoulder once again, and we started off.

By Wazim's reckoning we were some way south of the quay, so we started walking along the river's edge, quickly finding a cattle path which climbed up the bank and onto higher ground. The city wall angled away on a line running east, away from the river, which bent around a broad, rising bluff of honey-coloured stone.

My wet clothes began to dry in the sun and, although I was exhausted, I found my spirits soaring. Every step brought me closer to a glad reunion with Padraig, Sydoni, and Yordanus, and that much closer to home. The Holy Rood was heavy on my shoulder, but I did not mind the weight. Considering what the Saviour King had endured on my behalf, I would have carried it from one end of the world to the other and back.

After a while, we came to a cluster of huts fronting small green fields of beans, melons, onions, and garlic. Smoke from the morning cook fires drifted across the trail, and I could smell bread and meat cooking. The scent made my stomach rumble, reminding me that I had not eaten in some time. I stopped and looked around. Wazim asked why we were stopping. 'Do you think we might beg something to eat?' I wondered.

'Yes,' he said, glancing around, 'but not here.' He started away again.

'Why?' I wondered. 'Is it because they are Muhammedans?'

'Worse,' said Wazim, lowering his voice. 'They are pagans. Idol worshippers. Very bad people.'

'How can you tell?' It seemed like an ordinary holding to me. There were thousands along the wide, winding river.

He would say no more, so we moved on, passing through one small settlement after another, until coming upon yet another where Wazim stopped. 'There are Copts here,' he declared.

'How can you tell?'

'A true Copt never dwells beyond sight of a church.' Extending his hand, he said, 'See?'

I looked where he was pointing and saw a small white building with a bell-shaped dome topped by a tiny crude iron cross; otherwise, the building was completely unremarkable in any way. 'We will soon have something to eat.'

We made our way to the little church where Wazim rapped on the door, which appeared to be little more than scrap wood and bits of planking rescued from the river. His summons was answered by an old man with a long white beard, and a black robe which covered him from the chin down. One eye was sunken, the socket hollow, and the other was watery and dim, but he greeted us with a toothless smile, pressing his hands together and bowing.

Wazim did likewise, and the two of them held a brief, but intense discussion filled with much gesturing and pointing. The old priest raised his head, brayed, and spat, and then, grasping me by the arm, he led us along the cramped beaten earth street to a tiny hovel of a house where he pounded on the door with the flat of his hand. A woman pulled back the door and peered out, just her nose and one eye showing. The priest spoke a few words to her, and she closed the door; it opened again a moment later, and a hand appeared holding two eggs.

The old Copt took the eggs, blessed the woman, and we continued on. This ritual was repeated at the next house, where we were given three round, floppy pieces of flat bread and two green onions. After three more houses we had amassed another egg and some salt, four dried figs, a slice of fresh melon, and a handful of honeyed dates – whereupon I called a halt to the foraging and told Wazim to thank the priest for helping us.

After exchanging a few words, Wazim reported, 'He will accept no thanks for allowing his people the blessing of giving succour to strangers in need. Today they have earned a great reward in Heaven.'

'Then offer them a blessing,' I replied. 'Tell him, gold and silver have I none, but what I possess I share freely: the blessing of the Three to be aiding you, abiding with you, and showering peace and plenty on you, and on your people, each day, all day, and forever.'

The old priest liked this blessing, and made Wazim repeat it twice so he would remember it. We took our leave and found a place on the high bank overlooking the river to eat our meal. I flattened some of the tall grass and made a place for the rood so that it would not rest on bare ground. Then I sat down beside it, tired to the bone, and began to eat.

The eggs had been boiled, so we peeled them and dipped them in the salt, likewise the green onions. After such a long fast, the plain and simple fare tasted better to me than a banquet. I sat, feeling the sun warm on my back as I gazed out across the river, and thought about the welcome I would soon receive, and beyond that, to the journey ahead. By this time tomorrow, I thought, we would be well on our way home.

After our meal, we moved on. As much as I would have liked to rest even a few moments longer, I was a thousand times more anxious to rejoin Padraig and the others. Brushing the crumbs from my lap, I rose reluctantly, adjusted my bundle of ruined parchments, shouldered the rood, and declared that if we were to reach the ship by midday, we would have to hurry.

We walked on a short distance and crested the bluff, coming in sight of the city walls once more; and just beyond the great sweeping bend in the river, I could see the wharf and the wide avenue leading to the city gates. Somewhere down there, amidst the dark clusters of ships and boats lining the busy quayside, Yordanus' ship *Persephone* was waiting to carry me out of Egypt.

Beyond the walls, smoke rose in twin columns from the centre of the city. 'That one,' Wazim told me, 'is the covered market.'

'And the other?' It seemed to arise from the base of a high stony bank which dominated the northern quarter.

'Ah, that is from the citadel.'

It could easily have been the palace that was set on fire instead. I realized the risk Wazim had taken in coming back for me. 'Thank you, Wazim Kadi,' I told him. 'It was a brave thing you did last night. I am forever in your debt.'

He made a little bow, saying, 'I did only what one Christian would do for another.'

'No,' I corrected, thinking of all the betrayal, deceit and disloyalty I had seen, 'you did far more than that, believe me. You risked your life for me, and I am grateful. I will not forget it.'

The cattle trails and pathways ran continuously along the Nile's lofty banks, linking one small riverside settlement to the next north and south, on both sides of the river, as far as the eye could see. We passed through the little holdings, and Wazim unfailingly greeted each and every person we met: an old woman bent double beneath a bundle of straw fully as big as herself; two naked boys carrying a string of fish between them; a man carrying a jug of milk in one hand, leading a cow with the other, and bearing his young daughter on his back; women on their way to market carrying brown ducks bound with string. Wazim greeted them all, and I remembered just how much I had missed in my long captivity.

As midday approached, so did the quayside; the trails and pathways became roads and grew busier the nearer the city gates we came. I had been searching for Yordanus' ship since sighting the river harbour, and as we came onto the quay, I caught sight of the familiar red mast rising amidst the untidy forest of rigging at the far end of the wharf. My steps quickened as I pushed through the crush of people thronging the docks, dragging Wazim in my wake. I was almost running by the time I saw the bright green hull and yellow keel of the *Persephone*.

Panting and sweating, I paused to catch my breath before hailing those on board. 'Go on, Da'ounk,' urged Wazim excitedly, 'they are waiting for you.'

'It is a long time since I ran like this,' I said, lowering the rood gently to the wharf. 'Let me wipe the sweat from my brow at least.'

As I did so, I heard a familiar voice call out: 'Duncan!'

Glancing up, I saw Padraig standing at the rail. He waved to me, and then called to someone on the deck of the ship before starting over the rail. My heart leapt, and I started forwards to meet him on the wharf. And then another face appeared above the rail, and the sight halted me in midstep: Gislebert, the Templar sergeant.

At the same moment, I saw two more Templars standing on the wharf below the prow. Turning to Wazim, I said, 'Quick, Wazim, do exactly as I say. Take the rood. Stay here and guard it with your life. I will explain later. Whatever happens, do not give it to anyone, understand?'

'Perfectly, my friend.' Taking the rough length of timber from me, he planted himself on the wharf.

I turned, took a half-dozen steps and was caught up in Padraig's strong embrace. 'Hallelujah!' he cried, fastening his arms around me and lifting me off my feet. 'You are alive and well, Duncan. All praise to the Swift Sure Hand and his preserving power!'

My joy at seeing Padraig once again was sharply cramped by Gislebert's watchful presence. I turned to Padraig and, with true thanksgiving in my heart, started at once for the ship, leaving poor Wazim to look on with a profoundly bewildered expression. But there was nothing for it; as much as he deserved to be included in the celebrations, I could not imperil the precious relic by allowing the Templars so much as a glimpse of it – at least not until I saw how matters stood aboard ship.

'I knew you would come for me,' I told Padraig, squeezing out the words between his fierce hugs and bone-rattling slaps on the back. 'I never doubted.'

'Oh, Duncan, Duncan,' he said, grabbing my face in both his hands, 'look at you now. Earth and sky bear witness, it seems as if you had just walked down to the end of the quay and here you are back again, hale and hearty as ever. Are you well, brother?'

Before I could answer, he said, 'There is so much to tell you. How I have prayed to see this day!' he laughed aloud, shaking his head in happy disbelief. 'Praise the Saving God of Grace! Praise him all you heavenly hosts! The son who was lost is found! Praise him you burning-eyed angels, you saints give voice and sing –'

'Listen, Padraig,' I said breaking in, hating to stifle his happiness. 'It is good to see you, too, but there is something I must tell you before we board the ship.'

He looked at me, blinking in merriment. 'Speak, brother. I will listen all day to hear the sound of your voice.'

'I am in earnest, Padraig. Hear me.'

The priest became serious. 'Go on then. I am listening.'

We were nearly at the ship. 'There is no time to explain. We must leave Cairo as soon as possible. We must get rid of Gislebert and the Templars – send him on an errand and cast off at once.'

'That soon?'

'Even sooner would be better.'

The priest accepted this without question. 'So be it.'

'Duncan!' The voice drew my glance. It was Yordanus, waving his arms and calling out to me in glad welcome; standing next to him was his dark-haired daughter. Sydoni's smile was more subtle. I could not tell whether she was happy to see me, or merely amused by my dishevelled appearance.

'Duncan, my son, my son!' He snatched me up and clasped me to his bosom the instant I clambered over the rail and onto *Persephone*'s deck. 'Thanks be to God, you are safe, and here you are at last . . .' the old man's eyes began to fill with tears. 'At long last, here you are.' He embraced me warmly. 'God and all his angels be praised, you are safe.' He patted me on the shoulder and arms, as if to reassure himself that I was, indeed, returned in the flesh.

'Welcome, Duncan,' said Sydoni, her voice soft and low. She smiled and demurely offered her cheek. 'It is good to see you safe.' Compared to her father's effusive welcome, hers not only lacked warmth, but was ambivalent as well – though not from any timidity, I thought, for the glance of her dark eye was as proud as ever.

Braving her coolness, I gave her a kiss on the cheek and pressed her hand in mine. 'It is good to see you, Sydoni.'

Gislebert, who had been standing a little apart, watching, now stepped before me. Extending his hand, he said, 'Praise God, my friend. We have been working for your release these many days.' I took his hand and thanked him. 'We are only glad you are free.'

'Indeed, yes,' said Yordanus, breaking in. 'You were never forgotten for a moment, I can assure you. Welcome, Duncan,' he said, seizing my hand. The old trader beamed with good pleasure and danced from one foot to the other, unable to contain himself. 'Welcome, my boy. Praise Christ, our mighty redeemer.'

'Is this all you have with you?' asked Gislebert, indicating my crude bundle of soggy parchments.

'Yes,' I told him. 'I kept a record of my imprisonment, and I hoped to bring it out with me. Alas, they are ruined.'

'Allow me to have a look,' said Padraig, lifting the sodden sling from me.

'And who was that with you on the wharf?' Gislebert said, looking back towards the crowded quayside. For someone who was only glad for my freedom, the Templar sergeant seemed unduly concerned with the particulars of my release.

'That is Wazim,' I replied, truthfully enough, 'a guide who helped me find the ship.'

'How did you know we were waiting with the ship?' He could not keep the suspicion out of his tone.

Yordanus and Padraig both heard it and regarded the Templar with disapproval. Sydoni, however, appeared interested to hear my reply; leaning against the rail in a crisp blue mantle, her arms folded over her breast, she lifted an eyebrow – a sceptical judge inviting me to make my best explanation.

'How else would we come for him?' Yordanus chided; stepping forwards quickly, he embraced me again. 'Come, let us celebrate the return of our friend! Padraig, let us fill the cups and drink to his safe return.'

'Forgive me,' Gislebert said haughtily. 'I merely wished to know if you had seen Commander de Bracineaux?'

'How should I have seen him?' I asked, smiling. 'Was he looking for me?'

'When the riots began, he went to the palace to see if he might rescue you,' the sergeant answered. 'I imagined that was how you were freed.'

'I pray something has not gone wrong,' suggested Padraig quickly. The canny priest had seen his chance and taken it. 'Perhaps you should see what has happened to him.'

Gislebert frowned with indecision. He disliked the turn things had taken, but was not quick enough to see how to forestall the thing. 'I think the priest is right,' added Yordanus innocently. 'Yes, go at once, Gislebert. He may need you.'

'My orders were to wait here with you,' the sergeant replied dully.

'And you have done that,' said Sydoni suddenly; she stepped forwards, took his arm and turned him towards the rail. 'All is well, thanks to you and the good commander's vigilance. We can fend for ourselves here – at least long enough for you to see if your help is required elsewhere.'

Sergeant Gislebert's frown deepened. At Sydoni's gentle leading, he found himself at the rail. Unable to disagree, he said, 'Very well, if you think –'

'Do not worry about us,' Sydoni told him. 'You must consider your duty to your commander now.'

'No doubt he will welcome word of Duncan's return,' suggested Padraig. 'It would be well to tell him as soon as possible, lest he trouble himself unnecessarily.'

The Templar climbed reluctantly over the rail. 'I will inform the commander that Duncan has returned,' he said and, with a last dubious look at me, he dropped to the wharf. He called the two Templars on the dock to accompany him, and the three of them hurried away together. We watched until they were out of sight.

'Yordanus,' I said, 'how soon can the ship be made ready to sail?'

Taken aback by the question, he hesitated. 'You want to leave? But the commander will be exp –'

'How soon?' I insisted.

'Well, as soon as we can lay in some provisions,' he replied thoughtfully. 'I know you must be anxious to –'

'We can get provisions along the way,' said Sydoni. To me she said, 'We can cast off at once, if that is what you wish.'

'We cannot leave Commander de Bracineaux here without at least –' began Yordanus.

'Father, I think Duncan is attempting to avoid the Templars,' Sydoni said, looking to me for confirmation.

'It is true,' I confessed. 'I know you have laboured mightily on my behalf, but I fear I must ask you to aid me a little longer. There is some deceit at work here, and I fear de Bracineaux is not to be trusted. We must leave at once.'

'The pilot is sleeping below,' Sydoni said. 'I will wake him. You and Padraig make ready to cast off.'

I was puzzled by the sudden change in her disposition, but there was no time to wonder about it just then. 'I will fetch Wazim,' I told Padraig, already sliding over the rail. 'Begin casting off.'

I hastened back to where I had left Wazim, and found him sitting cross-legged on the dock, his eyes closed, the sacred relic nowhere to be seen. 'Where is the rood?' I demanded sharply. 'What have you done with it?'

'Calm yourself, my friend.' He smiled and stood, and I saw that he had been sitting on it. 'May God forgive me,' he chuckled, bending to retrieve the sacred object, 'but what thieves do not see, they do not steal.'

Stripping off my mantle, I quickly wrapped it around the holy cross and then we hurried back to the ship. The pilot and his two crewmen had been roused, and were lazily going about the task of getting the ship ready to sail. Yordanus and the others already knew Wazim, of course, and they welcomed him, and asked what had caused our delay. 'We expected you last night,' said Yordanus.

Leaving Wazim to explain, I went to secure the rood below deck. Curious, Padraig started to follow, but I asked him to stay behind and keep anyone from intruding on me. 'I will tell you everything,' I promised, 'just as soon as we have put this city behind us.'

I descended the short wooden steps, aware that Sydoni was watching me all the while. I hid the rood among the baskets of stores and supplies in the hold of the ship, and then rejoined the others on deck. I stood at the rail and nervously watched the quay for any sign of the Templars. But de Bracineaux did not appear. A few moments later, *Persephone* pushed away from the dock, and we left Cairo behind for good and forever.

FORTY-FOUR

The green-bordered Nile spread its slow, gentle curves before us, bearing swift *Persephone* north to Alexandria and the sea. I stood at the bow as the tiny riverbank settlements receded, and watched the twin columns of smoke rising in the distance – all that could be seen of Cairo now, and soon that was gone, too, blended and vanished in the heavy blue summer haze.

Leaving the rail, I descended to the hold, retrieved the prize and rejoined the others gathered around the mast where Wazim Kadi had been telling them about our escape from the palace. Yordanus and Sydoni were seated on cushions, and Padraig reclined on his elbow on a rug, listening to the little jailer as he spun the dull dross of our ordinary trials into the gleaming gold of great adventure.

'And this!' Wazim said proudly, waving his hand with a grand flourish as I lay the bundle on the rug before the seated listeners. '*This* is the Holy Rood of Christ, rescued from the treasure house of Khalifa al-Hafiz.'

Padraig rolled up onto his knees, and Yordanus and Sydoni leaned forwards eagerly as I slowly unwrapped the sacred relic. I pulled away the cloth to reveal the dark, deeply grooved length of ancient timber. Padraig gasped, and reached out a hand, hesitated, and stopped short.

'Go on,' I said. The priest lowered his hand and with trembling fingers, stroked the age-polished wood. The sunlight revealed a feature in the wood I had never seen before – a narrow cleft, sharp and very deep, in the centre of the piece, much, I imagine, like that which would be made by driving a spike into the wood.

Padraig's fingers found the cleft, and he gasped again. 'On this rough beam our Blessed Saviour King, the Holy One of God, shed his lifeblood for our redemption,' he said, his voice losing solidity as the tears began to stream down his cheeks. 'See here,' he said, 'this rough beam bears witness that our hope is not in vain.'

Pressing his finger to the hole in the wood, the weeping priest said, 'Here the cruel spike was driven which split the vein, divided bone and sinew, and slew the Blessed Jesu. But the wisdom of the All Wise Father encompasses things undreamed in human hearts. In Him, all divisions are united, all torn and broken lives made whole.

'Through the nail-riven body, the rent between time and eternity is joined. In the dying of the Only Begotten, life everlasting is born. For the Swift Sure Hand did not leave him in the grave, but raised him up. And all who cling to this black and Holy Rood shall likewise be raised up on the final day.'

We were silent then for a time, gazing on the holy object, filling our eyes with the homely crudeness of the relic, even as we filled our hearts with the certain knowledge of God's power to bend all things to his redeeming purpose.

'We heard in Antioch that the rood was lost,' Yordanus said, after a long silence. 'I never expected to see it with my own eyes.' He, too, lowered his hand and reverently stroked the rood – much, I expect, as people have done since that morning when the women ran from the empty tomb to tell the twelve that the Master's corpse was missing. For the faithful, it is a natural response, like that of lovers linking hands, to reverence the beloved with a touch.

'Thank you, Duncan,' he said, his eyes growing misty. 'I know I shall not abide this world much longer.'

'Papa, no,' chided Sydoni gently.

'Look at me,' he said. 'It is the simple truth; I am an old man. But I will go to my reward with a better courage now, thanks to Duncan.'

'All gratitude goes to you, Yordanus,' I replied. 'If not for you, I would still be a prisoner, and the rood would be lost to the world.'

'Not at all,' he replied, waving off the compliment. 'Our friend Renaud was working tirelessly on your behalf from the very first.'

His words did not square with what I had seen of de Bracineaux in the caliph's treasure house. But I held my tongue and let him finish.

'I see now why you wished to leave Cairo without delay,' Yordanus said, 'but maybe now you will not mind telling me why you were so anxious to leave the Templars behind.' When I hesitated, he said, 'Was it because you feared they would take it from you?'

'If they knew I had it, nothing would stop them trying to get it back.'

'But it rightly belongs to them,' Yordanus pointed out. 'At least, it belongs in Antioch.'

I heartily disagreed, but did not have it in me to dispute Yordanus. So, instead, I said, 'Tell me how you knew to look for me in Cairo.'

'Ah, now that is a tale in itself,' said Padraig, making himself comfortable.

'But if we are going to tell it,' Sydoni said, 'then I will fetch the cups.' Wazim liked the sound of that and scurried off to help her, returning a few moments later with his arms full of round, wheel-like loaves and two jugs of wine. Sydoni followed with a wooden tray on which were stacked a number of bowls. One of them was filled with olive oil and crushed garlic, and another had salt mixed with black pepper. She set the tray on the deck and handed around the cups.

'At first we did not know you had been taken,' Yordanus confessed, pouring wine into his bowl; he passed the jar to me. I poured and handed it to Padraig. 'We thought you were right behind as we raced to escape the Seljuqs, and it was not until Padraig looked back that we discovered you were no longer with us.'

'Would that I had looked back sooner,' said Padraig, passing the jar to Wazim.

Sydoni, meanwhile, had begun breaking bread into another of the bowls, which she then ranged before us. 'By the time we rode back to find you,' she said, 'the Seljuqs had taken you.'

'We found your horse,' added Yordanus, 'but that was all. There was nothing for it but to ride back to Anazarbus for help.' He shook his head sadly. 'What a terrible, terrible business.'

'Why?' I asked. It was exactly what I would have done if our places had been reversed.

'The Seljuqs did not content themselves with destroying Bohemond's army,' Yordanus replied solemnly. 'They decided to punish the Armenians for withholding the tribute. They attacked the city. It must have happened just after we departed. There were Seljuqs inside the city already, and as the royal family and nobles were attending to Prince Leo's funeral, it was a simple matter to bar the church doors and take over the garrison.'

'Those who resisted were killed,' Sydoni added sadly.

Yordanus took a piece of bread and dipped it in the olive oil and then the salt, chewed thoughtfully, and said, 'Although there was very little resistance.'

'What about Roupen and his family?' I asked, a weight of sorrow beginning to descend upon me.

'A great many people fled the city,' Padraig said. 'We met them on the road and they told us the royal family had been killed at their prayers – although this was far from certain.'

'No one knew anything for certain, save that the Seljuqs were in command.' Sydoni offered me the bowl of bread. 'They had closed the gates and no one was allowed in or out of the city.'

'We had no choice but to turn around and ride for Mamistra,' said Padraig. 'It is an eight-day journey, as you know – well, we made it in six, and regretted every day that it kept us from finding you. I wish there had been another way, but what else could we do? Our best hope lay in getting to Antioch as swiftly as possible. As soon as we reached Mamistra, we sailed for Saint Symeon, and then hastened to Antioch to alert the garrison there what had happened.'

'Bohemond's defeat left Antioch's defences decimated,' Yordanus observed. 'The idiot prince had taken his entire force, leaving only the Templars behind. It was a foolish, foolish thing. Mark my words, he will answer for it before the Judgement Throne on the last day.'

I nodded, dipping my bread, and began to chew glumly. 'Amir Ghazi realized his great good fortune,' I told them. 'He did not waste a moment, but marched directly to Damascus to rally support for an attack on Antioch.'

'Aye,' agreed Yordanus readily, 'we were there when it came!'

'Commander de Bracineaux sent to Jerusalem for troops to help defend the city. We spent a fair few anxious days wondering which army would reach Antioch first – the Templars or Seljuqs,' said Padraig. 'In the end, it was the Templars who arrived first, but Amir Ghazi was close behind. The city had but two days to prepare, and then the Seljuqs appeared and promptly mounted a siege. At first it was not so bad, but as the siege wore on, a plague of dysentery broke out and good water became difficult to find.'

'If relief had not come from Jerusalem,' added Sydoni, pouring more wine for me, 'I do not know what we would have done.'

We ate our bread and sipped our wine, and though it felt strange to me after spending so much time imprisoned on my own, I found myself gradually adjusting to the pleasures of human companionship once more. Peculiar too, I thought, to hear someone speak of events that intimately concerned me, but which I knew only in part.

I looked at those gathered around me, glancing from one face to the next, silently thanking them for their fealty and perseverance on my behalf. Yordanus, keen as a youth, slender still, wearing his age but lightly ... and beside him, Sydoni, she of the dark hair and soulful eyes, distant, watchful, a secret waiting to be known ... Wazim, smiling, his brown head bobbing, traversing an uncertain world with quiet courage and bountiful good will ... and Padraig, true friend of my soul, wise guide and boon companion for a pilgrimage or a lifetime ... I was blessed beyond measure and, as the sun warmed my back, and the wine warmed my stomach, I knew myself to be held in the strong arms of a love greater than any I could have thought or imagined.

'What happened?' I asked, suddenly wishing the day would never end, that I could sit with these friends forever, just like this, and time would cease.

'After the Templars left Jerusalem,' Yordanus replied, 'King Baldwin sent to Jaffa and Acre for troops to help protect the Holy City in their absence. They were a long time coming, because soldiers are needed everywhere these days and few can be spared.' He shook his head ruefully. 'Bohemond's profligate stupidity will cost the Holy Land dearly, and for years to come.'

'Eventually, Baldwin succeeded in raising enough of an army to relieve Antioch,' said Padraig, taking up the tale. 'The siege lasted longer than Ghazi anticipated, and by the time Baldwin arrived, most of the Seljuq support had dwindled away. The rest fled at the sight of Baldwin's troops, even though there were fewer than seven hundred knights in all.'

'The Seljuqs have no heart for a pitched battle,' Wazim put in. 'Stand up to them and they turn tail and run. They are cowardly dogs all of them.'

'God knows it is true,' agreed Yordanus. 'No one was happier than we were to see Baldwin riding through the gates of the city leading the crusaders in triumph – all the more since he brought word that a few of Bohemond's knights had survived the massacre, and these were taken to Damascus to be ransomed. The Seljuqs set a high price on the survivors – ten thousand dinars.

'I still have many old friends in Damascus, and we made arrangements to go there at once – which we did. Unfortunately, things did not go well for us in Damascus. We encountered great difficulty in getting reliable information from the atabeg's courtiers. They told us you were there and they would release you if I paid the ransom. But when I brought the money, they could not find you.' He paused, shaking his head. 'We feared you had been executed.'

'Prisoners without ransom are often killed for the pleasure of their captors,' offered Wazim.

'But then Renaud arrived,' said Padraig.

'He came to Damascus?' I could not keep the suspicion out of my voice. Sydoni marked my distrust with a knowing expression, although no one else seemed to notice. 'Why?'

'Also to ransom prisoners,' Yordanus replied. 'It was fortunate for us that he came when he did, because he was able to discover what had happened to you.'

Yes, I thought – no doubt the Fida'in told him. To Yordanus I said, 'You learned I had been taken to Cairo.'

'And so we came on as soon as we could.'

'When did you arrive?'

'Seven days ago,' said Padraig.

I tried to work out in my mind what day that would have been, but I could no longer remember where one day left off and another began. 'Then you were here before the trouble started?'

'Wazir Hasan slaughtered the amirs but two days ago,' Wazim said.

'Yes,' agreed Yordanus, 'that was when the trouble began.'

'I see.' I knew in my bones I was right about Renaud, but I did not care to speak ill of him before Yordanus, who was his friend.

'You look troubled,' said Padraig. 'Is something wrong?'

'I am tired,' I said. 'I have not talked so much in a long time. I had forgotten how taxing it can be.'

'You should rest now,' suggested Sydoni. 'There are quarters below deck where you will not be disturbed.' She rose. 'Come with me, I will show you.'

'Yes, go with her. We can talk again this evening,' the old man said. 'Sydoni, make him comfortable.'

I rose to my knees and, taking up the Black Rood, placed it in Padraig's hands – along with the responsibility of looking after it. 'Do you think you might find a safe place for this?'

'Gladly and with honour,' he said, accepting the precious relic with a bow of respect.

I retrieved my mantle and followed Sydoni forwards to a hatch in the deck with wooden steps leading down to a small, bare room set apart from the larger holding area below deck where cargo and stocks of provisions were kept. Quiet and dark – the only light came from a small grated opening in the deck above – it was the room she and her father shared, and it contained two low straw pallets set in boxes between the great curving ribs of the ship's hull. The pallets were spread with linen cloths and cushions to make a soft, inviting bed.

I thanked her and sat down on the edge of the box to remove my boots. She watched me for a moment, making no move to leave. 'I owe you a very great debt of gratitude, you and your father,' I told her. 'I intend to repay you – at least, I mean to try.'

She smiled. 'There is no need.'

I thanked her again, but instead of leaving me to sleep, she sat down on the edge of the box beside me, and I caught a beguiling whiff of sweet sandalwood and spice from her clothes and hair. 'You are worried about de Bracineaux.' She arched an eyebrow as if daring me to contradict her.

'Is it so obvious?'

'Not to my father, perhaps,' she allowed, 'but he tends to see only what he wants to see.'

'And you, Sydoni? What do you see?'

'I see a man who winces every time the Templar's name is breathed aloud.'

'I do not wince.'

'Like an old woman with a toothache.'

'An old woman . . .' I did not care for her choice of comparison.

She laughed and the sound charmed even as it humbled. 'It is something to do with the Holy Rood.'

'Yes,' I admitted. 'I know that much is obvious.'

She nodded, waiting for me to say more. When I did not, she sniffed, 'Well, you do not have to say anything if it taxes you overmuch.'

'I want to tell you. It is just that it is not so easily told.'

'People only say that,' she observed tartly, 'when they cannot decide how much to leave out.'

I had forgotten how very changeable she could be; like intemperate weather, Sydoni could be mild and calm one moment, and hurling thunderbolts the next.

'If I thought to leave anything out,' I replied, quickly losing my patience, 'it was only to spare your feelings.'

'My feelings?' She held her head to one side and regarded me as if I were mad. 'I have no feelings for Commander de Bracineaux.'

'Your father's feelings then. I know they are friends.'

'Tch! You demand that we depart Cairo with unseemly haste,' she snapped, 'for the purpose of eluding the Templars, and now you think to protect my father's finer feelings?'

I was tired, and it was futile arguing with her in any event. 'I suspect the Templars are in league with the Fida'in,' I told her.

'I knew it!' she cried, seizing my arm in her excitement. 'I *knew* he was lying to us. The good and kind de Bracineaux, lying through his wicked teeth.'

Needless to say, her reaction – gratifying as it was in its shameless intensity – took me aback.

'He told us he was doing all he could to secure your release,' she said, the words tumbling out in a rush. 'When father grew impatient, he told us to wait and pray, and leave everything to him, that negotiations had reached a precarious stage – the least word or action out of place, and we would risk losing everything, he said. Lies – it was all lies.'

'And that was when Yordanus approached the Copts,' I surmised.

'Indeed, it was his first thought,' Sydoni replied. 'He wanted to make contact with them the day we arrived, but had promised de Bracineaux he would let the Templars try first. After waiting three days, he and Padraig decided that it would harm nothing to have our friends look into matters. The Copts of Cairo,' she added proudly, 'have been living with the Saracens a very long time; they have many influential contacts throughout the city.'

'If not for your friends,' I declared, 'I have no doubt I would still be a prisoner in the caliph's palace. De Bracineaux did not care about me – at least, I was far from foremost in his thoughts.'

'He wanted the Holy Rood,' Sydoni said. 'You were just an excuse to help him get it. He used you, just as he used my father.' She regarded me wonderingly. 'But how did you discover he was with the Fida'in?'

'I saw them together.' I yawned, exhaustion overcoming me. 'They were trying to break into the treasure house.'

'To recover the rood.'

'Yes – that is, I believe that is what they were after.'

She stood abruptly. 'Sleep now. I will wake you for supper.'

'Sydoni,' I said, and realized how much I enjoyed saying her name, 'please do not tell Yordanus about my suspicions.'

'We must tell him. We cannot keep it from him.'

'I know. But let us wait until tonight at least. I want Padraig to hear it, too.'

'Very well,' she agreed. 'Tonight, then.'

She closed the door and I heard her climb the wooden steps and then her soft footfall on the deck above. I lay back on the soft-cushioned bed, my head in the place where Sydoni lay her head; and I fell asleep to the slow and gentle rocking of the ship beneath me, and the scent of sandalwood drifting through my dreams.

FORTY-FIVE

I awoke to a cool touch on my forehead and a warm breath in my ear. I had slept long and deep, and roused myself with difficulty. When I finally opened my eyes, Sydoni was gone and I wondered if I had dreamed her. I pulled on my boots and climbed back to the upper deck, emerging into a sky of radiant, deep-flamed red and gold, with darker shades of sapphire in the east where the first stars were already shining. Low green Egyptian hills were gliding slowly past, and goat bells across the water tinkled as the shepherd led his flock to the fold for the night.

Sydoni was kneeling before a low charcoal brazier cooking red fish on latticework spits. She ladled olive oil over the meat, which made the glowing coals sizzle and flare, and threw a delicious silvery cloud of smoke into the air; when the flames died down, she squeezed half the juice of a yellow lemon over the fish, glancing up at me as she did so. Her smile was ready and welcoming. 'Good evening,' she said.

'It smells wonderful,' I told her.

She held out a bowl of large flat yellow seeds. 'Try these.'

I tipped a few into my mouth and munched them. They had a salty flavour. 'Nice.'

'Parched squash seeds. The farmers make them. They also make this,' she said and, taking up a large earthenware jar, poured a clear, amber liquid into a large copper cup. The liquid frothed up with a white foam, and I smelled the flowery scent of good fresh ale as I raised the bowl to my lips. 'They call it Tears of the Crocodile.'

'Öl, by another name,' I said, savouring the sweet, bitter nut-like taste as it slid effortlessly down my throat. How long had it been since I had last lifted a cup of ale?

'The Egyptians say they invented ale,' Sydoni said, then shrugged lightly. 'But they say that about everything.'

'Padraig insists the Celts were first to make it – but he says that about everything.' I sipped the bittersweet brew with satisfaction, and breathed the soft fragrant air deep into my lungs. 'Where is Padraig?'

'He went below to say his prayers.' She turned the fish on the charcoal and squeezed more of the lemon over it. 'Vespers before the Holy Rood, he said.'

'The dreamer awakes!' called Yordanus. I turned as he came up from the stern where he had been talking to his pilot. Padraig and Wazim were not about.

'I feel as if I could take on an army,' I said.

'I hope you can eat like one,' said Sydoni. 'My father has decreed a celebration to honour your rescue. We stopped a little while ago at a market and bought everything in the settlement.'

'We want to honour your return as the occasion merits,' he said. 'God bless you, Duncan, but it is good to see you. I am sorry if I cannot refrain from saying it. I do not mean to embarrass you, but it *is* good to see you again.'

'And you, Yordanus,' I replied. 'Please, it does not embarrass me in the least. Indeed, there were times I thought I would not be seeing you, or anyone else, ever again.'

We talked of my captivity in the caliph's palace. Already, time was at work, blunting the sharp edges of that existence and bathing it in softer hues.

'Is that why you wrote it down?' asked Sydoni. I noticed how naturally she slipped in beside me, and remembered how much I missed her simple womanly graces.

'Just so,' I affirmed, and then remembered what had happened to it in the stream. 'But I fear it is ruined now. I will just have to remember as best I can without it.'

'Perhaps not,' said Padraig as he joined us, and I saw he was holding one of the scrolls from my bundle. 'This papyrus is remarkable in many ways. See here,' he peeled back a portion of the scroll to reveal the still damp surface, 'the ink has washed away, it is true, but a stain remains.'

I looked forlornly at the faint grey marks. 'It cannot be read like that.'

'No,' agreed Padraig casually, 'but it can be copied.'

'The monks of Ayios Moni excel in such work. They are always copying old scrolls and parchments. We can take your book to them,' Yordanus suggested eagerly.

'Papa,' said Sydoni, 'you presume too much. Perhaps Duncan does not wish to return with us to Cyprus.'

'No?' The old man's face fell, but he recovered himself quickly. 'Of course, I was forgetting myself. My friends, you have only to say where you wish to go, and this ship will take you there.' He looked from me to Padraig expectantly. 'Well?'

'I think,' said Sydoni, touching my arm lightly with her fingertips, 'it would be best to tell father what you told me.'

I nodded and drew a reluctant breath. 'I think none of us should return to Cyprus just yet,' I began. 'I have reason to believe that de Bracineaux and his men are in league with the Fida'in.'

'Impossible!' scoffed Yordanus. 'You are surely mistaken. Commander de Bracineaux would never contemplate such a thing.'

'If there is another explanation, I will gladly hear it and repent if I am wrong. But I know what I saw.'

This news proved so distressing to Yordanus that Sydoni suggested we all sit down and discuss it together over our cups. 'The meal will be a little time yet. Let us get this unpleasantness behind us before we eat.'

Wazim roused himself from his nap as we filled our cups, but declined to join us as we sat down on the rugs beside the mast; Sydoni put him to work helping prepare the meal instead. I related what Sydoni had told me about de Bracineaux's insistence on negotiating with the caliph himself. 'If he sought audience with the caliph, I never learned of it,' I told them. 'The first I knew of his presence was when I saw him in the tunnel helping the Fida'in break into the treasure house.'

'Are you certain they were Fida'in?'

'I did not know *who* they were,' I replied, and explained that it was Wazim who identified them from my description.

'He might have been mistaken,' Yordanus pointed out. 'It is possible, no?'

'It is possible,' I allowed. I called across to Wazim, and asked him if he had any doubt about who we had seen breaking into the treasure house.

'No, my lord,' he replied. 'They were the Hashishin.'

'But you did not see them, Wazim, did you?' asked Yordanus. 'You did not see them with your own eyes.'

'I did not need to see them,' he said, 'I could smell them. They smelled of the hashish smoke.'

'Much of the city was in flames last night,' the old man pointed out shrewdly, 'how could you be certain it was the hashish?'

He had sown the seed of doubt, but I remained convinced. I asked Wazim if anyone had come to the caliph's court to arrange ransom for me. 'No, my lord,' he replied again. 'No one ever came.'

'Might someone have come without your knowing?' wondered Yordanus. Although his manner was tactful and kindly, I could see what he was doing, and it made me uncomfortable. Had I been too hasty in my judgement of the Templars? Perhaps imprisonment had soured my good opinion of Renaud.

'I am a good jailer,' the little man answered. 'I make it my business to know such things. If anyone came seeking ransom for one of my prisoners, I would know of it. But no one ever came to the palace to offer ransom.'

'Who approached you on my behalf, Wazim?' I asked.

'Father Shenoute sent word and summoned me.'

'That is the Holy Patriarch of the Cairo church,' explained Padraig. 'When Renaud seemed to have trouble arranging the audience with the caliph, Yordanus and I went to the patriarch and asked if he could help. Father Shenoute made a few inquiries and found that Wazim was well placed to help us.'

Wazim nodded. 'Father Shenoute said I would be doing God's will if I helped Da'ounk to gain his freedom. When the riots began, I saw my chance and took it.'

'There, you see?' said Yordanus. 'It might all have been a mistake. I might simply have succeeded where the Templars failed. It does not mean they intended betraying you in any way.'

I conceded the point. 'It may be as you say,' I granted, 'but one thing bothers me still. If they only wished to help gain my freedom, why did they go to the treasure house first? When given the chance, why did they not seek my release?'

'I suppose they hoped to secure the Holy Rood,' said Yordanus.

'That very thing above all else,' I said, trying to keep an even temper.

'Can you blame them?' said Yordanus. 'It belongs to the church at Antioch. Blundering Bohemond lost it and they have a sacred duty to get it back.'

'They chose the relic above my life,' I said. 'Yet they told you nothing about that part of their enterprise. Why would they hide it from you?'

Yordanus spread his hands. 'That is something we must ask Commander de Bracineaux when next we see him.'

'What do you propose?' Padraig asked. I could tell from his tone and glance that he, like myself, was uneasy with the prospect of allowing the Templars to get their hands on the holy relic again.

'My friends, I believe this has been an unfortunate misunderstanding. I propose we sail home to Cyprus and, with your kind indulgence, I will send word to Renaud to come and meet us in Famagusta to discuss these matters. After all,' he said, 'the good Commander Renaud helped us immeasurably in Damascus. Before condemning him, we owe him a hearing, I think.'

Sydoni came and called us to our dinner then, and no more was said about the matter that night. It did not sit well with me, but I tried not to let it spoil the festive mood which Yordanus and Sydoni strove to instil in the evening's celebration. After a few more bowls of ale and Sydoni's delicious banquet I succeeded in putting my doubts about Renaud and the Templars to one side and enjoyed myself despite the troubling black cloud of foreboding hanging over me.

The meal was an inspiration of wholesome flavours prepared simply to allow the unadorned beauty of each dish to please with its own particular appeal. There was fish, and slow roasted peppers with garlic, olives, herbed flat bread made by the village women, and – my favourite – little chunks of lamb soaked in olive oil, sprinkled with dried herbs and roasted with tiny onions over the coals on slender wooden skewers.

We sat on the deck and talked and ate as night deepened around us. The flickering fires of passing houses and settlements spangled the river banks even as the stars dusted the sky above with glowing shards of light. The moon rose late and spilled its light onto the water to turn the lazily swirling liquid into molten silver. After a time, Yordanus bade us good night and went to his bed, then Padraig and Wazim likewise, leaving me alone with Sydoni.

We talked long into the night, enjoying the balmy air and the gentle music of the water rippling along the keel and steering paddle. The pilot kept the ship in the deep mid-river channel; from time to time, one of the crewmen would come to relieve him, and he would lie down on his mat in the stern for a time, only to awaken a little later to take the tiller once more. It was a fine night for sailing, and I was glad to be out on the water. Looking up into the great bowl of the heavens and the star-flecked sky, with no bound or hindrance in any direction as far as the eye could see, I began at last to understand that I was truly free.

Some time later, Sydoni bade me good night and went to her bed, but I remained on deck gazing up at the stars and listening to the sound of the dark river as the ship slid along the slowly winding waterway towards the sea. I slept a little towards dawn, but woke again at sunrise and went at once to the stern. The sky was bright pink in the east with grey shading to blue above, and not a cloud to be seen. The river had broadened considerably during the night, and the nearest bank was now a fair distance away.

There were no ships behind us, but two smaller boats kept pace one behind the other just ahead. I asked the pilot how long they had been there, and he said they had joined us at sunrise. 'They are fishing boats,' he told me in crude Latin. 'Do not worry, my friend. No one follows us.'

I thanked him but did not relax my vigil, keeping watch through that day and the next. Only when we had put sweltering Alexandria behind us, and entered the deep blue waters of the Mediterranean Sea, did I dare to believe we had made good our escape. Once under full sail, I allowed myself to rejoice in the knowledge that, despite the combined efforts of the Seljuqs and the Saracens, I was on my way home.

The voyage to Cyprus was swift and fair; the weather, though hot, was fine for sailing, and thanks to a favourable wind and bright, cloudless nights, we reached Cyprus in only three days. While the island was yet but a blue-brown hump looming in the sea haze, I prevailed upon Yordanus not to put in at Famagusta, but to use another port instead.

'But why?' he asked, genuinely mystified by my distrust and uneasiness.

Although I could think of several extremely compelling reasons to avoid Cyprus altogether, I merely replied, 'I would feel safer if our return was not widely known just yet.'

'But where is the danger?' the old trader countered innocently. 'I am certain the caliph has more important matters on his mind than the escape of a solitary prisoner. Still, if it would ease your mind, I will have a word with the magistrate and he will put the garrison on watch for a few days.'

'Father,' Sydoni scolded, 'we both know the magistrate is an officious gossip and meddler. The garrison is only a dozen old war dogs who bark far worse than they ever bite.' To me she said, 'We have a small house in Paphos on the other side of the island. We can stay there for as long as you like.'

Yordanus rolled his eyes and sighed heavily, but yielded to his daughter without further comment. I spoke to the pilot, who arranged it so that we did not make landfall until just after sunset; I wanted our arrival to arouse as little interest as possible. Accordingly, once ashore, we moved quickly through the lower, busy sea town and up the hill into a quieter quarter, known as Nea Paphos, where, scattered in amongst the large new estates of wealthy planters and merchants, the ruins of ancient fortresses and the crumbling palaces of long-dead kings could still be seen among the gnarled olive trees and thorn thickets on the hillside.

The house Yordanus kept here was less than a fourth the size of his great house in Famagusta, but it was more than adequate for our modest needs. It was surrounded by a high, white-washed wall which one entered from the road by a single, low wooden door. Once inside, the visitor entered a tidy square of courtyard kept perpetually and immaculately swept free of dust by a fearsome little bird-like housekeeper named Anna. A single large fig tree grew in the centre of the yard, surrounded by a few wooden benches; in one corner was a well which supplied the house's needs.

Anna let us in and, complaining about the lack of a timely warning, set about preparing a meal. Meanwhile, I secured the door to the courtyard. Yordanus watched me with a bemused expression, and when I was finished, asked if I was satisfied.

'It is stout enough,' I replied, rattling the iron bar in its holder. 'It will serve.'

'Good. Let us join the others and drink to a fortuitous return.'

As the main room of the house also served as kitchen, Anna would not allow us anywhere near the table until the food was ready; she chased us all back out into the courtyard where Padraig found a low bench and a number of stools, which he quickly arranged in a loose circle. Sydoni appeared with a jug of wine and an assortment of carved olivewood cups. She poured the wine and we all drank one another's health and prosperity, and long, happy, eventful lives.

'What will you do now, master?' Wazim asked me. I marked his use of that word – it was the second time he had called me that; the first time was in the tunnel.

'We will rest for a day or two,' I answered carelessly, 'and then Padraig and I will set about finding passage back to Caithness in Scotland.' I looked at the little Copt who had been my solitary friend in the caliph's palace. 'What about you, Wazim – what will you do?'

He thought for a moment. 'If Yordanus has no further need of me,' he said at last, his voice heavy with resignation, 'I will return to Alexandria.'

'Not Cairo?' I said lightly.

'Oh, I can never go back to Cairo, Da'ounk,' he replied. 'Truly, the khalifa would have me flayed alive and spit-roasted over hot coals.'

The little jailer had risked his life and given up his livelihood for me, and I had tossed him aside like a rag on which I had just blown my nose. 'I am sorry, Wazim. Forgive me, I was not thinking.'

'There is nothing to forgive. You must return to your own country. I understand.'

'You have served me admirably and well. As a true Christian brother, you have given unstintingly and at immense sacrifice for my benefit. Indeed, I would not be here now if not for you. I will not see your noble deed go unrewarded.'

He smiled to hear himself praised from my lips. 'I ask nothing of you, Da'ounk. God himself has prepared my reward.'

'I have no doubt of it, Wazim, my friend. Still, it may be some time before you collect that reward; it would please me to see you well settled and comfortable while you wait.'

I glanced over to where Padraig was sitting, and saw that he was following our conversation. My faithful *anam cara*, he gave me a nod of approval to let me know that yet another skirmish with the slippery adversary pride had been contested successfully.

Anna called us in to our supper then, and we went in to a meal of eggs and peppers with dried fish, wine, and olives. After the meal, we remained at the table long into the night, talking to Yordanus and Sydoni about how best to go about finding a ship to help us on our homeward journey. As we talked, it soon became apparent that Yordanus was less than enthusiastic about our leaving. He was intent on seeing de Bracineaux and myself reconciled, our differences mended and the Holy Rood returned to its rightful place.

I was against this, I confess, but felt deeply in Yordanus' debt, and was heartily reluctant to grieve him over this difference of opinion. We went to our beds that night with the matter unresolved, but I promised to give it my thoughtful consideration over the next few days. This pleased him, and he said no more about it, leaving me to my meditations.

Next morning, Padraig and I, with Sydoni's assistance, wrapped the Holy Rood in red silk and secured it in a stout wooden casket which Anna used to store her good shoes and feast-day clothes. We hid the sacred relic in the bottom of the box and replaced the clothes, adding a few shawls, a tablecloth, and such like. The box did not lock, but Sydoni said it was just as well. 'Someone searching for valuables will seize on anything that is locked,' she pointed out.

We placed the box under Padraig's bed and, satisfied that our treasure was safe enough for the time being, walked down to the harbour in the lower town where we arranged to be informed of any westbound ships departing Paphos harbour. I had the unhappy suspicion that we would have to go to a larger port to find passage, and that would increase the risk of discovery. Likewise, each day we waited heightened the risk as well, as I did not for a single instant believe that the Templars would easily give up searching for the sacred relic, nor allow anything to stand in their way of reclaiming it.

My sudden and unexplained appearance on the quay at Cairo had confounded Sergeant Gislebert, and I knew in my bones that de Bracineaux would quickly narrow his search to me – if only to satisfy himself that I did not have the relic in my possession. Thus, Yordanus' suggestion of sending word to him to meet us and discuss the matter had something to recommend it by way of surprise, but beyond that, try as I might, I could not think of a single good reason to meet with the Templars. I did not say as much to Yordanus, however, but merely begged more time to think the matter through.

'Take all the time you need,' the old man replied obligingly. 'While you are thinking, why not go up to the monastery and speak with the monks about restoring your damaged papyri? It is not far – you would only be gone a few days, and you could see something of Cyprus along the way.'

Padraig agreed that it was a good idea, so that is what we did.

FORTY-SIX

The people of Cyprus travel by donkey, and although exceedingly undignified, the sturdy little beasts are sure-footed and uncomplaining. They eat little and need less water than a horse or ox, and can endure heat and cold, and the hardships of the road far better than either of their larger stablemates. We hired three of the animals in Paphos – one each for Padraig and myself, and one to carry fodder and provisions for our journey. As Yordanus said, it was no great distance, but the people of the hill country beyond Paphos are very poor and the likelihood of finding suitable food or stabling along the way was slender indeed.

'It is best, I think, to travel lightly and make as few demands on the country folk as possible,' was how Yordanus tactfully put it.

So, early the next morning, we bundled a few things into a cloth bag and tied the bundle containing my still-soggy papyri – Padraig had determined that the best way to preserve the mess was to keep it wrapped in damp sheepskin – to the patient pack animal. Bidding farewell to Yordanus, Wazim, and Sydoni, we set off for the monastery of Ayios Moni, a refuge of learning and prayer deep in the hill country on the edge of the high Troodos mountains. The road was well-used and well marked, and the weather dry and fine, so the travelling was easy. Upon reaching the first high ridge I looked back to see Paphos glittering like a jewel in the shallow bowl of the bay, shimmering in the bright morning sunlight.

It was good to be with Padraig again, just the two of us, and I reflected that since beginning this pilgrimage, it had never been just the two of us together. We rode side-by-side, and I told him about my captivity with Amir Ghazi. As we climbed higher into the pine-forested hills, the air grew cooler and more pleasant. The breeze through the tall trees smelled of pine and reminded me of the Scottish woodlands, and I felt a pang of longing which was eased only by the assurance that we would be going home very soon.

We spent a good day in the saddle, stopping now and then to water the beasts from the roadside brook. We passed a few tiny settlements and, as Yordanus had warned us, they were mean places – tumbledown, soot-covered hovels with miserable dogs and dirty children standing in bare dirt yards looking silently and hungrily at us as we passed. At one such dwelling, Padraig was so moved by the want of a naked boy and his young sister that he gave them half our bread, some dried meat, and all the cheese we had brought with us.

Later, as the sun began to sink into the green valley to the west, we sought and found a clearing in the forest a short distance from the road where we made camp for the night. We made a fire of fragrant pine branches and cooked a simple meal of pease porridge, and slept on beds of pine needles with the stars shining down through the gaps in the lightly sighing trees.

We rose at daybreak and continued on, arriving at our destination just as the monastery bell tolled vespers. The gates were still open, so we went in and presented ourselves to the porter. They were Greeks for the most part, but we had no difficulty making ourselves understood. Padraig told the porter that he was also a priest, and that we were on pilgrimage, returning from the Holy Land – whereupon the simple monk became excited and ran off to find the abbot.

Abbot Demitrianos was a kindly and gentle man, humble in manner and appearance, with a head of wavy dark hair and a beard with two grey streaks either side of his mouth. Like the brothers under his care he dressed in a simple black robe that covered him from just below the chin to the tips of his toes; and like all the others, he wore a black, brimless peaked cap sewn with a tiny white cross on the front over his brow. Around his neck he wore a wooden cross on a braided leather loop, and he carried a short wooden staff in his hand.

Demitrianos received us like cousins long lost and lamented, and graciously welcomed us to the monastery. He ordered the porter to prepare the guest lodge and said, 'We are honoured to have someone who has been to the Holy Land. Perhaps, if you are not too exhausted from your journey, you might speak to us of your pilgrimage tonight at supper.'

'We would be most happy to share news of our travels with you,' Padraig told him. 'I must tell you, however, that owing to a great misfortune we did not reach Jerusalem. If you hoped to hear word of the Holy City, I fear we must disappoint you.'

'It makes no matter,' the abbot replied. 'Many of us have never travelled so far as Lefkosia or Salamis, and some have never been beyond the next valley. I am certain that anything you can tell us of the wider world will be respectfully and gratefully received.'

The little monastery of Ayios Moni, the good abbot told us, was very old, the first monks having come from Byzantium over seven hundred years ago. 'Before that,' he said, 'there was a temple to the goddess Hera; our chapel is built on the old temple's foundations. It is an ancient and holy place.'

When Padraig expressed an interest in hearing more about the monastery, the abbot became our guide and led us to each of the buildings in turn and showed us the treasures of their brotherhood, including the small, much faded and, it must be said, extremely crude icon of the Virgin Mary, which was believed to have been painted by none other than Saint Luke the Evangelist. Upon viewing this marvel, I did feel as if I had beheld a thing of immense age and undeniable consequence.

Although I lack a proper appreciation of such things, I do freely confess, what impressed me most was not the plaintive image of the young woman with large dark, melancholy eyes, but rather the worshipful reverence with which the monks handled their priceless relic. Their loving veneration was heartfelt and deep, and it shamed the arrogant crusaders with their careless desecration of the True Cross. The manifold profanations heaped upon that holy object by those who should have been its protectors amounted to a gross and terrible sacrilege. The humble adoration of the monks renewed my resolve to keep the Black Rood as far from the Templars' grasping hands as I possibly could.

The monks of Ayios Moni lived a simple life of prayer and toil, growing crops and vegetables, raising chickens and sheep – which they freely gave to the poor who came daily to their gates to beg for food and clothing. They were skilled in the healing arts, a practice for which they were justly renowned, dispensing their potions and medicines far and wide as any had need. They also tended vines from which they produced a sumptuous wine they served to their guests. The wine was sweet and heavy, and was reputed to possess curative powers because it was grown on hallowed ground.

The rules of their order forbade speaking during meals, but in observance of our visit, this rule was relaxed during our visit to allow them to listen to Padraig and me describe our sojourn in the Holy Land. In truth, Padraig did all the talking, as his Greek was far more eloquent than my own rough expression and he knew precisely what his fellow monks wanted to hear. Thus, I sat with the abbot at the high table, drinking my wine and eating a delicious stew of lamb and barley, while Padraig stood at the pulpit normally occupied by the brother reading the evening's lesson. He spoke well, adorning his talk with finely-observed word portraits of the people and places we had seen. He told them about my captivity among the Seljuqs and Saracens, and my escape – making it sound much more courageous than it felt at the time – drawing many appreciative murmurs from his listeners. When he finished, the entire community – thirty-five or forty monks in all, I think – stood in his honour while the abbot thanked him with a special blessing.

Following the meal, we were invited to Abbot Demitrianos' lodge for a special drink before night prayers. We walked across the quiet monastery yard in the balmy twilight, and I felt the deep peace of the place enfold me in its soft, inescapable embrace. The abbot's house was little more than a bare cell, but it had a hearth and a fleece-lined bed, several chairs and a table, on which stood simple olivewood cups and an earthenware jar. The abbot invited us to sit and poured a pale, slightly cloudy white liquid into the cups, which he passed to Padraig and me. He placed the palm of his hand over his cup and blessed the drink, whereupon we imbibed the sweet fire of the Ayios Moni monks: a delectable honeyed nectar that soothed even as it warmed, beguiling the unwary with a delightful smoky taste before stinging the senses into a lucid and delectable dizziness.

After only a few sips, I felt large and expansive, friend and brother to all mankind. It was with great reluctance that I set aside my cup, but when talk turned to the reason for our visit, I feared I might lose the power of speech if I drank any more of the wonderful elixir.

'We have it on good authority,' I began, as the kindly abbot watched me dreamily over the rim of his cup, 'that your community excels in the making and copying of manuscripts.'

'It is,' replied Demitrianos, 'a task in which we have long experience. If some small fame has travelled beyond these walls, I am glad, for it means that God's praise likewise increases.'

'As you know,' said Padraig, 'we have just arrived in Cyprus from Egypt where Duncan was a prisoner for many months.'

'Yes,' nodded the abbot with benign admiration, 'you showed great fortitude and forbearance in your captivity,' he told me. 'Our Lord was surely with you.'

'While he was a guest of the caliph,' Padraig continued, 'he wrote of his experiences –'

'I thought I would not live to see my young daughter,' I explained, 'and wanted her to know what had happened to her father.'

'A thoughtful and commendable bequest,' mused the abbot loftily. 'A very labour of love, to be sure.'

'Unfortunately,' I continued, 'all my work was ruined.' I went on to tell him what had taken place in the escape from the caliph's palace, leaving out any mention of the raid on the treasure house and the rescue of the Holy Rood.

Abbot Demitrianos frowned and clucked his tongue. 'Regrettable, to be sure.' He reached for the jar and offered to refresh our cups. 'More *alashi*?' I declined, but Padraig succumbed. 'Still,' the abbot continued, tipping the jar into his own cup, 'your life has been redeemed, all praise to Our Great Heavenly Father, and that is of inestimable value to your dear little daughter.' He raised his cup and imbibed deeply of the potent drink.

'As it happens,' said Padraig, 'this work was written on good papyrus, which the Egyptians use instead of parchment.'

'We know of it, to be sure,' replied the abbot contentedly. 'We call it *papuros*. Fine stuff, but very brittle, and lacking the durability of good parchment. I suppose, however, if you cannot obtain the sheep . . .' he sighed as if it were the chief lamentation of his life, 'what can you do?'

'This is why we have come to you,' Padraig said. 'We have brought the papyri with us in the hope that the wise brothers of Ayios Moni can help restore what has been lost.'

411

'To be sure.' The abbot slid a little down in his chair; he looked from one to the other of us with a slow blink of his eyes. 'Although it grieves me to tell you, my friends, experience tells me that nothing can be done. Papuros is very delicate, as I say; once ruined, it cannot be salvaged.' He lifted the jar. 'Are you certain you will not have more alashi?'

Again, I declined politely, and was surprised when Padraig helped himself, emptying the jar into his cup. 'I have no doubt that what you say is true,' the thirsty priest replied. 'Yet, it seems to me that the work might be copied.'

The bell for night prayers began tolling just then. Padraig stood. 'Ah, night prayers. I am keenly interested in attending the service tonight. Perhaps, with your kind permission, we might continue this discussion tomorrow. I think if you were to have a look at the papyri, you will see what I mean.' Turning to me, he said, 'Come, Duncan, we must hurry to the chapel. I thank you for your kindness, and bid you God's rest tonight, abbot.'

The abbot blessed us with a benediction and sent us off to prayers. We left him to his rest and, as I closed the door behind us, I noticed Padraig still clutched his drink in his hand. 'A lesser man would have surrendered long ago,' I told him.

'A lesser man *did*,' he replied, tipping the nearly full cup onto the ground. He lay the empty vessel beside the door, and we hurried to the chapel, taking our places at the rear of the small assembly of monks. There were two short benches either side of the door, and upon one an elderly brother sat with his hands folded in his lap, snoring softly; all the rest stood with their hands raised, palms upwards at shoulder height, intoning the prayer in a humming drone.

Padraig joined right in, but I did not know the prayer and found it difficult to follow the recitation. From time to time, one of the monks would raise his voice and call out a phrase and, just as I was beginning to grasp the prayer, suddenly the chant would change, and off they would go in a new direction. After a while, I gave up and sat down on the bench beside the sleeping brother until the service was over. He woke as I sat down, looked up blearily, smiled at me, and then went back to sleep. I wished him pleasant dreams.

The guest lodge was comfortable enough, if small; we woke the next morning well rested and ready to be about our business. After morning prayers we broke fast in the refectory with a meal of bread and honey, ripe olives and soft goat's cheese. The brothers asked us to tell them more about our experiences in the Holy Land, especially Antioch, where Paul, the great apostle, and his companion Barnabus the Generous had preached and worked. 'They came to Cyprus, too, you know,' one of the elder brothers informed us. 'Paphos was the first city to become Christian in all the old Roman empire. It is true.'

'Verily,' added another, 'you can still see where Paul was chained to the pillar and scourged for impugning the supremacy of the emperor.'

Padraig and I soon exhausted our small store of memories of Antioch. I wished I had more to tell them; I had spent but a single day there, and had seen almost nothing of the city. At least I was able to describe the Orontes valley and the famed white walls of Antioch rising up sheer from the river bank, and something of the wide main street leading to the citadel, as well as the citadel and palace.

Abbot Demitrianos entered while we were eating and joined us at table, helping himself to bread and cheese and joining in with the brothers. I liked him for his easy, unassuming ways, and his disregard for rank and ceremony. In this he reminded me of Emlyn, and I found myself wishing I was long since on my way home.

After the meal, the abbot took us to the scriptorium and introduced us to two of the senior monks who had the charge of the work of the monastery.

'I present to you, Brother Ambrosius,' the abbot said, indicating a small, round-shouldered monk with sparse white hair – the monk with whom I had shared a bench during prayers the night before. '. . . and Brother Tomas, our two most skilled and experienced scribes. If anything can be done for you, they will know.' The two bowed in humble deference to one another, and invited us inside. The room was small, but airy and light; a number of wide windows along the south wall allowed the sunlight to illumine the high work tables of the monks. Most of them were still at their morning meal, so we had the scriptorium to ourselves for the moment.

'My brothers,' said Padraig, 'we come to you with a problem, begging your help. You have heard me speak of Lord Duncan's captivity

413

among the Muhammedans.' The two nodded enthusiastically. 'As it happens, he used the time of his imprisonment to make a record of his experiences. Unfortunately, that record has been damaged.' Padraig went on to explain about the papyri and my escape through the underground canal.

When he finished, the abbot said, 'I have already warned our friends that there may not be any remedy for them. Nevertheless, I will let you decide.'

'Please,' said Brother Ambrosius, 'might we see the papuri in question?'

'It will be easier to make a determination once we have completed an examination of the documents in question,' added Brother Tomas.

'By all means,' said Padraig. I brought out the bundle, laid it on the nearest table, and began to unwrap the still-damp sheepskin.

Brother Ambrosius stopped me at once. 'Allow me,' he said, stepping in and staying my hand. 'Let us see what we have here.' He bent to his work, holding his head low over the skin as he carefully unpeeled the wet leather. Brother Tomas joined him on the opposite side of the table, and in a moment the two of them had exposed the tight roll of papyrus scrolls.

They gazed upon the soggy mass of slowly rotting matter as if at the corpse of a much-loved dog, and clucked their tongues sadly. There was a green tinge along the edges of the rolls, and the papyrus stank with a rancid odour. The two monks raised their eyes, looked at one another, and shook their heads. 'I fear it is as the abbot has said,' Ambrosius told me sadly. 'There is nothing to be done. The papuri can never be restored. I am sorry.'

Even though I was already resolved to this prospect, I still felt a twinge of disappointment.

'I am certain you are right,' replied Padraig quickly, 'and we anticipated as much. But perhaps you could tell me if I am right in thinking that these pages could be copied?'

This request occasioned a second, closer inspection, and a lengthy discussion between the two master scribes. They carefully pulled apart one section and carried it to the nearest window where they held it up to their faces and scrutinized it carefully. 'It could be done,' Tomas allowed cautiously. 'Each leaf of the papuros must be dried very slowly and flattened to prevent it from cracking to pieces.'

'Then,' Ambrosius continued, 'it might be possible to inscribe what was written thereon. Although it is Latin,' his voice took on a rueful tone, 'the hand is fair and open, the marks, however faint, could be traced and copied.'

'It would be a very great undertaking,' suggested Tomas, looking to his superior. 'But it could be done.'

'Truly, that is good news,' the abbot said. 'However, I fear we will not be able to shoulder this admirable labour for you. We are but a small community, and the pressure of work already begun is such that we would not be able to contemplate any new endeavours, however worthy, for a very long time.'

'I am prepared to pay you,' I offered. 'Such a service requires great skill and effort, I know. I would be more than happy to pay whatever you deem appropriate.'

'Please,' said Demitrianos, raising his hands in protest, 'you misunderstand me. I was not fishing for payment. It is not your silver I am after; I am telling you the truth, my friend. As much as I would like to help you,' he spread his hands, 'but –'

'Forgive me, abbot,' said Ambrosius, speaking up. 'Something has just occurred to me. A word?'

He led the abbot a little apart and the two of them spoke to one another quietly for a moment. I heard the abbot say, 'Very well.' And then he turned and smiled, and said, 'Our brother has just brought a matter to my attention which I have overlooked. He insists there may be a way we can help you – provided you are agreeable.'

'I assure you I am most agreeable to anything – within reason,' I allowed, 'and the limits of my purse.'

'The work we do here is not only for ourselves, but also for the wider world – for edification and learning, for posterity, for succeeding generations. This is why we take such great care – so that those who come after us will enjoy the benefit.' He made a gesture towards the elderly monk, who stood looking on hopefully. 'Brother Ambrosius reminds me that what you have written of your sojourn in the Holy Land might well prove a unique, and therefore valuable, reflection of our perishable age. He suggests that we should honour your request.'

'Indeed,' I said, pleased with the turn the thing had taken. 'I am glad to hear it.'

'There is just one stipulation,' Abbot Demitrianos said, raising a hand to check my eagerness. 'That we should be allowed to make not one, but *two* copies.'

'One copy for you, of course,' said Ambrosius, unable to restrain his eagerness, 'and one for our use.'

In truth, it had not occurred to me that my scribblings would be of any interest to anyone save myself and those of my family who cared about what had happened to me. While there was nothing in the papyri of which I was ashamed, I was not sure I wanted anyone else to read my mind and heart.

Before I could decide, however, Padraig nodded enthusiastically and said, 'An excellent solution. Of course! Nothing would please us more than to know that Lord Duncan's work might continue to serve in this way.'

'There is one other thing,' suggested the abbot, in a slightly embarrassed tone. 'I am reminded that the scriptorium is in need of a new roof. Needless to say, it would greatly contribute to our work if we did not have such a burden hanging over our heads as it were.'

'I understand completely,' I replied. 'I would be happy to stand the cost of a new roof for the scriptorium.'

Brothers Ambrosius and Tomas both clasped their hands in delight and praised the Great Creator for his bounteous provision. We thanked the brothers for the consideration, and arranged for a time to return and collect the finished copy; then, before the sun had quartered the sky, Padraig and I were on our way back to Paphos.

We arrived the evening of the next day to learn that Yordanus was gone.

FORTY-SEVEN

'He went where?' I said, disbelief making my voice harsh. Anger blazed up bright and hot as the sun beating down on my head, though I tried my best to quench it.

Sydoni bit her lip. She knew I was displeased, and was loath to withhold the truth from me – though it meant betraying her father's purpose. 'He went to Famagusta,' she said timidly. 'He took Wazim with him. I know you said –'

'When?' I demanded. 'How long has he been gone?'

'He departed the same day you left for the monastery. I suppose you are right to be angry. But he is only trying to help.'

'It will be no help to any of us if the Templars find us here.'

'He promised not to do anything without your consent,' she said half-heartedly.

'Then he should not have gone at all!' I snapped.

'He only went to see to his affairs – nothing more.' She was growing defensive. 'Never fear, my father will not betray your precious secret.'

'It was a foolish thing to do!'

'Peace!' said Padraig, entering the courtyard just then. 'The entire island will know of our business if you do not desist.' He cautioned us to leave off squabbling, and went to see that the rood was still safe in its box beneath his bed.

As much as I might have wished otherwise, Yordanus was gone and there was nothing to be done about that now. Still, I fussed and fumed, and finally Padraig sent me down the road to walk away my frustration. I stumped along in the hot sun, and felt the heat on my skin; soon I was sweating and tired, and though angry still, I had neither the will nor the strength to maintain it any longer. I stopped and looked around, and found myself at one

417

of the many ancient ruins that occupy the hilltops in that part of the island.

Little more than an overgrown mound now, with wild olive trees and bramble thickets, there were still a few sun-bleached sections of toppled columns to be seen, an arch and part of a wall – rising from the surrounding wrack like the enormous bones of a monstrous creature. My anger finally subdued, I sat down on the carved capital of a ruined column in the shade of a half-dead palm tree to rest and collect myself. I could see the bay from where I sat, and watched a few boats returning from the day's fishing, but there was no sign of the ship.

Padraig and I had arrived back in Paphos at midday and, upon coming in view of the shallow bay, I had suddenly become agitated. By the time we descended the hill overlooking the harbour, I knew what it was that disturbed me: *Persephone* was missing; the ship was not in the harbour, and nowhere to be seen.

We had hurried on to the house to be met by Sydoni, who took one look at my distraught expression and guessed what had caused my distress. She explained that she had told him not to go, but her father insisted he knew what he was doing, and anyway, he would be back before we returned.

In fact, he did not return until two days later.

I spent the intervening time stalking the hills and muttering about the ruins, waiting for Yordanus to return. I was sitting in my accustomed place in the shade when I saw a ship round the far headland and enter the bay just before sunset. I watched with growing expectation until I was certain it was the *Persephone*, and then I hurried back to the house to alert Sydoni and the others that Yordanus had returned.

While Sydoni and Anna fluttered around preparing food and drink for her father's return, the old trader stood in the courtyard and professed his trip to have been eminently successful, and that any worries I might have had were completely unfounded. Wazim stood with him, and the two of them assured me that nothing out of the ordinary had taken place. Padraig and I listened to their feeble justification for their disobedience.

'I know you instructed otherwise,' Yordanus allowed, 'and I did not lightly go against your wishes, believe me. Even so,' he raised his hands in appeasement, 'the day is soon coming when we must send word to Commander de Bracineaux at Antioch. I have instructed Gregior to begin making the necessary preparations for that journey. Also,' he added with a touch of self-righteous vindication, 'I needed to replenish my purse. Silver does not multiply of its own accord, you know, and travel is a costly business.'

There was no point in berating the man. 'Well, it is over and done now,' I said as graciously as possible. 'We will speak no more about it.'

'Very wise,' agreed Yordanus. Just then Anna came into the courtyard carrying a tray laden with bowls of food and baskets of bread; Sydoni emerged behind her with a tray of cups and a jug of wine. They placed the trays on one of the benches beneath the fig tree, and the four of us sat down to eat.

'I am anxious to learn about your trip to the monastery,' Yordanus said. 'Were the monks able to help you?'

'They were indeed,' replied Padraig. He told about the monastery and the agreement we had made to allow the papyri to be copied. 'They were only too happy to do it once they learned they could make a copy for themselves.'

'*And* a new roof for the scriptorium besides,' I said. The words came out sounding far more caustic than I intended. Both Padraig and Yordanus looked at me curiously.

'You seemed to find the agreement satisfactory at the time, brother.' Padraig scowls only rarely; thus, it speaks all the more eloquently of his displeasure. 'You have made a fine deception of hiding your disapproval until now.'

'I beg your pardon,' I muttered. 'I have misspoken. Forget I said anything.'

Sydoni joined us after awhile, and she and Padraig began discussing the hill country to the north and the many monastic settlements to be found in that part of the island. Yordanus meanwhile undertook a lengthy and pointless story for Wazim's amusement – all to do with some poor farmers in the hills near Paleapaphos who recently unearthed a treasure trove buried in a field they were ploughing; the find apparently consisted of several gold bands and an onyx chalice which they assumed was Roman, but which, upon examination by the Bishop of Paphos, turned out to be Greek. It was thought the items had once belonged to a potentate who had owned one of the ruined palaces in the area.

'I suppose they will be made to give up their find,' I remarked innocently. 'As always everyone else has a better claim on the treasure than those who discovered it.' Once again, my tone belied my true intent. The others regarded me with rank displeasure. 'What? Am I not allowed an opinion?'

After one or two more abortive attempts at joining in the conversation, I finally gave up, lapsing into a disgruntled and fidgety silence. As the evening dragged on, I found it increasingly difficult to sit still and listen to the idle prattling of the others. I sipped my wine and munched salty olives, all the while sinking deeper and deeper into a peculiarly fretful melancholy. When at last I could no longer endure the prattling, I stood so quickly I spilled my cup. I grumbled an apology and excused myself, saying my head hurt from too much sun and I was going to bed.

And that is where Padraig found me some while later; he had sat up talking with Sydoni and Yordanus and came in to find me still thrashing around, unable to sleep. He stood over me for a moment, and even though I could not see his expression in the darkness I could tell by his prickly manner that he was disgusted with me. I did my best to ignore him.

'I know you are not asleep,' he said at last, his voice sharp with disapproval.

'Is it any wonder? If you mean to stand over me all night neither one of us shall get any rest.'

'It is not myself keeping you awake. For a certainty, it is your own guilty conscience.'

His unjust accusation brought me upright. 'Guilty! What have I to feel guilty about?'

'You know what you did,' he said. 'Your own heart condemns you.'

'I have done nothing – unless treating everyone with the utmost courtesy is now become cause for reproach.'

'If I reproach you,' said Padraig with unmerited disdain, 'it is because you well deserve it. Every time Yordanus opened his mouth, you jumped down his throat. What were you thinking? The man is our host and benefactor. He has helped us in a thousand ways, and asks only for our friendship in return. Yet, you treat him like the lowest filth beneath your feet.'

'What cause has Yordanus to complain?' I replied petulantly. 'I was not the one who went behind *his* back and disobeyed *his* orders. Anyway, did I not forgive him? Why are you throwing this back in my face?'

'Listen to you now ... *disobeyed my orders* – who are you to issue commands to everyone else? Duncan the High and Mighty lifts his leg to fart and the whole world must dance to the tune – is that it?'

'You twist my words, disagreeable priest!' I growled angrily.

'Do I?' he sneered. 'Do I, indeed?'

'You do.'

'Perhaps they were twisted to begin with.'

'And what do you mean by that?'

'Think about it. Look you long and hard into your soul and repent of your vile and sinful conceit. It does you no credit, my lord.'

He turned away, leaving me to stew in my own bitter bile. His rebuke stung – all the more because I knew he was right. Though I was loath to admit it, the shrewd priest had read my soul aright. Proud as I was, I begrudged Yordanus his efforts on my behalf – not the least because I feared his meddling would result in my having to surrender the Black Rood to the Templars. Nor was that all. I resented having to depend on anyone – especially one I deemed less reliable than myself. In truth, in my long captivity I had grown used to trusting no one and relying only on myself to the extent that I now resented the intrusions of others into my affairs however well-intentioned, and viewed their small failings as wilful defiance of my authority.

These unhappy reflections kept me from my rest. I lay awake long into the night, staring into the darkness, restless and rankled, unable to sleep. Dawn was but a whisper away when I finally abandoned the effort. I rose from my troubled bed and went out, thinking to find some solace in the cool darkness of the quiet courtyard.

Lest I disturb the sleeping household, I crept as quietly as I could through the house, lifted the latch and slipped out through the half-open door, closing it silently behind me. I paused for a moment and looked up at the sky. The moon was down, and the stars were beginning to fade with the approach of daylight. The air was still and fine, and from some unseen corner, I heard the chirrup of a cricket . . .

421

and something else: a sliding plop, followed by a rapid dry scrabble across the bare earth.

The sound put me in mind of a rat scurrying back to its nest, but if so, it was a rat the size of a donkey. I stood motionless, listening, and when I heard the slow scrape of iron against wood, I moved slowly to the corner of the house and looked towards the gate.

A figure dressed all in black – little more than a shadow in the deeper shadow of the wall – stood at the gate, lifting the iron bar away. I started for the gate, moving as swiftly and silently as I could, and wishing I had some of Murdo's legendary stealth. I crossed to the fig tree, and as I stooped to crouch beneath it, I caught the faint whiff of the scent I had last smelled in the tunnels beneath the hareem in Cairo: the unmistakable tang of hashish.

My mind froze.

Fida'in!

There was no mistake. Pungent and sweet, with a musty, metallic odour, once smelled, the scent is not forgotten. I picked up one of the benches from beneath the tree and darted forwards.

The intruder heard me as I closed on him. He stepped back from the gate, swinging the iron bar as he turned.

I threw the bench before me, catching the iron bar as it came around, and forcing it back against his chest. I drove in behind the blow, slamming the bench hard against his chin. The Fida'i's jaw closed with a teeth-shattering clack as his head snapped back against the timber door just as his comrade on the other side started to push through. The door banged shut and the Arab intruder tried to squirm away. I heaved the bench into his chest, driving the air from his lungs; he slumped to the ground, his back to the door.

I dropped the bench and snatched up the iron bar. 'Padraig!' I shouted. 'Padraig, help!'

The Fida'i on the other side of the gate pressed hard against the door and succeeded in getting a hand and arm through the gap. The hand gripped a knife that sliced at me as I tried to force the iron bar back into the carrier. Seeing that I could not bar the gate with the intruder's arm in the way, I stepped back, and then hurled myself against the door. The attacker's arm snapped with a chunky pop like wet kindling.

'Padraig!' I shouted.

The howling Fida'i pulled his broken arm out of the way and I pressed the door closed with all my might. I shouted for Padraig again. At the same instant, there came a tremendous thump on the door as someone on the other side drove into it, trying to force it open once more.

There came a rush behind me. I spun around and caught the dull glint of metal streaking towards my neck. I threw my hands before my face and dodged away. The blow was ill-judged and hurried, catching me on the meaty part of the shoulder as I turned. The blade went in – it felt as if a red hot poker had been applied to my flesh.

Flailing with my fists, I stumbled backwards, falling over the body of the unconscious intruder on the ground beside the gate, and pulling the weapon from the grasp of my attacker as I went down. He leapt on me, straining to retrieve the blade still buried in my flesh. As he bent forwards, I kicked up hard into his groin – once, and again. He gave out a groan, staggered unsteadily, and collapsed onto his knees, holding himself.

Swift footsteps sounded on the earth beside me. My hand closed on the handle of the knife. I yanked it from my shoulder and made a wide, awkward swipe to keep my new assailant off balance. The man cried out, 'Duncan! It is me!'

The next thing I knew Padraig's hands were on me, pulling me to my feet. The Fida'i I had kicked was struggling to rise. Gasping, puffing, his eyes streaming with tears, he raised himself up on wobbly legs.

'May God forgive me,' Padraig said, and aimed a solid kick into the softness of the half-paralysed attacker's private parts. The man shrieked and pitched forwards, rolling in agony. He gagged and then vomited over himself, subsiding with a whimpering groan.

'Is that all?' Padraig whirled around, scouring the darkness for more Fida'in. 'Are there any more?'

'There were three of them,' I told him. Clutching my wounded arm, I looked at the two on the ground, both unconscious now. 'The other is outside still. I broke his arm.'

'Are you hurt badly? Here, let me see –'

As the priest reached a hand towards my wounded shoulder, there came a scream from inside the house.

Sydoni.

FORTY-EIGHT

I flew to the house with Padraig two steps ahead of me. He darted through the door and across the darkened room towards the sound of Sydoni's muffled screams. I started after him and collided with a black robed figure bent over something on the floor. The invader went sprawling and my feet slid out from under me. I fell, landing on my wounded shoulder in a glutinous pool.

Pain seared through me; my arm throbbed with a burning ache. I rolled onto my back and found myself lying next to Yordanus on a floor slick with his blood.

The Fida'in attacker lurched towards me. I saw his hands, pale in the darkness, fumbling frantically over the old man's unresisting body, and realized he was searching for his knife, which was hilt deep in Yordanus' neck. We both saw the weapon at the same time and grabbed for it. I was the quicker. My fingers closed on the hilt and I jerked the blade free.

The black-robed Arab lunged again, diving across Yordanus. I tried to roll away, but his hands found my throat and squeezed hard. I swung the knife backhanded with all my strength against the side of his head. The blade entered his temple with but little resistance. His limbs stiffened and his spine arched rigidly. He gave out a startled cry and began convulsing, his teeth chattering and gnashing as he writhed beside his victim on the floor. The spasms grew less violent, and after a moment he lay still.

I dragged myself onto my knees beside Yordanus. The old man's eyes gazed upward; his mouth was open slightly, as if preparing to speak, but no movement stirred his chest. He was gone.

From somewhere further back in the house I could hear voices. I rose and moved quickly towards the sound, and discovered it was coming from the room where Sydoni and Anna slept. The door was closed, but I could hear Padraig calming, reasonable; and Sydoni, frantic, pleading. I put my hand to the latch and, quietly as I could, lifted the wooden handle and pushed the door open.

In the light of a single candle, I saw Sydoni on the far side of the room, bending low over Anna's slumped body. Padraig was standing over her, his arms outstretched in an attitude of protection.

The Fida'i was standing with his back to the door. He glanced over his shoulder as the door opened, saw me, and said something in Arabic. Then he saw the knife in my hand and turned to confront me.

I saw the curved blade glint in the candlelight as he swung towards me and did not wait for him to see that I was wounded.

'Now, Padraig!' I shouted, charging headlong into the Arab intruder. He threw his arms wide to free his blade, and I pulled up at the last instant as Padraig, stepping in swiftly behind, seized the intruder's knife hand in both of his. The attacker swung on Padraig and I dived in, sliding the blade up under his ribs. Blood and hot damp air spewed from the wound.

The Fida'i struck me with his elbow, catching me on the jaw and knocking me off balance. I staggered back. Breaking free of Padraig's grasp, he leapt on me, knocking me to the floor, his knife blade slicing across the side of my face as I fell.

The curved blade rose in my assailant's hand and, helpless to prevent its descent, I shoved my knife up into his throat. The blade entered under the point of his chin, passing up into his mouth. He gave a strangled cry and tried to stab down at me, but Padraig now held his arm.

Gagging on the blade, he tried to pull it free, but I held tight to the hilt. Blood cascaded over his teeth, spilling down his chin and over my hands. The wretch toppled backward, choking on his tongue. His fingers raked at my hands, but I held firm.

'It is enough!' shouted Padraig. 'Duncan, it is enough.'

Still I held the blade, and gradually the struggling ceased. Only when he lay completely still did I withdraw the knife. '*Now* it is enough,' I said, slumping onto the floor.

Sydoni, terrified and shaking with fright, rushed to me. 'You are wounded,' she cried, her trembling fingers touching my cheek. 'Your face . . . your arm . . .'

'It is not so bad,' I told her. I raised a hand for Padraig to help me up.

'I have seen five of them,' I said as Padraig raised me to my feet. 'We must search the house. There may be more.' I looked at the crumpled body of the old woman; I did not have to ask whether she still lived. I would mourn the dead later, right now it was the living who needed my attention.

'Where is Wazim?'

Neither Sydoni or Padraig had seen him. 'Stay here and keep the door barred,' I instructed Sydoni. She glanced down at the dead Arab and shook her head. There was no time to argue with her, so I said, 'Come along then. But keep well back.'

We proceeded through the house, but did not find any more Fida'in. Upon reaching the kitchen, Sydoni saw her father lying on the floor. With a shriek of anguish, she rushed to gather his lifeless body into her arms. Although I wanted nothing more than to comfort her at that moment, I had to make certain there were no more Fida'in about. Padraig and I continued out into the courtyard and there found Wazim standing with a spear pointed at the Arab I had kicked and left unconscious. No longer inert, he was slumped against the outer gate, glaring at the little Egyptian and fending off the jabbing thrusts of Wazim's spear.

'Well done, Wazim,' I called, hurrying to join him.

At our appearance, the Arab straightened. Wazim, glad to be relieved of this dangerous duty glanced around at us, taking his eyes from his captive. The spearhead wavered and dipped as he turned. It was a fatal mistake. The Fida'i darted forwards and, before I could call a warning, reached behind his back and whipped out a slender dagger. Wazim, sensing the attack, raised the spear, catching the Arab in the pit of the stomach.

I watched in horror as the Fida'i grasped the spear and held it, then, with a great sweeping motion of his arm, drew the knife blade across Wazim's throat. The two of them fell to the ground together, one atop the other.

Padraig rolled the dying Arab aside, and I knelt over Wazim Kadi. I took his hand and he looked up at me and smiled. He moved his mouth, but he could not speak. 'I am sorry, my friend,' I told him. 'Go with God.'

426

He gave out a little sigh and his life passed from him. Padraig and I knelt beside his body for a time. Like the good Célé Dé he was, Padraig stretched his hands over the body, one palm at the forehead, one at the heart; he spoke a rune for the dead, and then prayed our friend on his way:

'The sleep of seven joys be thine, dear friend.

With waking to the peace of paradise,

With glad waking to eternal peace in paradise.'

We hurried on with our search, scouring every last corner of the house, yard, and outbuildings until we were satisfied that there were no more intruders to be found. Padraig put his hand on my shoulder. 'It is over.'

'No,' I told him. 'There is one more.'

Taking up Wazim's spear which Padraig had removed from the dead Arab, I crossed the courtyard and opened the gate to find the last of the Fida'in crouching beside the wall. He was rocking slowly back and forth, cradling his crushed arm across his body. He turned his head and looked at us as we stepped out onto the road. His eyes were half-lidded and his movements sluggish as he made to stand.

Padraig, holding out his empty hands, slowly advanced towards the injured Fida'i. 'Peace,' he said. 'Salaam.'

The Arab fumbled at his belt with his good hand and brought out a knife. Holding it at arm's length, he uttered a low growl of warning, his speech slurred and muttering.

'It must be the hashish,' I told Padraig, stepping quickly beside him.

'The killing will stop,' said Padraig, extending his hand once more. 'Give me your weapon.'

At that moment, a cock crowed in the yard of a house down the road. Away in the east, night was beginning to fade. The Arab made a clumsy swing with the knife to keep us back and then leaned against the wall, his face to the rising sun.

'Give me the knife,' said Padraig, extending his hand.

The Fida'i looked at us, his dark eyes glazed with drugged hatred. He drew a deep breath, put his head back.

'*La ilaha illa Allah!*' he shouted, and then turned the knife on himself, plunging it into his own heart. He slumped backward to the ground and rolled onto his side. A tremor passed through his

427

body, and he gave out a groan which ended in a death rattle. And then it was finished.

After a moment, I bent down and removed the knife. 'Great of Heaven, I pray that was the last of them,' Padraig said quietly.

'Amen.'

'How did they know where to find us?'

'Do you wonder?' I asked. I saw it so clearly in hindsight I could only marvel at my blindness to now. 'They must have been watching Yordanus' house in Famagusta. When he returned to Paphos, they followed him here.'

'But who could have sent them to Fam –' the priest began, and then halted. '. . . de Bracineaux.' Padraig turned to me, his face illumined by day's first light. 'You knew this would happen.'

'No,' I replied, shaking my head sadly. 'I feared it only.'

'Now that they know where to find us,' Padraig surmised, 'there is nothing to stop them sending more Fida'in. The Templars will not rest until they have achieved their aims.'

'We cannot stay here,' I said. Suddenly exhausted, I passed a hand over my face. My arm was throbbing, and I could feel the beat of pain in my head and all down my side.

The cock crowed again, and then everything grew strangely quiet. I swayed on my feet and my vision blurred. I looked at Padraig and I saw his mouth move but could no longer hear him speaking to me.

I remember very little after that. Only darkness, and a sense of tranquil motion . . . and then, nothing.

FORTY-NINE

Dearest Caitríona, my life, my light, my hope. If not for the poisoned blades of the wicked Hashishin, I should have been home long since.

As it is, I have been forced to endure another captivity – this time in a bare little cell within the walls of Ayios Moni. Abbot Demitrianos will forgive me for saying that while my clean, bare cell may be poorer by far than the sumptuous chamber I had within the caliph's palace, this new confinement is eminently superior in every way. I have had nothing but the best of care since my arrival these many months ago. Indeed, I do not hesitate to say it: if not for the healing skills of the monks here, I heartily doubt whether I would be drawing breath, much less lifting pen to write to you now, my soul.

Although I chafe at captivity once more, I endure with a high and hopeful heart, and thus resume the work which has occupied me during my long sojourn in Outremer. Kindly Brother Tomas visits me daily, bringing the list of difficulties his diligent scribes have encountered in their patient work of copying my poor scraps of ruined papyri onto fine, clean parchments. Sometimes it is a word they cannot read owing to the deterioration of the brittle and delicate papyrus; just as often, it is likely to be my ham-fisted script that has brought them to distraction.

Thus we sit together, the gentle brother and I; he asks me to supply the meaning which has perplexed them, and I embellish the tale with remembrances refined by hindsight. My indulgent taskmaster does not like it when I try to improve upon what I have written. He insists that it must be rendered as first I set it down. This, he tells me, assures a purity of authenticity – something the fastidious brothers seem overly keen to preserve, it seems to me. But then, I am no scholar, nor ever likely to be. Still, I cannot help myself; the memories come thick and fast, so vivid and clear; the more I tell, the more I remember. My patient scribes take it all down without complaining and, like busy weavers, make a whole cloth of ragged patches. So my tale grows in the making, expanding beneath the good brothers' diligent hands.

Abbot Demitrianos comes to see me every day also. He tells me that for the first few weeks I was, as he puts it, not of this world. Nor was I of the next world, either, I confess, for I remember nothing save recurrent periods of light and dark – days, perhaps, except they spun like the alternating spokes of a fast turning wheel – and this along with the soft and distant murmur of comforting voices, often with the scent of fragrant smoke. They say I hovered between life and death, and the times I smelled the smoke was when I drifted close to the heavenly altar and partook of the incense of paradise.

As to that, I cannot say I am the wiser for it. Any glories that might have been glimpsed through the veil were certainly lost on me; the all-obscuring shroud remained in place, secure from my prying eyes. Thus, the secrets of the Hereafter are safe for another season.

Later, when I awoke from my long sleep, the first thing I saw – once the daylight had ceased causing my eyes to water – was Sydoni's lovely face as she bathed my brow with a cooling cloth. For she, too, has been a constant visitor, rarely absent from my side for more than a few brief moments when she takes her own much-needed rest.

The Greek monks do not usually allow women to remain behind their protecting walls beyond sunset, but the wise abbot offered a special dispensation for Sydoni. In view of the circumstances, however, it was as much a necessity as a blessing – although, I imagine they would have had a fight on their hands had they tried to send her away. She has been a perpetual source of strength and comfort to me, and I have needed both – especially in those first days after waking when, too weak to lift my head from my pallet, she fed me and nursed me. I do believe Sydoni pulled me back from death's dark and silent gate by the sheer force of her unflagging resolve.

Padraig, too, has been a very champion – a hero the great Celts of old would not hesitate to welcome into their exalted companionship. Padraig has been the rock of salvation for me, my soul's true friend, my *anam cara* in word and unfailing deed. It is to Padraig's quick thinking that I owe my continued existence in the land of the living.

For, following my collapse in the road, the canny priest swiftly discerned that the severity of my wounds could not alone account for my sudden decline. He summoned Sydoni who confirmed that the Fida'in most often poison the blades of their knives so that should they fail to strike a killing blow, even the smallest cut will eventually prove fatal. He wasted not an instant, but bundled me in a robe and put me – along with the box containing the Holy Rood – in a borrowed wagon and carried me with all speed to Ayios Moni. If it was the monks who healed me with their shrewd knowledge, it was Padraig who gave them the chance.

Poor Sydoni faced the cruel dilemma of accompanying me to the monastery, or staying behind and seeing to her father's burial. Not that she had time to linger over the choice; Padraig needed help to get me to the monastery, and could not allow her to remain in any event. He foresaw the likelihood that another attack would be forthcoming as soon as those who instigated the first began to suspect it had failed.

Nor did his watchcare end there. Far from it. No sooner had he delivered me into the capable hands of the Greek brothers, than he hastened back to Paphos to move the ship. He sailed to Famagusta and, with the ship's pilot and crew, and Gregior and Omer's help, loaded the *Persephone* with as much of Yordanus' treasure as he could without raising local suspicion. He then hid the ship in a tiny cove on the north-western side of the island – a little fishing village called Latchi near the ancient Roman city of Polis – thus safeguarding our surest and best chance of making good our escape when the time comes to do so.

Having seen to these arrangements, he returned to the monastery to help relieve Sydoni in her long and selfless vigil at my bedside. They took it in turn to pray over me, and anoint my insensate body with holy oil and medicinal balms, which they rubbed into my half-dead flesh. Along with the Greek brothers, they worked the slow miracle of my recovery.

Two seasons passed while I hovered between this life and the next. I awoke one fine spring day with brilliant white light streaming in through the open window of my cell. I use the word 'awoke' for I know no other way to describe it. Yet, the sensation was unlike any awakening I have ever known. I opened my eyes and looked around and it was as if I had come into the world as a newborn infant, possessing neither memory nor knowledge of anything that had gone before. I raised a hand to shield my eyes, heard a gasp and turned my head towards the sound. I looked at the face of the woman clutching my hand and understood only that she was dear to me – I knew not how. Neither did I know her name, or anything about her. I loved her for the kindness in her face, and the joyful tears in her eyes.

And then I slept again.

This time it was a genuine sleep, deep and restful. When I opened my eyes on the next morning, Sydoni was there beside me, praying for my healing. The moment I beheld her graceful head bent over her folded hands, her arms resting on the edge of my bed, I knew I would live and not die. Each day thereafter, I enjoyed some small improvement – drinking my broth unaided, eating my first solid food, sitting upright, and the like. Although it would be a long time yet before I could walk unaided under my own strength, that day was the beginning of my recovery.

Though Sydoni and Padraig spent the greater portion of every day with me, I nevertheless had a great deal of time to think. As I grew stronger and could sustain the effort, I considered what had happened. At first my memories were vague, shadowy and unreal – through a glass darkly, as Padraig would say. But as I put my mind to it, more came clear, and still more, until I could at last recall the events of that terrible night.

Alas, it would have been better to allow the memory to sleep undisturbed. The horror of that painful night will haunt me for a long time, I fear. I lost good friends, and cannot help feeling that my own stubborn will is to blame. Padraig tells me this is foolishness, that I was not the one who sent the Fida'in to kill and recover the relic. That was Commander de Bracineaux's decision alone, and I believe in my bones that he is right.

Yet, as I have passed the days in contemplation, I cannot swear before the Judgement Throne that this is so. As much as I believe the Templar commander bears the responsibility, I have no real proof of his guilt – only hardened suspicion. True, de Bracineaux was the only person who knew where we could be found. Did he desire the holy relic so fervently he would kill for it? It must be remembered that it was Renaud who sent me to Yordanus to begin with. I ask myself, could he so easily betray his friends to death?

Perhaps he did not mean for anyone to be killed. But if that is the case, then why send the Fida'in? Why not come himself and demand the return of the relic?

Then again, it may be that he did not send them. Perhaps they came on their own accord, hoping to recover the holy relic and thereby win favour with the Templars for obscure reasons of their own. Maybe that is the way of it. Again, I cannot say. And I think no one will ever know.

Thus, although I do believe Renaud de Bracineaux was the author and agent of the bloody butchery of that awful night, the fact remains that I can offer no decisive proof one way or the other. I do know, however, that I am fully to blame for my part in it. If I had walked empty-handed from the caliph's palace Yordanus, Wazim, and Anna would still be alive today. I grieve for them, and I lament their cruel deaths. Before I leave this island, I will stand beside their graves and beg their forgiveness, as I have done a thousand times already in my heart.

Padraig says that each of life's experiences has great volumes to teach any ardent enough to seek the learning. So, I ask myself: what I will take from this strange pilgrimage of mine? Try as I might to reclaim something golden from the dross of this misbegotten enterprise, I cannot help hearing Nurmal of Mamistra's voice saying, *The enemy you meet today might be the friend you call upon tomorrow.*

I think of this, and I remember Emlyn telling me how the crusaders of the Great Pilgrimage, inflamed by blood lust and ignorant greed, slaughtered Greek and Jew, Armenian, Copt and Arab alike, recognizing no distinctions, lest any foe escape. On my pilgrimage, however, it has been the enemies of those first crusaders who have befriended me, while the friends I thought to trust were worse to me than enemies foresworn.

This has been a bitter lesson. I know now how my father feels, and why. I know why he set his face so adamantly against crusading, and against my going. I pray I may yet receive his forgiveness for my wilful disobedience.

Padraig, wise priest that he is, tells me I have no need to ask that which has been granted a thousand times already. He says the teaching of the Célé Dé is that each man must follow the light he is given, and that pilgrims on the True Path can never stray so long as they follow the Holy Light. I hope I have done that. God knows I have tried.

And now, dear Cait, my thoughts and prayers are turning ever and again towards home. I long for the day when I can see you and hold you and take you upon my knee and tell you how very much I have missed seeing your bright eyes and winsome smile. One day soon – it cannot be soon enough, dear heart – when the winter-stirred seas have grown calm and the winds fair, Padraig and I will raise sail and steer a homeward course. Rest assured, there is a good fast ship awaiting us, and once we loose the moorings there will be no more stopping, no more adventures, until we reach the Caithness coast.

In my heart, I am already on that homebound ship. Indeed, I can almost feel the fresh northern wind on my face and hear the ropes sing as fair *Persephone* bounds over the waves, carrying us around the broad headland and into the bay below Banvarð.

What will I bring with me?

Many extraordinary memories, a few scars, a little wisdom. I will bring the parchments the good brothers have so faithfully and carefully prepared. I will bring the Black Rood, of course, and that would be prize enough. Even so, I will bring with me another treasure: Sydoni herself, to be your mother, and my wife.

Dearest Cait, I know you will love her as much as I do. I pray the Swift Sure Hand smooths the way before us, for I cannot wait to see the two of you together under the same roof. When I have my family around me once more, I promise never again to let the wild, red-heathered hills of Scotland out of my sight. That is a vow I shall gladly keep.

EPILOGUE

November 30, 1901: Paphos, Cyprus

Paphos glistens in the warm autumn light. The white-washed houses of the fishermen shimmer as I gaze out upon a bay of hammered silver. The late afternoon air is soft and scented with lemon blossom, and I have been drowsing over my work far longer than I intended.

Here in this ancient fishing village, bathed by the sun and soft Mediterranean air, everyday life in rain-lashed Scotland seems very far away indeed. As Caitlin and I amble along the winding streets of this charming, quiet town it is difficult to imagine the bone-chilling North Sea gales roaring through Edinburgh as winter prepares to wring the final ounce of forbearance from the tough Scottish soul before grudgingly relinquishing its allotted span to a grim and dismal spring.

I exaggerate neither whit nor whisker when I say I have spent the most thoroughly luxurious and enjoyable holiday of my entire life. Although we have been here but a few weeks, I feel as if I know the timeless rhythms of village life like a native. In short, I am enamoured of this little island and its old-fashioned, homely charms. It may be dotty romanticism – the affliction of the Scotsman abroad – but I believe the local people have taken us to heart. At least, we have been here long enough for the Cypriots to begin to accept us as something more than the novelty we obviously are.

The little ladies – fishwives and widows, for the most part, dressed in black from head to foot, elaborate black shawls around their shoulders – now greet us enthusiastically when they see us on our morning expeditions to the market. And the shopkeepers and stallholders make much over Caitlin. Everyone wants to touch her; they pat her hands and stroke her hair, and treat her as if she were a goddess dropped into their midst: Aphrodite reborn as a Presbyterian with the smile of an angel and a voice that purrs in a rich Scottish brogue.

So enchanted with Cyprus are we, that I find myself hankering after a little cottage in Kato Paphos where Cait and I can potter around when my days of legal beavering are over. In the scant few weeks since our arrival, I feel myself positively reborn. I suppose the years of dull lawyering have taken their toll. Without my noticing, I had gradually sunk into the deadening routines of the dutiful drudge, going about my mundane affairs. Life had dwindled down to a comfortable, not to say monotonous, sameness that is as deadly to the soul as any sin.

I know now why I was sent to this haven – and why it was necessary for Caitlin to accompany me. Over the past few weeks I have been on a quest – a pilgrimage, if you like – which has transformed me utterly. I now know who I am and, more importantly, my ancestry and pedigree. I now know that my election to the Seven was no accident of chance. I belong to an ancient and noble lineage.

In these last blessed days of light and warmth before the darkness and cold of battle descends, I have been given an inestimable gift to carry me through the bitter times ahead.

In these last days, I have recaptured something of the intoxicating recklessness and abandon that I experienced when I last put pen to paper in that white-hot blaze of incendiary vision. At the time, I truly felt that I was losing my mind; that if I left off writing, even for a moment, the tenuous thread of sanity would slip from my sweaty grasp, and I would plunge headlong into the bottomless pit of dementia, there to live out my days perpetually seeking the thing I had lost, but never remembering what it was, or why it should matter so.

Such was the fever that drove me.

I have, of course, read that much-blotted missive – not once only, but several times, and am convinced in my own mind, at least, that I have made a credible job of setting forth the truth of what was communicated to me that night in the crypt. I mention this now, because if I imagined that my own pilgrimage had reached its conclusion, that notion was shattered forever at Ayios Moni.

Day after day, as I poured over the ancient manuscript, teasing out the meaning of that long-dead language, the fire slowly rekindled. And, upon turning over the last leaf, the transformation begun when I touched that bundle of mouldering parchment was complete. I see now that the lineage is long, and the quest begun all those ages ago continues. Where it will end, I cannot say, but I know I am in good company. Like Duncan, I am learning that, however dark and uncertain the path, we never travel alone: there are angels along the way waiting to help and befriend us.

Brave, stalwart Duncan seems to me, in many ways, closer than a brother. Almost an entire millennium stands between his day and mine, and yet I can hear his voice speaking to me across the years as if he were hovering at my shoulder. However mistaken I may be, I feel as if I know him as I have known few others. Moreover, I am reconfirmed in the realization that not only are the past and present woven of the same thread, the past is neither dead nor distant; it continues to exert a genuine and potent force on both present and future, on all that is and is to come.

In these last days I have come to believe that we are none of us so estranged from our ancestral heritage that we no longer feel its age-old rhythm in the pulse and flow of the blood through our veins. The lives of previous generations can be traced in the lines of our hands and the meditations of our hearts. For we are not ourselves alone; we are all that has gone before.